LAST STAND . . .

"What are you doin' here in the Territory all by your lonesome, mister?"

"I'm not the law, if that's what's bothering you," Dan said.

"Haw, haw," one of the men cackled. "Would you admit it if you was?"

"I have nothing to hide," said Dan. "I didn't cotton to the war, and I laid out up in St. Joe, Missouri. But I got lonesome for Texas, and that's where I'm headed."

To further his bluff, Dan holstered the Colt he still held in his hand.

"I'm Bart Scovill," the lead rider said, "and I've always had a hankerin' for a chestnut mare just like that one of yours."

"Good luck finding one," said Dan.

While Scovill had been talking, two of the mounted men had drawn their horses to the side so that they had a clear shot, and it was these that Daniel Strange was watching. When they went for their guns, Dan drew with lightning swiftness and shot them both out of their saddles. But four of them were on him before he was able to make another move.

"Jasper," said Scovill, "tie me a good thirteen-knot noose. . . ."

Death Rides a Chestnut Mare

Ralph Compton

A SIGNET BOOK

SIGNET
Published by the Penguin Group
Penguin Putnam Inc., 375 Hudson Street,
New York, New York 10014, U.S.A.
Penguin Books Ltd, 27 Wrights Lane,
London W8 5TZ, England
Penguin Books Australia Ltd,
Ringwood, Victoria, Australia
Penguin Books Canada Ltd, 10 Alcorn Avenue,
Toronto, Ontario, Canada M4V 3B2
Penguin Books (N.Z.) Ltd, 182–190 Wairau Road,
Auckland 10, New Zealand

Penguin Books Ltd, Registered Offices:
Harmondsworth, Middlesex, England

First published by Signet, an imprint of Dutton NAL,
a member of Penguin Putnam Inc.

First Printing, May, 1999
10 9 8 7 6 5 4 3 2 1

THE IMMORTAL COWBOY

This is respectfully dedicated to the "American Cowboy." His was the saga sparked by the turmoil that followed the Civil War, and the passing of more than a century has by no means diminished the flame.

True, the old days and the old ways are but treasured memories, and the old trails have grown dim with the ravage of time, but the spirit of the cowboy lives on.

In my travels—which include Texas, Oklahoma, Kansas, Nebraska, Colorado, Wyoming, New Mexico, and Arizona—there's something within me that remembers. While I am walking these plains and mountains for the first time, there is this feeling that a part of me is eternal, that I have known these old trails before. I believe it is the undying spirit of the frontier calling, allowing me, through the mind's eye, to step back into time. What is the appeal of the Old West of the American frontier?

It has been epitomized by some as the dark and bloody period in American history. Its heroes—Crockett, Bowie, Hickock, Earp—have been reviled and criticized. Yet the Old West lives on, larger than life.

It has become a symbol of freedom, when there was always another mountain to climb and another river to cross; when a dispute between two men was settled not with expensive lawyers, but with fists, knives, or guns. Barbaric? Maybe. But some things never change. When the cowboy rode into the pages of American history, he left behind a legacy that lives within the hearts of us all.

—*Ralph Compton*

Death Rides
a Chestnut Mare

Prologue

St. Joseph, Missouri. April 1, 1870.

"Margaret," said Daniel Strange to his wife, "Texas cattle can be had for three dollars a head in Texas. Drive them north to the railroad, and they'll bring thirty dollars and more. I can't pass up a chance at that kind of money."

"But you're the best gunsmith in Missouri," Margaret said, "and you've taught all the children the trade. Your father was a gunsmith and his father before him. Why must you give it all up and travel hundreds of miles for a herd of Texas cows? Why, you're one of the most respected men in town."

"And the most taken for granted," said Daniel Strange. "I'm owed thousands of dollars, and nobody pays. I've already arranged to sell the shop for five thousand dollars, which is more than it's worth. I can leave fifteen hundred dollars for you to manage on, until I can bring the cattle north."

"But there's just *you*, Daniel. You'll need men to help you drive the cattle."

"Texas is suffering through Reconstruction," Daniel said. "From what I've heard, I can get riders aplenty, paying them at the end of the drive."

"I have a bad feeling about this, Daniel," said Margaret. "Like if you go, I'll never see you again."

*   *   *

But Daniel Strange's mind was made up. On April 10, he rode out on a chestnut mare his daughter, Danielle, had named Sundown, bound for Texas. His wife, Margaret, wept, his twin sons, Jed and Tim, cussed the fate that kept them from going, and Danielle said not a word. While Jed and Tim had their father's blue eyes, they were not as tall. Danielle, on the other hand, had her father's height. With hat and boots, she was almost six feet. Her hair was dark as a raven's wing, and she had her mother's green eyes.

"Damn it, Ma," said fourteen-year-old Jed, "Tim and me should be goin' with him."

"Don't you swear at me, young man," Margaret snapped. "You and your brother will remain here and go to school, just as your father ordered. You don't see Danielle wanting to ride off on a cattle drive."

"She's just a girl," Tim scoffed. "What does she know about cattle, or anything else?"

Danielle turned and walked away, saying nothing. She had shared her mother's misgivings regarding Daniel Strange's journey to Texas, but she knew her father too well to try and cross him. She sat down on the front steps, watching the evening sun sink below the mountains far to the west. Despite her mother's objections, she had taken to wearing her gun belt with the Colt her father had taught her to use. She thought fondly of the days Daniel Strange had spent teaching her to draw and cock the weapon in a single motion. There had been countless days of constant practice, with advice on cleaning and oiling the weapon as well. There was practice shooting with her brothers, and Daniel Strange had been delighted when Danielle had outshot both of them. Not only had he been a master gunsmith, he had been a master of the weapon itself. Thus the offspring of Daniel Strange were proud of their ability to pull a Colt and fire in a split second. Instead of going back into the house where Jed and

Tim still complained, Danielle leaned on the corral fence, her eyes looking away into the distance, where she had last seen her father.

Daniel Strange regretted taking the chestnut mare, for it was the best horse they had, and he had given it to his daughter, Danielle. From St. Joe, he would ride almost due south, crossing Indian Territory into North Texas. The thirty-five-hundred dollars in his wallet would more than pay for the anticipated herd. There would be money enough for a chuck wagon and grub for the journey to Kansas. Dan Strange well knew the dangers of crossing Indian Territory, but trail herds were doing it on a regular basis. There was no other route that wouldn't be hundreds of miles longer. He simply had to be careful. Taking care to rest the chestnut mare, he made swift progress. After entering Indian Territory at the extreme northeastern corner, a four-day ride had taken him well into the heart of the Territory. He had seen nobody since leaving southern Missouri. His cook fires were small, and he doused them before dark. He had just lighted a fire to make his breakfast coffee when the chestnut mare nickered. There was an answering nicker, and Dan Strange drew his Colt. He well knew the Territory was a haven for renegades and killers, and prepared to bluff his way out, if he could. His heart sank when a dozen riders reined up a few yards away. They had the look of men on the dodge. Some of them wore two guns, and every man had a rifle in his saddle boot. Dan looked longingly at his own saddle and the Winchester in the boot, but he dared not risk going for it. Finally, the lead rider spoke.

"What are you doin' here in the Territory all by your lonesome, mister?"

"I'm not the law, if that's what's botherin' you," Dan said.

"Haw, haw," one of the men cackled. "Would you admit it if you was?"

"I have nothing to hide," said Dan. "I didn't cotton to the war, and I laid out up in St. Joe, Missouri. But I got lonesome for Texas, and that's where I'm headed."

To further his bluff, Dan holstered the Colt he still held in his hand.

"I'm Bart Scovill," the lead rider said, "and I've always had a hankerin' for a chestnut mare just like that one of yours."

"Good luck finding one," said Dan.

While Scovill had been talking, two of the mounted men had sidestepped their horses so that they had a clear shot, and it was these men Daniel Strange was watching. When they went for their guns, Dan drew with lightning swiftness and shot them both out of their saddles. But the other mounted men were firing now, and a slug ripped into Daniel Strange's shoulder, slamming him to the ground. Four of them were on him before he was able to move.

"Jasper," said Scovill, "tie a good thirteen-knot noose. Rufe, bring me that chestnut mare that this pilgrim's willing to die for."

"Take the horse," Dan Strange said desperately. "Let me go."

"A mite late for that," said Scovill. "You gunned down Reece Quay and Corbin Rucker, and the Good Book says an eye for an eye. They was my friends."

Ruse had saddled the chestnut mare, leading it to where Dan lay on the ground.

"Byler," Scovill said, "search him. He might have enough on him to buy all of us a drink or two."

Dan fought his way loose and was on his knees when Byler slugged him with the heavy muzzle of a Colt. The outlaws shouted in glee when Byler took the sheaf of bills from Dan's old wallet.

"Here," said Scovill. "Gimme that for safekeeping. Get him in his saddle. We'll string him up, take his horse, and ride."

Byler hoisted Dan Strange into his saddle, leading the chestnut mare to a giant oak. The noose was placed around Dan's neck, and the loose end of the rope flung over a limb. Bart Scovill slapped the flank of the chestnut, and the mare broke into a gallop, leaving the unconscious Daniel Strange dangling at the end of a rope. The outlaws were watching in morbid fascination, and nobody remembered the mare until the animal had a good head start.

"Damn it," Scovill shouted, "some of you catch that mare."

But the chestnut mare didn't like these men, and riderless, the animal lit out in a fast gallop toward home. The pursuing outlaws were quickly left behind. Finally, they gave up the search and returned to join their comrades. Dan Strange's dead body turned slowly, one way and then the other, in the light breeze from the west. Byler still held the empty wallet, and he flung it to the ground beneath the dangling corpse. The remaining ten outlaws didn't even bury Quay and Rucker, but mounted their horses and rode south.

Indian Territory. April 15, 1870.

Deputy U.S. Marshal Buck Jordan smelled the stench before he came upon the grisly mass of flesh hanging from an oak limb. His horse snorted, backstepping, and Jordan led the skittish animal well away from the scene of death. He tied his bandana over his nose and mouth and started back toward the hanging tree. That's when he saw what remained of the pair of outlaws Daniel Strange had shot.

"My God," said the lawman aloud, "the buzzards and coyotes have already got too much of you gents, they might as well have the rest."

Jordan cut the rope, easing Daniel Strange's body to the ground, and that's when he saw the empty wallet. He opened it and found a card that read *Daniel Strange, Gunsmith, St. Joseph, Missouri.*

"Well, old son," Jordan said to the lifeless man, "the bastards took everything but your shirt, britches, and boots. All I can do is bury you and try to get word to your next of kin."

Jordan carried a small folding spade behind his saddle for just such a need as this, and he buried Daniel Strange beneath the oak where he had died. Jordan then studied the sign left by the riders.

"Twelve horses left here, but two saddles were empty," Jordan said aloud. "That was good shootin', Daniel Strange. A damn shame there had to be so many of them, but it's the way of yellow coyotes to travel in packs."

Fort Smith, Arkansas. April 17, 1870.

Buck Jordan turned in his report to his superior and, having no better address, sent the empty wallet to the *Family of Daniel Strange, Gunsmith, St. Joe, Missouri.* With it he enclosed a letter explaining the circumstances and signed his name.

St. Joseph, Missouri. April 20, 1870.

It was already dark outside when the chestnut mare reached her home corral. Gaunt and trail-weary, she nickered.

"That's Sundown!" Danielle cried

"Oh, dear God," said Margaret Strange, "something's happened to Daniel."

"Maybe not," Danielle said. "I'll get a lantern."

Trailed by Margaret, Jed, Tim, and Danielle hurried to the corral. The mare nickered again, for she was among friends.

"She's stepped on the reins and broken them," said Danielle. "She's come a long way, riderless."

"Pa's hurt somewhere," Tim said. "We got to go find him."

"No," said Margaret, biting her lip to hold back the tears. "Your father's dead."

"I'll ride into town tomorrow," Danielle said, "and see if there's anything the sheriff can do."

It was a long, miserable night during which none of them slept. Danielle was ready to ride at dawn.

"Why is she ridin' in to talk to the sheriff?" Tim cried. "It ought to be Jed or me. This is man's work, and she's just a . . . a girl."

"Stop botherin' Ma," shouted Danielle. "Can't you see she's sick?"

Margaret Strange was ill with grief and worry. Upon reaching town, Danielle went first to Dr. Soble's office and told him the circumstances.

"I'll prescribe a sedative and look in on her," the physician promised.

Danielle then went to the sheriff's office, and he confirmed her fears.

"This parcel came yesterday," Sheriff Connally said. "It has no address except St. Joe, and the postmaster give it to me to deliver. He reckoned it might be important."

Danielle ripped away the brown paper, revealing her father's old wallet. She collapsed in a ladder-back chair, weeping. Sheriff Connally gathered up the brown paper wrapping, which still contained the letter from

Deputy U.S. Marshal Buck Jordan. Swiftly he read it, waiting for Danielle to compose herself. When she had, the old sheriff handed her the brief letter. As Danielle read the letter from Buck Jordan, her tears were replaced with fury.

"The low-down, murdering bastards!" she shouted. "There must be *something* we can do to make them pay."

"Now, girl," Sheriff Connally soothed, "it happened in Indian Territory. It's plumb full of thieves and killers, and there's no way of finding the varmints, even if we knowed who they are."

"There *must* be some way to find them, to make them pay," cried Danielle.

"Danielle," the old sheriff said, "your daddy's gone. There's nothing you can do that'll change that. Now don't go off and do somethin' foolish."

Danielle knew if the sheriff had any idea of the thirst for vengeance that possessed her, he would somehow foil the plan that was taking shape in her mind.

"I won't do anything foolish, Sheriff," said Danielle. "Thank you for your concern."

She mounted the chestnut mare and rode away. Connally watched her go. Despite her suddenly mild demeanor, he suspected trouble. He sighed. The girl was ready to raise hell and kick a chunk under it, and there was nothing he could do.

When Danielle returned home, Dr. Soble's buckboard stood in the yard. Jed and Tim met Danielle at the corral.

"You can't go in," said Tim. "Doc Soble ran us out. Did you learn anything in town?"

Wordlessly, not trusting herself to speak, Danielle handed them their father's beat-up old wallet. Tim took the ragged billfold, and both boys stared helplessly at it. Jed finally spoke.

"How . . . where . . . did you get it?"

"From the sheriff," Danielle said. "It came through the mail. Here's the letter that came with it."

She passed the letter to Jed, and Tim read it over his brother's shoulder. Finished, they spoke not a word, for their teeth were clenched in anger and tears crept down their cheeks. Suddenly, the front door opened, and Dr. Soble emerged. Danielle, Tim, and Jed waited at the doctor's buckboard.

"How is she?" Danielle asked anxiously.

"In shock," said Dr. Soble. "She has a weak heart, and another such shock could kill her. She's in bed. See that she stays there. I left some medication, and I'll be back the day after tomorrow."

Danielle, Jed, and Tim watched the doctor drive away. Not until his buckboard was lost to distance did anyone speak.

"We got to find the sons of bitches that done Pa in," Tim said.

"Damn right," said Jed. "I'm ready."

"Neither of you will be fourteen until June fifth," said Danielle, "and you're not going anywhere. You heard what Doc said about another shock killing Ma."

"But them bastards got to pay for what they done," Jed said.

"They will," said Danielle, "but we're not going to discuss it anymore until Ma's able to hear of it without it killing her. If either of you breaks the news to her, I can promise you there'll be hell to pay. Not from Doc, but from me."

They went on into the house, looking in on their sleeping mother. She seemed so thin and frail, Danielle wondered if she would *ever* be strong enough to learn the terrible truth of what had happened to Daniel Strange.

St. Joseph, Missouri. April 30, 1870.

It was ten days before Dr. Soble allowed Danielle to show Margaret Strange Dan's wallet and the letter that came with it. She wept long and hard, ceasing only when Jed and Tim entered the room.

"Ma," said Jed, "old man Summerfield's hired Tim and me to do his gunsmithing."

"Yeah," Tim said. "Business is awful. I think he's regrettin' ever buying the place from Pa. Jed and me ain't as good as Pa was, but we're better gunsmiths than old Summerfield or anybody else in town."

"The two of you are staying in school," Margaret Strange said. "It's what your father would want. Let Summerfield find someone else to do his gunsmithing."

"Ma," said Tim, "it takes money to live. Jed and me will each earn ten dollars a week, with a raise when business gets better."

It suited Danielle's plans for her brothers to take the gunsmithing work, for it would ease the shock when Danielle revealed her plans to her mother.

"Let them hire on as gunsmiths, Ma," Danielle said. "They're already near as good as Pa was, and they can read, write, and do sums. They're the men of the house now, and we'll need the money more than they need the schooling."

It was the inescapable truth, and Margaret Strange reluctantly gave in.

Danielle waited a month more before revealing her plans to avenge her father's death. Margaret, Danielle, Jed, and Tim had just finished supper, and were gathered around the table while Margaret read a chapter aloud from the family Bible.

"I have something to say," Danielle told them. "I was seventeen years old the thirtieth day of April, and I'm a woman. I'm as good with a gun as Pa was. I aim to find and punish his killers if it takes me the rest of my life."

"No," said Margaret. "This is no task for a woman. I forbid it."

"Woman, my eye," Tim said. "You're just a shirttail girl with big feet."

"I won't be going as a woman," said Danielle. "I'll cut my hair and dress like a man."

Jed laughed. "Some man. When you walk, your chest jiggles like two cougars fightin' in a sack."

Margaret slapped him. Hard. Despite her tough talk, Danielle found herself blushing furiously. Tim grinned broadly, obviously wishing to comment, but didn't speak lest he, too, incur his mother's wrath. Danielle said no more about her vendetta until her brothers had ridden to St. Joseph, to attend to their gunsmithing duties. Her mother would be difficult enough to win over, without the embarrassing comments of her brothers.

"Ma," said Danielle, "I haven't changed my mind about finding Pa's murderers."

"I said no, and I haven't changed *my* mind," Margaret Strange said. "Whatever gave you the idea you can function in a man's world? Why, every time you walk—"

"Oh, damn it, Ma, don't start *that* again," said Danielle. "I'll make myself a binder for my chest and wear a shirt a size too big. Nobody will ever know."*

"If you get shot and somebody has to undress you, they'll know," Margaret insisted.

"I don't aim to get shot," said Danielle. "You know how fast Pa was with a gun, and you know that I'm faster than he was."

Margaret Strange sighed. "I know you can take care of yourself under ordinary circumstances, and so could

*A binder was a band of cloth women used to flatten their breasts.

your father, but not against an outlaw gang. If I give my permission and anything happens to you, it would be the finish of me."

"I tell you, nothing's going to happen to me," Danielle said. "I know it was a gang that killed Pa, but I aim to find out who they are and go after them one at a time. I'm more grown up than you think, and I'm not about to do something foolish that could get me killed."

"But you have no money," said Margaret, "and with your father gone, we're going to need the little that we have."

"I have a hundred dollars," Danielle said. "Remember, Pa gave me fifty dollars for my birthday last year, and the year before. Besides, I'm good enough with a horse and rope to find work on a ranch if I have to."

Slowly but surely, Danielle overcame all her mother's objections. Margaret reluctantly cut the girl's hair to a length that might suit a man. Using strong fabric, Danielle doubled the material and then sewed it securely. Under one of her father's too-big shirts, there wouldn't be any "jiggling" going on.

Danielle wisely said nothing to Jed and Tim of her plans, and cautioned her mother not to. It would be difficult enough for Margaret, when her sons realized Danielle was gone to perform a task that they fancied their responsibility.

St. Joseph, Missouri. June 30, 1870.

Much against her wishes, Margaret helped Danielle prepare for her journey.

"You'd better take these shears with you, to trim your hair," Margaret said.

Danielle wore one of her father's shirts and placed two more in her saddlebag, with her extra Levi's. She buckled the gun belt around her lean waist, tying down the holster just above her right knee. A black, wide-brimmed Stetson completed her attire.

"Land sakes," said Margaret, "you *do* look like a man. Just be careful when and where you take your clothes off."

"Oh, Ma," Danielle said, embarrassed.

When all else had been done, Danielle went to the barn and saddled the chestnut mare. The good-byes had been said, and Margaret stood on the porch, watching Danielle ride away. Before crossing a ridge, Danielle turned and waved. There were tears in her eyes, a lump in her throat, and a nagging premonition that she might never see her mother again. Danielle carefully avoided St. Joseph, for there was hardly a person in town who wouldn't recognize the chestnut mare. She rode almost due south, bound for Fort Smith. Once there, she would talk to Deputy U.S. Marshal Buck Jordan.

Fort Smith, Arkansas. July 5, 1870.

Danielle was directed to the courthouse in which the marshal's office was located. A lawman sat behind a desk, barely noticing as she entered.

"What can I do for you, son?"

"Where can I find Deputy Marshal Buck Jordan?" Danielle inquired. Her voice was naturally low, like that of Daniel Strange himself, and she made it even lower to sound as much like a man as possible.

"The hotel, likely," said the lawman. "It's across the street, where he generally stays when he's in town."

"Jordan's in room four," the desk clerk told Danielle after she inquired about the deputy marshal.

Danielle knocked on the door several times before a voice answered from within.

"Who are you, and what do you want?"

"I'm Dan Strange," Danielle answered, making her voice huskier again. "You buried my father, and I want to talk to you if I may."

"I remember," said Jordan. "Come on in."

Danielle entered, and was dismayed to find Jordan sitting on the edge of the bed, wearing only his undershirt. She fought back a blush, forcing her eyes to meet his. She quickly explained her reason for being there.

"The only thing I didn't put in the letter," Jordan said, "was that your pa killed a pair of the bunch before they got him. Ten others rode away, leading two horses with empty saddles."

"Which way did they go?" Danielle asked.

"South," said Jordan. "Deeper into Indian Territory."

"You didn't pursue them?"

"They had a one-, maybe two-day start," Jordan said, "and there was ten of 'em. There was also rain that night, washing out their tracks."

"So they murdered my pa, and they're gettin' away with it," said Danielle.

"Look, kid," Jordan said, "Indian Territory's one hell of a big place. Outlaws come and go. You could spend years there without finding that particular bunch of killers, even if you could identify them. Besides, they may have ridden on to Texas, Kansas, or New Mexico."

"I appreciate what you did," said Danielle. "Now would you do me one more favor and draw me a map, so I can find my pa's grave?"

"Yeah," said Jordan. "Reach me my shirt off of that chair."

Danielle handed him the shirt, and from the pocket he took a notebook and the stub of a pencil. Quickly, he drew the map and tore the page from the notebook.

"Look for a big oak tree," Jordan said. "It's been hit by lightning, and one side of it's dead. Like I showed it on the map, it's almost due west from here."

"Thanks," said Danielle. Without a backward look, she walked out.

He had done little enough, but Danielle realized the lawman had been honest with her. There was no way of knowing where the outlaws had gone. Her only clue was her father's silver-mounted Colt, with an inlaid letter "D" in both grips.

"One of you took his Colt," she muttered under her breath. "When I find you, you son of a bitch, you'll tell me the names of the others before I kill you."

As she calmed down, aware of the vow she had just made, it occurred to her that she had never fired a gun in anger, nor had she ever killed. It wasn't going to be enough, just looking like a man. She would have to think like a man, like a killer. Finding a mercantile, she laid her Colt on the counter.

"I want two tins of shells for it," she told the storekeeper, in her man's voice.

"That's a handsome piece," said the storekeeper.

He brought the shells, and after buying enough supplies to last a week, Danielle rode out of Fort Smith, riding west along the Arkansas River. Darkness caught up with her before she found the landmark oak Jordan had mentioned. Rather than risk a fire, she ate a handful of jerked beef and drank from the river. Finding some decent graze, she picketed the chestnut mare, knowing that Sundown would warn her by nickering if anyone came near. She then lay down on one of her blankets, drawing the other one over her. She had removed only her hat and gun belt and held the fully loaded Colt in her hand. Sometime near dawn, the chestnut mare snorted a warning. Danielle rolled to the left just as two slugs ripped into the blanket on which she had been lying. She took in the situation in a heartbeat. There were two men, both with weapons drawn. They fired again, the slugs kicking dirt in her face. Belly-down, Danielle fired twice and the deadly duo were flung backwards into the brush by the force of the lead. Danielle was on her feet in an instant, fearing there might be more men, but all was quiet except for the restless Sundown, who smelled blood. With trembling hands, Danielle thumbed out the empty casings, replacing them with more shells. Bushwhacking was a cowardly act, and she had no doubt the pair were outlaws of some stripe, but why had they tried to kill her? She had acted swiftly, doing what she had to do, but as she looked at the two dead men, she became deathly ill, heaving. She forced herself to breathe deeply, and finally, after washing her face in the river, she mounted Sundown and again rode west.

It was late in the afternoon when Danielle reached the lightning-struck oak where Dan Strange had died. The mound—already grassed over—was where Jordan had told her it would be. She removed her hat, wiping tears from her eyes on the sleeve of her shirt.

"I'll get them for you, Pa," she said aloud. "If God's merciful and lets me live, I swear I'll gun them down to the last man."

Chapter 1

Danielle spent her second night in Indian Territory unmolested. As she lay looking at the glittering stars, it occurred to her she might actually have to join a band of outlaws to find the men she sought. Somewhere, one of the killers carried her father's Colt, and it was a unique piece that a man who lived by the gun would remember. *Could* she pass herself off as an outlaw among killers and thieves? It seemed the only way. She remembered Buck Jordan sitting on the edge of his bed, wearing only his undershirt. She realized she had led a sheltered life, and that men on the frontier were likely more crude than she even imagined. The kind of men she must associate with would soon become suspicious of her furious blushing. She drifted off to sleep. Tomorrow she would begin looking for a band of outlaws. The distressing thought crossed her mind that she might die the same senseless death as her father had, but that was the chance she had to take.

Indian Territory. July 8, 1870.

Three days into Indian Territory, Danielle encountered a group of men who could only be outlaws. It was late in the day when she smelled wood smoke.

Dismounting, leading the mare, she called out a challenge.

"Hello, the camp!"

A rustling in the brush was proof enough that one or more of the outlaws were preparing to cover her.

"Come in closer, where we can see you," a voice shouted. "Strangers ain't welcome."

"I'm Dan Strange," Danielle shouted back, "and my grub's running low. I was hoping for an invite to supper."

"Come on in," the voice invited, "but don't get too busy with your hands. We got you covered."

There were four men in camp, and two more who came out of the brush.

"Hell," said one of the men, "it's a shirttail kid that ain't old enough to shave."

"What are you doin' in the Territory, kid?" a second outlaw asked. "You won't find nobody here to change your diapers."

"I shot two *hombres* near Fort Smith," said Danielle, "and they had friends. It seemed like a good idea to move on."

It was time for a test, and one of the outlaws reached for his Colt. He froze before he cleared leather, for Danielle already had him covered.

"You're awful damn sudden with that iron, kid," said the man who had been about to draw. "Put it away. I was just testin' you. Part of our business is bein' suspicious. Who was the two *hombres* you gunned down?"

"I have no idea," Danielle said. "They came after me with guns drawn so I shot them."

"*You* shot *them* while they had the drop on you?"

"I did," said Danielle. "Wouldn't you?"

"If I was fast enough," the outlaw said.

The rest of the men laughed and relaxed. It was the

kind of action they could relate to, and the outlaw who had just been outdrawn introduced the bunch.

"I'm Caney Font. To your left is Cude Nations, Slack Hitchfelt, and Peavey Oden. The two varmints that just come out of the brush is Hargis Cox and Cletus Kirby."

"I've already told you my name," said Danielle.

"That's an unusual iron you're carryin'," Kirby said. "Mind if I have a look at it?"

"Nobody takes my Colt," said Danielle.

"The kid's smarter than he looks," Cude Nations said.

"Hell," said Kirby, "I never seen but one pistol like that, and I wanted a closer look. It looks like the same gun Bart Scovill had."

"Well, it's not." Danielle said. "A gunsmith in St. Joe made only four of these."

"I reckoned Scovill likely stole the one he had," said Kirby. "He ain't the kind to lay out money on a fancy iron. He claimed he had it made special, just for him, and it *did* have a letter 'D' inlaid in the butt plates." Danielle's ears pricked up at the mention of the gun.

"That don't make sense," Hargis Cox said. "Bart Scovill's got no 'D' in his name."

"You ain't knowed him as long as I have," said Caney Font. "His middle name is David, and there's times he calls himself Bart Davis."

"Where are you bound, kid?" Cude Nations asked.

"Away from Fort Smith," said Danielle.

The outlaws laughed. Her answer had told them nothing, and it was the kind of humor they could appreciate.

"We don't eat too high on the hog, kid," Caney Font said, "but you're welcome to stay to what there is."

The food was bacon, beans, and sourdough biscuits,

washed down with coffee. Danielle was ravenous, having had no breakfast.

"Kid," Caney Font said, after they had eaten, "we might could use that fast gun of yours. That is, if you ain't playin' games."

"Pick a target," said Danielle.

"What about this tin the beans was in?" Slack Hitchfelt said.

Without warning, Hitchfelt threw the tin into the air. In a split second, Danielle fired twice, drilling the can with both shots before it touched the ground.

"My God, that's some shootin'," said Caney Font. "How'd you learn to shoot like that, kid?"

"Practice," Danielle said, punching out the empty casings and reloading.

"How'd you like to ride with us to Wichita on a bank job?" asked Caney Font.

"I don't think so," Danielle said. "I have other business."

Cletus Kirby laughed. "What business is more important than money?"

"Killing the bastards that murdered my father," said Danielle.

"Then I reckon you ain't interested in joinin' us," Slack Hitchfelt said.

"No," said Danielle.

"Then I reckon it's unfortunate for you, kid," said Caney Font. "One word to the law in Wichita, and it'll all be over for us."

"I'm not going to Wichita," Danielle said.

"You're a sure enough killer, but you ain't no outlaw," said Peavey Oden.

Danielle saw it coming. She had refused to throw in with them, and having revealed their plans, they had to kill her. If they all drew simultaneously, she was doomed. But they had no prearranged signal. Peavy Oden drew first, with Hargis Cox and Cletus

Kirby a second behind. Danielle fired three times in a drumroll of sound, while the men who had drawn against her hadn't even gotten off a shot. The remaining three outlaws were careful not to move their hands.

"The rest of you—Font, Nations, and Hitchfelt—are welcome to saddle up and ride," said Danielle. "Make the mistake of following me, and now that I know your intentions, I'll gun you down without warning."

"We ain't about to follow you, kid," said Caney Font. "At least, I ain't."

"Me neither," Nations and Hitchfelt said in a single voice.

"Then saddle up and ride," said Danielle.

Careful to keep their hands free of their weapons, the trio saddled their horses and rode into the night. Danielle's hands trembled as she reloaded her Colt. While she had a lead toward one of her father's killers, she had already gunned down five men. When and where would it end? She saddled the chestnut mare and was about to mount when it occurred to her that she should search the dead outlaws. As distasteful as the task was, she found a total of a hundred and twenty dollars in the pockets of the dead men. Common sense soon overcame her guilt and she took the money.

Already tired of killing and outlaws, she rode south, toward the Red River and Texas. There was a chance the men she hunted had traveled as far from the scene of their crime as they could, and Texas was by far larger than Indian Territory. Danielle forded the Red at the familiar cattle crossing, near Doan's Store. Taking some of the money she had, she bought supplies she had been doing without, such as a small coffeepot, coffee, a skillet, canned beans, and some cornmeal. On second thought, sparing her bacon, she bought half a ham, which was all the chestnut mare could comfortably carry.

The storekeeper eyed her curiously, for he had seen all kinds come and go. They were getting younger all the time, he decided, with a sigh. Danielle continued riding south. Eventually, she came to the village of Paris, Texas. There was a general store, a livery, a hotel, and a sheriff's office. Adjoining the hotel was a cafe. Already tired of her own cooking, Danielle went to the cafe and ordered a meal. Once finished, she had a question for the owner.

"I'm looking for a gent name of Bart Scovill. His middle name is Dave, and sometimes he goes by that."

"Can't help you there," said the cafe's cook. "You might try Sheriff Monroe. He knows everybody within two hundred miles."

Danielle took a room at the hotel and went looking for Sheriff Monroe, finding him in his office, cleaning his Winchester.

"Barton Scovill is sheriff over to Mineral Wells, in Palo Pinto County. His kid run off up north somewhere to stay out of the war. I ain't seen him in near ten years. He'd be near thirty by now."

"I'd hate to ride all the way over there and find out he's the wrong *hombre*," Danielle said. "Do you know if his middle name is Dave, or David?"

"I got no idea," said Sheriff Monroe. "To tell the truth, my own son was killed in the war, and I got no respect for them that run off to avoid it."

"I can't say I blame you, Sheriff," Danielle said. "Thanks for your help."

Danielle took the chestnut mare to the livery, rubbed her down, and ordered a double portion of grain for her. She then took her saddlebags and Winchester to the small room she had rented. Clouds were building up in the west, and there would be rain before dark. She felt the need of a good night's rest in a warm bed, with a stall and grain for the chestnut mare. The first thing she did was lock the door, draw the window shade, and strip off all her clothes. She was well endowed enough that the binder was extremely uncomfortable, and she took it off gratefully. She then sat on the bed naked and cross-legged, cleaning and oiling her Colt. Again, she fully loaded it with six shells. Outside, the wind was screaming around the eaves, and there was the first pattering of rain on the windowpane. Danielle delayed supper until the rain subsided, enjoying the comfort of the rickety bed. By the time she reached the cafe, the rain had started again. Dusk was falling as she left the cafe, and that and the rain were all that saved her. Two slugs slammed into the cafe's wall, just inches from her head. Instantly, Danielle had her Colt out, but with the rain and darkness, there was no target. Reaching her room, she removed only her hat, boots, and gun belt. The Colt she placed under her pillow. But the night was peaceful, and Danielle lay awake wondering who had fired the shots at her the day before. Carefully, she made her way to the cafe for breakfast, and then to her room for her saddlebags and Winchester. She saddled the chestnut mare and rode east toward Dallas.

Dallas, Texas. July 11, 1870.

Dallas was the largest town Danielle had ever visited, and she was somewhat in awe of it. She dismounted before a livery, and the first person she saw was Slack Hitchfelt.

"Hold it, kid," he said, his hands raised. "I don't want no trouble."

"You missed last night," said Danielle. "Sure you don't want to try again?"

"I ain't drawin' on you, kid, now or ever," Hitchfelt said.

"Where's your scruffy partners, Font and Nations?"

"I dunno," said Hitchfelt. "We busted up. Said they was ridin' north. To Dodge City, likely."

"I'm sorry to hear that," Danielle said. "You deserved one another."

Danielle kept her eye on Hitchfelt until he rode away. She then left the chestnut mare at the livery, taking her saddlebags and her Winchester. The rain had continued most of the day, with every indication it would last the night. Danielle got herself a cheap room in an out-of-the-way hotel, returning to it after supper. She propped a ladder-back chair under the doorknob and slept with her Colt in her hand.

Mineral Wells, Texas. July 13, 1870.

It wasn't difficult to find the sheriff's office. Danielle had bought a second Colt, and she placed the gun her father had given her in her saddlebag, replacing it with the ordinary Colt in her holster. If Bart—or Dave—Scovill was around, the fancy weapon would immediately arouse his suspicion. She would use her mother's maiden name if there was a chance her true family name might reveal her mission to the killers.

"Sheriff," she said, "I'm Daniel Faulkner, and I'm looking for work of just any kind. Do you know of anybody that's hiring?"

"Not a soul, kid," said the sheriff. "The war chewed everybody up and spit 'em out. Nobody has anything but a few cows, and they're all but worthless unless you can get 'em to the railroad, and it takes money to do that."

While Danielle was in the sheriff's office, a young

man reined up outside and came in. Two things about him immediately caught Danielle's attention. A lawman's star was pinned on his vest, and in his holster was the silver-mounted Colt with a "D" on the grip. This man was one of her father's killers!

"Excuse my poor manners," said the sheriff. "I'm Barton Scovill, and this is my son, Dave, who's also my deputy. Dave, this is Daniel Faulkner."

The younger Scovill nodded. Not trusting herself to speak, Danielle stepped out the door, closing it behind her. She paused by the chestnut mare, seeking to calm herself and ease her shaking hands. The irony of it struck her, and it might have been amusing under different circumstances, but as things stood, the first of the men she must kill to avenge her father was a deputy sheriff. There was no mistaking the pistol that had belonged to her father, and no doubt she'd get the rope if she were captured for killing Scovill. She had to devise a plan, and so she went looking for a livery for the chestnut mare, and an obscure hotel for herself. Finding both, she took her saddlebags and Winchester to her room, where she stretched out on the bed to think.

"Damn it," she said aloud, "I must get close enough to do the job, and still manage to escape without being seen."

Just then she recalled seeing a notice posted on the hotel's front window. Saturday night there was to be a Palo Pinto County dance. She got up and went downstairs.

"What about that Palo Pinto dance?" she asked the desk clerk. "Would it be worth my time, staying over for it?"

"If you like pretty girls," said the desk clerk. "They'll be here from all over."

"Then I reckon I'll stay," Danielle said.

Dallas, Texas. July 16, 1870.

Danielle hated to part with the money, but she needed some fashionable female clothes, and she couldn't afford to be seen buying them in Mineral Wells. In Dallas, her first item was a bonnet to conceal her short-cropped hair. It wasn't uncommon for a cowboy to buy clothing for his intended, and nobody gave this "cowboy" a second look. Danielle bought a divided riding skirt in pale green to match her eyes, and a white blouse with fancy white ruffles. Finally, she bought a pair of fancy half-boots. She bought no underclothing, and the blouse was the actual size she wore. The "jiggle" that so amused her brothers suited her purpose, and other women would brand her a brazen hussy, but she must intrigue her intended victim enough to draw him away from the dance. Taking her purchases, she rode back to Mineral Wells. She entered the rear door to the hotel, making her way up the back stairs. In her room, she tried on the clothes, tying the bonnet so as to best conceal her short hair. Finally, she stood admiring herself in a cracked mirror on the dresser.

"Danielle Strange," she said aloud, "you look like a whore, but to a man that's a killer lowdown enough to have hanged my pa, a whore would be just his style."

Now there was nothing to do except wait four days for the planned dance. Meanwhile, Danielle learned it was to be a street dance at the farthest end of town, near a second livery across from a general store. A visit to the livery revealed overhead beams that were suited to Danielle's purpose.

Mineral Wells, Texas. July 20, 1870.

Danielle waited until the dance was in full swing before slipping out the hotel's back door and down the stairs. Soon she was mingling with the crowd. A bandstand had been built in front of the livery, and besides the caller, there were four musicians. One played a guitar, the second a banjo, the third a fiddle, and the fourth a mouth harp. A sixth man was beating time with the straws on the fiddle.*

The moment the men spotted Danielle, there was almost a fist fight over who was to have the first dance. It was a while before Scovill got his chance.

"Tarnation," said Scovill, "where have you been all my life?"

"Around," Danielle said coolly. "Where have *you* been?"

"I was in the war," said Scovill, lying.

"The war ended five years ago," Danielle said. "Did you get home crawling on your belly?"

"By God, if you was a man, I wouldn't take that."

Danielle laughed tauntingly. "If I was a man, folks would be wondering if you stand or squat."

"You brazen bitch," he said, shoving her away from him.

But there were a dozen men waiting to take his place, and despite Danielle's macabre reason for being there, she was beginning to enjoy the dance. As she had expected, Scovill couldn't stay away.

"Do you drink whiskey?" he asked.

Danielle laughed. "What do you think?"

Danielle had never tasted whiskey in her life, but it might be her only chance to get Scovill away from the crowd.

"I got a bottle stashed in a rear stall in the livery barn," Scovill said. "Give me a few minutes and come

---

*In traditional hoedowns, sometimes the only instrument would be a fiddle. The "straws" were often porcupine quills. A man "beating the straws" stood beside the fiddler, tapping the "straws" against the body of the instrument. It created a drumlike effect, providing the fiddler some rhythm.

on back. Be careful you ain't seen. Whiskey ain't allowed."

After Scovill had been gone for what she judged ten minutes, Danielle ducked into the shadow of the barn roof's overhang. The two swinging front doors of the livery were closed. Only a full moon lighted the wide open doors in the rear.

"Here," said Scovill. "Have a drink."

"Not yet," Danielle said.

She loosened the waist of her divided skirt, allowing it to drop to the ground. She wore nothing beneath it, and Scovill caught his breath.

Scovill laughed. "The drink can wait. There's an empty stall over there with some hay."

In the stall, he quickly shucked his gun belt and was bent over, tugging at his boots. Danielle took the opportunity to grab her father's Colt from Scovill's holster and struck him across the back of the head with it. He folded like an empty sack. Quickly, Danielle dressed herself and, taking a rope hanging outside the stall door, fashioned a noose. She had never tied one before, but the result would serve the purpose. Once she had the business end of it around Scovill's neck, she threw the loose end over an overhead beam. It took all her strength to hoist Scovill off the ground. She then tied the loose end of the rope to one of the poles separating the stalls and, with a leather thong, tied Scovill's hands behind his back. He began to groan as he came to his senses. His eyes began to bulge, and he kicked as the cruel rope bit into his throat.

"Now you know how my father felt when you hanged him in Indian Territory," Danielle said.

Taking her father's gun belt, holster, and the silver-mounted Colt, she slipped out the livery's back door. Keeping to darkened areas, she hurried back to her hotel. Going up the back stairs to her room, she saw nobody. Everybody was still at the dance. Once in her room, she locked the door and stripped off her female finery. She placed it all in her saddlebags and donned her cowboy clothing. Carefully, she placed her father's gun belt and Colt with her female clothes and her own initialed silver-mounted Colt. Again, the Colt she placed in her holster was the plain one. Being caught with either of the silver-mounted Colts would brand her as Scovill's killer.

Danielle lay awake, unable to sleep, in her mind's eye watching Dave Scovill strangle to death. Near midnight, the dance broke up. Suddenly, there were three distant shots. It was a signal for trouble, and it was from the livery where Scovill had been hanged. Obviously, he had been found when the livery closed. Come the dawn, Danielle went to the mercantile and bought a knee-length duster. Returning to her hotel room, she buckled the Colt her father had made for her on her right hip. She then buckled her father's belt around her waist, so that the weapon was butt forward, for a cross-hand draw. Trying on the knee-length duster, she found it adequately concealed the two fancy weapons.

Wearing the duster, Danielle sought out a cafe for breakfast. She passed the sheriff's office and was astounded to find the place packed and men milling around outside.

"What's happened?" she innocently asked a by-stander.

"Last night during the dance, some bastard hanged Sheriff Scovill's kid in the livery barn, right while the dance was goin' on."

"Any idea who did it?"

"The sheriff figures it might have been some men back from the war. Dave Scovill run off up north until the war was over and didn't come back until a few days ago. There's a lot of folks that lost kin in the war, and they didn't like Scovill. Trouble is, they all got alibis. Wasn't robbery. He still had money in his pockets, but whoever done him in, took his fancy silver-mounted pistol."

It was time for Danielle to saddle up and ride on. Looking back, she realized she had made one bad mistake. In her hurry to hang Scovill, she had neglected to force from him the names of his nine companions. From now on, her task would be doubly hard. Finished with breakfast, she saddled the chestnut mare and rode northwest toward Dodge. Scovill had returned to Texas because it was his home. With Reconstruction going on in Texas, might not the rest of the outlaws have ridden to Dodge, Abilene, or Wichita?

Dodge City, Kansas. July 24, 1870.

Danielle reached Dodge late in the afternoon and, taking a room at the Dodge House, went to Delmonico's for supper. Afterward, she found the sheriff's office. Sheriff Harrington was a friendly man, well liked by the town.

"Sheriff," said Danielle, "I'm Daniel Faulkner. I'm looking for men returned from the war. Some of them knew my father, and I owe them."

"If they don't have names," Harrington said, "you won't have much luck."

"No, I don't have any names," said Danielle, "but I owe them."

"Why not run some ads in the weekly newspaper?" Harrington suggested. It was a brilliant idea.

Danielle found the newspaper office, asked for pencil and paper, and carefully composed an ad that read:

To whom it may concern; am interested in finding men who rode with Bart Scovill in Indian Territory recently. Payment involved. Ask for Faulkner, at Dodge House.

There was a three-day wait until the paper came out on Saturday, with a few more days to see if anybody went after the bait. The stay in Dodge had eaten a hole in Danielle's wallet. In another two weeks, she would be forced to find work, just to eat. Thursday came and went with no response to her advertising. Not until Friday was there a nibble.

"Who's there?" Danielle asked in response to a knock on her door.

"I'm answerin' your ad," said a voice. "Do I come in, or not?"

Danielle unlocked and opened the door.

The man had the look of a down-and-out cowboy, with a Colt tied down on his right hip. He stood in the doorway, looking around, as though expecting a trap.

"There's nobody here but me," Danielle said. "Shut the door."

He closed the door and stood leaning against it, saying nothing.

"I'm Daniel Faulkner," said Danielle. "Who are you?"

"I'm Levi Jasper, and it's me that's entitled to ask the questions. Why are you looking for Scovill's friends?"

"Scovill and me had a job planned. He claimed he could get a gang together that he used to ride with. Then the damn fool got himself killed by some bounty hunter looking for draft dodgers. Now there's still a twenty-five-thousand-dollar military payroll that will soon be on its way to Fort Worth, and I can't handle it alone. Can you find the rest of the outfit?"

"I dunno," said Jasper, "and don't know that they'll be interested. They're scattered all over the West. They could be in St. Louis, New Orleans, Kansas City, Denver, and God knows where else."

"Are *you* interested?"

"Maybe, after I learn more about it. You ramroddin' the deal?"

"Not necessarily," Danielle said. "I just want a piece of it.

"Good," said Jasper. "I ain't sure the boys would ride with a shirttail *segundo*, even if we can find 'em. You aim to advertise in more newspapers?"

"If I had some specific names, I would," Danielle said. "Scovill never told me the names of the men he had in mind. I took a long chance, advertising for you. Tell me the names of the *hombres* I'm looking for, so I can ask for them by name."

"I dunno. . . ."

"Oh, hell," said Danielle, "just forget it. I'm just seventeen years old, and if you're so afraid of me, I don't want you on this job. I'll find somebody else."

"Damn it, nobody accuses Levi Jasper of bein' afraid. I can give you the names of the Scovill gang, and we'll pull this damn job of yours. One thing, though. I'm the *segundo*. When you find these varmints, tell 'em about Scovill, and that you're part of the gang. Let 'em believe I planned the thing."

"I will," said Danielle. "Now write down those names and where you expect me to find them. We don't have that much time."

Chapter 2

Danielle saddled the chestnut mare and rode east to Kansas City. She regretted losing out on Levi Jasper, but she had alerted the sheriff to her presence. Undoubtedly, Jasper had asked for her at the hotel, leaving her wide open to suspicion had anything happened to him. At least she had the names of the rest of the gang that had murdered her father. Levi Jasper would have to wait for another time and place. With her money running low, Danielle made her camp by a stream and picketed the chestnut mare nearby. She had no idea what she would use for money. Worse, if she was lucky enough to find work, the trail she followed would grow colder by the day.

Suddenly, the chestnut mare snorted. Danielle rolled to her left, her Colt in her hand, as the intruder's weapon roared twice. He had anticipated her move, and both slugs struck the ground just inches from her. There was no moon, but the starlight and muzzle flash was enough. Danielle fired twice. There was a groan and the sound of Jasper's body striking the ground. What had she said or done that had warned Levi Jasper? After having thought about it, the outlaw had apparently become suspicious, and whatever he had perceived as a mistake on his part, he had tried to undo. But Danielle still had the names— real or fictitious—of the remaining eight outlaws. She wouldn't need to spend anything more on advertising.

"Since you won't be needin' it, Jasper, I'll just see how much money you have in your pockets."

There was a considerable roll of bills, and Danielle took it without remorse. Saddling the chestnut mare, she continued east toward Kansas City. She must lose her trail among many others before Levi Jasper's body was discovered. Two hours later, she reached a little river town whose name she didn't know. But it had a hotel of sorts, a livery, a cafe, and some other buildings, including a general store. One sleepy old hostler was dozing in a chair before the livery. He sat up and looked around when he heard the chestnut mare coming.

"Stay where you are, old-timer," said Danielle. "I'll unsaddle, put her in a stall, and fork down some hay."

"I'm obliged," the hostler said.

With the mare safely in the livery, Danielle took a room at the one-story hotel. By the light of a lamp, feeling a little guilty, Danielle separated the roll of bills on the bed and was astounded to find there was more than six hundred dollars! Undoubtedly it was stolen, but from who, when, and where? Her conscience bothered her some, but there was no way to return the money, and besides, Danielle needed it desperately.

"The Lord works in mysterious ways" her mother was fond of saying, and Danielle said a silent prayer of thanks. Slowly, she began changing her mind about riding to Kansas City. She would be very close to St. Joe and home, and getting under way again would be hell without Jed and Tim finding her and following. With that in mind, she changed directions, riding to the southeast. Since she had no idea where to go next, why not New Orleans?

Springfield, Missouri. July 28, 1870.

Reaching Springfield, she left the chestnut mare at a livery and rented herself a modest hotel room. She had lived in Missouri all her life, but had never been south. A huge lump rose in her throat when she recalled what her father had once said.

"Someday, Danielle, when we've got money, we'll all board one of the big steamers and ride all the way to New Orleans."

But Daniel Strange's good intentions died with him, and there would be no steamboat ride to New Orleans. Instead, Danielle was riding obscure trails, seeking his cold-blooded killers. Eight of them remained at large, and she had no idea how long her quest would take. Jed and Tim might be grown and her mother dead by the time vengeance was hers, which was a chilling thought.

After supper, there seemed little to do except go to bed or make the rounds of the various saloons. Danielle chose the saloons, and since she didn't drink, she invested a few dollars in games of chance. A one-dollar bet on a roulette wheel won her ten dollars, more than she had lost all night. There were poker games in progress, and never having played before, Danielle left them alone. She could watch, however, listening to the conversation of the players. One of them mentioned a name that immediately caught her attention.

"Too bad about that killing in Indian Territory a while back. But they got just one of the men. Pete Rizner rode like hell and escaped. The law ain't done nothin', and Pete's mad as hell. He's swearin' one of the bunch of renegades was Rufe Gaddis, from right here in Missouri."

"Pardner," said Danielle, "my pa was killed by outlaws in Indian Territory not too long ago, and I'm wondering if the outfit you're talking abut might not be the same lot. I'd like to talk to Pete Rizner. Where can I find him?"

"Likely at the Busted Flush saloon," one of the men said. "His brother owns it. Good luck, kid."

The Busted Flush wasn't doing a thriving business, and all the occupants watched as Danielle entered. She went immediately to the barkeep.

"Where can I find Pete Rizner?" she asked.

"Who wants to know, and why?" asked the barkeep.

"I'm Daniel Strange, and I'm after the bastards that killed my pa in Indian Territory a few months ago. I'd like to know if they're still there, or if they've scattered."

A man slid his chair back and stood up, and when Danielle looked at him, he spoke.

"I'm Rizner, kid. Take a seat, and I'll tell you all I know."

Danielle drew back a chair and sat down at the table.

"Drink?" Rizner asked.

"No, thanks," said Danielle.

"It was gettin' on toward dark," Rizner said. "We seen these riders coming, and they all had their Winchesters out. There was eight of 'em, and I yelled for my pard to mount up and ride. I jumped on my horse and lit out, but my partner grabbed his Winchester and tried to stand 'em off. They rode him down, and he didn't get a one of 'em. I'd swear on a Bible the lead rider was Rufe Gaddis. You know him?"

"No," Danielle said, "I'm after the bunch that robbed and murdered my Pa. It looks as though it could be the same outfit. Where were you attacked?"

"Maybe a hundred miles north of Dallas, not too far north of the Red," said Rizner. "Ride careful, kid, and good luck."

Danielle didn't bother with any more saloons. From the information she had received, it seemed almost a certainty that the outlaws she was seeking had never left Indian Territory, or had soon returned. Danielle prepared to ride out at first light. Unless there had been rain in the Territory recently, there still might be tracks.

Indian Territory. August 1, 1870.*

Weary after more than three hundred miles, Danielle was looking for a stream by which she might spend the night when she came upon a grisly scene that made her blood run cold. There was a scattering of human bones, and a skull that still had its hair. There were the ripped, shredded remains of a man's clothing. The leg bones from the knees down were still shrouded in run-over, knee-length boots. There were tracks in abundance, and they all led south. Sundown, the chestnut mare, snorted, not liking this place of death. It was too late to follow the trail with darkness, but a few minutes away and far to the west, golden fingers of lightning galloped across the horizon. Danielle mounted and rode south, following the trail as long as she could see. There would be rain before dawn, and the trail would be washed out. Danielle made her camp on the north bank of Red River, wondering why the outlaws had suddenly returned to Texas after the killing.

She covered herself with her slicker for some protection against the expected rain, which started about midnight. There was no dry wood for a fire, which was just as well, for the smoke would have announced her presence. Breakfast was a handful of jerked beef,

*Near present-day town of Lawton, Oklahoma.

and through a drizzling rain, she crossed the Red River into Texas. She had ridden three or four miles when a voice suddenly spoke from a nearby thicket.

"You're covered. Rein up and identify yourself."

Danielle reined up, carefully keeping her hands on her saddle horn.

A young man stepped out with a Winchester, and he looked no older than Danielle.

"What are you doing here?" he asked.

"I'm Daniel Strange," said Danielle, "and I'm no outlaw or killer. Last April my pa was robbed and killed in Indian Territory, and I'm after the bastards who did it. I found what I thought was their trail late yesterday, but the rain last night washed it out. They all rode south, and having no trail to follow, I was just taking my chances."

"I'm Tuck Carlyle," the young man said, leaning the Winchester against a shrub. "This is our spread, for what it's worth. I live here with my sister, Carrie, and Audrey, my ma. Pa went off to war and never come back. The damn outlaws from Indian Territory have been rustlin' us blind. They hit us again night before last and already had the jump on me before I found out what they'd done."

"If it's the same bunch I'm after," said Danielle, "there's eight of them. That's a hell of an outfit for just you to be trailing them."

Tuck laughed. "Then there's at least one more gent that's as big a fool as I am, and that's *you*. You're trailing them, too."

"There wasn't anyone else," Danielle said. "My two brothers are barely fourteen."

"You don't look much older than that yourself," said Tuck.

"I'm just barely eighteen," Danielle said, "but I can ride, rope, and shoot."

"I believe you," said Tuck. "Have you caught up to any of the killers yet?"

"Two of them," Danielle said, "and I know the names of the others. Or at least the names they're using."

Tuck Carlyle whistled long and low. Westerners did not ask or answer foolish questions, and this young rider being alive was proof enough that two outlaws were dead.

"Trailing the varmints after last night's rain is a waste of time," Tuck said. "Why don't you ride on back to the house with me? You can meet Ma and my sister, Carrie, and have some breakfast."

"You talked me into it," said Danielle. "All I've had is a little jerked beef."

"Let's ride then," Tuck said. "God, could I use a cup of hot coffee, but we haven't had any since before the war."

"The war's been over for five years," said Danielle.

"No money," Tuck said gloomily. "Texans don't have a damn thing to sell except cows, and us little ranchers can't get 'em to market. We'd have to drive to Abilene, right across Indian Territory. Them damn outlaws would love having them delivered, instead of having to come and get 'em."

"Are other small ranchers having the same problem getting their cows to market?"

"All I know of," said Tuck. "Nobody has money for an outfit, and they can't afford the riders they'd need for a gather."

"If maybe half a dozen small ranchers went in together," Danielle said, "you might have enough riders to gather everybody's cows, one ranch at a time. With the gather done, you could take a rider or two from every ranch and drive the herd to Abilene."

"By God, that might work," said Tuck. "I can think of four others that's as desperate as we are."

"How big is your spread?" Danielle asked.

"A full section," said Tuck. "It's 640 acres."

"Hell's bells," Danielle said, "if that's a small ranch, how large is a *big* one?"

Tuck laughed. "When I call us a small outfit, I mean we don't have that much stock."

"You could sell some of the land if you had to," said Danielle.

"We may have it taken from us," Tuck said, "but we'll never sell. This section of land has been in our family for four generations. It has an everlasting spring, with the best water for fifty miles around. The only potential buyer is Upton Wilks. He owns sections to the east and west of ours, and he's sittin' back like a damned old buzzard, just waitin' for us to default on our taxes."

"If it's not improper for me to ask," Danielle said, "how *are* you paying your taxes?"

"My aunt in St. Louis—Ma's sister—married well," said Tuck. "She's kept our taxes paid, God bless her, so we wouldn't lose the place. Now this damned Upton Wilks is tired of waiting. He's trying to force my sister, Carrie, to marry him, and that would just about amount to *giving* him our spread."

"How does Carrie feel about him?"

"She hates his guts," Tuck said. "He's old enough to be her daddy, drinks like a fish, and goes to a whorehouse in Dallas every Saturday night. That's his good points."

Danielle laughed, in spite of herself.

"I'd give the place up before I'd have her marry that sorry old bastard," said Tuck.

"I don't blame you," Danielle said. "A girl shouldn't have to make a sacrifice like that. There must be some other way. Since we're both after the same gang, maybe I'll stick around for a few days, if I won't be in the way."

"You won't be," said Tuck. "We don't have a bunk-house, but we have a big log ranch house. There's plenty of room."

"I'll contribute something toward my keep," Danielle said. "I don't have a lot of money, but I do have a five-pound sack of coffee beans."

"Merciful God," said Tuck, "if you was a girl, I'd marry you for that."

Danielle laughed, feeling more at ease with him all the time. She was truly amazed that she had adapted so well to the ways of men. They were generally crude, and without even a shred of modesty among their own kind. She no longer blushed at anything said or done in her presence. She had already acquired enough swear words to hold her own with the best of them. Prior to leaving home, she hadn't been around men except for her father and brothers. She recalled the time when she had been fifteen and her brothers Jed and Tim were thirteen. She had followed them to the creek that July, watched them strip and splash around. But to her horror, the boys discovered her. When they told her mother, Margaret Strange caught the tail of Danielle's skirt, lifted it waist-high, and spanked her bare bottom. Jed and Tim had never let her forget it. She now felt old and wise in the ways of men, her childhood gone forever.

The Carlyle ranch house, when they reached it, was truly grand, the product of a bygone era. A huge wraparound porch covered the front and each side of the house. Danielle had a sudden attack of homesickness. Tuck's mother stood on the porch, watching them ride up, reminding the girl of her own mother.

"I brought some company, Ma," said Tuck. "This is Daniel Strange. He's hunting that same bunch of outlaws that's stealing our cattle."

"Welcome, Daniel," Mrs. Carlyle said. "Get down and come in."

A young girl—obviously Tuck's sister, Carrie—
stepped out on the porch. She looked at Danielle with
obvious interest, making Danielle nervous.

"Daniel," said Tuck, "this is my sister, Carrie.
We're trying to marry her off to somebody so Upton
Wilks will leave her alone."

The implication was obvious, and Carrie hung her
head, blushing furiously.

"Tuck," said Mrs. Carlyle, "don't tease your sister
about that. You and Daniel come on into the house,
and I'll scare up some breakfast. We have bacon, ham,
and eggs, but we've been out of coffee for years."

"Flour too," Carrie added.

"I have some supplies, including flour and coffee,"
said Danielle. "It's risky, building a fire to cook, when
you're tracking outlaws in the Territory."

"We surely will appreciate the coffee and flour,"
said Mrs. Carlyle, "and you're welcome to stay with
us as long as you like, sharing what we have."

"Lord," Danielle said, "I haven't had an egg since
I left St. Joe, Missouri."

"Your home is there?" Mrs. Carlyle asked.

"Yes," said Danielle. "My mother and two brothers
are there."

"You're so young, your mother must be worried
sick," Mrs. Carlyle said. "What have those outlaws
done to bring you this far from home?"

"They robbed and murdered my pa in Indian Territory," said Danielle. "Jed and Tim, my twin brothers,
are only fourteen."

"You don't look much older than that, yourself,"
Mrs. Carlyle said.

"I'm a little past seventeen," said Danielle, "and
there was nobody else to track down Pa's killers."

"He's already killed two of them and learned the
names of the others," Tuck said.

Danielle spread out the provisions from her saddlebags on the big kitchen table. Every eye was on the five-pound bag of coffee beans, and Danielle was glad she had bought them.

"Ma," said Carrie, "I'll make us some coffee. The rest can wait."

"It sure can," Tuck said. "Do we even have a coffee-pot anymore?"

"Yes," said Mrs. Carlyle, "but I have no idea where it is."

"You can search for it later," Tuck said. "For now, boil it in an open pot, and we'll add some cold water to settle the grounds."

"I'll go ahead and start breakfast," said Mrs. Carlyle. "Carrie and I have already eaten, but I'd dearly love to have a biscuit."

"Ma," Tuck said, "I've told Daniel our problems here, and he's come up with a way we can get our cows to market at Abilene. Tell her what you told me, Daniel."

"Dear God, yes," said Mrs. Carlyle.

Quickly, Danielle repeated what she had suggested to Tuck as they had ridden in.

"But we have no money for an outfit," Carrie said.

"I have some money," said Danielle. "It would buy enough grub to get you there with your herds."

"But you'll need what you have as you search for those killers," Mrs. Carlyle said. "It wouldn't be fair to you."

"I believe it would be more than fair," Danielle said. "I think that bunch of outlaws in Indian Territory will come after the herd. So you see, I have a selfish reason for wanting you to make that drive to Abilene. I'll be going with you."

"God bless you for making the offer," Mrs. Carlyle said. "Tuck, what do you think?"

"I think we'd better talk to Elmer Dumont, Cyrus Baldwin, Enos Chadman, and Wallace Flagg," said

Tuck. "It'll take all of us, I think, and since Daniel has offered to stake us with the necessary grub, the first hundred head of cattle we gather should be his."

"No," Danielle said. "You'll need your money. Besides, your herd will be bait enough to attract that bunch of outlaws I'm trailing."

"No matter," said Mrs. Carlyle. "You've brought us hope, and there will be five of us small ranchers. Any one of us can spare you twenty head. Tuck, when you talk to the others, be sure you tell them Daniel has a stake in this drive."

"But I feel guilty, taking some of your stock," Danielle protested.

"Without your help, we couldn't raise enough money for the drive, and neither could the others," said Tuck. "I'll want you to go with me and talk to the others. This sounds like the makings of a miracle, and I'm not sure they'll take me serious."

"Then I'll go with you," Danielle said. "We must have a couple of pack mules, and each rider will need spare horses. We must see how many can be had."

"Damn the luck," said Carrie, "we won't have enough horses, and I don't know of anybody with mules."

"We'll find them," Danielle replied. "First, let's see if we can line up those other ranchers for the drive."

"I'd like to go," said Carrie, "but there won't be enough horses."

"Somebody must have a wagon," Danielle said. "We could fix it up with seats for some of you, and still have room for our grub."

"That's a better idea than pack mules," said Tuck. "I doubt the others will be willing to leave their families behind."

"Besides the three of you," Danielle said, "how many other people will be involved?"

"Elmer Dumont has a wife and a son about my

age," said Tuck. "Cyrus Baldwin has a wife and two sons old enough to work cattle. Enos Chadman has a wife, a daughter, and a son. Wallace Flagg has a wife and two sons."

"Including me, there'll be nineteen of us," Danielle said. "For those who don't have a horse, the wagon will have to do."

"Every girl my age can tend cattle," said Carrie. "The wives can go in the wagon."

"We'll suggest that," Tuck added. "With us so close to Indian Territory, a man would object to leaving his wife and daughters behind. We'll need plenty of ammunition, too."

"I thought Texans weren't allowed to have guns during Reconstruction," said Danielle.

"Only those who served in the war against the Union," Tuck said. "I have a Colt and a Henry rifle. I'm sure the others will be armed, but they may lack ammunition."

"I have three hundred dollars to buy what we'll need," said Danielle.

"That should be more than enough," Tuck said, "but we may have to go to Dallas for the ammunition."

"Then take a wagon and go to Dallas after everything," said Mrs. Carlyle. "None of us are that well known in Dallas, while going to a smaller town would be like telling everybody what we intend to do."

"Everybody will know anyway, Ma," Tuck explained. "You can't keep a roundup secret, but we can try. We'll buy supplies in Dallas, and the way I see it, we have four weeks to get the herd together. It's already the first week in August. If we can't get away from here by September first, there'll be snow before we can reach Abilene."

"Then let's pay a visit to those other four ranchers today," Danielle said. "If each of the five of you can get cattle to market this fall, you'll have the money for a much bigger drive next spring."

"Bless you, son," Mrs. Carlyle beamed. "It will be our salvation."

"There's a rider coming," Carrie announced. "Oh, God, it's Upton Wilks. Please, Tuck, don't you or Daniel leave while he's here."

"We'll wait awhile then," said Tuck. "He *would* show up now."

From his very attitude, Danielle decided she didn't like Upton Wilks. He wore a fancy silk shirt and new boots. As though he owned all of Texas, he reined up, dismounted, and pounded on the door. He had the ruddy face of a drinking man, and most of his hair was gone. Tuck opened the door.

"What do you want, Wilks?" Tuck demanded. "You know you're not welcome here."

"Maybe I'll wait for Miss Carrie to tell me that," retorted Wilks. "I'm here to call on her."

Carrie rose to the occasion, responding in a manner that shocked them all, especially Danielle.

"I choose not to see you, Mr. Wilks. This young man, Daniel Strange, is now working for us, and I prefer his company to yours. Now please go."

Wilks's eyes narrowed and fixed on Danielle. "What Upton Wilks wants, Upton Wilks gets," he said.

"Not necessarily," said Danielle, her cold green eyes boring into his. "Carrie's told you to leave. Now go, while you still can."

"I don't take orders from no snot-nosed kid," Wilks said. "You want me to go, why don't you make me?"

With blinding speed, Danielle drew her right-hand Colt. Wilks's left earlobe vanished with a spurt of blood.

"Damn you," Wilks bawled. "You shot me!"

He clawed for his Colt and Danielle held her fire until he cleared leather. Then she shot the gun from his hand. Ruined, it clattered to the floor. Wilks's ear had bled heavily down his face, so that it looked as though his throat had been cut. With a deathly white face, he backed toward the door, his voice shaking with anger. "You'd better go back to where you come from, you young fool. I'll have you hunted down like a yellow coyote."

"Mr. Wilks pays others to do what he's not man enough to do himself," Carrie said. "Just be sure you watch your back, Daniel."

Speech failed Wilks. He mounted his horse and, spurring the animal cruelly, galloped away.

"Carrie," scolded Mrs. Carlyle, "you shouldn't have antagonized him. Having him think Daniel's here to see you wasn't the truth. You might have gotten him killed."

Tuck laughed. "I don't think so, Ma. I saw John Wesley Hardin draw once, and he was slow as molasses compared to Daniel."

"I'm sorry, Daniel," said Carrie, "but what I said was the truth. Everybody that's ever been on the outs with Upton Wilks has ended up dead. He hires a lot of men, some of them no better than outlaws."

"Carrie," Danielle said, "if you have to stomp a snake, don't put it off till the varmint bites you. I wouldn't be surprised to find Wilks behind the rustling."

"He has enough riders," said Tuck.

"No matter," Danielle said. "We'll go ahead with our plans. If Wilks is on the prod, I'll take care of him when the time comes. Tuck, you and me had better have some of that hot coffee and go calling on those other ranchers."

The first of the four ranchers they called on was Elmer Dumont. All of them—including Dumont's son, Barney, and his, wife Anthea—gathered around the dining table. Danielle and Tuck, speaking by turns, revealed the proposed plan to the Dumont family.

"Count us in," Elmer Dumont said. "If somethin' ain't done, we can't last the winter."

"We got maybe seven hundred head left, Pa," said Barney.

"I think we'd better limit the drive to five hundred head per outfit," Daniel said. "We'll be shy on remuda horses. Twenty-five hundred head will be more than enough to see all of you through the winter and provide enough money for another drive in the spring."

"With Daniel puttin' up money for grub and ammunition, I aim to see that he gets the first hundred head when we reach Abilene," Tuck said. "Does anybody disagree with that?"

"My God, no," said Dumont. "I'd give fifty head, myself."

"We'll be back," Tuck said. "We're callin' on Cyrus Baldwin, Enos Chadman, and Wallace Flagg. Then we'll all meet together and lay some plans."

Chapter 3

Cyrus Baldwin, his wife, Teresa, and his sons, Abram and Clement, listened while Tuck Carlyle and Danielle outlined the plan to save the small ranchers by driving a trail herd to Abilene.

"It's a great plan," Baldwin said. "We should be ashamed of ourselves for not thinking of it on our own, instead of sitting here starving."

"Before you give me too much credit," said Danielle, "remember that my purpose is to lure that bunch of outlaws into the open. I figure a herd of cattle will do it."

"Let them come," Baldwin said. "At least we'll have a chance to fight for our herds. As it is now, they're stealing us blind. The only way we can stop that is to take our own cows to market, and to kill as many of these thieving bastards as we can."

"We can count on you then," said Tuck.

"You sure can," said the four Baldwins together.

"We'll need extra horses, a team of good mules, and a wagon," Danielle said. "Can you help us?"

"If we're all going on the drive," Baldwin said, "we can take all four of our horses. I believe both Enos Chadman and Wallace Flagg have wagons and mules."

"We're calling on them next," said Tuck. "Unless you hear something different from us, then be at our place at noon tomorrow. We must start the gather soon, and finish the drive, if we're going to do it before snow flies."

Enos Chadman, his wife, Maureen, their son, Eric, and their daughter, Katrina, received the news of the proposed gather and drive with enthusiasm.

"We have a wagon and a team of mules," said Chadman. "You're welcome to make use of them."

"Wallace Flagg also has a wagon and mules," Maureen said. "Perhaps we can take both the wagons."

"We may have to," said Chadman. "With all you ladies going, you may be riding the wagons so that the riders can have an extra horse or two."

"We'll talk to Wallace about maybe using his mules and wagon," Tuck said. "Unless we tell you otherwise, be at our place at noon tomorrow. We have to make plans and decide what supplies we'll need."

"While the rest of you start the gather, Tuck and me can go to Dallas for supplies and ammunition," said Danielle.

Wallace Flagg, his sons, Floyd and Edward, and wife, Tilda, were as responsive as the other small ranchers had been.

"We'll be glad to take our mules and wagon," Flagg said, "but be sure when you go for supplies that you get a couple of sacks of grain."

"We'll get the grain," said Tuck. "I figure each animal should have a ration of grain three times a week."

The Carlyle Ranch. North Texas. August 5, 1870.

Wallace Flagg, along with his sons and wife, arrived first. Tilda Flagg drove the wagon. Next came Enos Chadman, his wife, his son, and daughter. His wife drove the wagon. Cyrus Baldwin and his family were next to arrive. Last to arrive was Elmer Dumont, with his wife and son. There was an impressive display of livestock, about eight mules and eighteen horses in total. Some of the horses were being led, because most of the women rode on the wagons.

"Thanks to Daniel," Mrs. Carlyle announced, "we have coffee."

There were whoops of joy from all those gathered, for they had been forced to do without many things before, during, and after the war. Sipping their coffee, they gathered on the porch. There were chairs for the ladies while the men hunkered down, rocking back on their boot heels.

"Ma has paper and pencil," said Tuck, "and she'll make the list. Each of you sing out the provisions you think we'll need. Don't bother with ammunition. We'll get to that and the weapons after we've decided on everything else."

As the list grew, Danielle worried that the three hundred dollars she had promised to provide wouldn't be nearly enough. Finally, they were ready to discuss weapons and ammunition.

"Thanks to the Comanches, every damn one of us has a rifle," said Wallace Flagg, "and if I ain't mistaken, they're all sixteen-shot Henrys."

"Anybody got any other kind?" Tuck asked.

Nobody spoke, and they quickly moved on to revolvers.

"Now," said Tuck, "all of you with pistols raise your hands."

All the men and their sons raised their hands.

"That's eleven including me," Danielle said. "What make?"

"Colt," they all answered at once.

"All of them may not work," said Wallace Flagg. "We ain't been able to afford parts."

"Anybody with a weapon that doesn't work," Danielle said, "give Mrs. Carlyle your name. My pa was a gunsmith, and I learned the trade. We'll hold off on our trip to Dallas until we know which gun parts we need. Between Indians and outlaws, we need every weapon in perfect condition."

Before day's end, Danielle and Tuck had their list of needed provisions and a second list of necessary gun parts.

"Take my wagon," Wallace Flagg offered. "The bed's a little longer than usual."

"I'll take my wagon and teams home," said Enos Chadman, "but we'll plan on using them for the drive. If nothing else, we can put the canvas up, keepin' our bedrolls dry."

"I feel good about this drive," Mrs. Carlyle said when the last of their visitors had gone.

"So do I," said Tuck. "These other ranchers are all older than Daniel or me, yet they have agreed to throw in with us. I think we should head for Dallas in the morning."

"How far?" Danielle asked.

"About eighty miles," said Tuck. "Figure three days there with an empty wagon, maybe five days returning with a load."

"We could be gone a week or more then," Danielle said. "As it is, we'll be until the middle of August starting the drive."

"No help for that," Tuck said. "We'll need time for the gather. Maybe we can make up some of what we've lost after we're on the trail."

When supper was over at the Carlyle place, Mrs. Carlyle spoke.

"Tuck, you and Daniel should get to bed early, getting as much rest as you can."

"I aim to do just that," said Tuck. "You coming, Daniel?"

"Not yet," Danielle said. "This is my favorite time of the day, and I think I'll sit on the porch for a while."

Danielle went out, thankful the Carlyles had a large house. What would she have done had Mrs. Carlyle suggested Danielle share a room with Tuck? She sat down on the porch steps as the last rosy glow of the western sun gave way to purple twilight. To her total surprise, Carrie Carlyle came out and sat down beside Danielle. Uncomfortably close.

"May I sit with you?" Carrie asked.

"It's all right with me," said Danielle.

"What will you do when you've tracked down the men who murdered your pa?" Carrie asked.

"I haven't thought much about it," said Danielle. "It may take me a lifetime."

"Then you'd never have a home, wife, or family," Carrie said.

"I reckon not," replied Danielle. "Is that what you want, a place of your own?"

Danielle could have kicked herself for asking such a perfectly ridiculous question.

"I want a place of my own, and a man," Carrie said, moving even closer. "That's why I was thinking . . . hoping . . . you might come back here. I've never been with a man before, and I'd like you to . . . to. . . ." Her voice trailed off.

"Carrie," said Danielle uncomfortably, "you're still young. I'll have to settle somewhere after this search is done. I can't say I won't come back here, but I can't make any promise either."

"I hope you do," Carrie said. "There's nobody around here my age except Dumont's son, Barney, Baldwin's sons, Abram and Clement, Chadman's son, Eric, and the sons of old Wallace Flagg, Floyd and Edward."

Danielle laughed. "Hell, Carrie, there's six of them. Can't you be comfortable with at least one?"

"Damn it, you don't understand," said Carrie. "They've all been looking at me, but all they want is to get me in the hayloft with my clothes off. You're not like that, are you?"

"No," Danielle said, more uncomfortable than ever. "I've sworn to find Pa's killers, and that comes ahead of any plans of my own. Until you find a man who appeals to you, stay out of the hayloft."

"I've found one, and he doesn't want me," said Carrie miserably.

It was well past time to put an end to the conversation, and Danielle did so.

"With Tuck and me getting an early start, I'd better get some sleep."

Tuck and Danielle were ready to start at first light. Along the way, they rattled past the Wallace place, waving their hats. Traveling due south, they stopped only to rest the mules. They saw nobody else. Reaching a creek just before sundown, they unharnessed the mules, allowing the tired animals to roll.

"I aim to dunk myself in that creek for a few minutes," Tuck said. "How about you?"

"No," said Danielle, her heart beating fast. "I'm hungry, and I'll get supper started."

She tried her best not to notice Tuck Carlyle as he shucked his boots and clothing, but found it an impossible task. She watched him splash around in the creek, and unfamiliar feelings crept over her, sending chills up her spine. Tuck caught her watching him, and he struck a ridiculous, exaggerated pose. Danielle forced herself to laugh, hoping she was far enough away that he couldn't see her blush. Never having had experience with a man, she was becoming far too interested in Tucker Carlyle. She tried to rid him from her mind, but there was always that vision of him standing there naked in the creek, laughing at her. She lay awake long after Tuck began snoring, and when she finally slept, he crept into her troubled dreams.

Dallas, Texas. August 10, 1870.

There was no trouble along the trail to Dallas. The only difficulty was Danielle's newly discovered infatuation with Tuck Carlyle. There were times when she dreamed of donning her female clothing, telling him the truth, and allowing him to have his way with her. But she quickly put all such thoughts from her mind. She must avenge her father before she did anything else. But there was a troublesome possibility that kept raising its ugly head. Suppose—now or later—when Tuck learned she was a woman, he didn't want her? There was no accounting for male pride. She swore like a man, looked, sounded, and acted like a man, and could draw and shoot like hell wouldn't have it. She found herself worrying more and more what the consequences might be of her having assumed the role of a man. Just as they were approaching Dallas, Tuck caught her off guard with a question.

"Dan, you want to find a cheap hotel room? Ma gave me the few dollars she had."

"Save it," Danielle said. "The weather's warm, and our camp won't cost anything. With so much to buy, you may have to add your few dollars to mine."

"Yeah," said Tuck, "I keep forgetting just how much we need. Since we have all of the afternoon ahead of us, let's find a mercantile and get them started on our provisions and ammunition list. Meanwhile, we can track down a gunsmith for the parts we need."

With the roll of bills she had taken from Levi Jasper, Danielle had well over six hundred dollars, but she had set a limit of three hundred for the trail drive.

However it came out, she would still need money to keep herself fed and supplied with ammunition. But there was much to be gained. Unanimously, she had been promised a hundred head of cattle, and if they brought as much as thirty dollars a head, that would be three thousand dollars! They left the wagon at the mercantile with instructions to load the supplies and ammunition as their list specified.

"Dallas is a right smart of a town," Tuck said. "If we ride, it'll have to be bareback, on a couple of the mules."

"Then let's ride the mules," said Danielle.

Tuck laughed. "We won't have to worry about robbers. They'll figure if we had anything worth stealing, we wouldn't be riding mules without saddles."

Eventually they found a gunsmith and, for fifteen dollars, got the springs and various other parts needed to restore all their Colts to working condition. Tuck insisted on paying the gunsmith from the little money his mother had given him.

"You should have let me pay for that," Danielle said.

"We'll be lucky if you have enough to pay for all the provisions we're getting at the mercantile," said Tuck. "It's still too soon to return to the mercantile. Let's go into some of the big saloons and see what they're like."

"I don't drink," Danielle said.

"Neither do I," said Tuck, "but I may never get to Dallas again, and I'd like to have a look at some of it."

They entered a prosperous-looking place called the Four Aces, and it being early in the afternoon, there were few patrons. Five men sat at a table, playing poker. Two women sat on bar stools and eyed the new arrivals with interest.

"Let's watch the poker game a few minutes," Tuck

said. "Maybe I can sit in for a hand or two. I still
have five dollars."

"Table stakes, dollar limit," said the house dealer
as Tuck and Danielle approached.

"I'll stand back out of the way and watch," said
Danielle.

She didn't approve of Tuck taking part in the game,
and she was sure Mrs. Carlyle had not given Tuck her
last few dollars for such a purpose. But she said nothing. Tuck hooked the rung of a chair with his boot,
pulled it out, and sat down. He lost three pots before
he started winning. He seemed to have forgotten Danielle as she stood with her back to the wall, watching
the game. To her dismay, one of the painted women
approached her.

"Hello, cowboy," drawled the woman. "I'm Viola.
While your friend's at the table, I can show you a
good time upstairs. Just twenty-five dollars."

"No," Danielle replied. "I'm not interested."

"So you don't have twenty-five dollars," said the
whore. "How about fifteen?"

"Ma'am," Danielle said coldly, "I wouldn't have it
if it was free. Now leave me the hell alone."

Viola slapped Danielle across the face, and Danielle
had to grit her teeth to avoid a similar response. A
man didn't strike a woman—not even an insolent saloon whore. It was time to leave the saloon, and Danielle did so, waiting outside on the boardwalk for
Tuck. He soon joined her.

"I won fifty dollars," he said. "What got the saloon
woman on the prod?"

"She wanted to take me upstairs for twenty-five dollars," said Danielle, "and when I refused, she came
down to fifteen dollars. I told her I wouldn't go upstairs with her if she was free."

Tuck laughed. "Sooner or later, you'll have to get
your ashes hauled."

"My *what?*"

"Oh, hell," said Tuck, "you *know*. Get with a woman."

"There's no time or money for that," Danielle said, "even if I was so inclined. I reckon you've already been there, have you?"

"No," said Tuck sheepishly, "but I did look through a window once, watching Carrie taking a bath in a washtub."

Danielle laughed. "I don't think that counts. A man shouldn't do that to his sister."

"Damn it," said Tuck, "there's not a female within riding distance of our place, except Katrina Chadman."

"She's pretty," Danielle said, trying mightily to hide her jealousy.

"She's also just sixteen," said Tuck. "From what I hear, I think her ma dresses her in cast-iron underpants."

Danielle laughed, slapping her thighs with her hat, as a man would do.

"Give her another year or two," Tuck continued, "and some varmint will have his loop on her. Barney Dumont, Eric Chadman, Abram and Clement Baldwin, and the Flagg boys, Floyd and Edward, are all makin' eyes at her. What chance would I have?"

"None, if you don't get off your hunkers and make a bid," said Danielle. "You could always take her swimming. You don't look too bad in your bare hide."

"I might have known if anybody ever said that to me, it'd be some *hombre*," Tuck said.

"You have fifty dollars," said Danielle. "While you're here, you could always buy yourself a heavy hammer and a good chisel."

"What for?" Tuck demanded.

Danielle chuckled. "For the cast-iron underpants."

Tuck laughed in spite of himself. They reined up

before the mercantile, where the other two mules were tied to a hitch rail. The canvas on their wagon had been raised, and one look told them the loading—or most of it—had been done. Barrels of flour sat on the floor of the wagon bed, while lighter goods were piled as high as the wagon bows would permit.

"My God," said Tuck, "I hope we can pay for all this."

"We might as well find out," Danielle said. "Come on."

"Three hundred and thirty-five dollars," said the storekeeper. "I had to cut back to half the sugar and coffee beans you wanted, so's I'd have some for my regular customers."

Wordlessly, Tuck handed Danielle thirty-five dollars with a wink while she counted out the three hundred. It was ironic that the fifty dollars he had won in the saloon had paid for the needed gun parts, with enough left to pay the mercantile.

They harnessed the mules, and only when they mounted the wagon box did Tuck say anything.

"Well, I'm broke. There goes the hammer and chisel."

Danielle laughed. "Maybe you won't need it until we reach Abilene. By then, you'll have the money. Or maybe you can get in solid enough with Enos Chadman, he'll let you have the key."

Tuck Carlyle actually blushed, and Danielle laughed. She had learned much in the ways of men, and when it came to cowboy humor, she was giving as good as she got.

"There'll be rain sometime tonight," said Tuck, changing the subject.

"At least we have a wagon canvas to protect the load," Danielle said. "I reckon we'll get wet, but we'll be wet many more times before we get to Abilene."

North of Dallas. August 14, 1870.

"We're making good time," said Tuck. "All the way from our ranch to Dallas and back to here in four days. We've come a good twenty-five miles today. If the rain don't bring mud hub-deep, we'll be home in another two days."

But the rain started just before dark and didn't diminish until the next morning.

"Damn," Tuck groaned, "we ain't going anywhere with this load. Not until there's been a couple of days of sun."

They picketed the mules and sat down on the wagon tongue, allowing the morning sun to dry their sodden hats, boots, and clothing.

By way of conversation, Danielle spoke.

"If we find and gun these varmints down, there may be others who'll continue rustling your cattle. What of them?"

"If we make this drive successfully," Tuck said, "we'll have money to hire riders and protect our stock. With cows selling for three dollars a head in Texas, we might actually buy some. Three thousand dollars would buy a thousand head. That many cows driven to the railroad in Kansas, my God, that's thirty thousand dollars."

"Don't let me gun down your dreams," said Danielle, "but we'll be reaching the railroad late in the season. Cattle buyers may not be paying as much as we're expecting."

"Maybe not," Tuck said, "but there's a chance they'll pay *more* than we're expecting. There likely won't be another herd until spring."

Conversation lagged. Having already commented on the rain, the mud, the delay, the rustlers, and the possible price of cattle in Kansas, there seemed little else to say.

"That night, while I was on the porch, Carrie sat with me awhile," said Danielle. "She tried to make me promise I'd come back to your place after I've avenged my pa."

Tuck laughed. "You could do worse. Carrie's two years younger than me. By the time you get back to our place, Carrie will be a prize for some varmint. She'll be chomping at the bit to do something."

"She's chomping at the bit *now*," Danielle said. "She's likely to do something foolish."

"I reckon," said Tuck. "Has any woman ever done anything else, when it comes to a man? She'll likely be wantin' to share your blankets before we reach Abilene."

"Tuck Carlyle, that's no way to speak of your sister," Danielle said heatedly.

"Whoa," said Tuck. "Don't go jumping on me. It was you that suggested she's after you like an old hen after a grasshopper. If she aims to bed down with some *hombre*, then I hope it's you, instead of one of the Dumont, Baldwin, Chadman, or Flagg boys."

"Sorry," Danielle said, "but I'm not beddin' with anybody until I've found and disposed of my pa's killers. Why don't you talk to Carrie, and give her some advice?"

"She'd tell me where to stick my advice," said Tuck. "She always has before. If you promised to come back here, it might keep her out of trouble."

"I can't use a lie to protect her," Danielle said. "Before my search ends, I could be dead. Besides, after I'm gone, she'll forget. The Dumont, Baldwin, Chadman, and Flagg boys may begin to look a little more promising."

Tuck laughed. "All any of them want is to take her somewhere and get her clothes off. Ain't you old enough to figure that out?"

"I reckon," said Danielle, holding on to her temper.

"While you're in Abilene, buy her some of those cast-iron underpants with the money, and throw away the key."

That silenced him, and for a long time, neither of them spoke.

"There's more clouds over yonder to the west. Unless it rains itself out before it gets to us, there could be more rain late tonight," Tuck finally said.

"Oh, damn it," Danielle said, "we'll *never* get to Abilene. We may never get back to your ranch."

But the rain ceased before it reached them, and the following morning Tuck came up with an idea.

"Why don't we hitch up the teams and see how far we can get today? I don't think I can stand another day sittin' on that wagon tongue, discussing cast-iron underpants for my sister, Carrie."

Danielle laughed. "Maybe I'll tell her that's what you aim to buy for her in Abilene."

"I don't care a damn," said Tuck. "I've done told her everything a girl should know, and maybe more. I told her if she wants a snot-nose kid before she's seventeen, to just do anything that strikes her fancy. I got cussed out for my efforts."

Despite the still muddy ground, Tuck and Danielle harnessed the teams and began their journey to the north. Tuck drove, steering the teams away from low places and keeping to high ground.

"You're good with a team and wagon," Danielle said.

"I'm good at most everything I've tried," said Tuck. "Of course," he said, winking, "I got a few things I ain't tried."

"One of them being Katrina, I suppose," Danielle said.

"Hell, I can dream, can't I?" said Tuck. "I saw her watching you while we were there at the Chadmans.

Chadman's impressed with you. By the time we get to Abilene, you may have already been inside those underpants."

"Maybe," Danielle said, for once not blushing, "but I'll tell everybody else what I've told you and Carrie. My pa's killers come first."

Despite the mud, Tuck's expert handling of the teams managed to keep the wagon on high ground. He continued on until after sundown before unharnessing the tired mules.

"I figure we're not more than thirty-five miles from the ranch," said Tuck. "If all goes well, we'll be there late tomorrow. Not bad, three days to Dallas and four back, returning with a loaded wagon."

"Where *are* they, Ma?" Carrie complained. "They've been gone a week today."

Mrs. Carlyle laughed. "Who are you missing? Tuck or Daniel?"

"I miss them both," said Carrie. "The rest of the ranchers have gathered their five hundred head, and they're waiting on us."

"They've also promised to help Tuck and Daniel with our herd," Mrs. Carlyle said. "It shouldn't be more than a day, with so many riders."

"There was a full night of rain to the south of here, night before last," said Carrie. "The mud may be deep. They may still be three days away."

"We'll just have to wait and see," Mrs. Carlyle replied. "I'm sure they'll be here as soon as they can."

The Carlyle Ranch. North Texas. August 18, 1870.

It was late in the evening, sundown not more than an hour away. Despite the scolding of Mrs. Carlyle, Carrie stayed rooted to her spot, continuing to look to the south as far as she could see. Finally, on the horizon, a moving speck became visible. It eventually turned into two teams of mules and a wagon.

"They're coming, Ma! They're coming!" Carrie shouted, running for the house.

Mrs. Carlyle and Carrie were waiting on the porch when Tuck reined up the tired and sweating teams. He was alone on the wagon box.

"Where's Daniel?" Carrie inquired in a quavering voice.

"Oh, he met a girl in Dallas and decided to spend a few days with her."

"No," Carrie cried, bursting into tears.

"Tuck," Mrs. Carlyle scolded, "don't tease your sister. Daniel's horse is still out there in our barn."

The joke was over, and Danielle managed to squeeze out of the wagon, where she had concealed herself.

"Damn you, Tuck Carlyle, I hate you," Carrie shouted.

"It was partly my idea," said Danielle.

"Then I hate you too," Carrie snarled.

"We got to find her a man somewhere, Ma," said Tuck, apparently deadly serious, "else there's no tellin' what will be takin' her to the hayloft."

It was more than Carrie could stand. Speechless, her face flaming red, she ran into the house.

Chapter 4

The Carlyle Ranch. North Texas. August 19, 1870.

"The first thing we'd better do," Tuck said, "is get the word to Dumont, Baldwin, Chadman, and Flagg that we're back. If they'll help us gather our herd, we'll be on the trail to Abilene tomorrow."

"They promised," said Mrs. Carlyle.

"Maybe we'd better remind them we're ready to begin," Danielle said.

"Then let's go," said Tuck. "We're losing more time."

Only Carrie said nothing, but stared vacantly out the window.

Tuck and Danielle weren't even off the Carlyle spread when they met Barney Dumont.

"I was just comin' to see if you'd made it back," Barney said. "Pa said if you was back that I'm to take the word to Baldwin, Chadman, and Flagg. We can start your gather today, getting on the trail that much quicker."

"We're ready," said Tuck, "and we have the needed parts for the Colts, besides the wagonload of provisions and ammunition."

"Then I'll tell the others to get on over to your place just as quick as they can," said Barney.

"Bueno," Tuck said. "It's the moment of truth.

We'll have to find out if we have cows enough to make the drive."

At Upton Wilks's ranch, Wilks was receiving a report from Kazman, his *segundo*.

"They're gettin' ready for a drive," said Kazman. "Four of the outfits has rounded up at least five hundred head. There's nobody left 'cept the Carlyles."

"Why not the Carlyles?"

"Tuck and the young gent stayin' with 'em took off south a week ago, in old man Flagg's wagon. Today they come back. From the tracks, I'd say the wagon's loaded to the bows. They likely been to Dallas, buyin' food and ammunition."

"Where the hell would they get the money?" Wilks demanded.

"Somebody staked 'em," said Kazman. "Maybe that new gent that's stayin' with 'em."

"Looks like we'll have to take care of him," Wilks said. "Give 'em a couple of days on the trail, but before the herd becomes trail-wise and settles down, stampede the lot of them from here to yonder."

"It'll be hell, finding them longhorns in Indian Territory," said Kazman. "I was hopin' we could grab the herd and take 'em on to Abilene ourselves."

"Maybe we can," Wilks said, "but we'll need more riders. Not countin' you and me, we got eight riders. There's nineteen in that outfit, and every one of them, even including the women, can shoot. We'll wait until they're practically out of Indian Territory before we take the herd. Let them do most of the hard work."

"I like it," said Kazman. "Ambush?"

"Yes," Wilks replied. "Shoot them all dead. Then when they default on their taxes, I'll take over all their ranches dirt cheap. Take a pair of riders with you and ride into Indian Territory. We'll need four or five more riders. No petty thieves. We want killers."

*   *   *

Within the hour, riders began showing up at the Carlyle ranch. The Dumonts were the first to arrive, followed by the Baldwins. The Chadmans were next, followed closely by the Flaggs.

"I'll need daylight to repair your Colts," Danielle said. "The rest of you begin gathering the cattle. When I'm done with the Colts, I'll join you."

"It's important we have those Colts ready," Tuck said. "Go ahead and fix them."

Danielle spread out a blanket on the grass beneath a tree. She then began work on the half-dozen Colts, breaking them down one at a time. Finished with one, she started on the second one before Carrie joined her.

"I thought you hated me," said Danielle mildly.

"I don't, really," Carrie said. "I'm just disappointed in you."

"I'm sorry to have disappointed you," said Danielle, "but you knew when I first rode in that I was after my pa's killers. I won't find them settin' on my hunkers here."

"I suppose not," Carrie said with a sigh. With Danielle being busy, the conversation lagged, and Carrie wandered back to the house.

An hour past noon, the riders drove in the cattle they had gathered.

"More than two hundred head," said Tuck proudly. "We got to gather the rest, run all the five herds together, and post guards. The rustlers could clean us all out in one night."

After a hurried dinner, the riders went to finish the gather before dark, if they could. Danielle, having finished repairing the Colts, went with them.

"Most of the varmints are holed up in thickets where there's shade," said Tuck. "We'll have to run them out of there."

"I've never worked cattle," Danielle said. "I don't know how much help I'll be, here or on the trail to Abilene."

"The secret to trail driving," said Tuck, "is keepin' the varmints bunched. Keep 'em on the heels of one another, so that every critter has a pair of horns right at her behind. It generally takes a few days—maybe a week—for them to get trail-wise and settle down."

Danielle rode into the brush with the other riders and was amazed at all the longhorns they flushed out. Some of the riders circled the growing gather, seeing to it that none of the cattle made a break for the thickets. With many riders, the gather proceeded quickly.

"I think we got enough," said Tuck, an hour before sundown. "Let's run a tally."

"I count five hundred and thirty head," Elmer Dumont said.

"I count five hundred and twenty-seven," said Cyrus Baldwin.

"Five hundred and thirty-two," Enos Chadman said.

"I count five hundred and twenty-five," said Wallace.

"Our herds has got a few more than five hundred," Elmer Dumont concluded. "We generally accept the lowest tally. Does that suit you, Tuck?"

"Yeah," said Tuck. "I'm glad to see this many. I was afraid, with all the rustling, we'd have trouble finding five hundred."

"You got lots of scrub thickets, especially near the spring runoff," said Wallace Flagg. "I believe we could drag out another five hundred if we had to."

"Let the others wait until spring," Tuck said. "It's important to get our gather on the trail to Abilene as soon as we can."

The gather was driven to the Carlyle ranch and herded in with more than two thousand of their kind.

"We got twelve men," said Enos Chadman. "We got to keep watch. I think with the herd bunched right here near the barn, we can get by with six men and two watches."

"It's always the men," Carrie Carlyle said. "I can shoot as well as any man here."

"No doubt you can, ma'am," said Chadman, "and I expect you'll get a chance to prove it before we reach Abilene. Get yourself one last good night's sleep in a bed."

The Trail North. August 20, 1870.

The first day on the trail, the cattle were predictably wild, seeking to break away and return to their old grazing meadows and shaded thickets. At her own request, Danielle rode drag. The chestnut mare quickly learned what was expected of her. When a cow quit the bunch, the mare was after her. Danielle had little more to do than just stay in the saddle.

"I reckon we've come ten miles," Enos Chadman said when they had bedded down the herd for the night.

"Lucky to do as well as that with a new herd," said Cyrus Baldwin.

"Starting tonight," Carrie said, "we'll need more than six on each watch. I'm offering to stand either watch."

"So am I," Katrina Chadman said.

"We may not need you," said Tuck. "We have enough men for a first and a second watch. The rest of you can just sleep with your guns handy."

"No," Katrina said. "We've already decided the women will do the cooking, and I can ride better than I can cook."

Her response brought a roar of laughter, and the

question was finally resolved when it was decided that Carrie would join the first watch, and Katrina the second.

"You ladies ride careful," said Enos Chadman. "If one of you gets spooked and shoots a cow, you'll end up washing dishes the rest of the way to Abilene."

On the first watch was Danielle, Tuck, Katrina, Elmer Dumont and his son, Barney, Chadman's son, Eric, and Wallace Flagg's sons, Floyd and Edward. Carrie had hoped to be part of the first watch, and she watched Katrina Chadman with some envy. Katrina was a year older than Carrie, and Carrie wanted to prove herself in front of Danielle.

Supper was over, and it was time for the first watch to mount up. The cattle were restless, being on the trail for the first time, and the riders were kept busy by bunch quitters. Danielle's task was made simpler by the chestnut mare. The horse seemed to sense when a cow was about to break away, and was there to head her. There was a moon, and it was Danielle's first opportunity to see Katrina Chadman close up. The girl had long blond hair that she wore in a single braid, and she rode her horse like she was part of it. For a few minutes Tuck rode alongside her, the two of them laughing. Danielle suffered a new emotion. As she watched them, flames of jealousy rose up, threatening to engulf her.

"Damn you, Katrina," said Danielle under her breath, "you haven't seen him jaybird naked in the creek."

The cattle finally settled down, and by the time the second watch came on at midnight, there were no more bunch quitters. Breakfast was an orderly affair, with Anthea Dumont, Teresa Baldwin, Maureen Chadman, Tilda Flagg, and Audrey Carlyle doing the cooking.

"This is the best I been fed in ten years," said Elmer

Dumont. "A man could start to liking these trail drives."

"A man generally don't have his women folks along to fix the grub," said Tuck. "We all know it's hard times in Texas, and we didn't dare leave them there."

"There's a stronger reason than that," Maureen Chadman said. "Katrina and me haven't had a stitch of new clothes since before the war, and we're practically naked. Surely we'll get enough for the herd so we don't go home in rags."

"We'll just have to hope we get a good price," said Enos Chadman uncomfortably.

"Katrina's cast-iron underpants are startin' to rust," Tuck said softly, standing behind Danielle.

"If anybody would know, it would be you," said Danielle coldly. "You spent the night following her around, instead of watching the herd."

"So what the hell is it to you?" Tuck demanded. "Sooner or later, she's got to give in to some *hombre*. Why not me? You reckon I can't do her justice?"

"I don't doubt that you can," said Danielle. "And neither does she. I just want to get this damn herd to Abilene, so I can get on with my life."

"You mean to get on with your killing," Tuck said.

"Well, just what the hell would *you* have done if your pa had been strung up without cause?"

"I deserved that," said Tuck. "I'd do the same thing you're doing."

Their second day on the trail was little better than the first. "We should reach Red River tomorrow," Elmer Dumont said. "From there on, every night will be a danger. They can even set up an ambush and pick us off in broad daylight."

"There's always the old Indian trick," said Wallace Flagg. "Stampede the herd, and when we separate to gather them, get us one at a time."

The third day on the trail, the cattle had begun to

settle down. The drive reached the Red River, making camp on the Texas side.

"This could be our last peaceful night," Cyrus Baldwin warned. "From here on, it could be Indians, outlaws, or both."

The night was still, and Danielle lay in her blankets, unable to sleep. She kept hearing Katrina laugh, and had no doubt Tuck Carlyle was keeping her amused. On Danielle's mind was the sobering realization that unless that murdering pack of outlaws died somewhere in Indian Territory, she would have to ride away and leave Tuck to the wiles of Katrina. At midnight, when it was time to change watches, Danielle spoke to Tuck.

"Well, did you get the key?"

"Not tonight," Tuck said cheerfully. "Maybe tomorrow night."

"Damn it," said Danielle, "like most men, you have only one thing on your mind."

"Then I reckon you don't," Tuck said. "Are you one of them fool *hombres* that prefers *other hombres* to women?"

"Tuck Carlyle, if we weren't on watch, I'd pistol-whip you for saying that."

"Just watch your damn tongue," said Tuck. "You're startin' to sound like a jealous female, and anytime you're of a mind to pistol-whip *me*, just keep in mind that I have a pistol too."

It silenced Danielle. Already, Tuck was suspicious of her. It was difficult, playing the part of a man when she most yearned to be a woman, but her resolve to find her father's killers was just as strong as ever. She would have to keep her silence, whatever Tuck and Katrina did. Danielle didn't realize it, but Tuck and Katrina were actually talking about her.

"I'd like to know Dan Strange a little better," Katrina said. "He keeps watching me, and he seems so nice."

"I reckon I'm not," said Tuck grimly.

"Sometimes you are," Katrina said, "and other times you're not. You think I haven't heard all the talk about my cast-iron underpants?"

"I didn't start that," said Tuck.

"I wouldn't expect you to admit it," Katrina said angrily, "but you repeated it."

"Hell, it's a reputation you created for yourself," said Tuck. "Your look-at-me-but-don't-touch attitude scares hell out of men."

"Everybody except you," Katrina said.

"And I'm gettin' exactly nowhere," said Tuck angrily. "Build yourself a reputation as a man-hater, and you won't need them cast-iron underpants."

Katrina laughed. "I'll give the key to the right man. Just don't get your hopes up too high, Tuck Carlyle."

Indian Territory. August 23, 1870.

The Red River crossing had been used many times before, and there was a shallows that allowed even the wagons to cross without difficulty. There was a trail of sorts, left by previous drives, and they followed it closely. Tuck was the point rider, and with the herd still behaving, he rode far ahead, seeking out a possible ambush. But all during their first day in Indian Territory, they saw nobody.

"From here on," said Elmer Dumont, "all of you on watch mustn't let anybody through your guard. Our lives and the herd are depending on you. No talking and no smoking, and when it's your turn to sleep, keep your horses saddled and picketed."

*   *   *

At the Wilks ranch, Kazman had just returned from Indian Territory. With him were four men, and he introduced them.

"These gents is Mitch Vesper, Elihu Dooling, Burt Keleing, and Chunk Peeler. I done told them what we got to do."

"Nothin' ain't been said about the pay," Dooling said. "This ain't one of them thirty-and-found jobs, is it?"

"Forty and found," said Wilks.

"Fifty and found," Dooling said. "If I got to shoot somebody, it'd better be worth my while."

There was quick agreement from Vesper, Keleing, and Peeler.

"Fifty and found, then," said Wilks, "but damn it, I want results."

"We can leave now and be in Indian Territory by midnight," Kazman said.

"I want you to get ahead of the herd and stampede them south," said Wilks. "There'll be no moon tonight, so don't go after the riders. Scatter the herd, and the riders will have to split up, looking for them. That's when we pick them off one or two at a time."

"Thirteen of us," Chunk Peeler said. "That's an unlucky number."

"Only if you don't do what you been hired to do," said Wilks. "Now get the rest of the bunch out of the bunkhouse, Kazman, and ride."

Within minutes, thirteen heavily armed men rode north toward Indian Territory.

Danielle noticed there was not much conversation between Tuck and Katrina, and she wasn't sure if it was by command or by choice. She was awake an hour before the second watch took to the saddle, and lay there listening. There was nothing to disturb the silence of the night except the occasional bawling of a cow.

An hour after the second watch had gone on duty, the raiders struck, riding in from the north. Bending low over the necks of their horses, they fired their pistols until it sounded like a small war in progress. The second watch fired at the elusive targets, their own shooting spooking the cattle all the more. The herd was on its feet in an instant, running south, seeking to escape these demons who swooped after them from the north. Tuck Carlyle and Wallace Flagg got ahead of the running longhorns, but they wouldn't be headed off, and the two cowboys had to ride for their lives to escape being trampled. The stampede thundered on, while those responsible for it fell back and vanished into the darkness. Slowly, the night watch made its way back to camp.

"Damn it," said Enos Chadman, "we didn't get a one of 'em."

"Well, at least they didn't get any of us, either," Elmer Dumont said. "That tells me that when we split up to gather the scattered herd, they'll try to gun us down."

"That bein' the case," said Tuck, "maybe we'd better let the cows go for a couple of days and trail the varmints that stampeded 'em."

"That's good thinking, up to a point," Wallace Flagg said, "but there's two problems. There must have been a dozen or more of the varmints, and you can be sure they'll split up, making it necessary for us to divide our forces. That will make it easy enough for them to gun us down from ambush."

"He's dead right," Cyrus Baldwin said.

"Damn it, we have to do *something*," said Tuck. "If we go after the cattle or rustlers, we're goin' to be split up. If it takes the whole outfit to pick up one cow at a time, we'll still be here *next* August."

"I think they stampeded the herd south so it'll be easier rounding them up, once they have disposed of us," Enos Chadman said. "When the herd begins to scatter, the riders will split up and get ahead of us, somewhere in Indian Territory."

"Maybe," said Wallace Flagg, "but I don't think so. Why scatter the herd all to hell and gone, unless they aim to scatter us for bushwhacking purposes during the gather?"

"Mr. Flagg's talking sense," Tuck Carlyle said. "I think if we separate while gathering the herd, that we'll be picked off one at a time."

"You think we should go after the rustlers, then," said Walter Flagg. "So do I. After we've gathered the herd, what's to stop them from stampeding it all over again? I think where we find one of these varmints, we'll find them all."

The argument raged back and forth until a decision was reached. Those from the first and second watches would trail the outlaws. The women—except for Katrina—would stay with the wagons. The tracks of shod horses were plain enough in the wake of the stampede, and as Flagg had predicted, once the herd had scattered, so had the riders.

"There's thirteen of us," Flagg said. "Let's split up into two groups, with each group tracking one rider. Unless they all come together in a bunch, we'll nail at least two of them."

Again Danielle was denied an opportunity to ride with Tuck, for he was on the first watch with Katrina. The sun was an hour high when they reached the point where the herd had begun to scatter. None of the tracks of shod horses continued south, but turned east or west.

"Damn it," said Elmer Dumont, "they're expecting us. They'll be holed up somewhere in Indian Territory."

"Give me one rider," Tuck said, "and if it's an ambush, we'll spring it."

"I'll go," said Danielle.

"You got it," Tuck said. "Ride a mile east of here, and then ride north. Look for the tracks of a rider who may have doubled back. I'll ride west and then north, doin' the same as you. As long as they're split up, they're at the same disadvantage we are."

Danielle rode east for almost a mile before turning north. Her Henry was cocked and ready, and she carried it under her arm. For several miles, there was no sign. Suddenly, she saw the tracks of a shod horse coming from the southeast. The tracks were fresh. It had to be one of the renegades, bound for a rendezvous somewhere to the north.

To the west, Tuck Carlyle had made a similar discovery. His rifle ready, he cautiously followed the trail of the single horse. His first and only warning came almost too late. His horse suddenly nickered, and somewhere ahead, another answered. There was a blaze of gunfire, barely missing him, and Tuck rolled out of the saddle. There was no sound of hoofbeats, which meant his man was holed up within rifle range.

"Come on," shouted Wallace Flagg. "Tuck's flushed somebody."

To the west, Danielle had no warning. The first slug snatched the hat from her head, and the second whipped through the baggy front of her shirt, leaving her thankful she had an uncomfortable binder around her chest. She rolled out of the saddle as though she had been hit, taking her Henry with her. She lay still, counting on her adversary to show himself. When she heard footsteps, she resisted the temptation to turn her head. Whoever was coming to see if she was alive or dead must soon come within her view. He did, finally.

"Just a damn kid," he said aloud.

"With a gun," said Danielle. She drew her Colt from flat on her back and fired twice.

She waited a few minutes, Colt in her hand, until she decided the bushwhacker had been alone. She then knelt beside him and began going through his pockets. She found only a bill of sale for a horse and an envelope addressed to Mitch Vesper. There was nothing in the envelope. On the back of it had been scribbled meaningless numbers. She then mounted the chestnut mare and rode back to meet her comrades. They had joined Tuck and were all looking at the bushwhacker he had shot.

"Did you find a name on him?" Danielle asked.

"Elihu Dooling," said Tuck. "Is he one of the bunch you're after?"

"No," Danielle said, "and neither is the one I shot. Either I'm barking up the wrong tree, or this bunch has added some new faces."

"They had more than eight men last night," said Tuck. "That means they've added to their gang."

"Daniel and Tuck," Elmer Dumont said, "that was a good piece of work. The rest of the varmints will have to come together sooner or later. I say we run 'em down, one at a time if we have to."

"It could become a Mexican standoff," said Cyrus Baldwin. "If they're after the herd, they can't round 'em up while they're dodgin' lead. Neither can we."

"It all comes down to who can hold out the longest," Wallace Flagg said. "This bunch will be just as aware as we are that we're not much more than a month away from snow. Every day we spend tracking them is one day less before snow flies."

"Well, damn it," said Enos Chadman, "what choice do we have? We know this bunch of owlhoots stampeded the herd with one thought in mind. They're countin' on us to split up in ones and twos, gathering the herd. That's when they'll come gunning for us."

"Then we have no choice except to track them down first," Danielle said.

"That's how it looks to me," said Chadman, his grateful eyes on Danielle.

"I'll agree with that," Wallace Flagg said. "Hell, I'd rather make the drive through the snow than to dodge bushwhacker bullets from here to Abilene."

It was a sentiment they all shared, and they again began seeking tracks of shod horses that belonged to the outlaws. Elmer Dumont and his son, Barney, were the next to flush out one of the rustlers. Barney took a slug through his left thigh, while Elmer was unscathed. It was he who had killed the bushwhacker. Quickly, the rest of the outfit gathered. Elmer went through the dead man's pockets, finding only a pocket knife and a few dollars.

"No name, then," said Danielle, disappointed.

"None," Elmer said. "Barney, you'd better ride back to the wagons and have your ma take care of that leg wound."

"There's a medicine kit and a gallon jug of whiskey in the wagon," said Tuck. "Barney, can you make it alone?"

"I can make it," the white-faced Barney said. "Go after the others."

Danielle sneaked a look at Katrina, and the girl's face was ashen. Tuck helped Barney mount his horse, and when he had ridden away, the others mounted, leaving the dead outlaw where he lay.

"The buzzards and coyotes will eat well," Wallace Flagg said. "If we can gun down two or three more, it might make believers of the others."

Losing Barney Dumont, they had twelve riders.

"We're at a disadvantage," said Tuck, "because they can be holed up under cover. For that reason, I think we should ride in pairs."

"I'll vote for that," Danielle replied. "With two of

us after the same bushwhacker, he'll be forced to divide his attention."

"Katrina rides with me," stated Enos Chadman.

Nobody disagreed or complained, for Katrina was still pale and obviously afraid. She gripped her saddle horn with both hands, keeping her head down, refusing to look at any of them. Danielle felt sorry for her, but she thought Tuck looked a little disgusted.

Floyd and Edward Flagg rode into the next ambush, coming out of the fight unscathed. They were searching the dead outlaw when the rest of their outfit arrived.

"Does he have a name?" Danielle asked anxiously.

"Yeah," said Floyd. "It's in his wallet. Chunk Peeler."

"Damn," Danielle said, "four of them, and not one of the eight I'm looking for."

"All of these might be the killers you're looking for," said Tuck. "The names you have may not even be their real names."

"I know," Danielle said softly. "I know. But I won't give up the search until I'm certain each of the men who killed my father is dead."

Chapter 5

Indian Territory. August 24, 1870.

The riders found no more of the outlaws, and sundown wasn't more than an hour distant. Wallace Flagg spoke.

"We'd better get back to the wagons if we want supper. We can't afford a fire after dark. We haven't seen any of that bunch, but that don't mean they won't be throwing lead our way."

"It's cloudy in the west," Danielle said, "and there's the smell of rain. It'll wash out all the tracks by morning."

"Probably," said Flagg, "but it'll be dark soon. We can't trail them at night."

Disappointed as Danielle was, there was no denying the truth of Flagg's words. When they returned to the wagons, supper was almost ready.

"I think we'd all better stand watch all night," Enos Chadman said. "It'd be just like the varmints to wait for the rain, and using it for cover, storm the camp."

"I agree with that," said Elmer Dumont. "I'd feel safer wide awake, with my old Henry rifle cocked and ready."

"We have a dozen men," Cyrus Baldwin said. "That's a pretty strong defense."

"Don't forget the women," said Teresa, his wife. "There's not a woman among us who can't shoot. I can't speak for anyone else, but I'm staying awake with my rifle."

All the women—even Katrina—added their voices to the clamor.

"Then it's settled," Wallace said. "Every one of us will be waiting, weapons ready for a possible attack."

Danielle said nothing, hoping the outlaws *would* attack. It might be her last chance, for ahead of her might lie long, hopeless trails. Two hours into the night, the rain started. It came down in torrents, but still there was no sign of the outlaws.

Kazman and his remaining eight men were quarreling among themselves as to what their next move would be.

"Using the rain for cover, we can fire into their camp," Kazman argued.

"Yeah," said Rufe Gaddis. "Givin' 'em a muzzle flash to shoot at. We already lost four men, without saltin' down one of them. I don't aim to become the fifth."

"Me neither," Julius Byler said. "I'm gettin' out of here now, while I got this rain to cover my tracks. Trail herdin' cattle is hard work, at best. They can have it."

Quickly, the rest of the outlaws agreed to the proposal.

"Upton Wilks ain't gonna like this," Kazman warned. "For fifty and found, he expects a lot of a man."

"Don't make a damn to me *what* Wilks thinks," said Chancy Burke, " 'cause I won't be goin' back there. Fifty dollars a month, my aching hindquarters. I need ten times that just to live like I want to."

There were shouts of approval from the other seven outlaws, and they began saddling their horses. They rode west, across Indian Territory, toward the little panhandle town of Mobeetie, Texas. Kazman stood there cursing them, dreading to face Upton Wilks. Finally, he mounted his horse and, riding wide of the cow camp, used the storm as cover to return to the Wilks place. Kazman reached Wilks's bunkhouse well after midnight. The house was dark, and in the morning he would have to face the wrath of Upton Wilks. He unsaddled his horse in the barn and went to the bunkhouse to get what sleep he could.

"So the bastards walked out on me," Wilks stormed, "and you let them go?"

"What the hell was I supposed to do?" Kazman demanded. "There was eight of them and one of me, and they'd just seen them shirttail ranchers gun down four of our outfit. I come back to tell you, which was all I could do. While I'm at it, I might as well tell you I ain't ridin' back to Indian Territory to round up more killers. This is a hell-for-leather outfit you sent us after. There's nineteen of 'em, and even the women can shoot. And I got a little more to say to you. What you want calls for gun wages, and you're just too damn cheap to pay."

"Are you finished?" Wilks inquired in a dangerously low voice.

"I am, and in more ways than one," said Kazman. "I've had more than enough of you and your dirty work. I'm drifting."

Kazman started for the door, but some sixth sense warned him. When Kazman turned, Wilks already had his pistol in his hand. Kazman drew and fired twice, and not until he was sure Wilks was dead did he make a move. He then proceeded to rip apart the Wilks house, eventually finding three hundred dollars.

"Thanks, you cheap old bastard," said Kazman. "This will see me through to somethin' better."

Kazman rode out, elated when the storm started

again. When Wilks was discovered, the rain would have washed away the tracks of Kazman's horse. The law might be suspicious of him, but suspicion wasn't proof. Besides, it was a big land, this frontier, and the law would never find him in Arizona or California.

"I think they've given up on us," said Wallace Flagg. "It's rained all night without a shot bein' fired, and they couldn't ask for better cover than this rain."

"There's a muzzle flash, even in the rain," Elmer Dumont said. "They'd have been some mighty good targets for return fire."

"It looks like the rain's set in for the rest of the day," said Cyrus Baldwin, "and I'm not the kind to set here and wait on outlaws who may or may not still be around. I say we begin gathering the herd and get on with the drive."

"By God, I'm with Cyrus," Wallace Flagg said.

The women kept their silence, while the rest of the men agreed to continue the drive as soon as the herd could be rounded up. There was enough dry wood in the possum belly of one of the wagons, so they had breakfast with hot coffee.

"It's unlikely any of the herd would have run far enough to cross the Red River," Elmer Dumont said, "so we should find them between here and there. Barney, you stay here, and stay off that wounded leg."

"Aw, hell," said Barney, "I ain't hurt that bad." But he obeyed his father. The others saddled up, mounted, and rode south.

"Cows have a habit of drifting with a storm," Wallace Flagg said. "I think we should be riding toward the east."

Accepting Flagg's suggestion, they rode southeast, and were soon rewarded by finding their first small bunch of cattle.

"We can pick these up on our way back," said Enos Chadman. "We should find the rest of 'em a mite farther down, maybe grazing alongside the Red."

Chadman's optimism was justified, for the grass was good along the north bank of the Red, and the cattle hadn't crossed the river. But the small herd had the wind and rain at their backs, and they resisted all efforts to turn them around.

"Damn it," Wallace Flagg said, "as long as the wind's blowing that rain out of the west, this bunch of critters ain't of a mind to go with us."

"But somehow we *got* to turn 'em around," said Tuck Carlyle. "If we don't, they'll just drift with the storm, taking them farther and farther away."

"There's maybe three hundred in that bunch," Enos Chadman said. "Let's get ahead of them and start firing our rifles. We got to make them more afraid of us than they are of the storm."

When the dozen men began firing their rifles, the cattle bawled in confusion. Finally, they turned and, facing the storm, galloped west.

"She's clearin' up back yonder to the west," said Cyrus Baldwin. "Give it another hour or so, and the rain will be done."

Baldwin's prediction proved accurate, and before noon the wind had died to a whisper and the rain had ceased entirely.

"No way we'll round up the rest of 'em today," Tuck said.

"We couldn't move out tomorrow, even if we had 'em all rounded up," said Wallace Flagg. "After all this rain, our supply wagon would soon be hub-deep in mud. While we gather the herd, the sun may dry the ground enough for us to start the day after tomorrow."

The riders continued their gather until almost sundown.

"Let's run a tally," Tuck Carlyle suggested. "I'd like to know how many more we got to find."

"Go to it," said Flagg. "Elmer, you and Cyrus run tallies too, and we'll take whatever is the low count."

Tuck had the low count of seven hundred head.

"Not bad, considerin' the storm," Enos Chadman said. "That's almost a third of 'em. I expect we'll get the rest tomorrow."

It was too late to ride after another bunch of cows, and supper would soon be ready. The riders unsaddled their horses, rubbed them down, and turned them loose to graze. The sun had been shining since noon, and much of the standing water had begun to dry up. As the riders settled down to supper, Katrina made it a point to sit next to Tuck Carlyle. For all the good it did her, she might as well not have existed.

"Tuck," Katrina said softly, "I'm sorry for the . . . things I said."

"Don't be," said Tuck. "I say what I think, and you have the same right."

The conversation immediately stopped, for Katrina feared she would drive him even further away if she said anything more. Because of Barney Dumont's wound, he soon had a fever, and Danielle was moved to the first watch. As they circled the gathered herd, it was only a matter of time before Danielle found Katrina riding beside her.

"Tuck's angry with me," said Katrina. "Has he said anything . . . about me?"

"Not to me," Danielle said. "I think he's the kind to settle his own problems. Maybe you should talk to him."

"He won't talk to me," said Katrina miserably. "I was scared silly when the shooting started, and everybody was watching me. I'm a disgrace."

"It's a good time to be scared, when the lead starts flying," Danielle said. "Besides, you're just a girl, and it's not your place to be gunning down rustlers."

"That's the trouble," said Katrina. "Everybody sees me as a foolish girl who can't do much of anything, and I've proven them right. In case you haven't heard what the other men are saying, I wear cast-iron underpants."

Danielle laughed. "Do you?"

"Hell, no," Katrina said. "There's nothing under my Levi's but my own hide. They call me names because I won't go into the hayloft with any two-legged critter that asks me."

"It's a woman's right to refuse," said Danielle.

"You sure don't talk like the rest of the men around here," Katrina said. "I thought Tuck was different, but I'm changing my mind. I like you better than I do him. You're good with a gun, but there's a gentle side to you. Something only a woman would notice."

Danielle's heart beat fast, for she was treading on dangerous ground. All she needed was for poor confused Katrina to develop a romantic interest in her, if only to make Tuck jealous.

Weighing her words carefully, Danielle spoke. "Why don't you just leave Tuck Carlyle alone for a while? He's still young, and so are you. Besides Tuck's sister, Carrie, you're the only unattached female on this drive. Leave Tuck be, and it'll worry the hell out of him."

Katrina laughed. "Thanks. I'll do that, and if you don't mind, perhaps I'll build a fire under him by talking to you."

"That might work," said Danielle, "but don't push him too far." Katrina walked away grinning.

Danielle felt sick to her stomach. She saw herself as a hypocrite, telling Katrina how to win Tucker Carlyle while she—Danielle—was interested in Tuck herself. But Katrina had an edge. She would be there

long after Danielle had ridden away in search of her
father's killers. Danielle bit her lower lip and said
some words under her breath that would have shocked
her mother beyond recovery. Danielle didn't know
Tuck was nearby, until he spoke to her from the
darkness.

"Well, *amigo*, did you get the key to the cast-iron
underpants?"

"Tuck," Danielle said, "it's cruel of you to keep
repeating that. She needs a friend."

"And now she has one," said Tuck. "You."

"Only if you play the part of a damn fool and drive
her away," Danielle said. "But I'll be riding on, once
we reach Abilene. I can't afford to have Katrina interested in me, for a number of reasons."

"We still may run into that bunch of outlaws," said
Tuck, changing the subject.

"I'm doubting it more and more," Danielle said.
"There's too many of us, and we're all armed. The
bunch I'm lookin' for is the kind who would kill and
rob one man, like they did my pa. If the odds aren't
favoring them, they'll back off."

Indian Territory. August 26, 1870.

The next morning the outfit set out downriver, seeking the rest of their herd. Their women would stand
watch over the seven hundred cattle they had gathered
the day before. When the sun had been up an hour,
both riders and horses were sweating. The cattle, when
they began finding them, were scattered. Single cows
grazed alone.

"We got our work cut out for us," Enos Chadman
said. "It'll be one damn cow at a time. We'll be lucky
if we find the rest of 'em in two or three days."

The riders split up, each going after one or two cows. Danielle watched Katrina as she went after the wandering cattle. Danielle felt some envy. While Katrina had been frightened during the gunfire, she was adept at gathering the strays. With doubled lariat, she swatted the behinds of troublesome steers and cows, bending them to her will. She would make some proud rancher a worthy wife, Danielle thought gloomily.

"Time for another tally, before we herd these in with what we got yesterday," Wallace Flagg said.

Enos Chadman had the low count of six hundred and twenty-five.

"Just barely half of them," said Cyrus Baldwin. "Two more days, if the rest are all over hell, like those we found today."

"We're just almighty lucky they stopped shy of crossin' the Red," Enos Chadman said. "Otherwise, and we might have been trailing them all the way to their home range, starting this drive from the very beginning."

"We might have been deeper into Indian Territory at the time of the stampede," said Tuck. "I've never been there, but I've heard it's hell, tracking stampeded cattle. The deeper you are into the Territory, the more danger."

"I've ridden across it," Danielle said, "and parts of it are wilderness. A cow—or a man— could hide there forever without being found."

Their day's gather was driven back to camp and bedded down with those gathered the day before. Barney Dumont was still feverish, and would have to drink some of the whiskey during the night. Danielle remained on the first watch, and wasn't in the least surprised when she again found Katrina riding alongside her.

"I've been watching how well you handle cattle,"

Danielle said. "My pa was a gunsmith, and I'm having to learn this business by watching the rest of you."

"Thank you," said Katrina. "You're better at it than you think. I remember what you said about leaving Tuck alone, and I caught him watching me all day."

Danielle laughed uneasily. "He thought he had you hooked, and now he's not quite so sure. Most men don't like it when things don't work out the way they've planned."

"You say some curious things, to be a man," Katrina said. "Most men will fight until hell freezes, even when they know they're wrong. I have the feeling you're not like that at all."

"I try not to be," said Danielle. "Ma tried to change my pa's mind about selling his gunsmithing business and going to Texas for a herd of cattle. The more she tried, the more stubborn he became. All his pride and stubbornness got him was a lonely grave here in Indian Territory."

"I'm surprised you weren't riding with him," Katrina said. "If it had been my pa, my brother, Eric, would have been hell-bent on going along."

Danielle thought fast. "He didn't want my mother left here alone. Then, after we knew Pa was dead, Ma changed her mind about me going, because she knew I'd be going anyway."

Katrina laughed. "You just described yourself the same way you have described most other men. Prideful and stubborn."

"Damn." said Danielle, "you've discovered my secret. I'm just like all the others."

"No," Katrina said. "There's something strangely different about you."

Danielle sighed. Was this curious girl seeing through her disguise, looking beyond her lowered voice, her man's clothing, and fast gun? She made a silent resolu-

tion to avoid Katrina as much as she could, hoping—
yet dreading—that Tuck Carlyle's interest in her might
be renewed.

Indian Territory. August 28, 1870.

Gathering the remainder of the herd required two
more days.

"We started with 2,625 head," said Wallace Flagg,
"and we now have 2,605. I think we'd better end this
gather, take our small loss, and head for Abilene. I'd
hate to be here looking for those twenty cows when
the first snow flies."

Flagg's suggestion was met with unanimous approval, and the next morning, the drive again headed
north. The hot August sun had sucked up standing
puddles of water, there was no mud, and the wagons
followed the herd without difficulty. The first and second watches were continued, and there was no further
sign of the expected outlaws. Danielle was glad for
the sake of the small ranchers, but disappointed with
her own position. She had been virtually certain the
outlaws would try to take the herd. Now, having seen
four of their number quickly shot down, the others
had apparently given up. Tuck had barely spoken to
her since she had begun talking to Katrina, and Danielle was surprised to find him riding beside her, in
drag position.

"What are you doing with the drag?" Danielle
asked. "You think these cows will find their way to
Abilene without you leading them?"

Tuck laughed. "They'll have about as much chance
with me leading 'em. I've never been to Abilene. I just
hope we can avoid any more outlaws and stampedes."

"I just wish I knew whether or not the bunch of

outlaws that stampeded the herd is the same outfit that murdered my pa. The more I think about it, the more certain I am that the killers aren't using their real names. The names I have may mean exactly nothing."

"Yet, when we reach Abilene, you still aim to go looking for them," Tuck stated.

"Yes," said Danielle. "I made a promise, and I'll live or die by it."

Tuck's sister, Carrie, had said virtually nothing to Danielle since the drive had begun, and it came as a surprise when she found Carrie riding along beside her during the first watch.

"You've been avoiding me," Carrie said. "What does Katrina Chadman have that I don't have? Besides the cast-iron underpants, of course."

"She has feelings for that thick-headed brother of yours," said Danielle. "She needs somebody to tell her there's nothing wrong with her. She needs a friend, and I haven't seen any of the rest of you being overly friendly."

"I've never been her friend, because she seemed snooty and stuck up," Carrie said. "I can't see that she has anything I *don't* have, but she acts like she does."

"It's a defense against the way she's been treated," said Danielle. "How would *you* feel if men started spreading the word that *you* have cast-iron underpants?"

"I think I'd be flattered," Carrie said. "Nobody notices me except Barney Dumont, and he's about as romantic as a corral post."

Danielle laughed. "Do you want me to spread the word that you have cast-iron underpants too?"

Carrie sighed. "I suppose not. Perhaps someday a man will see me for what I am. Whatever that may be. Do you still plan to leave us when we reach Abilene?"

"I must," said Danielle, "unless somewhere between here and there, I run into those outlaws who murdered my pa."

"I'll hate to see you go," Carrie said. "You're too nice to be shot in the back by some devil of an outlaw."

"I've learned to watch my back," said Danielle, "but I appreciate the kind words."

Abilene, Kansas. September 15, 1870.

The outfit reached Abilene without further stampede, Indian attacks, or outlaw trouble. There were two cattle buyers who hadn't left town, and Wallace Flagg called on both of them.

"I got us a deal," Flagg said. "We're definitely the last herd of the season, and all our beef is prime. We're getting thirty-five dollars a head."

Flagg collected the money, and the first thing he did was count out $3,500 of it to Danielle. He then divided what was left by five, and the five ranchers each had a little more than $18,000.

"Dear God," said Wallace Flagg's wife, weeping, "I never expected to see so much in my whole life."

"We have Dan Strange to thank for suggesting this drive," Tuck Carlyle said. "All of us, on our own, were sittin' there starving, waiting for the rustlers to drive off the cattle we had left. Now we'll have enough to make a bigger drive next year."

Amid shouting and cheering, Danielle felt a little guilty. She had taken $3,500 of their money, after investing only $300. But she was grateful, and told them so.

"I don't feel like I've earned this money," Danielle said, "but God bless every one of you for it. Now I won't have to always sleep on the ground, living on jerked beef."

The time had come for Danielle to say good-bye, and she found it far more difficult than she had expected. Carrie and Katrina further dampened her enthusiasm by weeping, while all she got from Tuck was a handshake. Mounting the chestnut mare, she rode west, having no destination in mind. Far beyond the Kansas plains lay Colorado. She had heard Denver was a thriving town, and being so far west, it might be the very place that would appeal to outlaws ready to hole up for the winter. She would go there, but her progress was interrupted by a blizzard that had blown in from the high plains. She fought snow and howling wind for the last few miles, before reaching the little town of Hays.

Hays, Kansas. September 20, 1870.

With the Union Pacific railroad coming through Hays, there were many cafes, hotels, and boarding-houses. After leaving her horse at a nearby livery, Danielle took a room on the first floor of one of the hotels. There was already a foot of snow on the ground, and a man from the restaurant was shoveling a path to the hotel. Danielle decided to go ahead and eat before the storm became more intense. In the cafe sat a man she had seen in the hotel lobby. He wore at least a three-day beard and a pair of tied-down Colts, and he eyed Danielle as he had in the hotel lobby. He left the cafe before Danielle finished her meal. When she left, darkness had fallen, and the swirling snow blinded her. There was a sudden muzzle flash in the whiteout, and quickly returning the fire, Danielle dropped to her knees, unhurt. She heard the unmistakable sound of a body thudding to the ground. She waited to see if anyone had been drawn by the shooting, although she was unable to see the front of the cafe or the hotel. Minutes passed and nobody appeared. She approached the inert form and saw that it was the man from the cafe, his intense eyes now rolled back. Searching the dead man quickly, Danielle found only a worn wallet. She placed it in the pocket of her Levi's and hurried on to the hotel. She found a fire had already been started in the stove in her room, and that it was comfortably warm. Locking the door, she lighted a lamp and sat down on the bed to find out whom she had killed. The dead man's wallet contained no identification. There was a hundred dollars, however, and she took it. From the man's behavior, she was virtually certain he was on the dodge, but why had he come after her? She was leaving yet another dead man along her back-trail, without the slightest idea why he had tried to kill her. She added more chunks of wood to the already glowing stove and prepared for bed. She thought of the many nights she had slept in her clothes and, despite the risk, stripped them all off. She had worn the binder around her chest so tight, her ribs were sore, and she sighed in blessed relief when she was without the bothersome binder. When she lay down for the night, the howling wind whipped snow against the window, and she was doubly thankful for a soft bed and a warm room.

When Danielle awakened next morning, the fire in the stove had apparently gone out, for the room was cold. She lay there dreading to get up. Finally wrapping a blanket about herself, she got up and looked out the window. There was an unbroken expanse of snow, and it was still falling. Some buildings had drifts all the way up to the windowsills. The room was colder than Danielle had imagined, and hurrying back to the bed, she lay there shivering. Unanswered questions still galloped through her mind. Who *was* the gunman she had been forced to shoot, and why had he tried to kill her? An obvious answer was that he was probably an outlaw who feared being followed by a lawman. But Danielle had said or done nothing to lead the stranger to suspect she represented the law. It would be to her advantage to leave town before the melting snow revealed the dead man, but she dared not attempt it with snow up to a horse's belly. She considered the possible ways the law might connect her to the killing, and decided there was only one. While she had been in the cafe, the man had scarcely taken his eyes off her. There had been others in the cafe, including several cooks. Had any of them noticed the dead man's interest in the stranger with a tied-down Colt?

Resuming her identity as a man, Danielle donned the sheep-skin-lined coat and gloves she had bought in Abilene. She then left the hotel for the cafe. She was dismayed when she discovered the only other person in the cafe wore a lawman's star. One of the cooks spoke to the sheriff, and he stood up, coming toward Danielle's table.

"I'm Sheriff Edelman," said the lawman. "Yesterday, there was a killer in town name of Gib Hunter, wanted in Texas, Missouri, and Kansas. When he left the cafe, he never went back to his hotel room. His horse is still at the livery. Do you know anything about him?"

"Only what you've just told me," Danielle said. "I'm Dan Strange, from St. Joe, and I got caught in this blizzard on my way west. Why would you expect me to know anything about this Gib Hunter?"

"I've been told Hunter had his eyes on you last night, after you came in for supper," said the lawman. "Since I have no other clues, I thought there might be a connection."

"I saw him watching me," Danielle said, "and I

can't imagine why, unless he mistook me for some-body else. He left the cafe ahead of me, and I went straight to the hotel."

"Snowin' like it was, a man with killing on his mind could stage one hell of an ambush, couldn't he?"

Chapter 6

Sheriff Edelman's question took Danielle by surprise, and she recovered as quickly as she could.

"I'm not a bounty hunter, sheriff, if that's what you're thinking."

"Glad to hear it," Edelman said, "and the possibility *had* crossed my mind. All over the frontier, there are men who are man-hunters. They make their living hunting down wanted men with prices on their heads. Texas is willing to pay a thousand dollars for Gib Hunter, dead or alive."

"From what you've told me," said Danielle, "Hunter had been here several days. If you recognized him, why didn't you arrest him then?"

"I wanted to be sure," Sheriff Edelman said, "so I sent telegrams to authorities in Texas, Kansas, and Missouri. It took a while to get answers."

"Maybe one of the bounty hunters got him," said Danielle.

"I doubt it," Sheriff Edelman said. "He was in the cafe last night, and even then, snow was up to a sow's ear. Something happened to him after he left the cafe and before he reached the hotel. His bed hasn't been slept in."

"So I'm a suspect," said Danielle.

"Frankly, yes," Sheriff Edelman said. "It has all the earmarks of a bounty killing. You and Gib Hunter were the only strangers in town. Maybe you *ain't* a bounty hunter, but this owlhoot had no way of knowin' that. It could have well been his reason for watching you in the cafe, and reason enough for him to use the storm as cover, bushwhacking you when you left."

"Well, he's gone," said Danielle. "Can't you be satisfied with that?"

"It ain't that easy for a lawman," Sheriff Edelman said. "Wanted men are unpredictable. You never know when they're goin' to get suspicious, like Hunter was last night, and it's damn near impossible to prove one of 'em's dead if you can't produce a body. Come on, kid, tell me what happened after you left the cafe last night."

Danielle sighed. She had fired in self-defense, and Hunter's Colt would prove it. There seemed little doubt that Sheriff Edelman would not stop short of hearing the truth of it. It was time for a decision, and Danielle made it.

"All right, Sheriff," said Danielle. "When I left the cafe, it was snowing so hard that I couldn't see my hand in front of my face. Somebody fired at me, and even through the swirling snow, I could see the muzzle flash, so I returned fire. You'll find him there just a few feet from the western wall of the hotel. I'd never seen the man until last night, and I'm claiming self-defense."

"I won't dispute that," Sheriff Edelman said. "I just need to find him so we can close the book. There'll be an inquest in the morning, and you'll have to testify. But with deep snow and maybe more comin', you can't go anywhere. Besides, soon as I can verify that Hunter's dead, the state of Texas will owe you a thousand dollars."

"I told you I'm no bounty hunter," said Danielle, "and I don't want any reward. All I did was defend myself. Claim the reward in my name, and then see that it goes to a needy cause, such as an orphanage or church."

"I'll do that," Sheriff Edelman said. "I'll see you at half-past eight tomorrow morning, and we'll go to the courthouse for the inquest. Now I'd better get some men with shovels to dig out Gib Hunter."

Somehow, Danielle felt better for having told the lawman the truth. He was right about the snow, and there was no way she could leave until it began to melt. By then, Hunter's body would have been found. The snow finally ceased in the late afternoon and there was a dramatic drop in the temperature. A big thermometer outside the hotel's front door said it was ten below zero. Danielle kept to herself, never allowing the fire in her stove to burn too low.

True to his word, Sheriff Edelman was at the hotel the next morning. Danielle was in the hotel lobby, waiting.

"We'd better get started," Sheriff Edelman said. "Snow's still mighty deep."

"I reckon you found him, then," said Danielle.

"Yeah," Sheriff Edelman said, "and there's proof enough of what you told me. His Colt had been fired and was still in his hand. I'll testify to that."

With Danielle's story and Sheriff Edelman's testimony, the inquest lasted not more than a quarter hour. Hunter's death was ruled self-defense. With some relief, she started back toward the hotel. There was little to do until the snow began to melt, and not until the following day did the clouds begin to break up enough for the sun to emerge. Danielle was thoroughly sick of the hotel and the cafe next door, silently vowing to ride out if some of the snow had melted.

Mobeetie, Texas. September 25, 1870.

The eight outlaws who had deserted Upton Wilks had reached Mobeetie just in time to hole up in the hotel before the snow storm had begun.

"If we ain't goin' back to Indian Territory," Rufe Gaddis said, "I think we should split up. Eight of us in a bunch attracts too much attention. I've already heard talk here in the hotel. Somebody's wonderin' who we are and why we're here."

"I think you're right," said Julius Byler. "We'd better split."

Chancy Burke, Saul Delmano, Newt Grago, Snakehead Kalpana, Blade Hogue, and Brice Levan quickly agreed.

"I crave warm weather," said Snakehead Kalpana. "I'm bound for south Texas."

"Yeah," Newt Grago said. "You aim to run them Mex horses across the border into Texas. Better men than you have been strung up for that."

When the snow had finally melted enough to permit travel, the eight outlaws split up, each going his separate way.

Hays, Kansas. September 25, 1870.

Danielle judged the snow had melted enough for her to continue her journey to Denver. Before riding out, she paused at the sheriff's office to tell Edelman she was leaving.

"Good luck, kid," Sheriff Edelman said. "Don't turn your back on strangers."

The hotel clerk had told Danielle it was just a little under three hundred miles to Denver, so Danielle took her time. There were still snow drifts so deep, it was necessary to dismount and lead the chestnut mare.

An hour before sundown, Danielle found a secluded canyon where there was water. The canyon rim was high enough to keep out the cold night wind. After a hurried supper, she put out her fire. The chestnut mare had been picketed near the stream, where there was still some graze. Confident that the horse would warn her of any danger, Danielle rolled in her blankets at the foot of the canyon rim, where the snow had melted and the ground was dry. She slept undisturbed, awakening as the first gray light of dawn crept into the eastern sky. After a quick breakfast, she again rode west. Much of the snow had melted, being replaced with mud as the sun thawed the ground and sucked up the moisture. About two hours before sundown she came upon two sets of horse tracks leading from the southeast. While catching up to them could possibly be dangerous, they might be two of the very outlaws she sought. Her first warning came when the chestnut mare nickered and a distant horse answered. Danielle reined up.

"Hello, the camp!" Danielle shouted. "I come in peace."

"Come on," said a cautious voice. "Just keep your hands where I can see 'em."

Both men stood with their revolvers cocked and ready.

"My name is Dan Strange, and I'm from St. Joe, Missouri, on my way to Denver."

The men were young, in their early twenties, Danielle judged, and they looked like out-of-work, line-riding cowboys. Danielle had made no threatening moves, and the pair slid their weapons back into their holsters.

"I'm Herb Sellers," said the rider who had called out the challenge. "My *amigo* here is Jesse Burris. Our grub's running low and we're out of coffee, but you're welcome to take part in what there is."

"I just left a trail drive in Abilene," Danielle said, "and I stocked up on supplies. Why don't you let me supply the grub for supper? I have coffee, too."

"That's the best offer I've had lately," said Sellers. "We holed up in Dodge, waiting out the storm, and town living just about busted us."

"Yeah," Burris said. "We done been starved out of Texas. Where in tarnation did you find a trail herd bound for Abilene? Ain't no money in Texas. It's been picked clean, and the buzzards is still there."

"Five small ranchers risked everything they had, driving 2,600 head to Abilene," said Danielle. "Come spring, they'll have money enough to take a larger herd."

"Straight across Indian Territory," said Sellers. "Any trouble with rustlers?"

"Some," Danielle admitted. "After we killed four of them, the others decided to ride on to other parts."

The two men laughed, appreciating the droll humor.

"We aim to do some bounty hunting," said Sellers. "Catching outlaws pays rewards, and I don't know of nobody needin' it worse than we do. We heard that Gib Hunter had been seen in Dodge and might be headed for Denver. That's a thousand-dollar bounty."

"No more," Danielle said. "Hunter tried to bushwhack somebody during the storm, and was gunned down in Hays. I was waiting out the storm myself."

"Damn the luck," said Sellers. "We're having trouble getting the names of outlaws with prices on their heads. Lawmen don't like bounty hunters."

"That's one reason we're bound for Denver," Burris said. "I got an uncle there, and he's working for the Pinkertons. We're hoping he can supply us a list of outlaws and the bounties on their heads."

While Danielle wasn't concerned with the bounty, the possibility of a list of the names of outlaws on the dodge appealed to her. These two down-at-the-heels cowboys seemed to be exactly as they had described themselves. Danielle decided to take a chance and, after supper, told the pair of her search for the outlaws who had murdered her father.

"I'm not after these men for the bounty," Danielle said. "I don't know if there's bounty on them, but of the ten of them still loose, I can tell you the names they were using in Indian Territory."

"Then maybe we can work out a trade," Burris said. "If my uncle in Denver can get us a list of wanted men with bounties on their heads, you can compare the names you have to the names on the list."

"I'd be obliged," said Danielle. "I'm hunting them down because I don't want any of them to go free. If there's money on their heads, then you're welcome to it. I just want them dead."

On a page from a small notebook, Danielle wrote down the names of the outlaws that she remembered.

"Nobody on here I've ever heard of," Jesse Burris said, "but that don't mean anything. Outlaws change their names like the rest of us change our socks. It'll be something to compare to our list if we're lucky enough to get one."

Danielle had no cause to doubt the sincerity of the two young bounty hunters, but she slept with her Colt in her hand. Danielle supplied the food and coffee for breakfast, and the trio set out for Denver. Except for deep canyons where the sun didn't often shine, the snow had melted, leaving a quagmire of mud.

Denver, Colorado. September 27, 1870.

There was nothing fancy about the Denver House, but its rooms weren't expensive, and Danielle rented two of them.

"You shouldn't of done that," said Herb Sellers. "We can't repay you until we collect some bounties."

"Let me look at your list of known outlaws," Danielle said, "and that will be payment enough."

"I aim to call on the Pinkertons and talk to my uncle in the morning," Burris said.

The more Danielle thought about it, the less likely it seemed the Pinkerton listing of known outlaws would be of any value. From what she had heard, the Pinkerton Agency was most often called upon to seek out bank and train robbers. The outlaws who had hanged Daniel Strange in Indian Territory began to seem more and more like a ragtag lot of renegades left over from those infamous days following the war. But Danielle had not a single lead, and a Pinkerton list would be better than nothing. Danielle bought supper for the three of them at a small cafe.

"Jesse and me aim to hit some of the saloons tonight," Herb said. "Want to come with us?"

"I reckon not," said Danielle. "I'm tired of sleeping on the ground, and I want to enjoy a warm bed." If the two were out of grub and low on money, the last place they should be going was to a saloon, Danielle thought. But it was the way of the frontier not to offer advice or opinions unless asked.

After the recent snow, there had been a warming trend and it seemed a shame to retire to her room so early. After Herb Sellers and Jesse Burris had left, Danielle changed her mind. Without taking her chestnut from the livery stable, she would walk to the places of business nearest the hotel. One of them—the Pretty Girl Saloon*—was across the street from her hotel. The Pretty Girl was a two-story affair, and the bottom floor was well lighted. There was a bar all

---

*The first Pretty Girl Saloon was in New Orleans. They caught on rapidly in the west.

along one side of the room, while the rest of it was occupied by a roulette wheel, several billiard tables, and more than a dozen tables topped with green felt for poker and black jack. A winding staircase led to the second floor. Waitresses dressed in flowing fancy gowns carried drinks to tables where the different games were in progress. Danielle stopped one of the waitresses.

"What's upstairs?"

"High-stakes poker and faro," the waitress said. "It'll cost you a hundred dollars to go up there, but you get a hundred dollars' worth of credit at the poker or faro tables."

While Danielle didn't care for poker, she had played faro—or "twenty-one"—with her father and brothers many times, and she understood the game. She still had more than $3,300, and feeling bold, she took five double eagles from her Levi's pocket and exchanged them for chips.

"First door on the left, at the head of the stairs," the waitress said.

Danielle climbed the stairs, opened the door, and got the shock of her life. All over the huge gambling hall there were young women who wore nothing except a short jacket that covered the arms and shoulders and red slippers on their feet. Danielle had no interest in naked women and was about to leave, when she recalled she had paid a hundred dollars to come to the second floor. Obviously, the girls were there to take a man's mind off how much he had lost or was likely to lose. Danielle took her handful of five-dollar chips to one of the faro tables.

"Minimum bet five dollars," said the dealer.

Danielle lost five times in a row, and then she started winning. One of the naked girls was at her side, urging her to visit the bar, but Danielle wouldn't be distracted. Not until she had won more than three hundred dollars did she leave the table. There were some vain attempts to lure her to the poker tables, where the saloon might recover some of its money, but Danielle wasn't tempted. With a last look at the naked women, she stepped out into the hall, closing the door behind her. Reaching the street, she walked for an hour before returning to the hotel. She secretly hoped Sellers and Burris were as broke as they had implied, so that Burris wouldn't be hung over and sick when it was time to visit the Pinkerton office.

Danielle was awake at first light. She was sitting on the bed, tugging on her boots, when there was a knock on her door.

"Who's there?" she inquired.

"Sellers and Burris," said a voice.

Danielle got up, unlocked the door, and let them in.

"We got in a poker game and, between us, won more'n five hundred dollars," Jesse Burris said.

"That's risky when you can't afford to lose," said Danielle.

"Hell, we know that," Sellers said, "but we had so little, it didn't make much difference between that and stone broke. Let's get breakfast. We're buying."

After eating, they returned to the hotel, where they paid for another night.

"You want to go with us to the Pinkerton office?" Jesse Burris asked.

"I reckon not," said Danielle. "You'll likely be more successful if they don't think you have a gang of bounty hunters. I'll be here when you return."

Danielle waited for almost four hours before the young bounty hunters returned.

"We got a list of thirty men with prices on their heads," Jesse Burris said. "Look at it and see if any of the names sound familiar."

Eagerly, Danielle took the list, reading it twice.

"Well," said Herb, "have you found any of 'em?"

"Just two," Danielle said. "Rufe Gaddis and Julius Byler."

"Since you already knew their names, and the same names are on the Pinkerton list, it sounds like they're using their real names," said Jesse Burris.

"It does seem that way," Danielle said. "I just wonder if some of the others on this list are the men I want, using different names."

"One thing I learned from the Pinkertons might be helpful to you," Jesse Burris said. "In southern New Mexico, southern Arizona, and other territories where there's a lot of silver and gold mining going on, there's plenty of outlaws."

"I'm surprised the Pinkertons would tell you that," said Danielle. "Seems to me they'd be anxious to cover that territory themselves."

"They've tried," Burris said. "Three Pinkerton men were sent there almost six months ago, and they haven't been heard from. They're presumed dead."

"Damn," said Danielle, "I can't believe the Pinkertons would take that without fighting back. I thought they were tougher than that."

"They're plenty tough and dedicated," Burris said, "but they bleed just like anybody else when they're bushwhacked or shot in the back."

Danielle sighed. "I don't know where to start."

"Neither do we," said Herb Sellers. "Now that we got a stake, we're gonna stay here one more night and try our luck at the poker tables."

"Don't risk all you have," Danielle cautioned. "These outlaws may be scattered from here to yonder, and it may take some time to collect a bounty."

"That's good advice," said Jesse Burris. "I think we'll do well to take it."

"I think so, too," Herb Sellers said. "You've been a lot of help to us, Dan. In a way, I reckon we're all in the same business. If you ever get your tail caught in a crack, be sure we'll side you till hell freezes."

"I'm obliged," said Danielle. "If I'm there, and you need me and my gun, you got it."

Danielle had supper with Sellers and Burris. Afterward, the pair set out for the saloons and poker tables. Danielle, still two hundred dollars ahead after the previous night at the Pretty Girl Saloon, decided to return there. It seemed immoral to her, naked women wandering among the tables, fetching drinks. More and more, however, Danielle was becoming accustomed to this man's world. The naked girls drew men like flies drawn to a honey jug. She wondered how a man kept his mind on the game, with a naked female to distract him. Suppose they discovered she wasn't a man? Would she be asked to leave?

Reaching the saloon, Danielle paid her hundred dollars, received her credit in chips, and made her way up the stairs. She opened the door into the gambling hall, and immediately a pair of the naked women were there to greet her.

"I remember you from last night, cowboy," said one of the women. "You won big."

"I reckon," Danielle said. "You just have to keep your mind on the game."

Danielle headed for a faro table, while the two naked women looked at one another questioningly. It had been their specific duty to watch for the return of this stranger who seemed to have no interest in naked women and kept his mind on the game. The naked pair hurried to the faro table and watched Danielle win the first three hands. She lost one and then won the next two. Occasionally she lost a hand, but won more often than she lost. So engrossed was she in the game, she failed to see the man with a tied-down revolver quietly leave the hall. Danielle decided it was time to back off after she had won four hundred dollars.

"You're on a roll, cowboy," one of the girls said. "Don't be in a hurry."

"Thanks," Danielle said, "but it's past my bedtime."

She had taken seven hundred dollars of the saloon's money in two days, and she fully understood the hard looks she had received from the dealers as she prepared to leave. She had ignored the naked women, defied the odds, and she had won. Now she had only to cross the street to her hotel. She felt like her luck had run out at the Pretty Girl Saloon. Her feeling was confirmed when, from the darkness between the hotel and the building adjoining it, there came a blaze of gunfire. The first slug ripped through Danielle's left arm between wrist and elbow, but it didn't affect her aim. Lightning quick, she drew her Colt and fired twice. Once to the left and then once to the right of the muzzle flash. Three men—one of them the desk clerk—rushed out of the hotel.

"What's going on out here?" the desk clerk demanded.

"Somebody tried to bushwhack me," replied Danielle, "and I shot back. I reckon you'd better send for the sheriff."

Sheriff Hollis arrived soon after with a lantern. Scarcely looking at Danielle, Hollis headed for the dark area between the hotel and the adjoining building. There he hunkered down, and in the pale light from the lantern, it became obvious he was examining the body of a man. Slowly the sheriff returned to the street where Danielle stood, blood dripping off the fingers of her left hand.

"Come on," said Sheriff Hollis. "We'll have Doc take care of your wound. Then you'll go to my office and tell me what this is all about."

"It's about me being bushwhacked," Danielle said. "I fired back."

"Two hits in the dark," said Sheriff Hollis. "I don't often see shooting like that."

Danielle said nothing. When they reached the doctor's house, he quickly cleaned and bandaged Danielle's wounded arm. Danielle then followed Sheriff Hollis back to his office.

"Now," Sheriff Hollis said, "you have some talking to do. Start with your name."

"Daniel Strange. I had just left the Pretty Girl Saloon and was on my way back to my hotel. I didn't fire until somebody fired at me."

"I believe you," said Sheriff Hollis. "This is not the first time this has happened here, but it's the first time anybody's nailed a bushwhacker. His name is Belk Sanders. Have you heard of him?"

"Not until just now," Danielle said. "I'd just won four hundred dollars playing blackjack at the Pretty Girl Saloon. Sanders must have been there, leaving ahead of me. But the cost of going upstairs is a hundred dollars' worth of gambling chips. I doubt anyone would be able to afford that very often, and it makes me wonder if the saloon didn't hire him to bushwhack the winners and take back the money."

"I've thought of that, myself," Sheriff Hollis said, "but there's no proof. Tonight's the fourth time a winner from the Pretty Girl has been bushwhacked. The first three weren't as sudden with a pistol as you."

"How long has this Belk Sanders been around here?" Danielle asked. "What does he do besides hang around in saloons?"

"Nothing, as far as I know," said Sheriff Hollis, "but he always seemed to be flush. I think maybe you solved one of my problems tonight."

"Will you need me for an inquest?" Danielle asked. "I'm claiming self-defense."

"You'll have no trouble with the court," said Sheriff Hollis, "and I don't think you'll have to be here. Three men in the hotel, including the desk clerk, saw the muzzle flash from Sanders's gun before you fired. I've never seen a more obvious case of self-defense."

"I'll be at the hotel tonight, and until sometime tomorrow, if you need me," Danielle said. "I want to be sure this wound is going to heal before I ride on."

"Good thinking," said Sheriff Hollis. "Get yourself a quart of whiskey. It'll take care of a fever and kill any infection."

Danielle returned to the Pretty Girl Saloon, but only for some whiskey, which she was able to buy at the downstairs bar. From there, she returned to her hotel. By then, her wounded arm had begun to hurt, and she took a dose of the laudanum the doctor had given her. The quart of whiskey she placed on the table beside the bed. She awakened the next morning with a temperature, and forced herself to drink some of the liquor. It was a terrible experience, for Danielle had never tasted whiskey before. She choked the stuff down, wondering if it wouldn't do more harm to her insides than the bullet had done to her arm. She counted her blessings, for Sanders had fired twice. Had his second shot hit her, it might have been necessary for the doctor to undress her in order to treat the wound. That would have given the lawman and the town something to talk about, and would explain why the Pretty Girl Saloon's naked women hadn't taken her mind off her game of twenty-one. Danielle was soon sick from the whiskey, and long before she was ready to get up, there was a knock on her door.

"It's Herb and Jesse," a voice said. "We're invitin' you to breakfast."

"I can't eat," said Danielle. "I had some whiskey last night, and I'm sick. I reckon I'll be here another night. If you're still here at suppertime, I'll join you."

The day dragged on, and it was late afternoon before Danielle felt like getting up. But when there was a knock on her door, she was ready.

"Burris and Sellers," said a voice through the door. "It's suppertime."

Danielle let them in, and although her shirt sleeve concealed her bandaged arm, the two of them looked at her with renewed interest.

"We heard what happened last night," Jesse Burris said. "The desk clerk's talking about it to anybody who'll listen."

"My God, that was some shootin'," said Herb Sellers enthusiastically. "You nailed the varmint twice, with only a muzzle flash to shoot at. When you start teachin' lessons for using a sixgun, I aim to sign up."

Danielle laughed. "My pa was the best gunsmith in all of Missouri. He taught me to draw and shoot."

"Maybe there's a reward on this gent you shot last night," Jesse Burris said.

"If there is, I don't want it," said Danielle. "I shot him because he shot at me. Now tell me about your night at the poker tables."

"Nothin' to brag about," Herb Sellers said. "Between us, we lost a hundred dollars, and when we managed to win it back, we quit. Is that Pretty Girl Saloon all it's cracked up to be?"

"I don't know about the poker," said Danielle, "but the faro game is honest. You have to play with a naked woman beside you."

Chapter 7

Denver, Colorado. September 30, 1870.

Danielle spent one more night in Denver, feeling the need to visit some more saloons. It was unlikely the men she was hunting would be well heeled enough to visit the Pretty Girl Saloon, and she silently rebuked herself for having spent two nights there. However, her stake was now $3,600. Wisely spent, it would last her many months. One of the first saloons she found was The Broken Spoke, and as she entered, one of the bouncers spoke.

"Poker tables are in the back, behind the curtain, kid."

Since Danielle had sworn off any further bouts with whiskey, there was no excuse for hanging around the bar, so pushing aside the curtain, she went on to the poker area.

"Table stakes, dollar limit," said one of the dealers.

"Too rich for my blood," Danielle said. "I'd like to watch for a while. Maybe I'll learn something."

"I don't want you lookin' over my shoulder," said one of the players. "It makes me nervous."

One of the other men laughed. "Levan's nervous because he ain't won a pot tonight, and the way he's playin' his cards, he ain't likely to."

Levan! Could it be Brice Levan, from the death list?
Danielle stayed there a few more minutes without

learning anything more about Levan. Finally, she left the saloon, hiding in the darkness near where the horses were tied. Sooner or later, Levan would have to leave, and if he was playing poker badly, it shouldn't be long. When he finally exited the saloon, he staggered a little. He had tied his horse's reins securely to the hitching rail, and cursing, he fumbled with the knot. Danielle stepped out of the shadows with a Colt steady in her hand.

"I'm looking for a man named Levan," Danielle said. "What's your first name?"

"None of your damn business," said Levan.

"I'm making it my business," Danielle said. "Identify yourself and tell me where you've been during the past year. If you don't, I'll shoot you just on general principles."

Danielle cocked the Colt for effect, and Levan spoke.

"My name's Henry Levan, and I'm called Hank. Up to the first of September, I was in Alamosa, at Clay Allison's horse ranch. I was there most of a year, and was let go when Allison sold most of his stock. Does that satisfy you?"*

"Not entirely," said Danielle, "but I suppose it'll have to do. Where do you come from, Levan?"

"Down south of Santa Fe, along the Rio," Levan said. "Too damn many sheep down there to suit me."

"Then mount up and ride," said Danielle. "You're not the man I'm looking for."

Levan fumbled with his horse's reins. Danielle held her Colt on him until he had freed the reins and mounted his horse. When he rode away, she followed at a safe distance. The shabby boardinghouse where

---

*Clay Allison was a dangerous man with a gun. Discharged from the Confederacy for insanity, he moved to New Mexico. There, he killed a sheriff who came to arrest him for another killing. He then left New Mexico, starting a horse ranch in southern Colorado.

Levan eventually reined up had an unattended stable, and he led his horse inside. When he came out, starting for the boardinghouse, he carried only his rifle. When he was gone, Danielle slipped into the stable, seeking Levan's horse. When she found it, the saddle was on a nearby rail, with saddlebags intact. She fumbled around in the dark, avoiding a change of clothes and a box of shells. Finally, her hands touched paper that felt like an envelope. Removing that, she felt around, seeking something more, but there was nothing. Quickly slipping out of the stable, Danielle rode back to the Denver House. Leaving the chestnut mare in the nearby livery, she hurried up to her room and lighted a lamp. What she had retrieved from Levan's saddlebag was actually a letter. It had been postmarked in Santa Fe and was addressed to Henry Levan, Alamosa, Colorado.

"Oh, damn," said Danielle in disgust. "Damn the luck."

Then, as though by divine inspiration, a thought came to her mind. There had to be other Levans somewhere near Santa Fe for Henry Levan to be receiving mail from there. Without feeling guilty, she withdrew the single sheet of paper and read the letter. It was dated May 1, 1870, and from its tone, had been written by Levan's mother. She urged Henry Levan to come home. One sentence quickly caught Danielle's eye: *Your brother has been gone for two months, riding to Texas with a bunch of outlaws.*

Danielle read the letter several more times without learning anything new. Everything pointed to Henry Levan's brother as one of the men Danielle was after, but where was he? Had he returned home, or was he still with the band of outlaws?

"Damn it, I'll ride to Santa Fe and find out," Danielle said aloud.

Inquiring, she learned that Alamosa was a little

more than two hundred miles due south of Denver. Since she was bound for Santa Fe, ever farther south, she decided to stop at the Allison ranch in Alamosa. Allison should be able to confirm or deny that Levan had been there for almost a year. Danielle made the rounds of half a dozen other saloons without learning anything helpful. At dawn, after riding to the mercantile to replenish her supplies, she rode south.

Alamosa, Colorado. October 3, 1870.

Alamosa wasn't a large town, and it was near dark when Danielle rode in. She took a room in the only hotel and led the chestnut mare across the street to the livery. She had no desire to go looking for the Allison ranch in the dark. There were several cafes, and she chose the one nearest the hotel. There were few patrons, and they left well ahead of Danielle. After paying for her meal, she questioned the cook about the Allison place.

"Allison's place is maybe ten miles east of here," the cook said, "but if you're looking for work, you won't find it there. He's done let most of his riders go. Old Crazy Clay may be gettin' ready to move on. He's about wore out his welcome around here."

"What's he done?" Danielle asked.

"It'd be easier to tell you what he *ain't* done," said the cook. "Two Saturdays in a row he's hoorawed the town. He rode in wearin' nothing but his hat and boots, screeching and shootin' like a crazy man. Swore he'd shoot anybody lookin' out the windows at him, but most of the ladies in town looked anyway. He didn't shoot nobody, but he's just so damn unpredictable as to what he'll do next. Ain't been long since he killed a man with a Bowie knife."

"Why?" Danielle asked.

"Him and his neighbor had an argument over a land boundary. To settle it, they dug a grave and the both of 'em got down in it with knives. The winner had to bury the loser, and old Clay's still walkin'."

"Maybe you can tell me what I need to know," said Danielle. "There used to be a gent name of Henry Levan working there. I need to know if he's still there, or if he's left, where he went."

"He's gone, far as I know," the cook said. "September first, Allison let four riders go, and they stopped here for grub. Levan was one of 'em."

"How long was Levan here?" Danielle asked.

"Not quite a year, as I recall. You ain't the law, are you?"

Danielle laughed. "No. I'm pretty well acquainted with Levan, and I reckoned I'd talk to him if he was still around."

"I expect he's gone looking for a place to hole up for the winter," said the cook.

The Clay Allison Ranch. October 4, 1870.

Allison stood on the porch, watching Danielle ride in. With his fancy garb, sandy hair, and smoothly shaven face, he was a handsome man. Danielle thought with amusement of him riding naked through town, women peeking at him. Danielle reined up.

"Step down," Allison said.

Danielle dismounted, but stopped short of the porch, noting that he carried two tied-down revolvers. Allison said nothing, so she spoke.

"My name is Daniel Strange, and I'm looking for a gent named Levan. I was told that he worked here for a while."

"Are you the law? I'm Clay Allison, and lawmen aren't welcome on my property."

"No," Danielle said, "I'm not the law."

"Levan worked for me not quite a year," said Allison. "I let him and three others go on September first. I got no idea where they went, but I know Levan has kin somewhere south of Santa Fe. Now I'd suggest you mount up and ride on."

In the West, it was considered rude not to invite a stranger in, if only for a drink of cold water, but being asked to leave for no reason was unthinkable. Danielle decided she didn't like Clay Allison. Without a word, she mounted Sundown and rode south.

Santa Fe, New Mexico. October 5, 1870.

The ride from Alamosa to Santa Fe was a little more than a hundred miles. Taking the time to rest the horse, Danielle rode in just as the first stars began appearing in the purple heavens. Santa Fe was an old, old town, established by the Spanish, and their influence was still everywhere. To Danielle it looked as big as Denver. Eventually, she found a little hotel with a cafe directly across the street. She left the chestnut mare at a livery on the street that ran behind the hotel and, walking back to the lobby, took a room for the night. The wind from the west was cold, and there was a dirty smudge of clouds far to the west as the setting sun had slipped over the horizon. It looked like another storm might be on the way. If that was the case, it should be obvious by morning. Danielle had no desire to be caught in the wilds somewhere to the south if there was snow. She would wait out the storm in Santa Fe, where there was shelter and warm food.

By dawn, a flurry of snow was blowing out of the west, and by the time Danielle had breakfast, the flakes were much larger. The wind was cold, slipping its icy fingers beneath her sheep-skin-lined coat. Danielle returned to her room at the hotel and, from the wood stacked in the hall, built up the fire in the stove. She brought in more wood for the night and, after locking the door, slid the back of a chair under the knob. She then treated herself to the luxury of stripping off all her clothing and removing the hated binder, finally freeing her breasts of its constricting grasp. With the storm raging outside and the wind howling around the eaves, there was little to do except sleep, and Danielle did just that. Undisturbed, she slumbered the day through, arising in the late afternoon. One look out the window told her that not only had the storm continued to blow, it had become more intense. Starting with the binder, she dressed. She buckled on her Colt, pulled her hat down low, and then added her heavy coat and gloves. She had to get to the cafe for supper, and it was a fight, for the snow was already to her knees. There was nobody inside the cafe except the cook.

"You might as well close and go home," Danielle said.

"I can't," said the cook. "This *is* home. I live in the back of the place."

Two more men came in while Danielle was eating, and one of them wore a lawman's star. The two ordered their meal and took seats at one of the tables, gratefully sipping hot coffee.

"Charlie," said the cook to the lawman, "how's it goin' with them cattlemen and sheepmen down along the Rio?"

"Not worth a damn," Charlie said. "Me and Vince rode down there for nothin', havin' to fight our way back through a blizzard. Old man Levan's killin' mad, and he's ready to go after the cattlemen with guns, when he can't prove anything. Somebody rim-rocked near a thousand head of his sheep."*

---

*"Rim-rocking" consisted of driving a herd of sheep off a cliff.

"Maybe he's right," said Vince, the lawman's companion. "Who else but the cattlemen would of done that?"

"Hell, I don't know," the lawman said. "All I know is this whole damn country is under my jurisdiction, and I can't spend all my time with old man Levan's sheep. I've done all I can do to avoid a range war between sheepmen and cattlemen. I reckon the winner will be whoever can afford the most hired guns."

Danielle listened with interest, a plan taking shape in her mind. Suppose she asked for and got a gunman's role with the sheepmen or cattlemen? Sooner or later, if he was alive, Brice Levan would be coming home. Even if he did not, some of the other killers hired by one side or the other might be men on her death list. Danielle returned to her hotel room, preparing for another dreary day of waiting out the storm.

To the south, on the eastern bank of the Rio Grande, Sam Levan's hired guns kept a roaring fire going in the bunkhouse stove. There were Gus Haddock, Dud Menges, Warnell Prinz, Sal Wooler, and Jasper Witheres.

"Old man Sam's mad enough to walk into hell and slap the devil's face," Dud Menges said. "By the time the sheriff and his deputy got here, the snow had covered the tracks of that bunch that rim-rocked the sheep. Wasn't nothing could be done."

"He'll end up blamin' us," said Gus Haddock, "and there's no way in hell so few of us can keep watch over three sheep camps at the same time. Markwardt's cow nurses just hit one of the unguarded camps, and by the time we can get there, they're gone. They'll split up, and like the sheriff says, there ain't a damn bit of evidence."

"He's got two Mex sheep herders at each of the

three camps," Dud Menges said. "If he wasn't so
damn cheap, he could arm them with Winchesters."

"But we get fightin' wages," said Warnell Prinz.
"The sheep herders don't."

"We need more men," Sal Wooler said.

"There's folks in hell wantin' cold spring water,"
Jasper Witheres said. "Their chance of gettin' it is
about the equal of old Sam hirin' more guns. I think,
once this storm has passed, he'll send us to the Adolph
Markwardt spread to raise hell, with or without any
evidence. Who else but a bunch of cow nurses would
want to run a flock of woolies off a bluff?"

At Adolph Markwardt's bunkhouse, there was considerable jubilation. Markwardt himself had come to
congratulate his men. With him, he had brought two
bottles of whiskey.

"You won't be able to ride for a couple of days,"
Markwardt said. "Get all the rest you can, for you've
earned it. The sheriff was by here in the midst of the
storm, and was on his way back to Santa Fe. Naturally
I told him all of you was in the bunkhouse, waiting
out the storm. I told him he could see for himself, but
he didn't bother. It's a comfort knowin' we're law-
abidin' folks, ain't it?"

"It is, for a fact," said Nat Horan. "Wasn't our fault
them sheep didn't have the sense to stop running
when they got to that drop-off."

"The damn four-legged locusts don't belong in cattle country," Lon McLean said.

"Yeah," said his brother Oscar, "but what we're
fightin' for is open range. Accordin' to the law, sheep
have as much right there as cattle, but we *need* that
range. We got just too many cows for the 640 acres
we have. We need two more sections."

"The sheepmen have set up camp there," Isaac Taylor said, "and they ain't likely to be movin' until there's some shootin' in their direction."

"After we've gunned down a few of them," said Joel Wells, "that's when the sheriff will come lookin' for us."

"Not if it's self-defense," Markwardt said. "We raise enough hell with them sheep, and Sam Levan will send his riders after us. For anybody trespassin' on my property, tryin' to gun us down, we got the right to shoot in self-defense."

Nat Horan laughed. "From ambush?"

"Whatever suits your fancy," said Markwardt. "I think after we rim-rock another two or three flocks of sheep, Sam Levan and his bunch will come looking for us."

During the second day of the storm, the snow ceased. With nothing to do but eat and sleep, Danielle was fed up with the inactivity. But the snow was deep, and travel would be all but impossible. Danielle went to the livery and requested a measure of grain every day for the chestnut mare. She would need it, because of the intense cold. The temperature was already well below zero. The day after the snow ceased, the sun came out, but had little effect, for the snow was at least two feet and frozen solid. Danielle waited another two days before deciding to resume her journey. She had not asked directions to either camp, for she had heard the sheriff say that the feud was taking place in his county. There was little doubt the bleating of sheep would lead her to Sam Levan's spread. If he refused to hire her, she must then seek out the cattlemen. During the cold months, even wanted men looked for a place to hole up, and the chance to draw gun wages might be tempting to the men on her death list. Within less than an hour, she could see the fair-sized herd of sheep. Two shepherds and two sheep dogs were with the flock, which looked to number a thousand or more. Danielle reined up, and one of the shepherds raised his eyebrows in question.

"Where might I find Mr. Levan, the owner of these sheep?" Danielle asked.

"At the *rancho, señor,*" said the Mexican, pointing.

Well before Danielle reached the Levan house, a pack of dogs came yelping to greet her.

"Here, you dogs," a bull voice bellowed. "Get the hell back to the house."

The pack turned and trotted back the way they had come, allowing Danielle to ride to within a few feet of the porch. Sam Levan looked her over thoroughly before he spoke, and there was no friendliness in his voice.

"Who are you, and what do you want?"

"I'm Daniel Strange, and I'm looking for work."

"You should know there's a range war goin' on here," Levan said. "I pay gun wages of a hundred a month, plus ammunition."

"I can live with that," said Danielle.

"You don't look like no gunman to me," Levan said. "Hell, you ain't even old enough to shave."

"That has nothing to do with drawing and firing a gun," said Danielle.

Sam Levan didn't see her hand move, yet he found himself looking into the muzzle of a Colt. Danielle slipped the weapon back into its holster.

"Not bad," Levan said, "but a fast draw don't mean you can hit what you shoot at."

"True enough," said Danielle. "Choose me a target."

Wordlessly, Levan took a silver dollar from his pocket and flung it into the air. As it started its descent, Danielle drew and fired once. When Sam Levan recovered the coin, there was a dent in the center of it. He eyed Danielle with grudging respect, and then he spoke.

"You'll do, kid. The missus will feed you breakfast and supper in the kitchen. There's five other men, and plenty of room in the bunkhouse."

"Thanks," Danielle said. "Am I allowed to keep my horse in your barn?"

"Yes," said Levan. "There's a couple of sacks of grain in the tack room."

Danielle led the chestnut mare to the barn, found an empty stall, and took the time to rub the animal down. She was in no hurry to meet the five strangers in the bunkhouse. The five were seated around the stove in various stages of undress. One of the men took a look at her youthful face and laughed. Gus Haddock suddenly found himself face-to-face with a cocked, rock-steady Colt.

"What is it about me that you find so funny?" Danielle demanded.

"Not a thing, kid," said Haddock, now serious. "Not a damn thing."

"I'm Daniel Strange," Danielle said, holstering the Colt. "Are any of you *segundo*?"

"No," said Dud Menges. "Sam Levan gives all the orders."

Starting with himself, Menges introduced the small outfit to Danielle.

"Why are all of you hanging around in the bunkhouse?" Danielle asked. "Enough of the snow's melted for you to be riding."

"We ride when Levan says," said Warnell Prinz, "and he ain't said."

Danielle said no more. In the snow on the ground, and in the mud which would follow, it would be impossible for riders not to leave abundant horse tracks. At suppertime the outfit trooped into the kitchen, lining up to use the washbasin and towel. A thin woman was carrying dishes of food from the big stove to a long, X-frame table. Along each side of the table was a backless bench.

"Eppie," said Levan, "this is Daniel Strange, a new rider I just hired."

Eppie barely nodded, saying nothing. She looked exactly like the harried woman who might have written the pathetic letter Danielle had taken from Henry Levan's saddlebag. It was an uncomfortable meal for Danielle, for the dark eyes of Eppie Levan seemed to have been stricken with a thousand years of heartbreak and despair. Danielle was much younger than the other riders and suspected Eppie Levan was seeing in her the faces of her own sons who seemed lost to her. Suppose Brice Levan gave up his outlaw ways and, in coming home, found himself face-to-face with Danielle? Could she kill him for his part in murdering her father? After supper, the outfit returned to the bunkhouse. There were enough bunks for a dozen men, and Danielle chose an empty one farthest from the stove. It would be reason enough to sleep fully dressed.

Levan's Sheep Ranch. October 10, 1870.

When the snow had melted and most of the mud had dried up, Sam Levan came looking for his riders.

"I want all of you to spend the next few days riding from one sheep camp to another," said Levan. "I know what Markwardt's trying to do. He reckons if he costs me enough, I'll come after him and his bunch. Then he'll call in the law."

"You reckon they aim to rim-rock more sheep, then," Warnell Prinz said.

"I do," said Levan. "They know I can't go on taking losses like the last one, and that I can't call in the law without proof. Our only chance, short of attacking the Markwardt outfit, is to catch them stampeding our sheep. Then I figure we're justified in shooting the varmints without answering to the law."

It was sound thinking, and Danielle admired the old sheepman for seeking a way out of what seemed an impossible situation without breaking the law. Danielle followed the rest of the outfit along the Rio to the first sheep camp, and seeing no danger there, they rode on to the second and third camps. Still, there was no sign of trouble.

"Instead of three separate camps," said Danielle, "why not combine all the shepherds and all the sheep into one bunch? They'd be easier to protect, wouldn't they?"

"Kid, you don't know much about sheep, do you?" Gus Haddock said. "Get all them woolies into one pile, and they'd eat the grass down to the roots and beyond. Scatterin' them into three camps, they still got to be moved every other day. That's why we need the range the damn cattlemen don't aim for us to have."

"I can understand why they feel that way," said Danielle. "Does it bother you, forcing sheep onto range where they're not wanted, where you might be shot?"

"Kid, there ain't nothin' sacred about cows," Haddock said, "and I don't like or dislike sheep. I'm here because it pays a hundred a month an' found. I been shot at for a hell of a lot less."

Haddock's companions laughed, and it gave Danielle something to think about. Suppose the rest of the men she had sworn to kill had sold their guns somewhere on the frontier? Already, she could understand a drifting rider's need to hire on somewhere for the winter, but it made her task far more difficult. She had no way of knowing whether or not Brice Levan would *ever* come home. Riding with outlaws, perhaps he was already dead. There had to be a limit as to how long she could remain with Levan, before giving up and moving on.

Reaching the third sheep camp and finding all was well, there was nothing to do except return to the first camp.

"What about tonight?" Danielle asked. "After we've been in the saddle all day, are we expected to ride all night?"

"So far," said Warnell Prinz, "the cattlemen have only stampeded the sheep during the daytime. We don't know why."

"I do," Sal Wooler said. "Them Mex herders has got dogs. Without 'em, it's hell tryin' to keep all them sheep headed the same way. I wouldn't want to try it at night."

Three days and nights passed without the Markwardt outfit bothering any of the three sheep camps. The strain was beginning to tell on old Sam Levan, and he spoke to all his riders at suppertime.

"I'm a patient man, but if Markwardt's bunch ain't made some move by sundown tomorrow, then we're goin' to."

"I reckon you aim to rim-rock some cows, then," said Dud Menges.

"Only if we have to," Levan said. "We'll start with a stampede tomorrow night. I want his herd scattered from here to the Mexican border. If *that* don't get his attention, then we'll try somethin' else."

"Then he'll be sendin' the law after us," said Gus Haddock.

"He can't send the law after us for stampedin' his cows any more than we could send the law after him for rim-rocking our sheep," Levan said. "At least his damn cows will be alive, wherever they end up. That's more than can be said for my sheep."

"Unless it rains, they'll have tracks to follow," said Sal Wooler.

"Let them follow," Levan said. "I want to put *them* in the position of having to break the law by coming after us."

"You mean with guns," said Jasper Witheres.

"That's exactly what I mean," Levan said. "When an *hombre* shoots at you, whatever his reason, then you got the right to shoot back. It's just the way things is."

Supper was a somber meal. Eppie Levan looked more harried than ever, and each of the men seemed lost in his own thoughts. Danielle had hired out her gun, and now there was a very real chance she would be using it for a purpose she had never intended.

The Adolph Markwardt Ranch. October 14, 1870.

"Startin' tonight," Markwardt told his riders, "we're going to be watching our herds after dark."

"Hell," said Oscar McLean, "there ain't but six of us. Who's gonna be watching them in the daytime?"

"Nobody," Markwardt said. "You don't need daylight to scatter cows from here to yonder, and I reckon Sam Levan knows that. If him and his outfit shows up on my range with mischief on their minds, then we can gun the varmints down."

"It'll be the start of a range war," said Nat Horan.

"Then so be it," Markwardt said. "This is the frontier, and a man can't claim nothin' he ain't strong enough to hold on to."

Chapter 8

Most of Adolph Markwardt's cattle were strung out along the Rio Grande, where there was still a little graze. Markwardt's outfit was watching from the west side of the river, and since there was no moon, they were not immediately aware of the Levan sheep outfit's arrival. Suddenly, the night blossomed with gunfire, and the spooked cattle lit out downriver, picking up others as they went.

"Let's go get 'em!" Nat Horan shouted.

He and his four companions galloped across the river, drawing their guns when they judged they were within range. But the marauders made poor targets, leaning over the necks of their horses. Finally, when the galloping herd was thoroughly spooked, they split up. Knowing the futility of pursuing them individually in the dark, Markwardt's outfit reined up to rest their heaving horses

"Damn," spat Isaac Taylor, "old Adolph will have our heads on a plate."

"Not mine," Oscar McLean said.

"Nor mine," echoed his brother Lon. "It's pitch dark out here. A man can't fight what he can't see."

"Well," Joel Wells asked, "do we ride in and admit they got the jump on us?"

"Not me," said Nat Horan. "I been cussed by Markwardt before, and I ain't about to take it again. I say we wait for first light, round up them cows, and drive 'em up yonder where they was."

"Without telling Markwardt?" Joel Wells asked.

"Not unless one of you wants to volunteer," replied Nat Horan. "After all, they just run the hell out of the herd. None of 'em's likely to die from that,"

"That's an invite for them to come back tonight and stampede 'em again," Joel Wells said. "Hell, we'll be up all night listening to the cattle run, and all the next day rounding them up."

"No we won't," said Nat Horan. "Tonight we'll be over there among the cows, ridin' around the herd. At first sign of any riders, we cut down on them."

"With graze so damn skimpy, that bunch will be strung for miles downriver," Oscar said. "How do you aim to keep 'em together long enough for just five of us to keep watch on them all?"

"We get down here a couple of hours before dark and bunch the varmints," Nat Horan said. "The only time we can legally shoot them damn sheepmen is when they're over here on Markwardt's holdings."

"They ain't exactly a wet-behind-the-ears bunch," said Joel Wells. "Old Adolph ain't done enough thinkin' on this. Soon as we gun down one of them sheepmen, it'll be hell from then on."

"Not if we gun 'em down on Adolph's spread, stampedin' his cattle," Nat Horan said. "The law can't touch us."

"It ain't the law that bothers me," said Joel Wells. "It's a range war. A man has to live like a hermit, afraid to ride to town on Saturday night, 'cause he never knows when he'll be shot in the back. There ain't no damn rules. It's shoot or be shot, every day, seven days a week."

"You can always take your bedroll and drift," Lon McLean said, "but you'll have to winter somewhere. It ain't often a man can draw a hundred and found."

"You're right about that," said Joel Wells, "and I ain't got enough money to even keep me alive until spring. I reckon I'll stay and take the risk with the rest of you."

The five of them set out at first light, driving the scattered cattle back upriver. It was two hours past sunrise when they finally gathered the last of them, and before them they could merge the new arrivals with those already gathered, Adolph Markwardt rode out from behind some brush. He reined up and, for an uncomfortably long time, said nothing. Finally, he spoke.

"So they stampeded the herd right under your noses."

"It was black as the inside of a stovepipe last night," Nat Horan said. "A man can't shoot what he can't see, and they never fired back. They just scattered the herd."

"So all of you decided to keep it from me by rounding them up on the quiet," Adolph said.

"We done the best we could," said Oscar McLean.

"Yeah," his brother Lon said. "It's easy to cuss somebody else because he fails to do something *you* couldn't of done yourself."

Adolph Markwardt's hand trembled over the butt of his revolver, but he knew better. He had hired these men for their deadly speed and accuracy with a gun. He relaxed, and when he spoke, there was no anger in his voice.

"Maybe you're right, McLean. Tonight and every night, until this thing is finished, I'll be ridin' watch with you. Now herd them cows together and git on to the house. The cook is holdin' breakfast for you. After that, git what sleep you can. We got a night's work ahead of us."

With that, he wheeled his horse and rode away. Not

until he was well beyond hearing did any of his riders speak.

"Hell's bells on a tomcat," said Joel Wells. "I looked for him to spout fire and brimstone."

Oscar McLean laughed. "Maybe the old dragon's fire went out."

"I wouldn't get too cocky too soon," Nat Horan said. "He'll keep us circlin' them cows so long we won't even have time to dismount and go to the bushes.'

Levan's Sheep Camp. October 17, 1870.

"I don't understand it," said Sam Levan at breakfast. "After we scattered his herd halfway to Mexico, old Adolph should of raised hell. I reckon we'll give him another dose tonight. There's *got* to be a limit to how much of that he'll take before comin' after us."

His riders said nothing. In a gunfight with Markwardt's outfit, any or all of them could die. It was the price a man might have to pay for having sold his gun. Danielle had begun wearing her father's Colt in addition to her own. Her own weapon was tied down on her right hip, while her father's was tied down on her left hip, butt forward for a cross-hand draw. None of this had escaped the others.

"Kid," said Gus Haddock, "you're mighty young to be totin' a matched pair of irons like that. Where'd you get 'em?"

"My pa made four of them," Danielle said. "He was a gunsmith."

"They're fine-lookin' weapons," said Sal Wooler, "but they could get you killed. The last damn thing a man on the dodge needs is a brace of pistols with his initial carved into the grips."

"I'm not on the dodge," Danielle said.

"You likely will be, before this thing between Sam Levan and Adolph Markwardt's over and done," said Jasper Witheres.

Danielle had mixed emotions, not doubting what Wooler had said about the danger of going on the dodge with a pair of fancy pistols. But there was a reason for her toting what appeared to be a matched pair of Colts. With a silver initial inlaid in the grips, they weren't the kind that a man was likely to forget, once having seen them. Wouldn't the men who had murdered her father remember the fancy Colt with inlaid silver? It was a calculated risk, but the killers might recognize the weapon as having belonged to Daniel Strange and, suspecting her vow of vengeance, come after *her*. If she couldn't find them, then let them begin looking for her.

"I'd bet my saddle old Markwardt give his riders hell for us stampedin' his herd," Dud Menges said. "I'm bettin' they're just waitin' for our patience to wear thin, figurin' we'll be back, just like Sam Levan aims for us to do tonight."

Levan's outfit spent the day riding from one of Levan's sheep camps to another, seeing nobody except the sheep herders.

Two hours after midnight, Sam Levan and his riders saddled their horses and crossed the Rio Grande. At the time of their last raid, cattle had been strung out for several miles along the river. Tonight they saw no cattle. Levan reined up, his outfit gathered around him.

"They've bunched the varmints upriver," said Levan. "It may be a mite harder for us to get them running. We'll circle around, comin' in from the north. Keep your heads down and your pistols blazing."

They rode a mile east of the river before riding north. Somewhere ahead, a cow bawled. The riders slowed their horses. They were getting close, and in the small hours of the morning, any sound—even the creak of saddle leather—could be heard from a great distance. Again there was no moon, and the meager starlight would be of little or no help to the Markwardt outfit. Sam Levan was the lead rider, and when he saw the dim shadows that made up the dozing cattle herd, he cut loose with a fearful shriek and began firing his revolver. The cattle scrambled to their feet and noticed the six riders closing in on them. They began to mill in confusion, and the muzzle flashes from the guns of Levan's riders offered excellent targets for the defenders. It was a standoff, for Markwardt and his riders had headed the herd before they could run. Two of Levan's riders were sagging in their saddles as though hard hit. Shouting a warning, Levan wheeled his horse and galloped upriver, the way he had come. His riders immediately followed. Danielle had not been hit, keeping her head low on the neck of the chestnut mare. They reached the Levan ranch house, and in the light from the window, Danielle could see that it was Gus Haddock and Dud Menges who had been hit. They slid from their saddles and would have fallen, had they not been supported by their comrades.

"Get them into the house," Levan ordered. "Then a couple of you take their horses to the barn and rub them down."

Once the wounded men were inside, Danielle, Warnell Prinz, Sal Wooler, and Jasper Witheres left to tend to the horses.

"My God," said Eppie Levan as she beheld the bloody shirts of the wounded men. "We must get a doctor for them."

"No," Sam Levan said. "When there's shooting involved, the doc will go straight to the law. Old Markwardt couldn't ask for any better evidence than that. We'll have to take care of them ourselves."

With his knife, Levan cut away the shirts of the wounded men, and to his relief, the injuries didn't look fatal. Both men had shoulder wounds, and the lead had evidently gone on through without striking bone. Eppie brought the medicine chest, and with disinfectant, Levan cleansed the wounds. He then bound them tight, using strips of an old sheet.

"We'll keep them here in the house for a day or two," Levan said. "They're likely to have some fever, and will need whiskey to kill any infection."

Eppie Levan seldom questioned anything the temperamental Levan did, but with her eyes on the wounded men, she spoke.

"It's started, Sam. One day you'll be brought in, tied across your saddle."

"Maybe," said Sam, "but I didn't start it. Markwardt's bunch rim-rocked a thousand head of our sheep. We only stampeded his cows. Tonight we couldn't do even that. The varmints was ready for us."

"And they'll be ready the next time," Eppie said. "Can't we make do with the section of land we own, and let them *have* the free range?"

"Hell no," said Levan defiantly. "Just because Markwardt raises cows, that don't give him divine right to all the free grass. Soon as Haddock and Menges is well enough to ride, we'll be goin' after them again."

Having unsaddled, rubbed down, and put away the horses, the rest of Levan's riders returned to the house to see how their wounded comrades had fared.

"They'll make it," Levan said. "Some of you help me get them into a spare bedroom."

Levan and Warnell Prinz carried Gus Haddock to the bed, while Sal Wooler and Jasper Witheres carried Dud Menges. Once the injured were in bed, Levan forced each man to take half a bottle of laudanum. They would sleep through much of the aftershock and pain. Prinz, Wooler, and Witheres returned to the parlor where Danielle waited. With two of the outfit wounded, they awaited orders from Sam Levan. They weren't long in coming.

"I want the rest of you to keep as close a watch on the sheep camps as you can," said Levan. "It's high time Markwardt and his outfit was comin' after us."

"We're considerably outgunned," Sal Wooler said.

"Damn it, I *know* that," Levan said. "I don't want a man of you killed over a few sheep, but do your best to keep them cow nurses from rim-rocking another flock."

After breakfast, Danielle, Prinz, Wooler, and Witheres rode out to begin their watch over the three sheep camps.

The Markwardt Ranch. October 18, 1870.

"Let's go get some sleep," Adolph Markwardt said, an hour after they had headed the intended stampede. "They won't be back tonight."

"We may have hit some of them," said Nat Horan. "We were within range, and all their muzzle flashes made pretty good targets."

"You boys done well," Markwardt said. "We may have just put an end to these late-night stampedes."

"I doubt it," said Oscar McLean. "Levan needs that free grass more than we do."

"All right by me," Markwardt said, "long as he's willing to risk his damn neck for it."

"Are we goin' after them now?" Isaac Taylor asked.

"Not yet," said Markwardt. "Give 'em a few days to lick their wounds, and they'll figure some other way of comin' after us."

* * *

Sam Levan rode into Santa Fe, to the mercantile.

"I need some dynamite," Levan said.

"Ain't got much," the storekeeper said. "Miners buy it up as quick as it comes in. I reckon I got a dozen sticks."

"That'll be enough," said Levan.

When Levan reached his ranch, he went to the bunkhouse, where he had the necessary privacy to cap and fuse the dynamite. Finished, he left it there. Had he taken it to the house, there would have been yet another tirade from Eppie. Just at sundown Danielle, Warnell Prinz, Sal Wooler, and Jasper Witheres rode in.

"Nothin' happened at any of the sheep camps today," said Jasper Witheres.

"I didn't expect it to," Sam Levan said. "We ain't pushed it far enough, but I think we will tonight. I'll meet you in the bunkhouse, after supper."

"How's Gus and Dud?" Danielle asked.

"Better," said Levan. "Eppie's been dosin' 'em with whiskey, and they're sweatin' like mules."

Supper was a silent affair, the four remaining riders wondering what old Sam Levan had in mind for them, with two of their companions out of the fight. Levan finished first, and by the time his riders left the supper table, Levan was waiting in the bunkhouse. His remaining four riders looked skeptical. Levan reached under one of the bunks, dragging out a gunnysack. From it, he took a stick of capped and fused dynamite.

"A dozen sticks," said Levan, "each with a seven-second fuse. All we got to do is fling three or four of these into the air above the Markwardt herd, and they'll run like hell wouldn't have it. This time, they won't have muzzle flashes to shoot at."

"My God," Warnell Prinz said, "The concussion from that could kill some cows. Maybe even a man."

"Damn it," said Levan, "ridin' in shouting and

shooting ain't got us nothing but two of the outfit shot. We can get close enough to fling this dynamite before they got any idea that we're there."

"No doubt we can," Jasper Witheres said, "but ain't you forgettin' we got two men out of the fight with wounds? This dynamite throwin' could be the very thing that'll blow old Adolph's mind. Why don't we wait until Haddock and Menges is healed? Then if them cow chasers comes after us, we won't be shorthanded."

"That makes sense to me," said Sal Wooler.

"And to me," Warnell Prinz agreed.

Danielle said nothing, and Sam Levan turned on her.

"Well, kid, ain't you standin' with the others?"

"I agree with their thinking," said Danielle, "but I'll ride with you. I don't cross a man who's paying me wages."

"Well, God bless my soul," Levan said. "The kid's got more sand than any of you."

"Aw, hell," said Warnell Prinz. "I still think we're bitin' off more than we can chew, but I'll ride with you."

Sam Levan looked at Sal Wooler and Jasper Witheres, and they nodded.

"I don't reckon they'll be expecting us again tonight," Levan said, "and we'll have that in our favor. We ride at midnight."

Danielle and her three companions retired to their bunks to get as much sleep as they could. For a long time Danielle lay thinking, pondering the wisdom of using dynamite. It seemed a cowardly thing to do, but nothing else had drawn the Markwardt outfit into an expected fight. When Danielle had ridden out of St. Joe, her mission seemed simple. All she had to do was track down the killers who had murdered her father, extracting revenge. Now she was about to take part in a raid that might cost innocent men their lives. To-night she would ride with Sam Levan, but the more she thought about it, the more convinced she became that she should just ride on. If some of the Markwardt outfit died, it would be reason enough for the county sheriff to come looking for Sam Levan. The very last thing Danielle wanted was to become a fugitive from the law. So sobering were her thoughts, she was wide awake when Sam Levan came to the bunkhouse at midnight.

"Each of us will take one stick of dynamite," Levan said. "We'll light the fuses, throw the dynamite, and get away from there before they know what's happen-ing. Here's a block of Lucifers.* Each of you be sure and take some."

Danielle took her stick of dynamite and broke off six of the Lucifers.

"Now let's saddle up and ride," said Levan. "Let's be done with this."

Danielle thought Levan seemed nervous, as though his iron-fisted resolve was not quite as strong as it had been. There was a very real possibility that so much exploding dynamite could kill Markwardt or some of his men. The county sheriff was well aware of the increasing bitterness between sheepmen and cattle-men. If one or more of the cattlemen died tonight, the lawman would most certainly come looking for Sam Levan, along with any of his outfit who had rid-den with him. The five of them rode out, nobody speaking, Levan taking the lead.

Adolph Markwardt and his five riders had most of the cows bedded down along the river bank, and they rode from one end of the herd to the other, and back again.

*"Lucifers" were the first matches, invented by an Englishman in 1827. In blocks, they could be separated, one or more, as needed.

"I still think we nailed a couple of 'em the last time they was here," Nat Horan said, "and I don't look for 'em to come back shorthanded."

"Never underestimate a damn sheepman," said Markwardt. "The varmints could give mules lessons in bein' stubborn."

The rest of the men laughed. In his own mind, each doubted there was a sheepman anywhere in the world who was more stubborn than Adolph Markwardt.

"It's hell, spendin' the night ridin' from one herd to the other," said Oscar McLean. "I think we ought to wait at one end."

"Oh, hell, don't give me that," Markwardt growled. "That's how they stampeded the herd the first time, with all of you gathered in a bunch at the wrong place. We don't know from what direction they're likely to ride in."

"They come in from the north last time," Joel Wells said. "I look for 'em to come in from the south if they try it again."

"I don't," said Isaac Taylor. "That would stampede the herd back toward the ranch."

"Isaac's probably right," Markwardt said. "I expect we'd better spend a little more time to the north of the herd."

Markwardt and his outfit had begun circling the herd toward the north when the first explosion came. Flung high into the air, the short-fused dynamite exploded directly over the herd. Five times explosions rocked the night and the cattle went crazy. To the south they ran, Markwardt and his riders frantically trying to head them off. But there was no stopping the stampede, and it thundered on.

"Damn them," said Markwardt. "The scurvy yellow coyotes."

"My God," Nat Horan said, "if we'd been any

closer to the north end of the herd, we'd all be dead men."

"Yeah," said Oscar McLean, "and that bunch didn't know we wasn't right there where they was throwin' the dynamite. How much longer before we ride over there and deliver a dose of lead?"

"Not much longer," Markwardt said. "The rest of you ride in and get what sleep you can. I expect them blasts killed some cows, and I aim to be here at first light, to find out just how many. Then I'll ride in for a talk with the sheriff. I'm bettin' Sam Levan bought that explosive in Santa Fe. If we can tie him to that, it may be the proof we'll need."

As Sam Levan and his companions rode away, nobody spoke. There had been no shots fired in response to the blasts, so none of them knew whether or not Markwardt's riders had been close enough to be hurt. While not lacking in courage, Danielle didn't want to find herself on the wrong side of the law for having been part of Sam Levan's outfit. Her quest—a vow of vengeance—was dangerous enough, without having to go on the dodge. As they drew near the Levan house, they could see lamplight streaming from several of the windows.

"Damn," said Levan, "I hope nothing's gone wrong here."

"A little soon for that, I think," Warnell Prinz said. "You want the rest of us to ride on to the house with you?"

"No," said Levan. "Go on to the bunkhouse and get what sleep you can."

When Levan entered the house, he heard voices in the kitchen, one of them Eppie's.

"What's goin' on in there?" Levan demanded.

"Oh, Sam," Eppie cried joyously, "Brice is here. He's come back to us."

When Sam Levan entered the kitchen, a lanky rider got up from the table. He was thin and hungry-looking, his clothing tattered and dirty, and his boots run over. Nothing was in order but the tied-down Colt on his right hip.

"Son, I'm glad to see you," said Levan, taking the young man's hand. "We got a fight in the making with old man Markwardt's cow outfit. I need all the help I can get."

"No," Eppie cried. "You're goin' to get yourself killed, Sam, and I won't let you take Brice with you."

"Ma," said Brice, "I can take care of myself. It's hard times in Texas, with no work for a line rider, so I'm back, asking for a bunk and grub for a while. I'll help Pa do whatever has to be done."

Eppie Levan said no more, for her wayward son was too much like his stubborn sire. Sam Levan grinned at Brice, and the two shook hands again.

Gus Haddock and Dub Menges had healed to the extent that they were able to come to the breakfast table, and were there when Levan and the rest of the outfit joined them. As they were about to begin eating, Brice Levan entered the kitchen.

"Any of you that ain't met him," said Sam, "this is my oldest son, Brice. He's . . . uh . . . been away." With the exception of Danielle, all the riders nodded. Apparently they knew the new arrival. Looking directly at Danielle, Brice Levan spoke.

"Who's the kid?"

"I'm almighty damn tired of being called the kid," Danielle said, getting to her feet. "My name is Daniel Strange."

"Uh . . . sorry," said Brice Levan. "No offense intended."

There was no doubt in Danielle's mind that Brice had seen her pair of Colts with silver initials inlaid in the grips, for his face went a shade whiter. She waited for Levan to sit down before seating herself on the other side of the table. He ate very little and seemed uncomfortable, for several times, he found Danielle staring directly at him. He was first to leave the table, returning to his room. Sam Levan knew something was wrong, but wasn't sure exactly what. He eyed Danielle with suspicion, and she ignored his curious stares.

Adolph Markwardt counted fifteen dead cows. He then mounted his horse and rode north toward Santa Fe. Arriving there, he rode directly to the office of Charlie Murdock, the county sheriff. Murdock listened patiently as Markwardt spoke, telling the lawman of his suspicions.

"Fifteen cows, huh?" said Murdock. "That still ain't quite as bad as a thousand sheep. I don't have a doubt in my mind that it was your outfit that rim-rocked them sheep, but I don't have any proof. Likewise, I don't have anything but your suspicions as to who it was that stampeded your cows. I can't arrest a man on *my* suspicions. What the hell am I supposed to do with yours?"

"If it ain't expecting too much," Markwardt growled, "you could ask around town and see who's been buying dynamite."

"There's no law against having dynamite," Sheriff Murdock said. "Every miner in the territory's got a few sticks of the stuff. You and Levan had better settle your differences before somebody's hurt or killed. I reckon you're a big man in the territory, but you let me find you've broken the law, I'll throw you in the *juzgado* as quick as I would a line-ridin' cowboy on Saturday night."

At Sam Levan's place, he and his outfit prepared to ride out to the various sheep camps. Gus Haddock and Dud Menges were still unable to ride, and remained at the house.

"What are we waitin' for?" Warnell Prinz demanded. "After what we done last night, them sheep are likely to catch hell."

"We're waitin' for Brice," said Sam. "Brice, where the hell are you?" he shouted.

Levan and his three companions were mounted, while Danielle still stood beside the chestnut mare. Brice Levan left the house, but instead of going to the corral for a horse, he started toward the mounted riders, his hard eyes on Danielle. A dozen yards away, he halted. Then he spoke.

"I don't like you, kid, and I won't ride with any outfit as long as you're in it."

"Oh," said Danielle calmly, "I reckon I remind you of somebody a bunch of cut-throat outlaws robbed and murdered in Indian Territory. He was my pa, and this left-hand Colt was his."

His face a mask of fury, Brice Levan drew. Danielle waited until the muzzle of his revolver had cleared leather, but he didn't get off a shot. With a cross-hand draw, Danielle drew her father's gleaming Colt. She fired twice, both slugs striking Levan in the chest. He stumbled, his knees gave away, and he fell.

Chapter 9

There was a shocked silence. Warnell Prinz, Sal Wooler, and Jasper Witheres made no move toward their guns. Dying, Brice Levan was trying to speak, and Sam knelt over him.

"It was . . . like he said, Pa," Brice said. "My bunch . . . robbed and hung . . . a man in Indian Territory . . ."

They were his final words. Sam Levan got to his feet and faced Danielle.

"Mount up and ride out," said Levan.

"I'll wait until the sheriff comes," Danielle said. "I want it understood that he was the first to draw."

"The sheriff won't be comin'," Levan said. "Four of us saw it, and it was a clear case of self-defense. That, and Brice confessed. I hate what you've done, but I can't fault you for doin' it. Now mount up and ride."

Danielle got on the chestnut mare and, nodding to her former companions, rode away. Eppie Levan had just left the house, and in the distance, Danielle could hear her anguished screams. Before leaving St. Joe, it had all seemed so simple—find the outlaws who had hanged her father and make them pay. Now she had to face the disturbing possibility that these seven other men might have families, just as Brice Levan had. It was a somber thought. She had hired on with Levan to pursue his best interests. Now she felt as if she had betrayed his trust, even though Brice Levan had admitted his guilt. She silently vowed never to sell her gun again, for any reason. She rode south along the Rio Grande, having heard one of the men say they were two days' ride from El Paso.

El Paso, Texas. October 22, 1870.

Weary, Danielle stabled the chestnut mare, skipped supper and, finding a hotel, slept the night through. As she started through the hotel lobby, the clerk spoke to her.

"Be careful. John Wesley Hardin's been seen in town."*

"Thanks," Danielle said. "I'll try to stay out of his way."

Danielle had heard of the gunman, for his reputation had been such that newspapers in St. Louis and Kansas City had carried stories about him. He carried two guns, and Danielle recalled a story that made her blood run cold. Inside a gunsmith's shop, testing a new pair of Colts, Hardin had chosen for a target an innocent man on the boardwalk outside. That was just one of many cruel acts attributed to the legendary gunman. After breakfast, Danielle went back to her hotel room, for few if any of the saloons would be open until noon. At eleven o'clock, she left the hotel and sought out the sheriff's office.

"I'm Daniel Strange."

"I'm Buford Powell," said the lawman. "What can I do for you?"

Danielle decided to tell the truth. She gave the law-

---

*Called the most dangerous gunman of his time, Hardin killed thirty-one men.

man the names of the seven men on her death list, and told him of her vow to hunt them down.

"None of those names sounds familiar," Sheriff Powell said, "but with outlaws, you can't be sure they aren't using other names. I know that between here and Laredo, Mex horses are being run across the border and sold in Texas, while Texas horses are being rustled and sold in Mexico. We have no names, and they wait for the dark of the moon. Not even the Texas Rangers have been able to stop them."

"It might be possible to join them and gather evidence," said Danielle.

"One of the rangers tried that," Sheriff Powell said. "He was never seen or heard from again. Was I you, I wouldn't go gettin' no similar ideas."

"Thanks for the information, Sheriff," said Danielle.

She quickly left the sheriff's office before the lawman got around to questioning her about her intentions. By then, the saloons were open. The Texas was one of the largest, and she went there first. She walked in, and then as though looking for someone she couldn't find, she left. There were no poker or faro games in progress, for it was still early, and being a nondrinker, Danielle couldn't justify her presence. She had to wait until evening. After supper, she found the saloons had come alive. In The Texas, two poker tables and a faro table were busy. The men seemed talkative enough, and hoping to learn something useful, Danielle sat in at the faro table.

"Two-dollar limit," said the dealer. "Table stakes."

Danielle quickly lost twenty dollars. Then she began winning, recovering her losses plus thirty dollars more. The rest of the men were looking at her with a mix of respect and anger, for all of them had lost money to her. At least one of the men was broke, and he appealed to the dealer.

"I got a pair of hosses—matched blacks—that I

picked up in Mexico. They're worth a hundred dollars apiece. Will you take them for security?" Danielle's eyes shot to the man at the mention of the horses' origins.

"We don't usually do this, Black Jack," said the dealer. "I'll grant you a hundred in credit for both of them."

"Done," Black Jack said. He sighed with relief as he suddenly began winning. When his winnings exceeded his losses, he dropped out and went to the bar. Danielle was ahead by fifty dollars, and when Black Jack left the saloon, she also withdrew from the game. Following Black Jack wasn't difficult. He had left his horse and the pair of blacks at a livery, and to Danielle's practiced eye, they indeed were worth a hundred dollars each, if not more. With the pair on lead ropes, Black Jack rode southeast, toward the border. Danielle followed at a safe distance, and not until she had crossed the border did she see Black Jack again. From behind a clump of brush, Black Jack suddenly stepped out, a Winchester leveled at her.

"Why are you followin' me, kid? Make it good, or I'll cut you in half."

"I like the looks of the pair of blacks you picked up in Mexico," Danielle said, "and I'd like to pick up a few for myself."

Without warning, with blinding speed, Danielle drew her right-hand Colt and fired. The lead slammed into the muzzle of the Winchester, tearing it out of Black Jack's hands. Her Colt holstered, Danielle eyed him calmly.

"Damn you," Black Jack bawled, "if you've ruint my Winchester . . ."

Danielle laughed. "You'll have to get yourself another one."

Ignoring Danielle, Black Jack retrieved the weapon,

examining it critically. Satisfied it wasn't seriously damaged, he again faced Danielle.

"Tarnation," said Black Jack, "I never seen such shootin'. Maybe there *is* as place for you, but it can't be just on my say-so. You'll have to prove yourself to my *amigos*."

"Lead on," Danielle said.

The outlaw camp was only a few miles south of the border. As they approached, there was a nicker from a distant horse, and Black Jack's horse responded. They rode on until they were challenged.

"Identify yourself," a voice shouted.

"Black Jack," the outlaw replied, "and I got company."

"Dismount and leave your horses there," the voice commanded.

Black Jack and Danielle dismounted. Ahead, in a small clearing beside a stream, stood four men. A coffeepot simmered over a small fire.

"Now," one of the men said, "who are you, and why are you here?"

"During a faro game, I heard Black Jack talking about picking up that pair of blacks in Mexico," said Danielle, "and I figured I'd like a hand in the game."

One of the outlaws laughed. "A kid that ain't even shaved, packin' two guns. Boy, one of them *Mejicanos* will have you for breakfast."

"I don't think so," said Black Jack. "I had the drop, had a Winchester coverin' him, and without me seein' him move, he shot the Winchester out of my hands."

Danielle said nothing, waiting for the outlaws to digest this new revelation. Quickly, they reached a decision, and they nodded at Black Jack.

"Who are you, kid, and where you from?" Black Jack asked.

"I don't answer to 'kid,' " said Danielle. "I'm Daniel Strange, and I'm from Missouri."

"I'm Black Jack Landis," said the outlaw. "The others is Joel Votaw, Revis Bronson, Hez Deshea, and Wes Pryor. Joel's our *segundo*."

"Black Jack," Votaw said, "I've warned you about leading horses through El Paso. With so many *Mejicanos* there, sooner or later, one of them's bound to recognize a horse, and then there'll be hell to pay. From now on, when you got the urge to ride to town, ride from here."

"Hell, there ain't nobody wise to me," said Black Jack.

"Oh?" Votaw said. "Then how come this two-gun man followed you back to camp? If he heard you shootin' off your mouth, then others heard. Next time, the *hombre* trailing you could be a ranger."

"After the war with Mexico, I've heard Americans can't legally cross the border into Mexico, and that Mexicans can't cross the border into the United States," said Danielle.

"That's the law," Revis Bronson said, "but it applies only if you get caught. There was at least one ranger that stepped over the line, and he ain't been seen since."

"You don't get shot at very often, then," said Danielle.

Black Jack Landis laughed. "Almost never. We take the horses at night. By first light, when the *Mejicanos* find our tracks, we are already across the river, in Texas. *Mejicanos* raise some very fine horses, but they're not fools. They don't consider 'em worth a dose of lead poisoning."

"I've heard talk that some sell Mexican horses in Texas, and Texas horses in Mexico," Danielle said. "Anything to that?"

"Some do," said Joel Votaw, "but we don't. Believe me, there ain't no love between the state of Texas and Mexico, and most Texans don't give a damn what happens on the other side of the border. As it is, if things get touchy in Mexico, we can cross the river into Texas, and the Mexes can't touch us. That could change almighty quick, if we was to run Texas horses across the border into Mexico."

"Damn right it could," Hez Deshea said.

"You're avoiding the law in Texas," said Danielle, "but what about Mexico?"

"Too much border," Wes Pryor said. "There's no way they can watch it all. *Mejicanos* cross the river into Texas, drivin' Texas horses into Mexico. They can't complain to the United States that Texans are violatin' their boundaries, because they're violatin' the Texas boundary. That's why nobody—not even the rangers—can stop it."

"Why are you camped in Mexico instead of Texas?" Danielle asked.

"You ain't earned the right to know that," said Joel Votaw. "Not until you've told us the truth. What's a younker that ain't old enough to shave and totin' two irons doin' in old Mexico?"

Danielle sighed. None of these men were the killers she sought. She quickly decided to tell them the truth. Or most of it. She told them of her father's murder and of her vow to track down the killers.

"I need money to continue my search," Danielle said. "There's seven more killers, and I'll never find them if I have to stop regular for a thirty-and-found riding job."

"That makes sense," said Joel Votaw, "but how do we know if you throw in with us, you won't shoot some *hombre* that'll attract the attention of the law? We can't allow that."

"If there's ever a possibility of the law stepping in, I'll vamoose," Danielle said.

Black Jack laughed. "I think we'd all vamoose if that happened."

"The men I'm after are outlaws and killers," said Danielle. "They're not going to call on the law for help."

"We been splittin' the money equal," Wes Pryor said. "If you join up with us, there'll be less money, split six ways."

"Show me what you're doing," said Danielle, "and I'll pull my weight. Your share may be even more."

"You've made a good case for yourself," Joel Votaw said. "I think we'll take you in for a while, as long as you don't get gun-happy and draw attention to us."

"I've never shot anybody except in self-defense," said Danielle.

"Bueno," Votaw said. "So far, we've took the horses we wanted without us doing any shooting. How good are you with horses?"

"I grew up with them," said Danielle. "I trained the chestnut mare I'm riding."

"We don't take a whole herd of horses," Votaw said, "because it's hard to control a herd at night. Each of us will take two lead ropes and lead two horses away. Come first light, when they can follow our tracks, we'll be across the border, in Texas."

"Only twelve horses for a night's work," said Danielle.

"The right horses will bring a hundred dollars apiece," Votaw said. "Two hundred for you for one night's work. At thirty and found, that's near seven months of line riding. If you can find the work."

"I've already learned the truth of that," said Danielle. "Where are you finding all these hundred-dollar horses?"

"A rich Spaniard, Alonzo Elfego, owns about half of Mexico," Votaw said, "and all his horses are blooded stock."

"Why doesn't he have riders watching them at night?" Danielle asked.

"There's too many of them, and they're scattered," said Votaw. "Besides, he has no idea when we're coming to visit him. We'll go tonight, and then give him a rest. There are other *ranchos* with plenty of good horses."

"Black Jack," said Hez Deshea, "why did you bring that pair of blacks with you? They should of brought top dollar in Texas."

"Cheap old bastard that was interested in 'em tried to knock my askin' price down to seventy-five dollars," Black Jack said. "That, and he got a little too interested in them Mex brands. I mounted up, rode out, and left him standin' there."

"You done right," said Votaw. "Brands are none of his damn business as long as he's gettin' a bill of sale."

"Where do you get bills of sale?" Danielle asked.

"A jackleg printer in El Paso makes 'em up for us," said Votaw.

Danielle nodded, digesting the information. Horse stealing was a hanging offense, but it seemed that these thieves had it down to a fine art. The only question in her mind was whether or not her alliance with the horse thieves would enable her to find any of the remaining men on her death list. Again Votaw spoke.

"Black Jack, you'd better take that pair of blacks back across the border, where we'll meet after tonight's raid. The rest of you get what sleep you can."

Black Jack mounted his horse, and with the pair of blacks following on lead ropes, he rode north. Danielle picketed the chestnut mare and, resting her head on her saddle, tipped her hat down over her eyes. After the blizzards on the high plains, the mild climate of old Mexico and the warm sun were welcome. She drifted off to sleep, rousing only when she heard a horse coming. Black Jack was returning. Shortly afterward, one of the bunch got a supper fire going. It was small, under a tree so the leaves would dissipate the smoke, and as soon as the coffee was hot, Revis Bronson put out the fire.

"When will we be going?" Danielle asked.

"Midnight," said Joel Votaw. "We ain't more than fifteen miles away."

Black Jack laughed. "Hell, we may be camped on Elfego's holdings right now."

The horse thieves all laughed, finding such a possibility amusing. Danielle had nothing more to say, and except for an occasional comment from one of the others, there was only silence. Danielle watched the stars, unable to sleep, thinking of the changes in her life. She might easily step over the line, becoming an outlaw, but how else was she to ever find the outlaws who had murdered her father, without associating with outlaws herself? Finally, Votaw gave an order.

"It's near midnight. Time to saddle up and ride."

Votaw gave each of them a pair lead ropes. They then saddled their horses, mounted, and rode south. There was no moon, and riding behind the others, Danielle could barely see them. They took their time, eventually reining up in the shadow of a stand of trees.

"We go from here on foot," Votaw said. "Once you've taken your horses, bring them here until we're all ready to ride."

Danielle had to concede that the thieves were smart. By starlight, it would be difficult to see men afoot, even if the herd was being watched. Dark as it was, they could still see the dim shapes of grazing horses. The horses raised their heads and snorted as they were approached. Danielle began to speak softly in a soothing tone that had proven effective in her handling of the chestnut mare. Suddenly, the night came alive with gunfire. Winchesters blazed from three different directions. There were entirely too many defenders. Danielle did not return the fire, for muzzle flashes would have been the finish of her. Besides, she had no intention of killing men for defending what was theirs. She reached the stand of trees where the horses had been picketed without being hit. Black Jack Landis hadn't been quite so lucky. He lay on the ground, groaning.

"Hard hit?" Danielle asked.

"My thigh," said Black Jack. "I can't mount my horse."

"Here, I'll help you," Danielle said.

By the time Black Jack was mounted, the rest of the horse thieves were galloping away to the north. None of them had horses except the ones they rode. Black Jack knew where they were headed, and Danielle followed him. There was a shallows in the river, and there they crossed the border into Texas. They reined up before a shack that had seen better days. The roof sagged in the middle, and what had once been a front porch had fallen in.

"All right," said Joel Votaw, "who's been hit, and how bad?"

"In the thigh," Black Jack said, "and it hurts like hell."

None of the others had been wounded.

"Bronson," said Votaw, "get a fire going in the fireplace. Then put some water on to boil so we can take care of Black Jack's wound."

"This is the first time we ever been shot at by old Alonzo Elfego's outfit," Black Jack said. "What the hell went wrong?"

"We got too damn overconfident," said Votaw. "It's been only a week since we took ten of Elfego's horses. Now we got to stay away until he's convinced we've backed off. I'd say he had a dozen men staked out with Winchesters. One of us could of been shot right through the head just as easy as Black Jack took one through his thigh."

"But Elfego's is the biggest horse ranch in Mexico," said Hez Deshea. "If we can't take horses from there, where else can we go?"

"I didn't say we can't go there again," Votaw said. "We'll just have to wait a month or so, until Elfego takes away them Mexes with Winchesters."

"Damn it," said Wes Pryor, "I'm near broke. I can't wait a month or two."

"Neither can I," Revis Bronson said as he stepped out of the dilapidated cabin. "When we started doin' this, we was selling horses every week."

"I need money too," said Joel Votaw, "but I don't need it bad enough to be shot dead. Any of you that can't wait a few days until Elfego's cooled down, feel free to ride out on your own."

"I ain't wantin' to bust up the outfit," Bronson said. "I reckon I can wait a few days."

"Then I'll stay on, too," said Pryor.

"I reckon I'll ride on," Danielle said, "but I won't be competing with any of you. I'll be riding to south Texas, looking for the bunch that killed my pa."

"Good luck," said Votaw. "Watch your back."

Votaw went into the shack. The water was boiling, and after cleansing Black Jack's leg wound, he bound it tight. Danielle stretched out, her head on her saddle, awaiting first light. Votaw came out, took a bottle of whiskey from his saddlebag, and returned to the cabin. Like Danielle, Bronson, Deshea, and Pryor tried to rest. Danielle lay awake, unsure as to the effect of her decision to ride on. As the eastern horizon began to gray with the first light of dawn, Danielle saddled the chestnut mare.

"Good luck," called Danielle to the others as she rode away.

Until she was out of sight, chills ran up and down her spine. It would have been easy for one of them to shoot her in the back, taking the chestnut mare and

the money in her saddlebag. But there were no shots.
Danielle rode back to El Paso. Stabling the chestnut
mare, she took a hotel room and slept until late afternoon. After supper, she again visited some of the saloons. Every saloon seemed to have a poster in the
window, and Danielle stopped to read one. It was simple and to the point.

> Señor Alonzo Elfego of Mexico will pay one thousand
> pesos for any hombre, dead or alive, who steals his
> horses.

Danielle felt a moment of guilt, for it had been only
an act of providence that had kept her from stepping
over the line and becoming a horse thief. She stopped
at another saloon, the Rio, where a faro game was in
progress. Danielle dragged out a chair and sat down.

"Five-dollar limit, kid," said the dealer. "No
credit."

"I don't recall asking for any credit," Danielle said,
dropping five double eagles on the green felt that lined
the tabletop.

Several of the men at the table grinned, expecting
this arrogant newcomer to soon get what he deserved.
But their grins faded as Danielle won five of the next
six pots. Every time she lost a pot, she more than
recovered her losses by winning the next three or four.

"I'm gettin' out of this," one of the gamblers
snarled, kicking back his chair. "I think the damn
house is slick-dealing cards to the kid. I ain't never
seen anybody win so often."

"Hank," said the house dealer, getting to his feet,
"I never slick-deal to anybody. Some folks is just better at the game than others, and if you can't afford to
lose, then just stay the hell away from the tables. Now
get out of here."

"If there's a problem," Danielle said, "I'll drop out."

"The problem's leavin', kid," said the dealer. "Win or lose, you're welcome to stay as long as you can cover your bets."

Danielle recovered her original hundred dollars, and won two hundred more. Leaving the saloon, she walked along the boardwalk. Suddenly a shadow moved from between two deserted buildings, and a voice spoke.

"Turn around, kid, and keep your hands where I can see 'em. I'm taking back all my money."

Danielle turned around slowly. The disgruntled gambler held a revolver on her. Quickly, she dropped to the ground as the pistol roared, almost in her ear. Before he could fire again, Danielle threw herself at his legs, and off balance, he fell. His head slammed into the strong wood of the boardwalk, and he lay still. The shot had been heard, and the sheriff, Buford Powell, was the first to arrive. Almost immediately, some of the men from the Rio Saloon were there, arriving in time to hear Danielle's explanation. The sheriff had a lantern, and set it down on the boardwalk.

"Let me see your guns, kid."

Danielle handed him the weapons. They were fully loaded, and had not been fired. The sheriff then took the gun from Hank's limp hand and found one load missing. There were many ways a man could fall from favor on the frontier, but there were three that stood head and shoulders above the rest: hitting a woman, mistreating a horse, or being a sore loser.

"The kid's lucky to be alive, Sheriff," said one of the men from the saloon. "I think Hank should be told when he wakes up that he's to stay away from the poker and faro tables in this town. This time, it was the kid. Next time, it could be any one of us."

"A couple of you tote him over to the jail," Sheriff Powell said. "I'll have some strong talk with him in the morning."

The sheriff took the gambler's revolver and followed the two men who lugged the still unconscious gambler. Some of the men from the saloon seemed inclined to further discuss the incident, but Danielle walked away. It seemed a good time to return to her room at the hotel.

"Well," said the desk clerk, "I see you didn't meet up with John Wesley Hardin. It's generally peaceful enough, except when he's in town."

For a long time Danielle lay awake, considering what her next move should be. When she had joined the horse thieves, she had felt there was a chance that one or more of the men she had sworn to kill might be in old Mexico. But after the raid on Elfego's horses had gone sour, she was forced to change her opinion. Not only was it illegal for persons from the United States to cross into Mexico, any American south of the border might be considered a horse thief, and shot on sight. She was convinced the men she sought were still scattered across the Southwest.

Returning from breakfast the next morning, Danielle stopped to question the young man at the lobby desk.

"How far is it to San Antonio?"

"Well over five hundred miles, and nothing much in between," said the desk clerk. "If you're ridin', you'd best take plenty of grub. But there's a stage once a week."

"Thanks," Danielle said.

Stage fares were expensive, so Danielle dismissed that possibility. It was a hot, dusty, and uncomfortable way to travel. She would ride, allowing the chestnut mare to take her time. Checking her saddlebags, Danielle found she was low on some items and rode by a mercantile to replenish them. To her dismay, as she was leaving the store, she met Hank, the sore loser from the saloon the night before. He had a bandage around his head, and his holster was empty. Apparently Sheriff Powell had kept his revolver.

"You young coyote," the gambler snarled, "nobody treats Hank Marshall like you done. One day, we'll meet up where you can't hide behind the law. Then you'll pay."

"Then you'd better shoot me in the back," said Danielle, "because you don't have the guts to face me. Try it, and I'll kill you."

Without a word, Marshall went on into the mercantile. Danielle mounted the chestnut mare and rode eastward. She was soon out of El Paso, and the plains before her looked bleak. There was no sign of human habitation for as far as she could see. As barren as the land appeared, there was water, but little or no wood for a fire. Danielle had a cold supper without coffee. There was no graze for the chestnut mare, and Danielle fed the animal a ration of grain she had brought along for that purpose. Picketing the mare nearby, she rolled in her blankets, her head on her saddle.

When Danielle arose the next morning, the weather was still mild, but far to the west, there was a dirty smudge of gray on the horizon. She saddled and mounted the chestnut mare and rode on toward San Antonio.

Chapter 10

The Trail to San Antonio. October 24, 1870.

By early afternoon, Danielle judged she was fifty miles out of El Paso, and that sometime during the coming night, she would be in for a soaking. The dark clouds from the west had begun moving in, and the wind was getting stronger. Danielle began looking for a place that might offer a little shelter, but there was nothing. It was then that she heard what sounded like a distant gunshot. She reined up, listening. The single shot was followed by a dozen more in quick succession. Somebody was under siege, and the odds didn't appear anywhere close to equal.

"Horse," said Danielle, "we ought to mind our own business, but somebody's in trouble down yonder toward the border."

Danielle kicked the chestnut into a slow gallop, reining her down to a walk as they drew nearer the shooting. Reaching a rise, she could see a shack below, and from brush that surrounded the shack, there were puffs of white smoke. There appeared to be three defenders, while the attackers numbered twice that many, perhaps more. Adjoining the shack was a corral, and in it were six horses, nickering in fear. The three men nearest the shack were in poor positions, for the attackers were on the opposite side of a ridge, where there was broken land and huge stones to cover them.

From powder smoke, Danielle counted eight riflemen firing toward the cabin. As one of the attackers shifted position, she saw the high crown of a Mexican sombrero. Danielle dismounted and, drawing her Henry rifle from the boot, set out to even up the odds. Her position was far better than that of the three defenders below, for the ridge on which she stood was higher than that on which the attackers were concealed. Her first shot ripped the Mexican's sombrero from his head, while her second shot slammed into the top of the stone behind which he was hiding, filling his eyes with dust. Danielle's intervention seemed to have given the three defenders renewed hope, for their firing grew more intense. Danielle held her fire, settling down on the rise, for if the attackers on the opposite ridge moved, she could see them. Suddenly, one of them did, seeking to get nearer the shack. Danielle fired, and the attacker fell, throwing up his hands. Another tried to improve his position, and Danielle's shot struck him in the shoulder, turning him around. He leaped for the stone behind which he had been concealed. Danielle quickly accounted for a third man, while the three men below continued firing. One of them scored a direct hit, and the four that remained ceased firing. Their attempts to move in closer had proven disastrous. It was time to back off.

"You on the ridge," shouted a voice from near the cabin, "can you see 'em? Have they retreated?"

"I think so," Danielle said. "Who were they, and who are you?"

"They're Mexicans that chased us across the border," said the voice. "I'm Roy Carnes, and my *amigos* are Jake Kazman and Maury Lyles."

"You've been rustling horses in Mexico, then, and driving them across the border," Danielle said. "Maybe I should have stayed out of it and let them take you."

"I swear we ain't rustled nobody's horses," Carnes shouted back. "Three of the horses in the corral is our personal mounts. The other three are wild as Texas jacks, without any brands. We trapped 'em wild, and before we could get 'em across the border, the damn Mexicans caught up to us. Come on down. There'll be a storm pretty quick."

The invitation was difficult to refuse, for the black clouds out of the west appeared to be dropping lower and lower. Already they had obscured the sun, and it was as though twilight had descended on the land. Leading the chestnut mare, Danielle descended the slope to the cabin below. The three men were waiting for her.

"Not a very good place for a cabin," Danielle said. "It's hard to defend."

"We know," said Carnes, "but there's water handy. We never expected them Mexes to foller us across the border. They never have before."

"Maybe you'd better think long and hard before crossing the border for more horses," Danielle said.

"I expect we will," Carnes said. "Who are you?"

"I'm Daniel Strange, bound for San Antonio."

"You're welcome to wait out the storm here with us," said Carnes. "We ain't got a bunk for you, but we can offer you a dry place to spread your blankets. Turn your horse into the corral with ours."

"Thanks," Danielle said. "It's looking pretty black over there. I'll accept your invite."

Removing her saddle and saddlebags, Danielle led the chestnut mare into the corral. It was a good time to see if Carnes had been lying about the newly acquired horses. But the trio appeared wild, and there wasn't a sign of a brand on any of them. Danielle followed the three men into the shack, finding it larger than she had expected. Danielle dropped her saddle and saddlebags in a corner. Carnes started a fire in the fireplace.

"Kazman," said Danielle, "your name's mighty familiar. I spent some time with friends north of Dallas, and I seem to recall having heard your name."

"No," Kazman said, a little too hurriedly. "I'm from south Texas, near San Antone."

"We ain't got much to offer in the way of grub," said Carnes. "When we break these wild horses, we got to ride into El Paso and stock up on supplies."

"I bought pretty heavy before leaving there," Danielle said. "While I'm here, and you're providing me shelter, I'll supply the grub. You got a coffeepot?"

"Yeah," said Maury Lyles, "but we been out of coffee beans for a week."

"I have some," Danielle said. "Maybe I can spare you enough to get you to El Paso."

"We'd be obliged," said Roy Carnes.

Outside, the wind had risen to a shriek, driving sheets of rain against the side of the cabin. Danielle felt the floor tremble beneath her feet. They all sat on the benches on each side of the table, Danielle covertly watching Jake Kazman. Without appearing to, he shifted his eyes toward Danielle's saddle and saddlebags, and then looked away. Danielle observed him from the corner of her eye, and realized if he *had* been in north Texas, he might well know of the trail drive in which Danielle had taken part. He might also suspect that she had earned considerable money when the cattle had been sold in Abilene. Outside, the storm roared on. Using Danielle's supplies, Carnes prepared supper. After eating, the conversation dribbled away to nothing. While Carnes and Lyles were at ease, Kazman was restless, and more than once Danielle caught him watching her.

"We might as well turn in for the night," Lyles said,

"unless the rest of you want to light the lantern and play some low-stakes poker."

"Thanks," said Danielle, "but I don't play poker."

"I don't play for low stakes," Carnes said, "and these other two jaybirds are likely as broke as I am. Besides, we've had a hard day, and I can use the sleep."

The three retired to their bunks, while Danielle took her place in the corner, her head on her saddle. The fire was allowed to burn itself out, and soon the cabin was in complete darkness. In the early hours of the morning, Danielle awakened, unsure as to what had disturbed her. The storm had ceased, for there was no roar of the wind or the sound of rain on the roof. Danielle lay on her back and, without moving the rest of her body, very slowly moved her right hand until it reached the butt of her Colt. Slowly she drew the weapon, and again she heard the sound that had awakened her. A floorboard creaked.

"You're covered," Danielle said. "A step closer, and I'll shoot."

"Hell," said Jake Kazman, "I was just goin' outside."

"Then turn around," Danielle said. "The door's behind you."

"Kazman," said Carnes, who was awake now, "I don't hold with botherin' an *hombre* that's stood by me or been a help to me in any way."

"Neither do I," Lyles added. "Nothin' but a flea-bitten yellow coyote eats another man's grub and then tries to rob him."

"You can't prove I had any such thing in mind," Kazman shouted, "and I won't take a charge from nobody. Nobody, by God!"

"You've been watching me ever since I got here," Danielle said, "and I'm accusing you of coming after me in the dark. When you say you don't know me, or don't know of me, you lie. If you're still here come daylight, be wearing your pistol. You'll need it."

"I ain't goin' nowhere without one of them wild horses," said Kazman. "One of them belongs to me."

"Then catch one of them, saddle your horse, and get the hell out of here," Roy Carnes said.

"That goes for me as well," said Maury Lyles. "I never liked you much, Kazman, and now I know why."

Carnes stirred up the coals and added some wood to the fire. Without a word, Kazman took his saddle and left the shack.

"You reckon we ought to watch the varmint?" Lyles asked. "He's likely to take all the horses. Maybe our mounts too."

"I'll watch him," said Carnes, taking his Winchester and stepping out the door.

"I swear we didn't know what he was when he joined up with us," said Lyles.

"I don't fault you and Carnes," Danielle said. "Despite what Kazman said, I still think he's from north Texas. A few weeks ago, I joined some Texas ranchers in gathering and getting a trail herd to Abilene. We gunned down four outlaws in Indian Territory, and I'm sure Kazman was one of those who escaped."

Nothing more was said until Carnes returned to the cabin.

"He's got his work cut out for him, with that wild horse," said Carnes.

"That's his problem," Lyles said. "I'm glad to be rid of him."

"He seems like a man that carries a grudge," said Danielle. "He's liable to sneak back and bushwhack one or both of you."

"You'd better watch your back trail," Carnes said. "He knows where you're headed, and I wouldn't put it past him, trailing you."

"I'll keep that in mind," said Danielle. "There's still time to get some sleep before first light. But I think we should shove the table up against the door."

It was still dark outside when the nickering of a horse awakened Danielle. She pulled on her boots, aware that Carnes and Lyles were moving about. Nobody spoke. Danielle heard her companions cocking their Winchesters, and she followed them outside. There was a frightened nicker from the chestnut mare, for a shadowy rider was attempting to mount the animal. Danielle whistled once, and the mare broke into a frenzy of bucking, flinging the would-be thief to the ground.

"Get up, you thieving bastard," Carnes shouted.

But there was a muzzle flash, and Carnes stumbled back against the cabin wall. In only a split second, Danielle drew and fired twice, to the right and the left of the muzzle flash. For a moment none of them moved, lest the intruder still lived. Finally, Maury Lyles spoke.

"How hard was you hit, Roy?"

"Shoulder," said Carnes.

"I'll get the lantern," Lyles said, "but I think we all know who the coyote is."

Lyles lighted the lantern, and they found themselves looking into the dead face of Jake Kazman. He had been shot twice.

"Tarnation, that's some shootin' in the dark," said Lyles to Danielle. "That skunk really had it in for you."

"Do you know if Kazman was his real name?" Danielle asked.

"That's the name he gave us," said Lyles. "I'd better patch up your shoulder, Roy."

After dragging Kazman away from the corral, they returned to the cabin. Lyles stirred up the fire and put on a pot of water to boil.

"I have a quart of whiskey in my saddlebag," Danielle said, "and I'll leave it with you. There may be infection."

"We're obliged," said Carnes. "We won't be ridin' to town until we break those three wild horses."

After dressing Carnes's wound, Lyles built up the fire and started breakfast, since first light wasn't far away. In the brightening sky, the stars had begun to retreat into the distant heavens. By the time they finished breakfast, the eastern horizon was illuminated with the first light of dawn.

"I have plenty of coffee beans," Danielle said. "I'll leave some with you to last until you can get to town. Do you want me to bury Kazman before I go?"

"No," said Lyles, "I'll take care of it. You've done us some mighty big favors, and we are obliged."

Carnes added, "If you hadn't come along and spooked Kazman, he might have shot us both in the back and took *all* the horses. You sure you can't stay and join in our horse hunting?"

"No," said Danielle. "My pa was robbed and murdered in Indian Territory by outlaws, and I aim to track them down. There's seven of them still alive, unless Kazman was one of them, using another name."

"Before you leave, I'll search Kazman," Lyles said. "You never know what you'll find in a dead man's pockets."

Lyles took a little more than an hour, digging a shallow grave and burying Kazman. He returned to the cabin and dropped six gold double eagles on the table.

"That's all he had on him," said Lyles. "I reckon it's yours, Daniel, since you gave him what he deserved."

"I don't want it," Danielle said. "Use it to stock up on grub and coffee beans."

Shortly afterward, Danielle rode away. She genuinely hated leaving the two genial cowboys, but she wanted nothing more to do with taking horses—wild or gentled—from old Mexico. She had thought at first that some of the killers she sought might have crossed the border into Mexico, and were hiding there. But now, with Mexicans so hostile toward all Americans, it seemed unlikely. Texas itself was large enough to hide the whole bunch, and she rode on toward San Antonio.

San Antonio, Texas. October 30, 1870.

Danielle took a room on the second floor of the Cattleman's Hotel. It was the exception among frontier hotels, for there was a dining room on the first floor. Every room had a deep pile carpet on the floor, with matching drapes at the window. Danielle sat down on the bed, which was firm enough that it didn't sag under her weight. It would be a welcome comfort, after four nights on the ground. There was a washbasin and a porcelain pitcher of water, and she took advantage of it, washing away the trail dust. One look in the mirror told her that her hair was getting entirely too long. She had to visit a barbershop, and soon. Since there was still daylight left, she decided to go for a haircut and be done with it. It was nearing the supper hour, and there were no other patrons in the shop.

"Cut it short," Danielle said. "I'm having trouble getting my hat to fit."

"Shave?" the barber asked.

"No," Danielle said. "Just cut my hair."

"There's a bathhouse in back, with plenty of soap and hot water," the barber said.

"Maybe later," said Danielle. "It's near suppertime, and I'm hungry."

The door opened, and a lanky man entered. A Colt was tied low on each hip.

"Haircut," said the stranger.

"You're next," the barber replied.

"King Fisher don't like to wait," said the new arrival. "I'll get in that other chair, and you take care of me. Then you can get back to the shavetail you're working on now."

"I was here first," Danielle said, "and he's goin' to finish with me. If you don't like it, wait until I'm out of this chair and settle with me."

Under her barber's cloth, there was the ominous sound of a Colt being cocked. There was no fear in Danielle's cold green eyes as they bored into King Fisher's.

"I'll come back another time," said King Fisher. Turning, he walked out the door.

"My God," the barber said, "do you know who that was?"

"I believe he said his name is King Fisher," Danielle said. "It means nothing to me."

"It should," said the barber. "He don't carry them two guns just for show, and at this particular time, Ben Thompson's in town. Him and King Fisher are friends. Sober, they're decent, but let 'em get drunk, and the devil couldn't ask for no better disciples."*

Danielle left the barbershop and returned to the hotel, where she took a table in the dining room. She had not even been served when King Fisher entered. With him was a smaller man, dressed all in black, with a frock coat and black silk top hat. The two took a table next to Danielle's, and she couldn't help hearing their talk.

*King Fisher and Ben Thompson (born in Knottingley, England, November 11, 1842) were dangerous men. Both were confirmed killers noted for their swiftness with a gun. They were notorious gamblers, and they each walked on both sides of the law, wearing the star until some drunken brawl or random killing got them dismissed. Both men were ambushed in a theater in San Antonio, in 1884. The killers were never caught.

"The kid at the next table pulled a gun and run me out of the barbershop," said King Fisher, loud enough for Danielle to hear.

Fisher's companion found that uproariously funny, pounding the table with his fist, but when he spoke, his voice was like cold steel.

"Nobody drives Ben Thompson away if he wants to go on living."

Danielle tried her best to ignore the pair, taking her time with her meal. As she got up to leave, Thompson spoke.

"I never seen a man with a butt-forward pistol who had any speed with a cross-hand draw."

In an instant, he found himself facing the barrel end of the butt-forward Colt from Danielle's left hip.

"There are exceptions," Danielle said coldly. She border-shifted the Colt back to her left hand, deftly slipping the weapon back into its holster, again butt forward.

It was King Fisher's turn to laugh. "Who *are* you, kid?"

"My name is not 'kid.' I'm Daniel Strange."

"I'm King Fisher, and the little *hombre* in the stovepipe hat is Ben Thompson. Let word of this get around, and Thompson may have to go back to England."

"I've never seen a fancy pair of irons like that," Thompson said. "May I see one?"

"Look all you like," said Danielle, "but they stay where they are."

Thompson's ruddy face turned ugly, but King Fisher took the edge off his anger.

"Come on, Thompson, let's go play some poker. This two-gun man's too tough for a pair of old dogs like us."

Danielle waited, allowing the pair to leave ahead of her. Referring to her youth, King Fisher had been just as insulting as Ben Thompson, and she didn't like either of them. The evening was still young, and there was little to occupy one's time except gambling tables in the various saloons. Danielle still had almost four thousand dollars, thanks to her success at the faro tables, and a town like San Antonio had many saloons. With a self-imposed limit of a hundred dollars, she set out to make the rounds. She had learned that the fancier the saloon, the higher the stakes. The first place she entered was called The Oro Palace and the faro dealer was asking for—and getting—ten-dollar bets. When a player left the table, Danielle sat down, dropping five double eagles on the felt-topped table before her. The other players paid her no attention until she won three pots in a row. She still had sixty dollars of her original hundred, plus her winnings. She lost two pots, and then won four in a row. The dealer had been watching her suspiciously but it was he, after all, who was dealing the cards. After winning back her initial hundred dollars and taking another two hundred from the house, Danielle dropped out. The house dealer seemed relieved.

Danielle found most saloons unpleasant, with brash, insensitive women determined to lead her upstairs. But the saloons were where men gathered, and as she sat at the faro table, she listened to talk around her, hoping for some word of the men who had killed her father. Quickly tiring, she returned to her hotel. In the lobby was a stack of newspapers.

"Take one," the clerk invited. "They're fresh in from Dallas."

Danielle took one, finding it to be larger than the average frontier newspaper. With news items from all over, one in particular caught her eye. It was datelined Wichita, and concerned the robbery of a Kansas-Pacific train. She read the article twice, grinding her teeth.

. . . two men—Rufe Gaddis and Julius Byler—were believed to be involved, but they had none of the gold, and refused to talk. They were released for lack of evidence.

Both the men were on Danielle's death list, but after their brush with the law, they would be long gone from Wichita. The Kansas town was almost at the edge of Indian Territory, and the pair might have gone there to hide. On the other hand, they might have gone west, or perhaps back east, toward St. Louis. Danielle lay down to sleep, wondering if she was wasting her time in south Texas.

The next morning, after breakfast, Danielle found the Texas Ranger office. A ranger sat at a battered desk, reading a newspaper. He looked up as she entered.

"I'm Daniel Strange."

"I'm Sage Jennings," said the ranger.

"I'm looking for some men—outlaws—who robbed and murdered my pa in Indian Territory," Danielle said. "There are seven of them still alive, and although I've managed to learn their names, I don't know that they aren't using other names by now. Do you have any wanted dodgers that I'd be allowed to see?"

"You're welcome to look through what I have," Jennings said, "but I doubt they'll be of much help. These are only outlaws wanted by the state of Texas."

"I'd like to look at them anyway," said Danielle.

Jennings brought out the dodgers, many of them yellowed with age. Some of them had a rough sketch of the wanted man, but the majority had only a name, the nature of the crime, and the reward, if any. Almost immediately, Danielle found a pair of yellowed pages with the names of Rufe Gaddis and Julius Byler.

There was a thousand dollars on the heads of each of them.

"This is two of them on my list," said Danielle.

"Those dodgers are mighty old," Jennings said. "Chances are, they're using some other names by now."

"No," said Danielle. "Yesterday, I saw both their names in a story in a Dallas newspaper. Gaddis and Byler were suspected of robbing a Kansas-Pacific train, but were let go for lack of evidence. The law in Wichita had them."

"By now they're somewhere in Indian Territory," Jennings said.

Danielle thumbed through the rest of the wanted dodgers without finding the names of any more of the men she sought.

"Just those two," said Danielle. "I'm obliged."

"A ranger keeps records of his own," Jennings said. "I'll check out Bible Two."*

From his shirt pocket, he took a small notebook and began thumbing through it.

"Here's something that might be of interest to you," said Jennings, "and it brings back some unpleasant memories for me. Gaddis and Byler didn't take part in the war. They're both Texans, and they stayed here and raised hell. When they finally stepped over the line to become thieves and killers, we haven't seen them since. Another *hombre* known to the rangers as Chancy Burke generally rode with them."

"Burke's on my list with Gaddis and Byler," said Danielle. "If they're all Texans, then I may not be wasting my time in Texas after all. What part of Texas did they call home?"

"In and around Waco," Jennings said, "and you

*Every Texas Ranger carried a personal Bible. In addition, he kept a record of outlaws wanted by the rangers, and this notebook was referred to as "Bible Two."

may be right. They still have families—law-abiding folks—living there, and I wouldn't be surprised if all of them don't slip back home for an occasional visit."

"I'm obliged to you for the information," said Danielle. "Maybe I'll ride to Waco and see what I can find."

"Then take some advice from somebody that's been there," Jennings said, "and don't tell anybody why you're in town. Everybody in the county is loyal to them three young varmints, and hostile as hell toward the rangers and other lawmen."

"I reckon they didn't do their hell-raising close to home," said Danielle.

"They didn't," Jennings said. "Their kin will admit they're wild, but they won't lift a hand to help the law track them down."

"Thanks," said Danielle. "I'll keep my silence."

"If you're successful in finding any or all three of them, I'd appreciate your sending me word," Jennings said.

"I will," said Danielle.

On the way to her hotel, Danielle met King Fisher and Ben Thompson walking unsteadily along the boardwalk. The pair looked as though they might have been up all night.

"Well, by God," King Fisher said, slapping his thigh with his hat, "it's the kid with the two big guns."

"He'll bleed like anybody else with a slug in him," said Thompson, fixing his bloodshot eyes on Danielle.

Danielle walked around them, chills racing up and down her spine. Would the drunken Thompson shoot her in the back? Nothing happened, and she began to relax.

Danielle saw no advantage to remaining in San Antonio. Remaining there, she might be confronted with either Ben Thompson or King Fisher, a confrontation that would profit her nothing. So taking her bedroll and saddlebags, she went to the livery where she had left the chestnut mare. Saddling the animal, she mounted and rode north, toward Waco.

Chapter 11

Waco, Texas. November 3, 1870.

Reaching Waco, Danielle stabled the chestnut mare and took a hotel room not too far away. Danielle found a cafe and had supper. While Waco wasn't nearly as large as San Antonio, it had its share of saloons. Recalling the warning from Sage Jennings, the Texas Ranger in San Antonio, she would make the rounds of the saloons first. Only then, if she learned nothing, would she speak to the county sheriff.

The first saloon she entered was The Bull's Horn, and except for a poker game, there was nothing going on. She watched for a few minutes, but nobody spoke, except for an occasional grunt of satisfaction as one of the men won a hand and raked in the money. The rest of the saloons in town proved to be much like the first. There were faro games going on in several of them, but Danielle avoided them, lest she draw attention to herself. People in Waco seemed especially closemouthed, and she expected some hostility when she had to ask questions. Since it seemed there was no other way, the next morning after breakfast, she set out to find the sheriff's office. It was small, with a pair of barred cells behind it.

"Sheriff, I'm Daniel Strange, and I need to ask a favor."

The lawman had gray hair, and the years had taken

their toll on his body. A Colt was tied down on his right hip. He looked Danielle over carefully before he spoke.

"I'm Sheriff Rucker. The last two-gun man through here got strung up. Now what do you want of me?"

"I'm looking for some word of Rufe Gaddis, Julius Byler, and Chancy Burke. They're from this area, I'm told."

"Far from here," Rucker said. "I ain't seen any of 'em for three years. Mind telling me why you're interested in them?"

There it was. There was no holding back the truth, which Rucker likely suspected already. Danielle sighed, then spoke.

"They were part of a group of men who robbed and hanged my pa in Indian Territory last spring."

"I reckon you got proof," said Sheriff Rucker.

"To my satisfaction," Danielle said. "I've tracked down three of them, and the second one gave me the names of the others. Where do you stand?"

"Right here in this county," said Sheriff Rucker. "I got no jurisdiction anywhere else, and unless some *hombres* ride in here to raise hell, I leave 'em alone."

"Even if they're wanted by the *rangers* for crimes in other places?"

"Even then," Rucker said. "Hell, the *rangers* ain't been sanctified. It wouldn't be the first time they've gone after the wrong men."

"How well are the Gaddis, Byler, and Burke families known around here?" Danielle asked.

"They're known and respected all over the county," said Rucker, "and they look after their own. They're clannish, and when you cut one, they all bleed."

"And they all vote," Danielle said.

"Yeah," said Sheriff Rucker, his face going red. "I won this office ten years ago, and an *hombre* like you could lose it for me in one day."

"Oh, I won't drag you into it," Danielle said in disgust.

She turned and left the office. When the liveryman brought her the chestnut mare, she had a question for him.

"I'm looking for work. Who are the most prominent ranchers in these parts?"

"Silas Burke, Damon Byler, and Luke Gaddis," said the liveryman, "but they won't be hiring. They can't afford no riders."

"Give me some directions anyway," Danielle said, "and I'll see for myself. I'm needin' to hire on somewhere for the winter."

It wasn't an unusual request from an unemployed, drifting rider, and the liveryman gave Danielle directions. The Burke spread was the closest, and she rode there first. When Danielle rode in, a man with graying hair and a body gone to fat stood on the front porch, a Winchester under his arm. Danielle reined up a few yards away.

"Who are you and what do you want?" the man growled.

"I'm Daniel Strange, and I'm looking for some line riding to see me through winter."

"I'm Silas Burke, and I ain't hiring. If I was, I wouldn't hire no two-gun stranger. We got too many cowboys here in the county that's needin' work. Had you asked, you could of learned that in town."

Two young men—Benjamin and Monroe—looking like younger versions of Silas, came out and stood beside their father.

"He looks like one of them damn rangers, Pa." said Benjamin. "Two guns."

"A mite unusual for a line rider," Silas said. "Boy, are you the law?"

"No," said Danielle, "and I'm not a bounty hunter. Why are you afraid of the law?"

"I ain't afraid of the law," Silas growled, "and if I was, it wouldn't be no business of yours. Now turn that horse around and ride."

There was no help for it. Danielle wheeled the chestnut mare, riding back the way she had come. After she was well out of sight, a horseman rode out of a thicket where he had been waiting, and rode on to the Burke place. Sheriff Rucker had some news for old Silas Burke.

Danielle rode on to the Byler spread, where she received the same cold reception.

"I ain't hiring," said Damon Byler, "and if I was, it wouldn't be no two-gun shavetail passin' through. Ride on."

Reaching the Gaddis ranch, Danielle prepared herself for yet another rebuff, and it wasn't long in coming. Luke Gaddis was waiting for her to ride in, and before she had a chance to speak, Gaddis shifted the shotgun under his arm.

"I ain't hiring," said Gaddis bluntly.

"You don't even know me," Danielle said.

"No," said Gaddis, "but I know *of* you and your kind. Sheriff Rucker's told me about you. Now turn your horse around and ride."

Danielle rode away, furious. Sheriff Rucker had violated a confidence, knowing well the effect it would have on the Burke, Byler, and Gaddis families. There was nothing more to do except ride back to town, and Danielle did so, unsure as to what her next move would be. If the three men she sought *did* return to Texas, they would immediately learn that they were being hunted. But Danielle still had some unpleasant surprises ahead. She reined up and dismounted at the livery.

"I got no room for another horse," the liveryman said.

Danielle made up her mind to remain in Waco one

more night. Returning to the hotel, she requested a room.

"Sorry," the desk clerk said. "We're full."

Danielle received the same treatment at other hotels and boardinghouses. She stopped at the cafe where she had eaten breakfast, and before she could sit down, one of the cooks spoke.

"You're not welcome here. Move on."

Danielle left, mounted the chestnut mare, and rode to the mercantile to replenish her supplies, including a bag of grain for the chestnut mare. She would sleep on the ground and prepare her own meals. But the store owner, looking embarrassed, turned her away.

"I got to live in this town," he said, "and I can't afford havin' them that don't like you comin' down on me. Sorry."

"The whole damn bunch of you deserve one another," spat Danielle in disgust.

She considered riding back to San Antonio and reporting the sheriff's behavior to Sage Jennings, the Texas Ranger, but changed her mind. Jennings had almost surely been to this town and, beyond a doubt, had met with the same hostility. Recalling that Fort Worth was only a few miles north, Danielle decided to go there. If the gold taken from the train by Gaddis and Byler had a government payroll, surely the post commander at Ft. Worth would know. He might even be sympathetic to her cause.

Fort Worth, Texas. November 5, 1870.

Arriving in Fort Worth, Danielle asked to speak to the post commander. Following a Sergeant Waymont, she was taken through the orderly room. Sergeant Waymont knocked on a door, and from inside the office, a voice spoke.

"Yes, who is it?"

"Sergeant Waymont, sir, and I have someone with me who wants to talk to you."

"Come in, Sergeant," the officer said.

Waymont entered, saluted, and had it returned. He stepped out the door, closing it behind him. Danielle was on her own. She spoke.

"I'm Daniel Strange, from St. Joe, Missouri."

"I'm Captain Ferguson. Sit down and tell me what you want of me."

"Maybe you can help me track down three killers I'm looking for," said Danielle.

"The military does not assist bounty hunters," Ferguson said.

"I'm not a bounty hunter," said Danielle. "The men I'm searching for were part of a gang that robbed and murdered my pa in Indian Territory."

"You are justified in your search for them, then," Ferguson said, "but I don't understand what you want of me. I presume you have no evidence."

"Only the confession of one of the men," said Danielle.

"Oh," Ferguson said. "Where is he?"

Danielle sighed. "He's dead."

"Then we're right back where we started," said Ferguson.

"Not quite," Danielle said. "When I was in San Antonio, in a Dallas newspaper I found a story about a train robbery near Wichita. Gaddis and Byler, two of the men I'm after, were involved in that holdup. They stole a military payroll, didn't they?"

After a long moment of silence, and just when Danielle had decided Ferguson wasn't going to reply, he did.

"I don't think I'm violating any rules, telling you this. Yes, it was a military payroll, bound for Fort

Dodge. A military escort was to have intercepted it at the end-of-track."*

"Those outlaws were successful in one train robbery," said Danielle, "and it's a safe bet they'll plan another one. How can I find out when there'll be another shipment?"

"You can't," Ferguson said. "That's confidential information."

"Not confidential enough to keep the outlaws from knowing it," said Danielle.

"No," Ferguson said with a sigh. "Privately, I believe we're being sold out by somebody with the Kansas-Pacific in Kansas City. But the railroad refuses to consider such a possibility, because there's no proof."

"Except that the thieves always seem to know which train is carrying a payroll," said Danielle. "Can you get me the names of the men employed by the railroad?"

"Probably," Ferguson said, "but for what purpose?"

"I want to see if any of the men I'm searching for are on that list," Danielle said. "If a name on that list matches a name on my list, he could well be the traitor that's selling out to the train robbers."

"I'll secure a list of the Kansas-Pacific employees on one condition," said Ferguson.

"I'm listening," Danielle said.

"Should we actually find on this list the name of one of the men you're searching for," said Ferguson, "I want him arrested by the proper authorities, not gunned down."

"If the proper authorities can take him, welcome," Danielle said. "If they can't, then he belongs to me. In case you don't know, three of the varmints on my list are from Waco, and two of them stole your last payroll. Your 'proper authority'—the county sheriff—

---

*The Kansas-Pacific rails didn't reach Dodge until 1872.

is more concerned with keeping his star than he is in tracking down hometown boys who are thieves and murderers."

"See here, young man," said Captain Ferguson coldly, "it is not the responsibility of military personnel to track down civilian thieves. Asking for an employee list from Kansas-Pacific would be exceeding my authority, and under the circumstances, I don't believe it is justified."

"Thank you for seeing me, Captain," Danielle said, getting to her feet.

"I'm not finished with you," said Ferguson.

"Maybe not," Danielle said, "but I'm finished with you. You're about as much help as that no-account sheriff in Waco."

Danielle left the office, mounted the chestnut mare, and rode north, bound for Indian Territory.

Meanwhile, Rufe Gaddis and Julius Byler had established a camp in Indian Territory, a few miles south of Wichita. Passing a bottle back and forth, they contemplated their next move.

"Damn it," Byler said, "if it wasn't for owin' Chancy Burke a third of what we got, we could take that twenty-five thousand and ride on."

Gaddis laughed. "We could ride on, anyway, taking it all. What would Burke do? For sure he couldn't complain to the law that we took his share of the money he helped us steal from the railroad."

"No," Byler agreed, "but he wouldn't feed us any more information about when there's a gold shipment coming. This is a sweet setup, and us gettin' greedy could ruin it."

"One thing bothers me," said Gaddis. "There ain't been a word out of the railroad after we took that twenty-five thousand. We can always stop the train by blocking the track or ripping out a rail, but what happens if there's a dozen armed guards in that mail coach?"

"I reckon that's all the more reason for Burke to get his share," Byler said. "It'll be up to him to warn us if the train's swarming with Pinkertons or soldiers."

"Tomorrow, then," Gaddis said, "we'd better ride to Kansas City and have some words with him. If a shipment's under heavy guard, he's got to warn us."

Leaving Fort Worth, Danielle reached the Red River before sundown. Rather than enter Indian Territory so near dark, she made camp on the south bank of the Red. Tomorrow, she would continue her journey to Wichita. The story she had read in the Dallas paper was somehow incomplete. It had provided the names of the thieves—Rufe Gaddis and Julius Byler—but how had that been possible? For certain, the two had not introduced themselves. She hoped the sheriff in Wichita could and would fill in the missing information.

The following morning, after a hurried breakfast, Danielle saddled the chestnut mare and crossed the Red. It was a good two-day ride just getting across Indian Territory. She wanted to get as much of the Territory behind her as she could on the first day. She kept the chestnut mare at a mile-eating gait, stopping once every hour to rest the animal. Near sundown, she found a spring and, not wishing to risk a fire, ate jerked beef and drank cold water. There was no graze, and she fed the horse the last of the grain.

"Sorry, old girl," said Danielle. "That will have to hold you until we reach Wichita."

Wichita, Kansas. November 8, 1870.

The first stars were already twinkling when Danielle rode into Wichita. Her initial concern was for the horse, and she left the mare at a livery, paying for extra rations of grain and a rubdown. The newer buildings in Wichita were strung out along the railroad track, with several cafes and a hotel among them. Danielle took a room then went to the nearest cafe. She was hungry, having eaten little but jerked beef since her first night in Waco. After eating, she decided against returning to the hotel immediately, going to a nearby saloon instead. In an obvious play for railroad business, it had been named The Railroad Saloon, and a sign in the plate glass window proclaimed it the largest and fanciest in Wichita. It wasn't much past the supper hour, but the place was already crowded with an abundance of poker and faro games in progress. So as not to attract unwanted attention, Danielle sat in on one of the faro games. Sticking to her limit, she dropped her five double eagles on the felt-topped table.

"Five-dollar limit," said the dealer.

Danielle won and lost, won and lost, and finally dropped out, breaking even. She was about to leave the saloon when a pair of familiar faces caught her eye. At one of the poker tables sat Herb Sellers and Jesse Burris, the two would-be bounty hunters she had last seen in Denver. Danielle slipped up behind Burris and poked him between his shoulder blades with her finger.

"You're under arrest, you varmint."

"Not now, damn it," said Burris. "I'm ahead."

Herb Sellers looked up and smiled, recognition in his eyes, but he remained where he was. For the next few hands, Danielle stood back and watched. Evidently, Herb and Jesse were doing well at the table, and it was almost an hour before they withdrew from the game.

"Well," Danielle said, after they had left the saloon, "how's the bounty hunting going?"

"Not worth a damn," said Burris. "We're surviving because we've been lucky at the poker tables, but how long does a run of luck last?"

"What about your manhunt, Daniel?" Sellers asked.

"I caught up to one of the outfit in New Mexico," said Danielle, "but that's all. I came here because there was a short story in a Dallas newspaper about two *hombres* robbing a Kansas-Pacific train of a government payroll. The newspaper printed the names of two of the men I'm searching for, so I came here to see what I could learn. Mostly, I want to know how the newspaper discovered their names."

"I can tell you that," said Burris. "Herb and me got here yesterday because there's a $2,500 bounty on the heads of each of the train robbers. They stopped the train four or five miles east of here, and after the robbery, the engineer backed the train into town. The sheriff got a quick posse together and picked up the trail of the robbers, who were bound for Indian Territory. But they found tracks of three horses, and eventually caught up to a woman whose horse had gone lame. She had been with the robbers, but hadn't taken part in the train robbery. She told the sheriff as much as she could—including the names of the train robbers—and the sheriff let her go."

"The newspaper account didn't tell it all," Danielle said. "There was no mention of the woman. She had to talk about Gaddis and Byler, but she might also have known something about the rest of that bunch that hanged my pa."

"She left last night on the eastbound train," said Herb. "The sheriff wouldn't even tell us her name."

"Sounds like the kind of treatment I got in Waco," Danielle said. "Rufe Gaddis, Julius Byler, and Chancy Burke are all from there, and they're all part of the gang that hanged my pa. I made the mistake of telling the sheriff why I was looking for them, and he made it a point tell the whole damn county why I was there. The Gaddis, Byler, and Burke families tell everybody when to jump and how high. I couldn't stable my horse, rent a room, or buy myself a meal."

"Then what did you do?" Jesse Burris asked.

"I rode to Fort Worth and met with Captain Ferguson, the post commander. He finally admitted it was a military payroll that Gaddis and Byler took, but he wasn't interested in the plan I had. I think Gaddis and Byler are being fed information by someone working for the railroad. I wanted Captain Ferguson to use his influence to get a list of the names of men who are involved with the Kansas-Pacific, but I couldn't meet his conditions. He wants to do everything by the book, allowing the authorities to make proper arrests. I don't care a damn about Gaddis and Byler being arrested for train robbery. I want the bastards dead."

"Burris and me was in that saloon right through supper," said Herb, "and I'm starved. Let's get somethin' to eat and talk about this some more."

"I've had supper," Danielle said, "but I can always use some more coffee."

They stopped at one of the cafes near the railroad. While Sellers and Burris waited for their food, the three of them sipped hot coffee.

"A damn shame the military wouldn't work with you," Burris said. "If Gaddis and Byler have somebody connected with the railroad feeding them information, they'll know when a train's carrying a payroll. But suppose we managed to get the names of every man with the Kansas-Pacific, and none of them are the men you're hunting? We still wouldn't have a clue as to who the Judas is, and you'd be no closer to finding the bunch you're looking for."

"True," Danielle said, "but at least I'd know that they're likely not in Kansas. Since I learned nothing in Waco, I'm really not sure where to go from here.

I'm thinking of going directly to the Kansas-Pacific
and asking them if any of the men on my list are
involved with the railroad."

"Maybe we'll go with you," said Burris.

"No," Danielle said. "Some folks frown on bounty
hunting, and that might interfere with my learning
anything. If I learn something you can use, I'll pass
it on."

"Then why don't we ride to Kansas City in the
morning?" Herb suggested. "I doubt we'll learn anything more here."

Kansas City, Kansas. November 10, 1870.

The trio reached Kansas City in the late afternoon.
There was the shriek of a whistle and the clanging of
a bell as a train pulled out for the end-of-track.

"Let's find a hotel and get the horses stabled," Danielle said. "Then I'll see what I can learn from the
railroad."

The town was large and growing, evidence enough
of the prosperity that followed the coming of the rails.
Danielle and her companions took rooms in one of
the hotels not far from the railroad yard. It was close
enough for Danielle to walk, and she did. Railroad
offices were housed in a larger building that was also
the terminal, and Danielle went in. A little man with
spectacles looked up from the telegraph instrument on
the table before him.

"I'm looking for someone who might be working
for the railroad," Danielle said. "Who do I need to
talk to about him?"

"Alan Steele," said the telegrapher. "He's personnel manager, but he's gone for the day. Nobody here
but me."

Danielle sighed. "I'll try again tomorrow."

Slowly, she walked back to the hotel, her spirits at a low ebb. It was becoming more and more difficult to live up to her vow to find the men who had hanged her father. Herb and Jesse were eagerly awaiting her return.

"All I learned," said Danielle, "is that I'll have to talk to the personnel director, and he's gone for the day."

"Some bounty hunters we are," Burris said. "We spend all our time waitin' for something or somebody, and now we're ridin' your shirttail, hoping you'll lead us to *hombres* we can't seem to find on our own."

"Hell, I'm about ready to ride into Indian Territory and join a bunch of outlaws," said Sellers. "There must be plenty of them with prices on their heads."

"I don't recommend that," Danielle said. "I've tried that, and if they take you in, you'll have to take part in whatever they're doing. You could end up on the wrong side of the law, with prices on *your* heads."

"I haven't put that much thought into it," said Sellers, "but I reckon you're right. I'm just not sure I'm cut out for bounty hunting. It all seemed so easy. You take a varmint in and collect the bounty. Trouble is, I never shot at a man in my life, and I wonder if I actually could. I doubt that any man with a price on his head will surrender, and that means he'll have to be brought in dead."

"I think so," Danielle agreed, "but you never know what you can do until it's shoot or be shot. The first *hombre* I shot was trying to kill me, and that left me no choice. If we can track down Gaddis and Byler, I'll let the two of you turn them in—or what's left of them—for the bounty."

"That's white of you," Sellers said, "but I don't take money that I ain't earned."

"Me neither," said Burris.

"Damn it," said Danielle, "you're looking at this all

wrong. I'm not bounty hunting, and I'll not be claiming any bounty. I want some varmints dead, and I won't take money just for keeping a vow I made on my pa's grave. If you're with me, and there's a bounty, you can take it or leave it. I don't want it. I'd feel like I was selling my pa's life for the money."

"I reckon that makes sense," Sellers said. "You're a generous man, Daniel Strange."

"Let's get some supper," said Burris, "and then check out the games in the saloons. It won't seem so much like we're wasting time if we can win some money."

"I'll risk a hundred, but no more," Danielle said.

The Wagon Wheel was the biggest and fanciest saloon in town, and that's where the trio went. Sellers and Burris took their seats at a table where a poker game was going on, while Danielle approached one of the faro tables.

"Five-dollar limit," said the dealer. "Show me your money."

Danielle dropped five double eagles on the green felt that covered the table. Some of the men around her cast sidelong glances at the twin Colts tied down on each hip. Losing the first three hands, Danielle then began to win. Sellers and Burris remained in the poker game as Danielle continued winning at faro. When her hundred-dollar stake increased to three hundred, she withdrew from the game. The relief on the dealer's face was obvious. She headed for the poker table where Sellers and Burris seemed engrossed in the game. They seemed to be doing well, especially Burris. There was a huge pile of chips before him, and as Danielle watched, he won another pot.

"I'm out," said one of the players in disgust.

But as he slid back his chair, Danielle could see that

he held a revolver under the table, and he wasted no time in using it. He stood up.

"Bucko," he said to Burris, "you're just a little too damn lucky to suit me."

Burris was caught totally by surprise, and as he went for his gun, his opponent fired.

But a second shot blended with his own, and he fell across the poker table. All eyes turned to Danielle, who still held a smoking Colt steady in her hand. Sellers was already kneeling over Burris.

"Is he alive?" Danielle asked.

"Yeah," said Sellers, "and he wasn't cheating. Some of you take a look at his cards."

They examined the cards Burris was holding, shaking their heads.

"That damn Winters had to be the worst poker player in town," said the house dealer. "When he's a big loser—which is most of the time—he's got to have a dog to kick."

"He won't be drawing any more bad poker hands," one of the men said. "He's stone cold dead."

One man had gone for a doctor, while another had gone for the sheriff. Doctor Avery and Sheriff Barnes arrived together.

"He'll live," the doctor said after examining Burris.

"Who's responsible for this?" the sheriff asked, his eyes on the dead gambler.

Chapter 12

"I shot him after he gunned down a friend of mine, Sheriff," Danielle said.

"The *hombre* Elmo Winters shot wasn't cheating, Sheriff," said a house dealer. "Elmo had a mad on because he was losing, like he usually does."

"I'll want you to come with me to the office," Sheriff Barnes told Danielle.

"Not until I've seen my friend back to the hotel," said Danielle.

"Me and the doctor can handle that," Herb Sellers said. "You got a stretcher, Doc?"

"Yes," said Doctor Avery. "I'll go get it."

"Some of you tote Elmo Winters over yonder to the carpenter shop," Sheriff Barnes said. "I'll ride out in the morning and see what Jubal and Ebeau wants to do with him."

Danielle followed Sheriff Barnes to his office, the lawman saying nothing until they were inside. Then he spoke.

"You can start by telling me who you are and what you're doing in town."

"I'm Daniel Strange, Sheriff, I mostly make my living gambling. You have some fine saloons here."

"We also have some snake-mean hell-raisers here," said Sheriff Barnes. "Elmo Winters, the *hombre* you shot, has family. There's his pa, Jubal, and his older brother, Ebeau. I'll tell you this for your own good, kid. Don't stay in town long enough for Jubal and Ebeau to find out you shot Elmo."

"I had cause to shoot him," Danielle said. "Are you denying that?"

"No," said Sheriff Barnes, "he's had that coming for a long time. But his old daddy and his brother won't settle for anything less than an eye-for-an-eye. I'll ride out in the morning and tell them, so you got a little time."

"I have business here, Sheriff," Danielle said, "and I'm not leaving until I've seen to it. I want peace, but not the kind that comes with the grave. You can tell Elmo's kin that if they come gunning for me, they'd better be wearing their burying clothes. Now, is there anything more you need from me?"

"I reckon not," Sheriff Barnes said. "There'll be an inquest tomorrow, but I think I'll be able to justify the shooting to the satisfaction of the court. There's witnesses aplenty."

"I'll be here at least through tomorrow if you want anything more of me."

Leaving the sheriff's office, Danielle returned to the hotel, knocking on the door to the room occupied by Herb Sellers and Jesse Burris. Herb opened the door and Danielle closed it behind her.

"How is he?" Danielle asked.

"Better than you'd expect, him being shot at such close range," said Herb. "I want to thank you for buying in. I'm sorry to say it took me as much by surprise as it did Jesse, and if Winters had got off a second shot, it would of been the end of Jesse Burris. What did the sheriff want?"

"Mostly to warn me to get out of town," Danielle said. "Elmo's pa, Jubal, and his brother, Ebeau, are the kind who'll likely come looking for me."

Jesse Burris slept, the doctor having given him some

laudanum, and for a long moment, Herb looked at his sleeping friend. Finally, he spoke.

"Jesse will be sorry he dragged you into his fight, Daniel, and I'm sorry, too. Both of us are big enough to stomp our own snakes."

"We've all been taking our chances," Danielle said. "Some men are poor losers. Elmo Winters was one of them. If his pa and brother come looking for trouble, they'll find it. How long does the doctor think Jesse will be laid up?"

"Maybe a week," Herb said. "I cashed in his chips, and he'd won more than four hundred dollars. I won about half that, so we'll be able to afford the hotel until he's healed. Do you still aim to visit the Kansas-Pacific tomorrow?"

"Yes," said Danielle. "I aim to learn something helpful if I can. If I can't, then I want to know it. Then I can move on."

"I'll stay close by," Herb said. "If Winters's kin come looking for you, I promise you'll not have to face them alone."

"I'm obliged," said Danielle, "but it was me that shot Elmo Winters, and I bought in of my own choosing. I'm not afraid of his pa or his brother. The only way they'll get me is to shoot me in the back."

Danielle returned to her own room. She bolted the door from inside and placed the back of a chair under the knob of the door. For a long time she lay awake, unable to sleep, yet too exhausted not to.

Danielle was awakened by a knock on her door.

"Who is it?" she asked.

"Herb," a voice replied. "I'm about to have breakfast and thought you might join me."

"I will," Danielle said. "Give me time to get up and get dressed."

Danielle dressed hurriedly and found Herb waiting in the hall.

"How's Jesse this morning?"

"Sleeping," said Herb. "No fever yet. The doctor's coming by sometime today."

Danielle and Herb had breakfast in a cafe, neither talking much, for it seemed there was little to be said. Danielle was thinking ahead to her meeting with Alan Steele, at the Kansas-Pacific offices, and was at a loss as to what she must do or where she must go if the railroad man refused to cooperate with her. Herb interrupted her thoughts.

"How long do you aim to stay here?"

"At least today and tonight," Danielle said. "It's near nine o'clock, and when I leave here, I'm going straight to the Kansas-Pacific offices. Go on back to the hotel, and I'll tell you what I learn, if anything."

The railroad terminal was a bustle of activity when Danielle arrived. In the outer office, a different telegrapher sat at the instrument, which was clattering out a message. Danielle waited until the machine was silent before speaking to the telegrapher.

"I'm Danielle Strange, and I need to talk to Alan Steele. Tell him it has to do with the recent train robbery."

The telegrapher wasted no time in getting the message to Steele, and Danielle was led down a hall to Steele's office. She entered, closing the door behind her. Steele nodded to a chair, and she sat down. Steele was a heavy man with bushy eyebrows and a ruddy face. His eyes met hers, and Danielle spoke.

"Mr. Steele, I'd like to help you find the men who recently took a military payroll from one of your trains."

"You're a bounty hunter, then," said Steele.

"No," Danielle said. "Last spring, a gang of outlaws robbed and murdered my pa. I have the names of those who are still alive. Gaddis and Byler, who robbed you, were part of the bunch I'm looking for. Another is Chancy Burke. All three men are from Waco, and they've been riding together. I have reason to believe they were working together on this robbery, and that they may be planning others."

"But you have no proof," said Steele.

"No," Danielle said, "and that's why I'm here. I want you to help me get that proof."

"And how do you propose I do that?"

"I think Gaddis and Byler are being fed information about these payroll shipments by someone on the inside," said Danielle. "Someone who works for the railroad."

"Now, see here," Steele said, becoming indignant, "this is all speculation. The payrolls are all brought here from Fort Leavenworth. If there's a leak, it could well be coming from that end."

"True," said Danielle, "but not likely. Will you allow me to see a list of the names of the men who work for the railroad?"

"No," Steele said. "I won't be a party to you killing someone purely on speculation and suspicion."

"Then take the names of the outlaws I'm looking for, and compare them to those of the men working for the railroad," Danielle said. "If none of these seven names appear on your roster, then I'll say no more."

"I suppose I can do that," said Steele.

Danielle handed him a sheet of paper on which she had written the names.

Steele studied the list, comparing it to his own. Finally, he looked up, and when he spoke, Danielle thought he seemed nervous, for his eyes didn't exactly meet hers.

"Nobody on your list works for the railroad," he said.

Danielle sighed. "I'm sorry to have taken your time, Mr. Steele."

Danielle closed the door behind her as she left the office. Steele waited until she was gone before he summoned a secretary. She looked at him questioningly, and he spoke.

"A few weeks ago we hired a freight handler, name of Chancy Burke. I want to see him here in my office, just as soon as possible."

Steele waited, clenching and unclenching his fists. The Kansas-Pacific already had too much bad press as a result of the payroll robberies. The last thing the railroad needed was for word to get out that one of its own employees was in cahoots with the men who had robbed the train. When Chancy Burke entered the room, there was an arrogance in his manner that Steele didn't like. A Colt was tied down on his right hip, and despite his having been in town for several months, he still dressed like a down-at-the-heels cowboy.

"Burke," said Steele, "I have it on good authority that you have been consorting with thieves and outlaws. I have learned that two of your closest companions—Rufe Gaddis and Julius Byler—may have gotten information from you on that payroll that was stolen. Do you have anything to say?"

"Not a damn thing," Burke said, "except you got no proof. I deny doin' anything."

"Then take a look at this," said Steele, handing to him the names of the seven outlaws Danielle had given him.

Quickly, Burke read the list of names, and when he again faced Steele, he had lost much of his arrogance.

"So you threw my name in with six other *hombres* I never heard of," Burke said. "That don't prove anything."

"I think it does," Steele said. "I got this list from a

young man who intends to kill all the men on that
list, including you, and I don't want you involved with
the railroad in any way when it happens. As of this
moment, you're fired, and if you're still in town after
today, I'll see that the sheriff knows what you've done.
Now get out."

"I'll go," said Burke, "but before I do, I owe you
something. You know too much, Mr. Railroad Man."

Burke drew his Colt and fired twice, the slugs striking Steele in the chest. Burke then left the office on
the run, exiting the building and making his way across
the tracks to the railroad yard. His horse had been
tied there, and he mounted in one leap, kicking the
animal into a gallop. In the Kansas-Pacific offices there
was total confusion. Women screamed and men
cursed. One of the telegraphers ran to find the sheriff
and a doctor, but Sheriff Barnes had already ridden
out to the Winters place. Doctor Avery took one look
at the bloody body of Alan Steele and shook his head.

"He died instantly," said Doctor Avery. "This is a
case for the sheriff."

Sheriff Barnes didn't relish reporting Elmo's death,
and his confrontation with Elmo's kin was even storm-
ier than he had expected.

"Fine damn sheriff you are," Jubal Winters bawled.
"A man can't go to town for a friendly game of cards
without bein' shot dead."

"It wasn't what I'd call a friendly game," said Sheriff Barnes. "Elmo had a mad on, for no other reason
than he was a big loser. He shot a man without cause."

"The other *hombre* was cheatin'," Ebeau Winters
said.

"Not according to what the witnesses and the house
dealer said," the sheriff replied. "I had Elmo taken to
the carpenter shop so a coffin could be built. Do you

aim to come and get him, or will the county have to bury him?"

"We'll come and get him," Jubal snarled. "We don't want a damn thing from you but the name of the bastard that killed Elmo."

"So you can ride to town and raise hell," said the sheriff. "No, I don't think so."

"Then we'll find out on our own," Jubal said. "The next damn coffin you build will be his."

"Elmo's dead from a case of bad judgment," said the sheriff, "and I'm asking you to let it go. If the two of you show up in town with killing on your minds, I swear I'll throw both of you in the *calabozo,* leaving you there till the Second Coming."

With that, Sheriff Barnes rode away, fully aware of the whispered cursing of Jubal and Ebeau Winters. He had no doubt the pair would defy him, or that when they came for Elmo's body, they would come seeking vengeance. When Sheriff Barnes rode in, he had most of the town watching for him. One of the railroad's telegraphers got to him first.

"Sheriff, Alan Steele's been shot and killed in his office."

Wearily, Sheriff Barnes nodded. He then rode toward the railroad terminal and began asking questions. He quickly learned that the young gunman who had shot Elmo Winters had been in Steele's office, and when he had left, Steele had sent for Chancy Burke, one of several newly hired freight handlers.

"So this *hombre* Burke did the killing," Sheriff Barnes said.

"Yeah," said one of the telegraphers. "After the shooting, I saw him running down the hall toward the back of the building, into the railroad yards. His horse is gone."

Sheriff Barnes found the death list Danielle had given Steele on the floor behind Steele's desk. Burke's name was on that list, and Barnes believed it had been a factor in the killing of Steele. Daniel Strange had visited Steele in his office, and immediately following Daniel's leaving, Steele had sent for Chancy Burke. It was time for a serious talk with the young rider who had killed Elmo Winters, and Sheriff Barnes headed for the hotel where the wounded Jesse Burris had been taken.

Danielle found Herb waiting for her, and she broke the bad news.

"Well, damn, I reckon that does it," said Herb.

"I don't think so," Danielle said. "When Steele read those names from my list, I was watching his face. Something in his eyes told me he was lying when he said none of the men on my list worked for the railroad."

"But without his help, there's nothing you can do," said Herb.

Suddenly, there was a knock on Danielle's door.

"Who's there?" Danielle asked.

"Sheriff Barnes."

Danielle opened the door, and Sheriff Barnes closed it behind him as he entered.

"You know my *amigo,* Herb Sellers, Sheriff," said Danielle.

"Yes," Sheriff Barnes said, "and he might want to leave the room. I have some serious questions to ask you."

"Let Herb stay, Sheriff," said Danielle. "I'll answer your questions."

"I know you were in Alan Steele's office at Kansas-Pacific earlier this morning. Why?"

"I wanted a favor from him, which he denied," Danielle said. "You knew I believed there might be an outlaw on the railroad payroll, feeding information to train robbers. I wanted Steele to let me go over a list of men who work for the railroad, but he refused. He requested that I give him a list of the suspects, which I did. He assured me that none of them worked for the railroad."

"Is this the list?" Sheriff Barnes asked, holding out the sheet of paper.

"It is," said Danielle. "Where did you get it?"

"I found it on the floor behind Steele's desk," Sheriff Barnes said. "After you left, he had a freight handler, Chancy Burke, report to his office. Burke shot and killed him, and then ran for it."

Danielle looked at Herb, and he seemed pleased. Danielle's suspicions had just been confirmed. But Sheriff Barnes wasn't finished. His eyes on Danielle, he came up with the question she had been expecting.

"The men on this list—why are you hunting them?"

"They robbed and murdered my pa in Indian Territory last spring," Danielle said. "On my pa's grave, I swore I'd track them down, and that they'd all die."

"What give you the idea that one of them worked for the railroad?" the sheriff asked.

"When I learned Rufe Gaddis and Julius Byler robbed a Kansas-Pacific train," Danielle said. "Gaddis, Byler, and Burke are all from Waco, Texas, and usually ride together. I had an idea Burke had a hand in the robbery, and the only logical answer seemed that he must be working for the railroad."

"Good thinking," Sheriff Barnes said. "It's a damn shame Steele didn't use what he had learned to a better advantage. After that robbery, the railroad's a mite skittish, afraid of more bad publicity."

"There'll be plenty of it now," said Danielle. "There'll be no hiding the fact that the railroad hired a thief and a murderer. It won't help the confidence of the military if they aim to ship future payrolls."

"I expect future payrolls to Dodge will go by wagon, with a military escort," Barnes said. "It won't be as quick as by train, but the military can protect it better. How much of what you've told me do you intend to tell the newspapers?"

"None of it, if it can be avoided," said Danielle.

"I'm afraid it can't," Sheriff Barnes said. "Indirectly, you were responsible for Steele's death, but it wasn't your fault that he used your information as he did. Still, it's expected of the law to come up with a motive for the killing, and I can't do that without you. The newspaper people are already at Kansas-Pacific, and they're going to be told that you were in Steele's office just before he sent for Chancy Burke. What will you tell them?"

"The truth, I reckon," Danielle said. "You have the list that I gave Steele, and Chancy Burke's name is on it. We can piece together the rest."

"Except for one thing," said Sheriff Barnes. "Why did Burke shoot Steele? Being fired is one thing, but I can't understand the need to kill a man. Steele wasn't even armed. I'm at a loss to explain why Burke didn't accept his dismissal and just quietly ride away. It seems that's probably what Steele expected. Now there'll be a murder charge against him."

There came a knock on Danielle's door.

"Who is it?" Danielle asked.

"Newspaper reporter," said the voice.

"You might as well get it over with," Sheriff Barnes said.

Danielle went to the door and let the man in. He was tall and thin, and had a nervous twitch. His head darted back and forth like that of an inquisitive rooster. But there was nothing slow about him.

"I'm Jud Dubose," he said, "and I'm here regarding the shooting of Alan Steele earlier today. You were in Steele's office just ahead of Chancy Burke, and we believe something you said or did caused Steele to summon Burke to the office. Would you tell me just how you fit into all this?"

"Yes," said Danielle, and she repeated everything she had told Sheriff Barnes.

"So Steele tried to cover it up, handling Burke on his own," Dubose said, "and Burke shot and killed him. May I see that death list you gave Steele to compare with names of employees on the railroad's payroll?"

"No," said Danielle. "Why should I allow you to publish it in the newspaper when it would only make things more difficult for me? These outlaws would change their names."

"That's suppressing evidence," Dubose said.

"Wrong," said Sheriff Barnes. "You can mention the list, and that Chancy Burke is one of the names on it, and it was he who did the shooting. But the rest of the names aren't any of your business. You know the motive, and you know the killer."

Clearly, Dubose didn't like it, but even without the rest of the names on the list, he had his story. Bowing to them all, he got up and left the hotel room.

"I'm obliged, Sheriff," Danielle said.

"You got enough trouble already," Sheriff Barnes said. "I rode out this morning to the Winters's place. Jubal and Ebeau are killing mad and are vowing revenge. Was I you, I'd stay close to the hotel for a while."

Chancy Burke rode to the outskirts of town, where he had a room in a cheap boardinghouse. To his surprise, he found his door unlocked. Drawing and cocking his Colt, he then kicked the door open. Rufe Gaddis and Julius Byler sat on the bed.

"What are you doin' here so early in the day?" Gaddis inquired.

"They got wise to me," said Burke, "and I had to shoot the varmint that fired me."

"Had to, or wanted to?" Byler asked.

"He knew too damn much," said Burke. "Somebody's huntin' all of our old gang. The death list he showed me included *hombres* we rode with in Indian Territory. Three names was missing. Bart Scovill, Levi Jasper, and Brice Levan wasn't on it, but I was, along with both of you."

"If somebody had the names of seven of us, he had them all," Gaddis said. "I reckon Scovill, Jasper, and Levan are dead."

"I think so, too," said Byler, "and thanks to you shootin' that railroad man, we'll likely have every damn bounty hunter and Pinkerton in the country after us."

"Then I'll just go my way, and you gents can go yours," Burke said, "but I won't be leavin' until I get my share of that twenty-five thousand you took from the train."

"You'll get it," said Gaddis, "and whether or not you go your own way is up to you. We know somebody's after us, maybe a bounty hunter, and we might be safer not ridin' alone."

"I'll likely have a price on my head before the day's done," Burke said. "Let's get out of here and head for Indian Territory for a while."

"We'll have to," said Byler. "That's where the gold's hid."

"I think we ought to wait until dark," Gaddis said. "There's a storm building, and it'll be raining by tonight. Somebody might discover our trail and decide to track us."

"I'm going down to the parlor for an evening paper," said Burke. "I'd like to see just how much they know about me, and if there's a price on my head."

The story was on page one, and they all gathered around to read it.

"Damn," Burke said, "there's a five-thousand-dollar bounty on me."

Gaddis laughed. "If they raise it to ten thousand, I'll take you in myself."

"Whoa," said Byler, "this ain't so damn funny. That death list the sheriff found on the floor of Steele's office come from a young gunman who's looking for us. Somehow, he's found out we're ridin' together."

"Yeah," Burke said, "and how does he know we're ridin' together?"

"He's likely been through Waco," said Gaddis. "It wouldn't take a man long to find out all of us are from there."

"This young gun-thrower's smart," Burke said. "Without any evidence, he figured out that I was keeping you gents informed about the gold shipments. I owe Steele something. If he had gone directly to the sheriff, and had allowed the sheriff to move in, I'd likely be in jail by now."

"The law's got our names on that death list now," said Gaddis, "and I think we should get the hell out of Kansas. That newspaper's linked all our names together, and the three of us have prices on our heads totaling ten thousand dollars."

"Then let's ride," Burke said. "Remember, that varmint that gave Alan Steele the list with all our names is still in town."

The three mounted and rode away toward Indian Territory.

Danielle whiled away her time in her hotel room, regretting having promised the sheriff she would remain in town another day. Looking out the window, she could see a gathering of clouds far to the west. She had considered circling the town, seeking the tracks of

Burke's horse, but with rain on the way, it would be of little use. Tomorrow she'd have to begin her search all over again. But there was the problem with Elmo Winters's kin. Noon came and went without a sign of them. Then there was a knock on her door.

"Who is it?" Danielle asked.

"Sheriff Barnes."

Danielle opened the door, allowing the lawman to enter.

"Well," said Sheriff Barnes, "they're here. They brought a wagon, and they're over at the carpenter shop, loadin' Elmo to take him home."

"How should I handle this, Sheriff?" Danielle asked.

"Any way you have to," said Barnes, "but don't go gunning for them. Let them make the first move, and if you're forced to shoot, then shoot. Everybody around here knows how they are, and if they come after you with guns, there's not a court in Kansas that'll blame you for defending yourself."

"Then I might as well circulate around town," Danielle said. "Otherwise, they'll likely come here to the hotel, and somebody here might be hurt."

"I wouldn't spend too much time on the street," said Sheriff Barnes. "Trouble with the Winters has never gone this far before, so I can't predict what they might do. They might climb up on a roof and bushwhack you."

"I don't believe in putting off something that must be done," Danielle said. "I'll go on and face them, and be done with it."

"Then I'll go with you," said Sheriff Barnes, "to be sure it's a fair fight."

Herb Sellers had heard the sheriff at Danielle's door, and had waited in the hall.

"I'm going along, too." Herb said.

Sheriff Barnes nodded, and the trio left the hotel.

The walk to the carpenter shop was short, and Jubal and Ebeau Winters were there standing beside a wagon, arguing with someone from the carpenter shop. As Sheriff Barnes and his companions drew near, Winters spoke.

"Sheriff, this varmint's expecting me to pay ten dollars for Elmo's coffin, and I ain't gonna do it. I didn't ask him to build it."

"I did," said Sheriff Barnes, "and I'll pay the ten dollars. Now you and Ebeau get out of town. I want no more trouble."

"We ain't goin' nowhere until we take care of the bastard that killed Elmo," Winters said.

"That would be me," said Danielle.

Sheriff Barnes and Herb moved out of the line of fire. Ebeau walked toward Danielle.

"Jubal," Sheriff Barnes said, "this is going to be fair, just between the two of them. If you pull iron, I'll shoot you myself."

Danielle waited, thumbs hooked in her gun belt. Her green eyes bored into Ebeau's, and he halted a dozen yards away.

"Draw, damn you," Ebeau shouted.

Danielle continued to wait, while Ebeau cursed. Then Danielle turned and began walking away, and that's when Ebeau Winters went for his gun.

"Daniel!" Herb shouted.

Danielle hit the ground and rolled, coming up with her right-hand Colt blazing. Ebeau had fired twice, but there was no third shot. Ebeau had died on his feet.

Chapter 13

As Ebeau Winters slumped to the ground, Jubal bawled like a fresh-cut bull and went for his gun. But Sheriff Barnes had been expecting that.

"Don't do it, Jubal," Barnes warned.

Jubal fought the urge to draw, finally dropping his shaking hands to his sides. His old face a mask of grief, he stared at the body of his second son.

"I'll help you get him in the wagon, Jubal," said Sheriff Barnes. "Then I'll ride out and help you bury them."

"I don't need no help from the likes of you," Jubal said.

But he couldn't handle Ebeau's body by himself, and he didn't object when Barnes lent a hand in getting Ebeau into the wagon beside Elmo's coffin. Wordlessly, Jubal climbed to the wagon seat, took the reins, and clucked to the team. Sheriff Barnes mounted his horse and followed the wagon.

"God, he took it hard," said Herb Sellers. "I thought you'd likely have to shoot him."

"I didn't want to shoot either of them," Danielle said.

"You didn't have any choice," said Herb. "He'd have shot you if he could. I reckon it's the curse of a man carryin' a gun. You got to shoot a man, just so's he don't shoot you."

"Let's get on back to the hotel," Danielle said. "I want to say *adios* to Jesse before I ride out."

"There's a storm comin'," said Herb. "Why don't you wait until tomorrow?"

"I don't want to have to shoot Jubal Winters," Danielle said.

But it was already early afternoon, and dark clouds hid the sun. The wind coming out of the southwest had begun to rise. Herb and Danielle had barely reached the hotel when the first drops of rain kicked up puffs of dust in the street.

"It's gonna blow long and hard," said Herb. "You'd better reconsider and lay over."

"I reckon you're right," Danielle said. "I'll likely spend enough time soaked to the hide, so I'd better enjoy a roof over my head while I can."

Suppertime was two hours away. When Danielle and Herb returned to the room that he shared with Jesse Burris, they found him awake, sitting on the edge of the bed, dressed except for his boots and hat.

"Where in tarnation do you think you're goin'?" Herb demanded.

"Out of this bed, and out of this hotel," said Jesse.

"I don't think so," Herb said. "The doc says you need a week to heal, and you ain't had any fever yet."

"No matter," said Jesse. "I was the cause of that shootin' in the saloon, and I reckon if that *hombre* that was shot has kin, they'll be ridin' in to settle up with somebody."

"You didn't shoot anybody," Danielle said. "I did."

"Elmo's pa and brother rode in looking for trouble earlier," said Herb, "and Daniel had to shoot Ebeau. Sheriff Barnes followed Jubal Winters home to help bury Elmo and Ebeau."

"All this over a damn poker game," Jesse said. "I wish I'd stayed out of it."

"You don't feel any worse than I do," said Danielle,

"but some men have no business at a poker table, and Elmo Winters was one of them. I'm sorry for his pa's sake."

"There should be a newspaper out today," Herb said. "I'll go to the lobby for one. I'd like to see what's been written about that shooting at the Kansas-Pacific offices."

"What shooting?" Jesse asked.

"Tell him about it, Daniel, while I go for the paper," said Herb.

Quickly, Danielle explained what had happened. By then, Herb had returned with the day's edition of the newspaper. He read the front page account aloud while Danielle and Jesse listened.

"At least they didn't print the rest of the names on your death list," Jesse said.

"No," said Danielle, "but they figured out the connection between Chancy Burke and Gaddis and Byler. Now the three of them know their names are on my list."

"Alan Steele died for nothing," Herb said. "If he had told Daniel the straight of it, he'd have saved the railroad any bad publicity. Now the very thing he tried to hide is printed in the newspaper for everybody to read."

"Some good may come of that," said Danielle. "While they printed only the names of Gaddis, Byler, and Burke, that may warn the rest of them they're being hunted. If I can't find them, maybe they'll find me."

"You'll need somebody to watch your back," Jesse said, "and I'm beholden' to you. If you can wait until the doc lets me get out of this bed, Herb and me can ride with you."

"I'm obliged," said Danielle, "but I aim to ride out in the morning, as soon as the storm blows itself out."

"There won't be any trail," Jesse said. "Where do you aim to start?"

"I reckon I'll ride back through Wichita, and from there into Indian Territory," said Danielle. "I figure that's the only place Chancy Burke will feel safe, with a bounty on his head and a murder on his back-trail."

"It's a hell of a place for one man to ride alone," Herb said.

"I have no choice," said Danielle, "and I have no right to ask you and Jesse to risk your lives for a cause that will gain you nothing but a bullet in the back."

Sheriff Barnes showed up at the hotel, water dripping off his slicker. He knocked on Danielle's door.

"Who is it?"

"The sheriff," Barnes said.

Danielle unlocked and opened the door, allowing the sheriff to enter.

"Remove your slicker and sit down," Danielle invited.

"I won't be here that long," said Barnes. "I just want to know how long you aim to stay in town."

"Until the storm blows itself out," Danielle said. "Why?"

"I got me a gut feeling Jubal Winters ain't finished with you," said Sheriff Barnes. "All the time I was with Jubal, helpin' him bury his boys, he didn't say a word. Something's on his mind, and I think it involves you."

"The last thing I want is to have to shoot Jubal Winters, Sheriff," said Danielle. "I aim to ride out in the morning, storm or not."

"You've been a decent *hombre,* and I hate to rush you, but I think it's for the best."

"So do I, Sheriff," Danielle said.

* * *

Jesse Burris was able to join Herb and Danielle at breakfast. There was little talk, for these young men had grown fond of Danielle, and she of them.

"Before you go," said Jesse, "write out the names of those seven men you're hunting. If we learn anything about them, we'll telegraph the Texas Ranger outpost in San Antonio."

"*Bueno,*" Danielle said. "Send it to Captain Sage Jennings. He knows me and what I have to do. I aim to cross Indian Territory and spend some tine in south Texas. Chancy Burke, Rufe Gaddis, and Julius Byler have kin there, and sooner or later, they'll be going back."

The sky was overcast with the threat of more rain as Danielle saddled the chestnut mare. Having already bid farewell to Herb and Jesse, she mounted and rode toward Wichita by simply following the Kansas-Pacific tracks.

But vengeful eyes had watched Danielle ride out of the livery. When she finally rode out of sight, Jubal Winters mounted his horse and followed. In his saddle boot was a fully loaded Winchester.

Wichita, Kansas. November 15, 1870.

Danielle estimated the distance to Wichita at close to a hundred and fifty miles. Taking her time and sparing the chestnut mare, she rode what she felt was halfway, and there made camp for the night. She picketed the horse so that the mare might warn her of any approaching danger. After a day of cold, miserable drizzle, the rain had finally ceased, and stars in the purple sky overhead were a welcome sight. Having no dry wood for a fire, Danielle ate jerked beef for breakfast, washing it down with water from a spring. She quickly fed the mare a measure of grain, and when the horse had eaten, she saddled up and rode on toward Wichita. She arrived in the late afternoon of the second day and decided to spend the night there, for she was not more than twenty miles from Indian Territory. She hadn't bothered talking to the sheriff of Wichita before riding on to Kansas City. She thought the sheriff might supply some additional details about the train robbery and the thieves, so she went looking for him.

"I didn't know a thing about the robbery," said Sheriff Bart Devlin. "By the time the engineer backed the train from end-of-track to here, the thieves were long gone. A posse and me followed 'em as far as Indian Territory, and it was comin' on dark."

"What about the woman you captured?" Danielle asked.

"Her horse went lame, and they left her behind," said Sheriff Devlin. "She was furious at them for leaving her, and she told me their names. She didn't seem to know anything else, so I let her go. What's your interest in this? Are you with the railroad?"

"No," Danielle said. "This is personal."

She then told the lawman of tracking the men who had murdered her father.

"I read about you in the Kansas City paper," said Devlin, "but they didn't say exactly why you were hunting the outlaws. They did say you was responsible for rooting out one of the varmints that worked for the railroad, passing along information on gold shipments."

"His name is Chancy Burke," Danielle said, "and like Gaddis and Byler, he's from near Waco."

"That would be a good place to go looking for them," said Sheriff Devlin.

"I've already been there," Danielle said. "If they're riding together, it seemed like a good idea to see if Chancy Burke might be working for the railroad. If

the railroad hadn't called Burke's hand, he might have
been captured or killed."

"The sheriff in Waco was of no help to you?"

"None," said Danielle. "He went out of his way to
warn the kin of Gaddis, Byler, and Burke that I was
there, and I was practically run out of town."

"Damn such a lawman," Sheriff Devlin muttered.
"It's enough to give us all a bad name."

"The woman you captured told you nothing except
the names of the thieves? Where did she team up with
Gaddis and Byler?"

"In St. Louis," said Sheriff Devlin, "and she was
goin' back there."

"She didn't tell you where Gaddis and Byler were
holed up before the robbery?"

"She didn't seem to know," Sheriff Devlin said.
"She wasn't familiar with the country, and from her
description, it sounded like Indian Territory. She said
they rode less than an hour before reaching the Kansas-
Pacific tracks."

"I'm obliged, Sheriff," said Danielle.

"Good luck," Sheriff Devlin said. "I hope you find
them. The railroad's on my back because I can't catch the
thieves, but I'm just a county sheriff. I can't watch their
damn railroad all the way from Kansas City to end-
of-track."

"They may get as far from here as they can," said
Danielle. "After killing that Kansas-Pacific man,
Burke's got a price on his head, just like Gaddis and
Byler."

Danielle stabled Sundown and took a room in one
of the hastily built hotels that faced the Kansas-Pacific
tracks. She entered a cafe, had supper, and it was
already dark when she left. The Railroad Saloon was
ablaze with light. Lighted lanterns had been hung
along the eaves of the building, and across the top of
its false front. There was a distant jangling of a piano

that was sorely in need of tuning. From within the saloon, shouts mingled with the clinks of glasses and bottles. Danielle went in, finding the place packed, a large number of the men appearing to have come in from end-of-track. Three poker games were in progress, but only one faro game. Danielle waited until one of the men kicked back his chair and left the table.

"I'm buying in," Danielle said.

"Welcome, kid, long as you got money," said the dealer. "Five-dollar bets."

Danielle dropped her five double eagles on the table and, in ten straight hands, lost half her stake.

"We know one thing for damn sure," said one of the players, "the kid ain't cheatin'."

Danielle kept her silence and, within an hour, had won back her stake and more than two hundred dollars additional. She then withdrew from the game.

"I've never seen such a run of luck," one of the gamblers said, his eyes on the house dealer. "It's almost like you was slick-dealing to the kid."

It was an open invitation to a fist-fight or a shooting, so Danielle hurriedly left the saloon and returned to her hotel room. She might well meet one of the disgruntled gamblers on the street and be forced into another senseless killing. Already, the Kansas City paper had referred to her as a "fast gun artist," and "a killer riding a vengeance trail."

Danielle arose early, had her breakfast, and rode out. She was only a few miles north of Indian Territory, but chose to ride west, toward the end-of-track. She would learn nothing from the railroad men, for they would surely be hostile toward her for indirectly being the cause of Alan Steele's death. However, before reaching end-of-track, she would ride south toward Indian Territory. There would be no tracks, no trail, and little chance of her finding any of the men she sought. But they were all Westerners, and she fully expected them to be holed up in Indian Territory or in Texas. At this moment, the trio responsible for the train robbery might be at home, in Waco.

As Danielle entered Indian Territory, chills crept up her spine, for it was a massive tangle of vines, thickets, brush, and tall trees. It was gloomy even when the sun was shining, for only a little sunlight filtered through the dense foliage. She reined up to rest the chestnut mare and stood beside the horse, looking back the way she had come. She saw nothing and, mounting, rode on. But something was bothering her, a strange foreboding that dug its claws into her and wouldn't let go. Again she reined up, dismounted, and walked a ways along her back-trail, without seeing anyone. She was about to mount and ride on, when the stillness was shattered by the roar of a rifle just ahead of her. The lead tore its way through her left thigh, and a second slug ripped into her right side, making a ragged exit wound. She fell on her back, remaining still, for she believed the bushwhacker would come close enough to be sure she was dead. She was losing blood, but dared not move. Finally she heard cautious footsteps approaching and, through half-closed eyes, could see the haggard, grinning face of Jubal Winters.

"You damn gun-slick," he snarled. "Kill my boys, will you?"

Jacking a shell into the chamber of the Winchester, he was about to shoot Danielle a third time when Danielle drew her right-hand Colt and fired twice. The slugs struck Jubal in the chest, and he died with a look of total surprise on his face. Danielle struggled to her feet and, using a rawhide thong from her saddle, wrapped and tied it tightly above the bleeding wound in her left thigh. But there was little she could do about the wound in her right side. The chestnut mare, spooked by the smell of blood, back-stepped.

"Damn it, Sundown," Danielle gasped, "hold still."

Three times she tried to mount the horse, and three times her left leg failed her. Using her right leg for support, she mounted from the off-side. She felt cold all over, and there was a growing weakness in her body. She turned the chestnut mare back the way she had come, hoping to reach Wichita before bleeding to death. She blacked out, holding to the saddle horn with both hands. Danielle had raised Sundown from a colt, and the horse knew something was terribly wrong. The animal stopped, perking up her ears. In the distance, a dog barked. The mare listened a moment and then, as though making up her mind, turned and trotted back into Indian Territory, toward the sound of the barking dog. The dog barked furiously as Sundown neared a run-down cabin.

"That awful man is coming back, Ma," said nine-year-old Anita Willard.

"Perhaps not," said her mother, Ann. "It doesn't sound like his horse."

The cabin's windows had no glass, and she had to open a shutter to see outside. Even with the threat of the dog, the chestnut mare waited patiently at the front stoop, seeking help for her young rider. Even as Ann Willard watched, Danielle fell from the saddle and lay still.

"Come on," said Ann. "He's hurt, and we must get him inside."

Once they had Danielle inside and stretched out on a bunk, Anita unsaddled the mare and led her to a corral where there were two other horses. Returning to the house, she found Ann Willard had stripped the injured rider and simply stood there staring.

"He . . . he's a woman," Anita said aghast.

"Yes," said Ann, "and we must do what we can for

her and get her out of here before Eph Snell returns.
Stir up the fire and put some water on to boil."

When the water was hot, Ann cleansed the wounds
as best she could, disinfecting them with whiskey from
a jug Eph Snell kept under his bunk. There was no
other medicine, and Danielle moaned in her sleep. She
didn't awaken until near dawn of the next day, her
face flushed and her eyes bright with fever.

"Water," she begged.

Anita brought a tin cup of water, and Danielle
drank it gratefully. Again she spoke.

"Where . . . am I, and who . . . are you?"

"I'm Ann Willard, and this is my daughter, Anita."

"I . . . I'm Danielle Strange. Do you . . . live here
alone?" Danielle asked.

"Only when Eph Snell's gone," said Ann.

"Eph Snell's a damn horse thief, and when he's
here, he's always drunk. I hate him," Anita said.

"Anita," said Ann, "that's no way for a young lady
to talk."

"Then I ain't a young lady," Anita said. "I want to
grow up and carry a gun so's I can shoot the varmints
I don't like."

Despite being racked with fever and pain, Danielle laughed.

"Anita," said Ann, "go get the jug of whiskey."

"I'll get it," Anita said, "but old Eph's gonna raise
hell when he finds we've been into his jug."

"God help us," said Ann with a sigh. "She's picking
up Snell's bad habits."

"Why are the two of you living with such a man?"
Danielle asked.

"My husband never returned from the war, and
Anita and me were starving back in New Orleans. I
met Snell, and he promised me a better life. Am I
permitted to know why you dress as a man?"

But Anita returned with the jug of whiskey just

then, and Danielle was forced to drink a cupful. Then, as Ann and Anita listened, she told them her story and of becoming Daniel Strange.

"Dear God," Ann said, "how old are you, Danielle?"

"Just past seventeen," said Danielle.

"See, Ma?" Anita cried. "She's only eight years older than me."

"I'm trusting the two of you to keep my secret," said Danielle. "As soon as I'm able to ride, I'll move on. I don't want to cause any trouble."

"There'll be trouble whether you're here or not," Anita said. "Last time, he beat Ma up something terrible."

"Don't you have somewhere else you can go?" Danielle asked.

"I have a sister in St. Louis who would take us in, but I don't know how we'd ever get there," said Ann.

"I'll help you as soon as I'm able," Danielle said. "Do you have horses?"

"Two, but only because Eph hasn't sold them," said Ann. "He's gone after more."

"He steals them in Texas," Anita said helpfully.

"That's a long ride from here," said Danielle. "When do you expect him to return?"

"Perhaps in another week," Ann said. "He's usually away for two weeks, and he's been gone only six days."

"Then maybe I can get the two of you on the way to St. Louis before he returns," said Danielle.

"But we have no money," Ann said.

"I do," said Danielle, "and all we have to do is reach Wichita. From there, you can take the train to Kansas City, and another on to St. Louis."

"You are so kind," said Ann. "I fear we can never repay you."

"You already have," Danielle said. "It's me that'll

never be able to repay *you*, because you saved my life."

"You need food," said Ann. "I'll make you some chicken soup."

She started toward the kitchen, but not before Danielle saw the tears on her cheeks. It was an opportune time for nine-year-old Anita to speak to this strange girl who dressed like a man and carried tied-down Colts. She sat down on the foot of the bed and spoke.

"Ma didn't tell you all of it. The last time Eph Snell came in drunk, he said I was old enough to be a woman, and he tore off all my clothes. Ma tried to stop him, and he beat her so bad, she couldn't get up off the floor."

"A poor excuse for a man," said Danielle. "Did he . . . bother you?"

"He was going to," Anita said, "but I ran outside and hid in the brush, naked. When he saddled his horse and rode away, I went back to take care of Ma."

"He won't lay a hand on either of you as long as I'm alive," said Danielle.

"Oh, I'm so glad you found us," Anita said. "The next time, I might not be able to get away from him."

Ann returned with a bowl of soup and a wedge of corn bread. Sore as Danielle was, she sat up long enough to eat, and immediately felt better.

"Now," said Ann, "we're going to leave you alone so you can sleep off that fever."

Danielle slept all day and part of the night. She awakened, sweating. Ann sat on the foot of the bed, and she spoke.

"The fever's broken. Now all you have to do is heal."

"I'm obliged," Danielle said. "You've done all this for me without knowing whether I've told you the truth about myself or not."

"I saw the truth in your eyes," said Ann, "but I'd

have helped you even if you were an outlaw. The Good Book says we should not judge as we be not judged. It wasn't up to me to decide if you were deserving or not. All I saw was the need."

"You're a good woman, Ann Willard," Danielle said.

"I'm a sinful woman," said Ann, her hands covering her face. "For five years I've been with Eph Snell because Anita and me were starving. I thought anything was better than that, but I don't anymore. Snell's a thief and a killer, and I fear what he may do if he comes back and finds you here."

"Put my guns where I can reach them," Danielle said, "and I'll promise you he'll get the surprise of his life."

"It's none of my business," said Ann, "but can you tell me who shot you, and why?"

"It's something I'm not proud of," Danielle said, "but I'll tell you the story."

For the next few minutes she told of having to shoot Elmo and Ebeau Winters, and finally of the necessity of killing old Jubal, after he had bushwhacked her.

"You didn't shoot anybody that didn't deserve it," said Anita, from behind the door.

"You're supposed to be in bed asleep," Ann said.

"I'm too excited to sleep," said Anita. "When can we leave?"

"Not until Danielle heals enough to ride," Ann said.

"Three more days," said Danielle. "Just so I'm healed enough that the wounds won't start bleeding again."

The three days came and went without a sign of Eph Snell. Danielle was up and limping about, again with her binder in place, dressed like a man.

"It's time we were going," Danielle said. "Do you have saddles for your horses?"

"No," said Ann, "but I'd crawl from here to Wichita on my hands and knees. We can ride bareback."

Ann gathered her own and Anita's few belongings, stuffing them in a gunnysack. The trio then rode north toward Wichita.

"I'll stay with you in Wichita until there's an eastbound train," Danielle said. "Once we reach town, you can sell the horses you're riding. That'll give you some extra money. I'll buy your train tickets from Wichita to St. Louis."

"You're too generous," said Ann. "I'd gladly sell the horses, but I don't have any bills of sale. I'm sure Eph stole them somewhere."

"I'll write you some bills of sale," Danielle said. "By the time Snell figures it all out, you'll be on your way to St. Louis, and well out of his reach."

The trio reached Wichita. Inquiring, Danielle learned the next eastbound from the end-of-track wouldn't reach Wichita until the following morning. Danielle bought two tickets to St. Louis, and Ann Willard wept for her generosity.

"Now I'll get us a hotel room for the night," said Danielle, "and we'll see about selling those two horses."

The bills of sale were not questioned, and Danielle collected seventy-five dollars for each of the horses.

"Here," Danielle said, handing the money to Ann. "The horses brought a hundred and fifty dollars, and I've added some to that."

Ann Willard was completely overwhelmed, and Anita's eyes sparkled like stars.

Leading three horses, Eph Snell reached the deserted cabin in Indian Territory. He swore when he found the corral empty, and it took him only a few minutes to find tracks of three horses heading north.

Leaving the three newly arrived horses in the corral, he mounted his horse and rode north, toward Wichita. He also carried a pair of tied-down Colts, and he had killing on his mind.

Chapter 14

Wichita, Kansas. November 22, 1870.

The eastbound was due at ten o'clock. Danielle had accompanied Ann and Anita to the railroad depot to await the train. Far down the track, they could hear the whistle blowing for the stop at Wichita.

"I can't believe we're actually leaving," Ann said. "I feel like I'm dreaming."

"We ain't gone yet," said Anita. "I won't feel safe until we're on the train and it's on its way."

With the clanging of its bell, the eastbound rolled in, and the locomotive began taking on water. The conductor stepped down from the one passenger coach, lowering the metal steps so that the passengers might enter. Up the track, beyond the train's caboose, there came a horseman at a fast gallop.

"Ma," Anita cried, "it's him!"

"Dear God," said Ann, "it's Eph Snell."

"Get aboard the train," Danielle said. "I'll delay him until you're gone."

"I can't let you do it," said Ann. "He'll kill you."

"I'll risk it," Danielle said. "Now get aboard the train."

Ann and Anita had just entered the passenger coach when Snell reined up. Dismounting, he started toward Danielle. She spoke quietly.

"That's far enough, Snell."

Snell laughed. "So you know me."

"I know *of* you," Danielle said. "You're a damn yellow-bellied, woman-beating coyote that walks on his hind legs like a man."

It was the ultimate insult, and Snell drew. He was fast—incredibly fast—but Danielle had her Colt roaring by the time Snell pulled the trigger. His slug spouted dust on the ground in front of him. From the locomotive, the fireman and engineer had watched the entire affair. Suddenly, Ann and Anita were out of the coach, running toward Danielle. At the sound of shooting, the station agent came running from the depot. He eyed Danielle as she reloaded her Colt, directing his question at her.

"What's the meaning of this?"

"Get the sheriff," Danielle said, "and I'll explain it all to him. I reckon you'd best keep this train here until the sheriff's talked to the fireman and engineer. They saw it all."

"I want to talk to the sheriff, too," said Ann to Danielle. "I won't leave until I know the law's not holding you responsible."

Others had heard the sound of distant gunfire, and men came on the run. One of them was Sheriff Bart Devlin. He eyed Danielle and spoke.

"Who's the dead man?"

"Eph Snell, a horse thief and likely a killer," Danielle said. "This is Ann and Anita Willard. I helped them to escape Snell, but he caught up to us and drew on me."

"He pulled iron first, Sheriff," the engineer said. "We saw him, didn't we, Slim?"

"Yeah," the fireman said, "and he was a fool. This young gent here could shoot the ears off John Wesley Hardin."

"Now, ma'am," Sheriff Devlin said to Ann, "suppose you tell me where you figure into all this."

Ann spoke swiftly, her eyes meeting those of Sheriff Devlin. When she paused to catch her breath, Anita spoke.

"He tore all my clothes off, and I had to hide from him in the woods."

Shouts of anger erupted from the men who had gathered around.

"Sheriff," said the station agent, "this train needs to be on its way. What more do you need of the fireman and engineer?"

"Probably nothing," Sheriff Devlin said, "but just in case, write down their names and addresses for me. Then they can go."

"I'm not going until I know you're not in trouble for shooting him," Ann told Danielle.

"Neither am I," said Anita defiantly.

"I know this young gent," Sheriff Devlin said, "and from what I've heard, I believe I can safely promise you there'll be no charges filed. In fact, if this dead varmint's been hiding out in Indian Territory, I may have a wanted dodger on him."

The fireman and engineer had mounted to the locomotive's cabin. A clanging of its bell and two blasts from the whistle announced the train's departure.

"Ann, it's time for you and Anita to get aboard," Danielle said. "Go in peace."

The two mounted the steps into the passenger coach, and as the train pulled out, they waved to Danielle for as long as they could see her. Two men had volunteered to remove Snell's body, taking it to the carpenter shop, where a coffin would be built. Sheriff Devlin spoke to Danielle.

"Come on to the office with me, and let's see if there's a dodger on Snell. Might even be a reward."

"I'm not concerned with a reward, Sheriff," Danielle said. "I shot him only to save my friends."

"A fine piece of work and a noble reason," said

Sheriff Devlin, "but if there's a reward, it belongs to you."

Danielle waited while Sheriff Devlin fanned through a stack of wanted dodgers.

"Ah," Devlin said, "here he is. He's wanted in Missouri and Texas for murder. There's a five-hundred-dollar reward, but it'll take me a few days to collect it."

"When you do," said Danielle, "send it to Ann Willard, in St. Louis. Send it to this address."

"I will," Devlin said, "and it's a fine thing you're doing. Ride careful, kid."

Danielle genuinely liked the old sheriff and didn't object to him calling her "kid." She had not completely healed from her wounds, and the drawing and firing of the Colt had somehow inflamed the wound in her right side. She felt a dull, throbbing ache, and after leaving the sheriff's office, she took a room at a hotel, for she dared not go to a doctor. First, she stabled Sundown. She then went to a saloon and, as much as she hated the stuff, bought a quart of whiskey. At the mercantile she bought a bottle of laudanum and returned to the hotel. She was hungry, but in no mood to eat. She didn't yet have a fever, and dosing herself with the laudanum, she went to bed and slept far into the night. When she awakened, her throat was dry and inflamed, and her face felt like it was afire. She drank a third of the bottle of whiskey and returned to the bed. When she again awakened, the sun beamed in through the room's single window, for she had slept well into the day. Her fever had broken, and her body was soaked with sweat. The ache of the wound in her side was gone, allowing her to sit up without pain. On the dresser was a porcelain pitcher half full of water, and she drank it all, right from the pitcher. Her belly grumbled, reminding her she had eaten nothing since her meager breakfast with

Ann and Anita the day before. Taking her time, she went to a cafe. After a satisfying meal of ham, eggs, biscuits, and hot coffee, she felt much better. She was tempted to ride on, but after having the wound in her side flare up again, she was reluctant to go until she had completely healed. She paid for another night at the hotel and spent most of the day stretched out on the bed, resting. In the late afternoon, there was a knock on her door.

"Who is it, and what do you want?"

"I'm Casper DeVero, and I want to talk to you," said a voice outside the door.

"About what?" Danielle asked, suspecting she already knew.

"About the heroic thing you did yesterday," said DeVero.

"I don't want to talk about it," Danielle said.

"Damn it," said DeVero, "the sheriff said you'd left town, and I had a hell of a time finding you. I'm a stringer for one of the Kansas City newspapers, and this is just the kind of human interest story they'll like. You'll be famous."

"I don't *want* to be famous," Danielle shouted. "Now leave me alone."

"Your choice," said DeVero. "Talk to me, and you'll get a sympathetic ear. But I can piece the story together if I have to, and you may not like some of the turns it takes. I will see that the story's published, with or without your help."

"Then do it without my help," Danielle shouted, "and leave me alone."

Later feeling better, Danielle went out for supper, encountering Sheriff Devlin in the cafe.

"I didn't know you were still in town," said Devlin. "We got a gent here name of DeVero, and he sells stories to the Kansas City newspapers. He's been looking for you."

"Unfortunately, he found me," Danielle said, "but I refused to talk to him. I'm still here only because I decided to rest a couple of days before riding on."

"I don't usually give advice unless it's asked for," said Devlin, "but it might have been better if you had talked to DeVero. There's certain gossipy folks in town that are likely to give you a reputation you won't like."

"Then they lie," Danielle said. "I did what was right."

"I believe you," said Sheriff Devlin, "but don't be surprised if DeVero hints at some funny business between you and this woman, Ann Willard."

"My God," Danielle said, "Ann's old enough to be my mother. If that yellow-bellied, two-legged coyote prints anything close to that, I'll kill him."

"Then I'd have to arrest you," said Devlin. "It's kind of a Mexican standoff. While he can't prove there was anything goin' on, you can't prove there wasn't. Writers have a way of hinting at things without actually accusing anybody, and this Ann Willard is an almighty handsome woman."

Sheriff Devlin departed, leaving Danielle alone with her thoughts. No longer hungry, she forced herself to eat, knowing her body had to gain strength. As she thought of DeVero and the lies he might tell, she decided to remain in Wichita long enough to read what he had to say. While she couldn't stop him from making her look bad in the press, she had no intention for it to appear she was running away.

Wichita, Kansas. November 27, 1870.

When the story appeared in the Kansas City newspaper, it was even worse than Sheriff Devlin had suggested it might be. Danielle was furious, and one particular paragraph made her killing mad. It said:

It appears the young gunman, Daniel Strange, may have gunned down Eph Snell over a woman they both wanted. Had Strange been consorting with a woman of questionable morals, when Eph Snell caught them?

There was much more, but Danielle refused to read it. A companion piece exploited the killing of Elmo and Ebeau Winters in Kansas City, suggesting that their father, Jubal, was also dead, since he had apparently disappeared. The only redeeming feature was a few lines quoting Sheriff Barnes, in which he stated flatly that Danielle had fired in self-defense. Grinding her teeth in frustration, Danielle went to supper. Tomorrow she would ride out, but the day wasn't over, and she expected the worst. It wasn't long in coming. There were half a dozen men in the cafe, and they grinned openly at her. Ordering her supper, she sat down to wait. In the distance there was a locomotive whistle, as the train neared Wichita on its way to the end-of-track. She had just begun to eat when the door opened and she was confronted by Herb Sellers and Jesse Burris.

"We put our horses in a boxcar and come here on the train," Jesse said. "We didn't know if you'd still be here or not." Uninvited, the two pulled out chairs and sat down.

"You read about me in the paper, I reckon," said Danielle bitterly. "Believe it if you like. I don't give a damn anymore."

"We'll believe it like *you* tell it," Herb said, "and we'll stomp hell out of anybody that makes anything more of it."

"I'm obliged," said Danielle, "but I don't want either of you in trouble with the law because of me.

The sheriff's already told me I can't shoot the no-account bastard that wrote the story, and that's the only thing that would give me any real satisfaction."

"We'll hit 'em where it hurts," Jesse Burris said. "When we've had supper, we'll make the rounds of all the saloons and win a pile of their money."

"You and Herb go ahead," said Danielle. "I'm going back to the hotel and rest. I aim to ride out early tomorrow."

After supper, Danielle parted company with the two genial bounty hunters. Her wound seemed to have healed, but there was still some weakness in her right arm. The wound in her left thigh had healed to the extent that she no longer limped. Locking her door and placing a ladder-back chair under the doorknob, she stripped off her clothes and got into bed. It was a blessed relief, being rid of the hated binder, and she suspected the pressure of it had slowed the healing of the wound in her right side. But there was no help for that. She thought fondly of Ann and Anita Willard, and the secret that they kept.

Wichita, Kansas. November 29, 1870.

Danielle was awakened by a knock on her door.

"Who is it, and what do you want?" she asked.

"Jesse and me," said Herb Sellers. "We was big winners last night, and we'll buy your breakfast."

"I'll eat with you," Danielle said, "but I'm barely awake. Wait for me in the lobby."

Danielle got up, feeling stronger. With the binder back in place, she was soon ready. She tipped her hat low over her eyes, buckled on her gun belts, and removed the back of the chair from beneath the doorknob. It was later than Danielle had believed, for the sun was already several hours high, its rays beaming through the lobby's open door.

"Herb and me slept late," Jesse said. "We won a pile last night, and we had to give the varmints a chance to win their money back."

Herb laughed. "They didn't win none of it back. Fact is, they lost some more, and we didn't run out. We stayed until the saloon closed."

The trio had breakfast at one of the cafes alongside the Kansas-Pacific tracks. There was little talk until they finished eating, and it was Herb who spoke.

"Would you take kindly to Jesse and me ridin' with you? We got nothing to hold us here, and I think we'd better avoid that saloon tonight."

"I reckon you're welcome to ride with me," said Danielle, "but I want one thing understood. Bounty or not, when I find these yellow coyotes I'm looking for, they'll belong to me. Then you're welcome to any bounty. All I want is their scurvy hides."

"When you find 'em, Herb and me will stand aside and let you get your satisfaction," Jesse said.

The bank was across the railroad tracks from the hotel, and as Danielle, Herb, and Jesse neared the hotel entrance, Herb stopped.

"What is it?" Jesse asked.

"Them three *hombres* that's headin' for the bank's front door just left their horses behind the building, and the hitch rail's out front," said Herb.

"No law against that," Jesse said.

"No," said Herb, "but somethin' about this don't look right. Let's wait a minute."

Across the tracks, the three men entered the bank. Facing the tellers, they drew their guns.

"Don't nobody try nothin' foolish," yelled one of the thieves, "and nobody gets hurt. We want them cash drawers opened, and we want only the big bills."

But one of the tellers had a Colt in his cash drawer.

When he drew it, one of the outlaws shot him. The teller's slug went wild, shattering the bank's front window with a tinkling crash. Fearfully, the other two tellers had emptied their cash drawers of large bills, and the outlaws scooped them up.

"The varmints are robbin' the bank!" Herb shouted as the echo of the shots faded.

Of a single mind, Herb, Jesse, and Danielle drew their Colts. Seconds later, the three robbers swung the bank's front door open, but before they could make a break for their horses, Herb challenged them.

"Halt, you varmints. You're covered."

But the three went for their guns. Danielle's Colt was roaring, and when Herb and Jesse began firing a second later, it sounded like rolling thunder. The three bank robbers went down as men poured from nearby saloons and businesses. A man stepped through the bank's front door with a shotgun under his arm, just as Sheriff Bart Devlin arrived. Devlin paid no attention to anybody except the three men who had been gunned down after leaving the bank. He found the trio dead, with the bills they had taken scattered about. The sheriff then turned his attention to the trio in front of the hotel. They were calmly reloading their Colts. The banker who had stepped out the door with the shotgun was the first to speak.

"Jenkins, one of my tellers, is hard-hit, Sheriff. But for those three young men before the hotel, these thieves would have escaped."

The sheriff said nothing, then crossing the street, he spoke to Danielle.

"I know you, but who are your friends?"

"Herb Sellers and Jesse Burris," Danielle said. "We just had breakfast, and it was Herb who thought there was something unusual about those three men leaving their horses behind the bank. When we heard the shots, we knew they were robbing the bank."

"A fine piece of work you gents have done," said Sheriff Devlin. "You just gunned down the Fenner gang. Three brothers gone bad, wanted for robbery and murder. I want to talk to all of you in my office, after these dead men are removed."

Some of the same men who had laughed at the cruel story in the Kansas City paper no longer laughed at Danielle. They moved aside respectfully, allowing Danielle, Herb, and Jesse to proceed along the boardwalk to Sheriff Devlin's office.

"There's a reward for them three *hombres,*" Sheriff Devlin said, when he returned to his office, "but I don't know how much. I'll have to look it up, and it'll take a few days to collect the money."

"I aim to ride out this morning," said Danielle. "See that Herb and Jesse get the reward. If Herb hadn't been suspicious, all of us would have been in the hotel when the robbery took place."

Sheriff Devlin sat down at his desk and began going through wanted dodgers. He found the one he was seeking and spread it out on the desk. The trio had been wanted for murder and robbery in Kansas, Missouri, and Texas. The combined rewards were more than six thousand dollars.

"Daniel, it ain't fair, Jesse and me takin' all that," said Herb. "Part of it's yours."

"No," Danielle said. "There's only one thing I want. If this Casper DeVero comes asking questions, don't tell him anything about me. I don't like him or his habits."

"There'll likely be no avoiding him," said Sheriff Devlin, "but I'll see that nothing is said to him that will be damaging to you. Anything he says about you in print is goin' to leave him looking like a fool, after that last piece he wrote. These varmints the three of you gunned down took twenty thousand dollars from that same bank last year. Morrison, the bank president, is grateful to you. He saw the whole thing as it happened. I'll see that Morrison gives DeVero a firsthand account."

Danielle, Herb, and Jesse left the sheriff's office and started back toward the hotel.

"I reckon the two of you made a pretty good start at bounty hunting," said Danielle.

"It's still not fair, us taking all the bounty," Jesse said.

"It is as far as I'm concerned," said Danielle. "I'm not of a mind to stay here longer than it takes to saddle my horse. That bounty will be enough eating money until you can track down some more outlaws with a price on their heads."

"I have a problem I never expected," Herb said. "I feel . . . well . . . guilty, gunning down a man for money."

"You shouldn't," said Danielle. "None of us *knew* there was a reward when we bought into that fight. We did the right thing, and if we hadn't taken those thieves by surprise, it might be one or all of us lying dead."

"That's right," Jesse said. "This same bunch robbed the same bank last year, but they won't ever do it again. Maybe it'll send a message to the rest of the thieves and killers holed up in Indian Territory."

The trio reached the hotel. Herb and Jesse waited in the hall while Danielle went into her room for her few belongings and saddlebags. It was time for parting, and Danielle was anxious to be gone. She genuinely liked these two cowboys, and while she didn't condemn them for bounty hunting, their motivation was entirely different from her own. How often had she read of men like Bill Hickok, John Wesley Hardin, and Ben Thompson, who had become legends as a result of their speed and accuracy with a gun? It was just such a name she didn't want, and yet the more often she had to use her guns, the more likely she was to find herself with the very same unwanted reputation. Reaching the livery, she paid her bill and saddled Sundown. She rode out quietly, glad to be escaping any further contact with the newspaperman, Casper DeVero. St. Joe wasn't that far from Kansas City, and for the first time, she wondered what her mother and brothers would think of the ridiculous story DeVero had written.

Indian Territory. December 1, 1870.

Danielle chose not to light a fire. Finding a source of water, she ate jerked beef for her supper. She then fed the chestnut mare a measure of grain. She had no illusions about finding any of the men she sought in Indian Territory, for it was a gloomy, dreary place. A man could remain there only so long, for thieves who had money would be eager to get to a town with saloons and whorehouses. Danielle spread her blankets near where Sundown was picketed, depending on the horse to warn her of any impending danger. But the night passed peacefully, and Danielle then rode south. Despite the difficulties she had experienced in Waco, she still believed some of the outlaws she was hunting were in Texas, and it was there she intended to go. She now regretted having left south Texas so quickly, for there was a good chance some of the fugitives from her list might be there. With only the river between Texas and old Mexico—despite her riding into an ambush while with Joel Votaw's outfit—she still believed that horse rustling flourished along the border. Done properly, there was little risk from authorities on either side of the river. Suddenly a distant horse nickered, and the chestnut mare answered. It was all the warning Danielle had. A rifle roared, and she rolled out of the saddle, going belly-down. One of the slugs had grazed Sundown, and the animal galloped away.

"All right, *hombre*," a voice challenged, "git up, keepin' your hands high."

There was no help for it, and Danielle got to her feet, careful to keep her hands away from the butts of her Colts. That these men were outlaws, she had no doubt.

"Now, come on," said the voice, "and don't do nothin' foolish."

There was a small clearing through which a stream flowed, and four men stood there with their hands near the butts of their revolvers. One of them spoke.

"Come on, Leroy. We got him covered."

A fifth man stepped out of the brush, carrying a Winchester. He wasted no time. His hard eyes met Danielle's, and Leroy spoke.

"Who are you, kid, and what are you doin' here?"

"I'm not the law, if that's what's botherin' you," Danielle said. "Thanks to you and your damned shooting, my horse ran away. Now get your no-account carcass out there and find her."

The rest of the outlaws laughed uproariously, and Leroy's face went bright red.

"Leroy," one of his companions said, "I never realized your daddy was so young."

That brought on a new round of laughter, and some violent cursing from Leroy. When they all became silent, Danielle was standing there with her thumbs hooked in her gunbelts just above the butts of her Colts.

"I hope you're done shootin', Leroy," said Danielle, "because I aim to shoot back."

But Leroy was furious. Dropping the Winchester, he went for his Colt. Danielle waited until he cleared leather and then, with blinding speed, shot the gun out of his hand.

"Anybody else?" Danielle asked, covering them.

Leroy stood there looking unbelievingly at his mangled Colt on the ground, while the other four men regarded Danielle with grudging respect.

"No need to get your tail feathers ruffled, kid," said one of the strangers warily. "Put away the iron. Sometimes, Leroy's a mite hard to convince. I'm Cass Herring, and these three gents beside me is Stubbs Potter, Jarvis Brooking, and Watt Slacker. Leroy Lomax you've already met."

Danielle punched out the empty shell casing and reloaded her Colt. Now there was no empty chamber, for the weapon was fully loaded, an observation that meant something to the five men who watched. Holstering the weapon, Danielle spoke.

"I'm Daniel Strange. Who you gents are, and what you're doing here is of no interest to me. I'm on my way to Texas, and thanks to Leroy here, I have no horse. Whatever you're riding, Leroy, saddle it and find my horse."

"Damned if I will," Leroy snarled.

"You're damned if you don't," said Danielle, her green eyes regarding him coldly. "It's cost you a Colt, so far. If you're still not convinced, I can shoot off a finger or a thumb."

Cass Herring laughed. "Leroy, I think you'd better round up the kid's horse."

Leroy stomped off into the brush, cursing as he went. Danielle relaxed. None of the other four men made any hostile moves. Instead, they regarded her curiously. It was Watt Slacker who finally spoke.

"Kid, where in tarnation did you learn to shoot like that?"

"My pa was a gunsmith in St. Joe, and he taught me," Danielle said. "He was robbed and hanged in

Indian Territory last April. Seven of the coyotes that killed him are alive somewhere, and I'm after them."

"I reckon you got some way of knowin' who they are, then," Stubbs Potter said.

"I have their names," said Danielle. "At least the names they were using."

"Name them," Cass Herring said. "We might be of some help to you. We been down to Laredo, where we got into a disagreement over the ownership of some horses."

Danielle named the men on her death list.

"One of them *hombres* I've heard of," said Herring. "This Snakehead Kalpana has been down to Brownsville, driving Mex horses across the border into Texas."

"Yeah," Stubbs Potter said. "The damn Spaniard loused up everything by gunning down a Texas lawman. They'll overlook a gent picking up a few Mex horses, but when he kills a man behind the star, he's in trouble."

"I'm obliged," said Danielle.

At that point, Leroy returned, leading Sundown. Without a word, he passed the reins to Danielle.

"We're bound for North Texas, kid," Cass Herring said, "and you're welcome to ride with us. It ain't safe for a man alone, here in Indian Territory."

"I'm obliged, and I'll join you," said Danielle. "Does that suit you, Leroy?"

"Hell, no," Leroy snarled. "You humiliated me, and I owe you for that."

"When you're ready," said Danielle. "I'll give you a head start."

Chapter 15

Danielle allowed the five men to lead out, for she didn't trust Leroy behind her out of her sight. She didn't like the way he had cut down on her with a Winchester, not knowing if she was friend or foe. The other four men seemed of a more even temperament.

"I figure we're maybe two hundred and fifty miles north of Fort Worth," Cass Herring said when they had made camp for the night.

"You're bound for Fort Worth, then," said Danielle.

"Yeah," Herring replied. "For the time being, any-way. It gets God-awful cold here in the Territory when them snowstorms blow down from the high plains."

"Hell, it snows in Texas, too," said Leroy sullenly.

"Not near as much as it does to the north," Herring replied. "If it gets bad enough, we can always ride farther south."

"I don't like south Texas," said Leroy. "Too damn many rangers there."

"You can always strike off on your own and go any place you damn please," Herring said, "but if you get gun-happy in Texas and get us in trouble with the rangers, then I'll personally gut-shoot you."

While none of them had admitted it, Danielle be-lieved they had been in Laredo—on the Mexican bor-der—rustling Mexican horses and selling them in Texas. They had then rode into Indian Territory to avoid any retribution for the lawman who had been shot. Danielle wondered if Leroy had done the killing, but there was no way of finding out unless she asked. For her own well-being, she couldn't afford to show too much interest in these men, who were undoubtedly on the dodge.

"We used the last of our coffee this morning," Cass Herring said. "How are you fixed for grub, kid?"

"I have enough coffee to see us through to Fort Worth," said Danielle. "I've got some jerked beef, bacon, and hardtack I'll share."*

"That's generous of you," Jarvis Brooking said. "We're near 'bout out of everything."

They rode on, stopping only to rest their horses, making night camp near a spring or a stream. At the end of the second day, Danielle estimated they were within fifty miles of Fort Worth. She had no reason for returning to the fort, since Captain Ferguson—the post commander—had refused her any help. Still, the sutler's store would be the nearest source of supplies, and sharing with her five companions had all but emptied her saddlebags. With much of the frontier still unsettled, civilians were allowed to buy supplies and goods from a military outpost's store.

Fort Worth, Texas. December 4, 1870.

In back of the sutler's store was a saloon, and Danielle's five companions went there first. Danielle had no intention of remaining at the fort overnight and, in the sutler's store, began replenishing her supplies. The very last person she wished to see was Captain Ferguson, but she soon heard footsteps behind her, and there he was. His manner was different, and when he spoke, there was some friendliness in his voice.

*Hardtack was an early version of today's soda crackers.

"You've been busy, young man. I received the Kansas City newspaper that told of the killing of a Kansas-Pacific railroad man. He refused to cooperate with you, didn't he?"

"Yes," Danielle said. "He didn't want any bad publicity for the railroad, but he got it anyway. One of the men on my list is Chancy Burke, and I was told by Alan Steele that Burke didn't work for the railroad. Steele confronted Burke himself, and after he shot and killed Steele, Burke escaped."

"I suppose I owe you an apology," said Ferguson. "If you had gone to Kansas City knowing Burke was with the railroad and feeding information to his outlaw friends, Steele might be alive today. I'm sorry I didn't make some effort to get that list of railroad men for you."

"We all make mistakes, Captain," Danielle said. "Your apology is accepted. Now I want to ask you something. Did you know Rufe Gaddis, Julius Byler, and Chancy Burke are all from Waco, and that they have families there?"

"No," said Ferguson. "It's news to me. Perhaps that's where they are now."

"I wouldn't be surprised," Danielle said, "but a lot of good it'll do me. I visited the Gaddis, Byler, and Burke families, and was ordered out of town. I couldn't stable my horse, buy a meal, or rent a room."

"Waco has an elected sheriff," said Ferguson. "You got no help there?"

"None, and no promise of any," Danielle said. "The sheriff's concerned only with the next election, and it was him that told the town I was looking for Gaddis, Byler, and Burke. He also made it a point to warn the families of the three outlaws, and their kin were waiting for me with guns."

"I can't promise you any help," said Captain Ferguson. "I suspect there are outlaws all over Texas, but there's nothing the military can do. We're already un-dermanned, and with Quanah Parker and his Coman-che followers raising hell, local lawmen and the rangers will have to deal with the outlaws."

"I understand," Danielle said, "but even the rangers have failed in Waco."

Shaking his head in frustration, Captain Ferguson walked away. When Danielle had her purchases bought and wrapped, she took them outside and stowed them in her saddlebags. She tied a sack of grain for Sundown to her bedroll behind the saddle. Feeling that she at least owed her five companions an *adios,* she went looking for them in the saloon behind the store. They did, after all, tell her that Snakehead Kalpana had been in south Texas, running horses across the border. If he had killed someone, especially a lawman, he might be long gone. She found all five of the men were gathered around a table, playing poker.

"I'm ridin' out," Danielle announced. "I just came to say *adios.*"

"Watch your back, kid," said Cass Herring. It was an underhanded compliment, for no man was likely to face her down when she drew with blinding speed. Potter, Brooking, and Slacker had words of farewell. Leroy Lomax glared at her murderously, for he was a big loser, having few chips before him.

"Don't expect nothin' from Leroy," Stubbs Potter said. "His ma weaned him on sour pickles, and he's went downhill from there."

There was laughter, some of it from strangers who had overheard the conversation. For a second, Dan-ielle's eyes met Leroy's, and she knew if their trails again crossed on the frontier, one of them would die. Danielle rode out slightly to the southwest so that she might avoid Waco, which lay due south of Fort Worth. She had no doubt that eventually she would be riding back to Waco, for with the whole town, including the sheriff, looking out for Gaddis, Byler, and Burke, it was a safe enough haven for the outlaws. She took heart in the possibility that Kalpana might not have been working alone, that some of the other killers she sought might be riding with him. From what she had learned at Fort Worth, Laredo, Texas was a border town some three hundred miles to the south. Since San Antonio was along the way, Danielle decided to stop and talk to the old ranger, Sage Jennings.

San Antonio, Texas. December 7, 1870.

Captain Jennings had heard of the killing of Alan Steele, of the Kansas-Pacific. Danielle filled in the details, and shaking his head, Jennings spoke.

"No damn wonder the frontier's neck-deep in outlaws. I reckon you've been to Waco?"

"I have, right after I left here before," Danielle said. She explained her run-ins with the sheriff and the Gaddis, Byler, and Burke families.

"I frankly don't know what we're going to do about that situation," said Jennings. "If we had some way of knowing when those three varmints slip back into Waco, I reckon we could take a posse and go after them. But it would be hell, trying to buffalo a whole town the size of Waco. Somebody would die, and not necessarily the outlaws."

"I got word that Snakehead Kalpana, one of the men I'm hunting, has been rustling on the other side of the border and bringing the horses into Texas. Do you know anything about that?"

"I didn't know the last time you were here," said Jennings, "but I do now. Kalpana has three men riding with him. He killed two men. One of them a Mexican officer, and the other a Texas Ranger. We want him, and we want him bad. He's worth twenty-five hundred dollars, dead or alive."

"If I find him," Danielle said, "you won't be getting him alive. I'm bound for Laredo."

"He hasn't been heard from around there since the killings," Captain Jennings said.

"I'm not surprised," said Danielle, "but there's a lot of border from Laredo south to Brownsville. I aim to ride all of it if I have to."

"I could swear you in as a ranger," Jennings said, "but it might hurt you more than it would help. A varmint that's killed one ranger couldn't hang any higher for killing another one. Just be careful, and remember, it's against federal law for you to cross the border into Mexico."

"Wherever Kalpana is, that's where I'm going," said Danielle, "and that includes south of the border."

"I didn't hear you say that," Jennings said. "Do what you have to do, and good luck."

Weary from the long ride from Fort Worth, Danielle stabled Sundown and took a room for the night. She lay down and slept awhile after supper, then decided to visit the Alamo Saloon. She had heard it was a favorite watering hole for King Fisher, Ben Thompson, and other gamblers. The saloon was even more luxurious than she had imagined. Instead of sawdust floors, there was deep-pile carpet, drapes on the windows, a mahogany bar, and two dozen tables devoted to poker and faro. Danielle wondered if her lucky streak had played out, or if she could still win. Placing five double eagles on a faro table, she bought in.

"Ten dollars a bet," the house dealer said.

It was the highest stakes Danielle had ever played for. At ten dollars a throw, she could lose her hundred dollars in a matter of minutes. On the other hand, if she won, the higher stakes put more money in her pocket. She quickly lost fifty dollars before she began winning. She almost immediately recovered her fifty dollars, and for an hour she averaged winning two pots out of three. Her companions at the table took their losses in stride, for they seemed to be affluent men. When Danielle had won three hundred dollars, she withdrew from the game. It didn't pay to win too much, too soon. She couldn't help wondering what these men would have thought or said, had they known she wasn't a man. Thinking back, she was amazed at the changes in her. She had learned to control herself and her emotions so that nothing men said or did caused her to blush. It bothered her, for when she reached the end of her vengeance trail, suppose she had become a hard woman, comfortable in saloons, among drunks and whores? She often thought of Tucker Carlyle, but she dared not ride back to the Carlyle ranch. Her good-byes had been difficult enough, and she didn't want to go through them again. She returned to her hotel, and as usual, she slid the back of a chair under the doorknob.

Danielle arose early and had breakfast in a nearby cafe. She then took her saddlebags and headed for the stable where she had left the chestnut mare. During their months on the trail, she had become much closer to Sundown, and the mare nickered her pleasure when Danielle came near. She rode slightly to the southwest, toward Laredo. If there had been trouble on the border at Laredo, it wasn't likely the outlaws were still there, but she couldn't overlook the possibility that they had simply holed up somewhere in the wilds of old Mexico until the incident was forgotten. Rustling horses in Mexico and driving them into Texas had become relatively easy, for as Captain Jennings had pointed out, even the combined efforts of the United States and Mexico were not enough to patrol the hundreds of miles of border.

Laredo, Texas. December 10, 1870.

Compared to San Antonio, Laredo wasn't much more than a wide place in the trail. The hotel was a single-story affair, the rooms were cheap, and there were only two cafes. But, as Danielle noted with amusement, there were six saloons. Darkness was falling when she reached town, and to her dismay, she found the livery closed. She pounded on the door with the butt of one of her Colts until the door creaked open. An old Mexican peered at Danielle in the fading light. Under his arm was a Winchester rifle.

"What you want, *señor*?"

"I want to stable my horse for the night," Danielle said. "What the hell's the idea of closing before dark?"

"*Mejicanos* come from across the river and take our horses," the old one replied.

"Tarnation," Danielle said, "don't you have a lawman or a sheriff?"

"*Sí,*" said the Mexican, "but he is one *hombre*. The border, she be great, *señor*."

The old man had told her essentially what she had already heard from Captain Sage Jennings, but she had learned something more. Apparently in retaliation, Texas horses were being run across the border into Mexico, or so it seemed. But suppose it wasn't Mexicans stealing Texas horses? Who could say that, after several killings, American outlaws hadn't holed up south of the border and begun running Texas horses into Mexico? Danielle took a room at the hotel and went to the nearest cafe to eat. Tomorrow morning she would seek out the sheriff and question him.

Three men were in the cafe when Danielle entered, and they turned to stare at her. Each wore a high-crowned Mexican sombrero, and their faces were obscured by maybe a week's growth of beard. Their tight-fitting black trousers and their red-embroidered vests showed much trail-dust. Their ruffled, once-white shirts were sweat-stained, and tied low on his right hip, each had a revolver. Danielle paused in the doorway, her eyes on the three, and they hastily resumed eating. The cook looked fearfully from Danielle to the Mexicans, and relaxed. The three were eating, apparently oblivious to Danielle. She spoke.

"Bring me a double portion of whatever you have."

"Beef stew, potatoes, apple pie, and coffee," said the cook "Tequila if you wish."

"No," Danielle said. "Coffee."

It was obvious the three men who had stared at Danielle were drinking tequila, for on their table sat a bottle a third-full of the potent liquor. Danielle watched them out of the corner of her eye and, from their flushed faces, decided they were drunk or close to it. When the cook brought Danielle's meal, she ate slowly, allowing the trio to finish ahead of her. They did and left the cafe without looking at Danielle again. It was just her and the cook, so she spoke.

"I thought it was illegal for Mexicans to cross the border into Texas, or for Texans to cross over into Mexico."

"That fool law was wrote in Washington," said the cook, "and that's a hell of a long ways from here. If the Mexes want to wade the branch and spend their *pesos* in Laredo, I ain't about to complain. I reckon you've noticed this ain't a very big town."

"I've noticed," Danielle said, "and I'm not concerned with Mexicans. I'm looking for Snakehead Kalpana, an American. I have business with him."

"Never heard of him," said the cook.

The furtive look in his eyes told Danielle he was lying. Drinking the last of her coffee, she paid for her meal and left the cafe. Returning to the hotel, she locked the door to her room and placed the back of a chair under the doorknob. Tomorrow she would seek out the sheriff, and for a long while, she lay awake wondering if his attitude toward the border crossings would be the same as those of the man in the cafe. If Kalpana and some of the other men felt safe south of the border, finding them would be all the more difficult.

Danielle arose at dawn, had breakfast, and went looking for the sheriff. There were only two cells in the jail, both empty. The sheriff looked to be in his forties, and he got to his feet when Danielle entered the office.

"Sheriff, I'm Daniel Strange, from St. Joseph, Missouri."

"Pleased to meet you," said the lawman. "I'm Tom Carson. What can I do for you?"

"Tell me if you know anything about Snakehead Kalpana," Danielle said.

"I know he's an outlaw and a killer, and that the Texas Rangers would dearly love for him to be the guest of honor at a necktie party. What's your interest in him?"

Quickly, Danielle again told the story of her father's murder in Indian Territory.

"I can't say I blame you," said the sheriff, "but you're almighty young to be ridin' the vengeance trail."

"Maybe," Danielle said, "but there was nobody else. My two brothers are younger than I am."

"I'll help you in any way that I can," said the sheriff, "but I suspect Kalpana and the bunch he's ridin' with have moved on. It was Kalpana who shot two men. One of them was a Mexican officer, and the other was a Texas Ranger."

"Speaking of the bunch Kalpana's riding with,"

Danielle said, "do you know the names of any of them?"

"No," said Sheriff Carson. "I'm familiar with Kalpana only because he spent his time in the saloons, gambling. Of course, that was before we learned he was rustling Mex horses and selling them in Texas, and before he shot and killed the Mexican and a ranger. He's got a hair-trigger temper, and when he loses at the poker table, he has a bad habit of accusing somebody of cheating him. I threatened to arrest him several times, but he would always back down. I reckon it's lucky for me that he did, because he carries a couple of tied-down Colts. From what I've heard, he's faster than forked lightning."

Danielle sighed. "I'm obliged, Sheriff Carson. I didn't really expect Kalpana to still be here, but this trail's not quite as cold as that I've been following. How much border is there between here and Brownsville?"

"A good two hundred miles," said Carson, "and all manner of little villages where a man on the dodge can hole up. He could even be south of the border. Mexicans are poor, and if an *Americano* has money, they'll take him in, whatever he's done."

"The border situation being what it is," Danielle said, "can you suggest anything that might be helpful to me?"

"Maybe," the lawman said. "As you ride on to Brownsville, follow the river. There's Del Rio and Eagle Pass, about a day's ride between them. You probably won't learn much at Del Rio, but King Fisher has a ranch near Eagle Pass.* It's common knowledge that King rides across the border, rounds up wild horses, and drives them into Texas, but you

---

*King Fisher's ranch was the Pendencia. He was a cowboy, a rustler, and a killer—he was fifteen when he killed his first man.

would be wise not to mention that. He might be willing to identify some of the men you're looking for if
he understands your reason. But he's almighty swift
with a pistol, and he don't like company. Are you
familiar with him?"

"Yes," said Danielle. "I ran into him and Ben
Thompson once, when I rode through San Antonio."

"Drunk, I reckon," Sheriff Carson said.

"Roostered to the eyeballs," said Danielle. "They
looked just about drunk enough to want to fight, so I
avoided them."

"Good thinking," Sheriff Carson said. "It's a damn
shame King Fisher walks on both sides of the law. He
could use his guns to help rid the border of thieves
and killers."

Del Rio, Texas. December 12, 1870.

It seemed there was nothing more Danielle could
learn in Laredo, so she rode along the Rio Grande
toward Del Rio. It was, as Sheriff Carson said, a good
day's ride, and the first stars were winking from the
heavens when Danielle rode in. The town seemed
smaller than Laredo, for Danielle counted only four
saloons. For some reason, there were two liveries, and
Danielle left Sundown at the one nearest the hotel.
She then took a room for the night and went to a cafe
for supper. Since it was already dark, she decided to
wait until the following morning to seek out Sheriff
Lon Guthrie. The cafe was nothing fancy, having a
big hanging sign outside that said simply EATS. Besides
the cook, there was only one man in the cafe, and he
wore a lawman's star. Danielle ordered her meal, then
took a chair across from the lawman. He looked questioningly at her.

"I reckon you're Sheriff Lon Guthrie," Danielle

said. "Sheriff Carson, in Laredo, said I should talk to you."

"I'm Guthrie," said the lawman. "Who are you, and why do you want to talk to me?"

"I'm Daniel Strange, and I'm looking for a varmint that's been rustling horses south of the border and driving them to Texas. He's one of ten outlaws who robbed and murdered my pa in Indian Territory. His name, far as I know, is Snakehead Kalpana."

"I've heard the name," Sheriff Guthrie said, "but I don't think he's spent any time here in Del Rio. Seeing as how we're right on the border, I'm always watching for strangers in the saloons and cafes."

"I'm obliged for the information," said Danielle. "In Laredo, Sheriff Carson suggested that on my way to Brownsville, I talk to Sheriff Rim Klady, in Eagle Pass. He told me that I should also talk to King Fisher, since he gathers wild horses in Mexico and drives them across the border into Texas."

"King Fisher's a hell-raising coyote that walks on his hind legs like a man," Sheriff Guthrie said. "I doubt he'd help you if he could, because some of those horses he rounds up in Mexico ain't wild. They're wearin' Mex brands. You'd best avoid him."

"If I don't learn anything in Eagle Pass," said Danielle, "I'll be riding on to Brownsville. With so much border, I can't believe these rustlers would give up easy pickings."

"Maybe you're right," Sheriff Guthrie said, "but Sam Duro's sheriff there, so don't be expecting too much."

"I'm obliged, Sheriff," said Danielle.

Sheriff Guthrie had finished his meal. He slid back his chair and stood up.

"Good luck, kid."

Danielle nodded, for the cook had just brought her supper. She ate, mulling over what Sheriff Guthrie had told her. While he hadn't really told her anything about the sheriff at Brownsville, he had implied much. Among the many good lawmen on the frontier, there was always an occasional one—if the price was right—who would turn his back on rustlers, outlaws, and killers. Danielle paid for her meal and returned to the hotel. Having already talked to Sheriff Guthrie, in the morning she could get an early start to Eagle Pass.

Eagle Pass, Texas. December 13, 1870.

The border town of Eagle Pass wasn't that much different from Del Rio. There were the same weather-beaten saloons, but only four this time. Danielle arrived before dark and, finding a livery, stabled Sundown. She then set out to find the sheriff's office. The door was locked, and peering through a window, Danielle could see no sign of life inside. There was an hour of daylight remaining, so Danielle decided to make the rounds of the saloons. In the third one, called the Eagle's Claw, she found the sheriff, involved in a poker game.

"Sheriff," Danielle said, "I have some business with you."

Sheriff Rim Klady turned and looked her over, his eyes pausing when they reached the two tied-down Colts on Danielle's hips. Finally, he spoke.

"Have you been robbed or shot somebody?"

"No," said Danielle. "I'm Daniel Strange, and it's about another matter."

"Then see me at the office in the morning," Sheriff Klady said.

The lawman had just won another pot. Dismissing Danielle, he raked in his winnings. Danielle left the saloon, furious. She took a room at the hotel. Tomorrow she might or might not be questioning the sheriff.

It seemed that a talk with King Fisher might be far more beneficial, if she could get to him.

The next morning, Danielle was sitting on the steps to the sheriff's office and the jail when the lawman arrived. She got up, allowing him to mount the steps and unlock the door. She followed him into the office.

"All right," said the sheriff, "I'm Rim Klady. Sit down and have your say."

Klady sat down in his chair behind his desk while Danielle took a ladder-back chair facing him. She quickly told her story, and by the time she was finished, the sheriff was shaking his head.

"The name 'Kalpana' don't mean nothing to me," Sheriff Klady said. "There's hundreds of miles of border, and rustlers ain't likely to drive stock across the border where there's a town with a lawman."

"I understand King Fisher has a ranch near here," said Danielle, "and that he rounds up wild horses in Mexico, driving them back into Texas."

Sheriff Klady's manner changed abruptly, and there was something in his eyes akin to fear. Finally, he spoke.

"I don't bother King Fisher, and he don't bother me. I don't see nothin' wrong with him capturing wild horses in Mexico."

"Except that the United States government has a law against him going there," Danielle said. "That doesn't concern you?"

"Hell, no," said the lawman. "The federals passed that damn law. Let them enforce it. If Mexicans want to come into Texas or Texans want to go into Mexico, there ain't enough lawmen on both sides of the border to stop 'em."

"You haven't been much help, Sheriff," Danielle said, "and I'm going to ask just one more favor of you. How do I find King Fisher's place?"

"Just ride along the river toward Brownsville," Sheriff Klady said. "The Rio borders his place to the south, and you'll see a sign pointin' toward the ranch. Just don't complain to me if he greets you with a Winchester and orders you to get the hell off his property."

"I'd never think of bothering you over a small matter like that, Sheriff," said Danielle. "I'm armed, and I'm not afraid to shoot back. *Adios.*"

The sheriff said nothing, and Danielle left, closing the door behind her. Mounting Sundown, she rode south, keeping the Rio in sight. As Sheriff Klady had said, there soon was a fork in the trail. A board with crude lettering had been nailed to a tree. It said:

This is King Fisher's road. Take the other.

Chapter 16

Ignoring the warning, Danielle took King Fisher's road. Of her welcome, she was very uncertain, for the only times she had seen King Fisher had been in San Antonio, when he and Ben Thompson had been very drunk. She finally rode out into a clearing and could see the ranch house in the distance. The place seemed deserted, but suddenly the stillness was shattered by a gunshot.

"Don't come any closer," a voice shouted. "You're not welcome here."

"I only want to talk to you," Danielle said. "I'm not the law."

"You're still not welcome here," said the distant voice.

Gritting her teeth, Danielle rode on. Would the man shoot her out of the saddle? She eventually reined up forty yards from the front porch. King Fisher stepped past the door, a Winchester under his arm. His dress could only be described as gaudy. His trousers were black with pinstripes, and over a white ruffled shirt, he wore a bright red tie. Around his middle was a red sash that matched the tie. His boots were fancy, and a white Stetson hat was tipped low over his eyes. On each hip in a tied-down holster was a revolver.

"I could have shot you dead and been within my rights," he snapped. "Haven't I seen you somewhere?"

"In San Antonio," said Danielle. "You and Ben Thompson were drunk."

"Since you're here," Fisher said, "who are you, and what the hell do you want of me?"

"I want some information," said Danielle, "and it in no way concerns you. I am Daniel Strange, and I'm hunting some men who robbed and hanged my pa in Indian Territory in the spring. One of those still alive—Snakehead Kalpana—has been rustling horses in old Mexico and driving them across the border into Texas. He killed a Mexican and a ranger near Laredo, but I doubt that he's given up rustling. I think he's just moved to another location along the border."

"Well, if you think he's here, or that I'd have any dealings with the likes of him, then you're barking up the wrong damn tree," Fisher said.

"I've been told that you trap wild horses in Mexico and drive them into Texas," said Danielle. "I was hoping you might have seen or heard of Kalpana."

"I want nothing to do with the kind that rustles another man's stock," Fisher said. "I've shot some *hombres* that was needful of it, but I've never stole a horse or a cow."*

"If you know nothing about Kalpana," said Danielle, "maybe you'll recognize some of these other varmints I'm looking for."

Quickly, she told him the names of the other six men, and Fisher shook his head.

"I'm obliged anyway," Danielle said.

"You got sand in your craw, kid," said King Fisher. "How old are you?"

"Old enough," Danielle said.

Fisher laughed. "A regular two-gun man, huh? Can you use them irons, or do you just carry 'em to scare hell out of folks?"

---

*Despite his assurances to the contrary, King Fisher had been known to rustle. He was only fifteen when he stole his first horse.

In a lightning cross-hand draw, Danielle drew the butt-forward Colt from her left hip. She fired once, the slug kicking up splinters from the porch. Then she spoke.

"I could have shot your ears off, but you've been decent to me. *Adios.*"

Holstering the Colt, she wheeled the chestnut mare and rode away. King Fisher stood there watching her until she was out of sight. Then he laughed to himself.

"You'll do, kid. You'll do."

When Danielle reached the river, she rode southeast. She had no idea how far she was from Brownsville and decided not to attempt to reach it in what was left of the day. She was rapidly running out of trails and needed to think. There was always a chance, she concluded, that she had miscalculated. Suppose Kalpana *had* left Laredo, but instead of riding deeper into south Texas, he had ridden west, toward El Paso? He might even have gone to southern Arizona, for there he would be just across the river from Mexico. There were so many possibilities, Danielle had to rest to put them all out of her mind.

Brownsville, Texas. December 16, 1870.

Clearly, nobody was enforcing federal law in Brownsville, for Mexicans were virtually everywhere. From the saloons there were drunken shouts in Spanish, and as Danielle rode along the main street, she saw many dark-eyed *señoritas* with their hair tied back, and some peons with colorful serapes about their shoulders. It appeared that most of the cafes and restaurants, if not Mexican owned, were at least Mexican operated. Before most of them, in colorful clothing and a high-crowned sombrero, a young boy praised his establishment's bill of fare in rapid Spanish. It looked like a wide-open town, Danielle thought, and might well be just the kind of place where Snakehead Kalpana would try to lose himself. Getting past the saloons, cafes, and street vendors, Danielle reached a quiet street down which she rode. She came upon a huge old house, and above the front door was a neatly painted sigm that read AMERICAN HOTEL. Reining up, she dismounted and knocked on the door. When it was eventually opened, there stood a gray-haired old man.

"I just rode through town," Danielle said, "and I like the look of your sign. I'll need a room for maybe two or three days."

"Come in," said her host. "My name is Ephiram Delaney. My wife, Ethel, is upstairs. I'll get her. Make yourself at home."

He proceeded to summon Ethel by shouting for her at the top of his voice.

"Damn it," Ethel shouted back, "do you have to wake the dead? I'm coming."

She came down the stairs, taking her time, a wisp of a woman as gray as old Ephiram. She looked at Danielle, a question in her eyes. Danielle spoke.

"I'm Daniel Strange, and I'll need a room for maybe three nights."

"Two dollars a night for the room," said Ethel, "or three-fifty if you want some grub twice a day."

"I'll take the room and the grub," Danielle said, handing her a gold eagle.

"Good choice," said Ephiram. "In these Mex cafes and cantinas, they load everything with chili peppers 'cept the coffee."

"Now," Danielle said, "is there a place close by where I can stable my horse?"

"Behind the house across the alley," Ephiram said, "but we can't afford no hostler."

"I won't need one," said Danielle.

"I'll get you a room ready while you're gone," Ethel said. "Just come on up. It'll be at the head of the stairs on the right."

Danielle led Sundown around the house and into the stable. It appeared to be empty, and Danielle chose a stall for the mare. She unsaddled the horse and, seeing hay in the loft above, climbed up and forked some down.

"Chew on that awhile, Sundown," said Danielle. "I'll be back before dark and bring you some grain."

Danielle found Ephiram seated on the front porch. Nodding to him, she again entered the house and mounted the stairs.

"In here," Ethel said.

The room could only be described as luxurious. There was a thick gray carpet on the floor, with rose-colored drapes at the window. The bed was brass with a multicolored coverlet. There were several extra chairs, upholstered in rose, and a wide dresser on which stood a porcelain water pitcher and matching basin. On the back of the door was a mirror, full length and uncracked.

"The chamberpot's under the bed," said Ethel with a wink.

"I'm obliged," Danielle said. "You have a fine place. I've never had better."

"Thank you," said Ethel, pleased. "We cater to Americans. Ephiram says one day we'll wake up and there won't be anybody but *Mejicanos* as far as the eye can see."

"It already looks that way uptown," Danielle said.

"It just about is," said Ethel. "Don't let 'em sell you any of that Mex whiskey, either. It's about a hundred and forty proof. Then when you're layin' there stiff as a post and can't get up, them human turkey buzzards—*Anglos* or *Mejicanos*—will pick your pockets clean."

"I'm obliged for the information," Danielle said, "but I don't drink or smoke."

"Praise be," said Ethel. "Last time we had a drinking man in here he passed out and his cigarette set the bed afire. Supper's at five, breakfast at seven."

As Danielle left the house, Ephiram sat nodding on the front porch. The Delaneys were in a residential section of quiet homes, and the area seemed a world apart from the center of town with its noisy *Mejicanos* and shifty-eyed *Anglos*. Danielle had already been warned not to expect too much of Brownsville Sheriff Sam Duro, but she went looking for the lawman anyway. She found his office and he was there, his booted feet on the desk and his hat tipped over his eyes. From somewhere came the sound of three rapid gunshots and a cry of anguish, but the sheriff remained where he was.

"Draw, you lazy varmint," Danielle shouted, kicking the desk.

Duro's swivel chair went over backward, coming to rest on top of him. He cursed as he fought to draw his revolver, and Danielle laughed. Finally, he sat up, shoving the chair off him, and began beating his crushed Stetson back into shape. Danielle stood there chuckling, allowing the disgruntled lawman to get to his feet and right his swivel chair.

"Damn you," Duro shouted, "that's a good way to get yourself shot dead. Who the hell are you, and what business do you have here?"

"Killing business when I find the right man," said Danielle. "I'm after an outlaw and a killer. You being the law here, I reckoned I'd better talk to you first."

"The law hereabouts don't work with bounty hunters," Sheriff Duro said.

"I'm not a bounty hunter," said Danielle. "I'm after the yellow coyotes who robbed and murdered my pa in Indian Territory. One of them in particular is

Snakehead Kalpana, and I have reason to believe he's here. Do you know him, or know of him?"

"No," Sheriff Duro said, "and I won't tolerate vigilantes any more than I'll tolerate the bounty hunters. The first damn sign of trouble that involves you, I'll lock you in the jail till hell freezes. You got that?"

"If I find the *hombre* I'm looking for, I aim to do what I came here to do," Danielle said steadily, "and if you try to stop me, you'd better be pretty damn sudden with a pistol. *You got that?*"

Danielle turned and left the sheriff's office, not even bothering to ask Duro about the rest of the men on her death list. There were more gunshots from the area where most of the saloons were. She decided that Duro was even more useless than Sheriff Rucker in Waco. She had little choice except to make the rounds of the saloons, hoping to gather a bit of information that might suggest a new trail. The biggest and noisiest of the saloons seemed to be a place appropriately called the Border Saloon. There were poker and faro games in progress, but Danielle didn't like the looks of the men gathered around the tables. She watched a faro game for a while and learned her suspicions had been well founded. A bearded man suddenly leaped to his feet, drew a Bowie knife, and lunged across the table. But the Mexican he had gone after was just as resourceful with his own blade, and under their weight the table collapsed. They rolled around on the floor, each man seizing the wrist of the other's knife hand. Two bouncers arrived to break up the fight, and their method was simple. Each of them seized a chair, slamming it down on the head of one of the men on the floor. When the two knife-wielders were beaten bloody and unconscious, the bouncers carried them outside, one at a time, and flung them into the street. By then, another table had been set up, and the interrupted faro game was again in progress. Danielle was about to leave when a woman screamed. It was one of the saloon girls. She lay on her back on the floor while a man astraddle her was ripping her clothes off. Danielle looked for the bouncers, but they were nowhere in sight. Nobody tried to help the unfortunate girl, and some of the men had gathered around to watch, laughing. Danielle drew her Colt, crossed the room, and slammed the muzzle of the weapon against the back of the attacker's head. He tumbled over, allowing the terrified girl to get to her feet. Drawing the remnants of her torn dress together, she ran up the winding stairway that led to the second floor. The saloon had become deathly silent, and not a man among them could meet Danielle's eyes. She holstered her Colt, awaiting she knew not what. Slowly, the man she had buffaloed got to his hands and knees, shaking his head. He then got unsteadily to his feet.

"Which one of you sons of bitches hit me?" he snarled.

"I did," said Danielle, "and I'm only sorry I didn't do it sooner."

He went for his gun, only to find himself covered by Danielle's Colt. Baring his teeth like a wolf, he snarled at her.

"Do you know who I am?"

"No," Danielle said calmly, "but I know *what* you are. You're a woman-beating coward, a yellow-bellied coyote that walks on his hind legs like a man."

"I'll kill you for that!" he shouted. "Reece McCandless swears it."

"I'm obliged for the warning," said Danielle. "I'll watch my back. Now get out of here, and the next time you reach for a gun, I'll kill you."

McCandless was a big man, and given a choice, he would have preferred being gut-shot to the humiliation he had endured. His face flaming red, he stumbled out of the saloon. As Danielle stepped out onto the boardwalk, she encountered Sheriff Sam Duro.

"Where the hell have *you* been?" Danielle asked. "The brute that just left here had a woman down on the floor, ripping her clothes off."

"I reckon you stepped in and saved her," said Sheriff Duro.

"I did," Danielle said, "and I only regret that I didn't shoot him."

"God help you if you had," Duro said. "That's Reece McCandless. Old Simon, his pa, owns half of Brownsville."

"Does he own you along with it?" Danielle asked.

"Kid," said Sheriff Duro, "I'm gonna pretend you didn't say that, because you're in enough trouble already. With any luck, you can mount your horse and be long gone from here before Simon McCandless learns what you've done."

"Sheriff," Danielle said, "I'll go when I'm ready, and I'm not ready. I called McCandless a woman-beating coward and a yellow-bellied coyote walking on his hind legs like a man, and I don't regret a word of it. I'm sticking to what I said, and I don't care a damn if old Simon McCandless is nine feet tall and feeds on raw meat."

Danielle left Sheriff Duro speechless. She went into one of the smaller cantinas, where a faro game was in progress, and decided to sit in.

"Five-dollar limit," said the dealer.

Danielle lost fifty dollars and was about to quit the game when one of the men across the table spoke to his companion.

"I'm tired of this damn town, neck-deep in *Mejicanos*. If Kalpana don't show up by tomorrow night, I'm ridin' on."

The other laughed. "After what he done in Laredo,

he'll likely have to spend the rest of his life south of the river."

Danielle listened eagerly, hoping to hear more, but the conversation took a new turn and Kalpana's name wasn't mentioned again. The reference to what Kalpana had done in Laredo led Danielle to believe it might have been him who had killed the Texas Ranger. After losing most of her hundred-dollar stake, Danielle began to go over her options. She wanted to remain in the game so that when the two strangers left, she could follow them. Their reference to Kalpana was the only mention of the man's name she had heard after many months on the trail. It wasn't a common name, and she believed it was the outlaw she sought. The two strangers had a run of extremely bad luck, and to cut their losses, they withdrew from the game and started toward the bar. Danielle won another hand just as the pair finished their drinks and were about to leave the saloon. She waited until they were outside on the boardwalk before following them. Eventually, they reached a two-story building, the bottom floor of which was a saloon. A faded sign said ROOMS FOR RENT UPSTAIRS. Danielle watched the pair ascend the outside stairs, waiting for a lamp to be lighted in one of the rooms. Lamplight soon flooded one of the front rooms facing the street. Since the two had returned to their room instead of going on to other saloons, Danielle didn't expect them to leave again before the next morning. When they did, she would be waiting for them. She returned to the Delaney house, finding Ethel on the front porch.

"Come set with me awhile," Ethel Delaney invited.

"Maybe later," said Danielle. "I promised my horse some grain."

She walked on around the house to the stable, and the chestnut mare nickered as she drew near. She

grained Sundown and then drew enough water from
the well to half fill the horse trough. She then returned
to the front porch and sat down in a cane-bottom
rocking chair.

"I thought I heard shooting a while ago," Ethel
said.

"You likely did," said Danielle. "A couple of
drunks. I reckon nobody got hurt."

"Wouldn't be nothin' done about it if somebody
had been killed," Ethel said. "You met Sam Duro?"

"Yes," said Danielle cautiously.

"He's a disgrace to the star that he wears," Ethel
said. "Outlaws get run out of other towns, and they
come here."

"I heard that," Ephiram said, joining them.

"I don't care," said Ethel. "It's the truth. I think
they pay Sam Duro to leave them be. I wish a company of rangers would come here and clean up this
town."

"Would do no good," Ephiram said. "Damn outlaws would just ride into Mexico and hole up there
until the rangers were gone. Who are you after, son?
Maybe we've heard of him."

He had caught Danielle entirely by surprise, and she
was forced to gather her thoughts before she replied.

"Who says I'm looking for anybody?"

Ephiram laughed. "I do. You don't pack them two
guns for show. I figure you got to be a peace officer
or a bounty hunter. In either case, this is your kind
of town."

"Ephiram," said Ethel, "when are you goin' to learn
to mind your own business?"

"No offense intended," Ephiram said sheepishly.

"None taken," said Danielle, "but you're wrong.
I'm no lawman and no bounty hunter."

She had already told Sheriff Sam Duro her purpose

for being in town, and could think of no reason why she shouldn't tell these friendly people the truth. Quickly, she did.

"I can't do nothin' about it," Ephiram said, "but I hear things. This Snakehead Kalpana was here, but he's spooked after shootin' that ranger in Laredo. He's somewhere on the other side of the border, and God only knows how many other outlaws are with him. You don't aim to ride into Mexico after him, do you?"

"Not unless there's no other way," said Danielle. "I overheard two men talking in one of the saloons a while ago, and Kalpana's name was mentioned. They're waiting for him, and startin' tomorrow, I aim to follow them."

"Watch your back, son," Ephiram said. "There's talk around town that the McCandless boy's gunning for you."

"Reece McCandless?" Ethel asked. "What on earth for?"

Ephiram laughed. "I forgot to tell you. Our young friend Daniel here was in one of the saloons where Reece McCandless was mistreating a saloon woman. Old Reece got himself buffaloed with the muzzle of a Colt, and he was laughed out of the saloon."

"I have no patience with women who work in saloons," said Ethel. "She was likely just getting what she deserved."

"Sorry," Danielle said, "but no woman deserves being mistreated by a bully."

"The McCandless family is a vicious flock of buzzards," aid Ephiram. "Reese is the only son, and it's shameful what he gets by with in this town. Long as you're here, you'd better ride carefully."

"I aim to," Danielle said. "I may have a long day tomorrow, so I think I'll turn in."

Brownsville, Texas. December 18, 1870.

Danielle was up and about well before breakfast time at the Delaney's, so she stopped to eat at one of the many cafes. While she was eating, she felt eyes upon her. Looking up quickly, she recognized the face at the window as that of the girl she had rescued from Reece McCandless. Just as quickly, the face was gone. Danielle paid for her breakfast and left the cafe, looking in both directions along the deserted street. She started along the main street's boardwalk to the old house to which she had followed the outlaws the night before.

"Look out, cowboy," a voice shouted.

Danielle went down on her left side, rolling off the boardwalk into the dusty street as shots ran out. She drew her right-hand Colt as she fell and, belly-down, began returning fire. But her assailant was firing from cover, the slugs kicking up dust all around her. Lead splintered the hitch rail over her head, while others slammed into the front wall of a store that had not yet opened for the day. It was a shoot-or-be-shot situation, and Danielle's only hope lay in rooting the bushwhacker out into the open. He had a Henry or a Winchester, for slugs kept coming, screaming closer with each volley. Danielle rolled to her knees and sprang to her feet. She ran, zigzagging her way toward the gunman's position. From the powder smoke, she found him firing from the window of a vacant building that faced the street. Danielle fired twice, and her lead came close enough to spook the bushwhacker. The firing from the window ceased. Danielle reloaded and holstered her Colt. The girl who had warned her stood fearfully in a doorway.

"I'm obliged to you," Danielle said. "I don't suppose you know who that was."

"Reece McCandless," said the girl. "He's been telling everybody who will listen that he intends to kill you."

"He won't if I kill him first," Danielle said. "What's your name?"

"Mary," said the girl. "If you kill him, old Simon McCandless will have every gunman in town after you. You'd better ride away while there's still time."

"When I'm ready, Danielle said, "and I'm not ready."

She continued along the boardwalk until she was across the street from the old house to which she had followed the two outlaws the night before. It would be far simpler if Kalpana came to them, she thought. Otherwise, she might have to trail them across the border. Danielle took up a position behind a vacant building. From there she could observe the stairway to the second floor of the house across the street. When the duo finally left, Danielle followed them, only to find they had gone out for breakfast. Finished, they returned to their room and Danielle saw no more of them the rest of the day. Not being in a mood for further conversation with the Delaneys, she returned to the American Saloon, where her trouble with McCandless had begun. It was barely dark outside, but the place seemed unusually crowded. Sheriff Sam Duro was there, and to her surprise, so was Reece McCandless. It was he who was shouting angrily.

"Damn you, I'll have your badge for this. I've been here all afternoon, and I got plenty of witnesses to prove it."

"Maybe," said Sheriff Duro, "but somebody slit that girl's throat, and I can't think of anybody with more reason than you."

"Whose throat's been slit?" Danielle asked.

"Mary," said a bystander. "You saved her from McCandless last night."

It was more than Danielle could stand. She approached Reece McCandless, and everybody backed away, including Sheriff Duro. When she spoke, her voice was like ice.

"You've been threatening to kill me, and you tried to back-shoot me this morning. All that saved me was Mary's shouted warning, and you got even with her for that, didn't you?"

"I don't have to answer your damn questions," McCandless said. "You ain't the law."

"No," said Danielle, "and for that reason, I only have to answer to my own conscience. I hear you've been threatening to kill me, and I'm going to offer you the chance. But this time you won't be under cover, trying to shoot me in the back. It's light enough outside. I'll meet you in the street."

"I won't do it," McCandless bawled. "I didn't shoot you this morning, and I ain't said nothin' about shootin' you."

"The hell you ain't," a salty-looking bystander said.

There were shouts of agreement from other men, and not liking the turn the situation was taking, Sheriff Duro yelled for quiet. Then he spoke to Danielle.

"You can't accuse a man of trying to bushwhack you without evidence, and you have only your suspicions. Get out of here and go about your business."

"I'm getting out," Danielle said, "but McCandless has threatened to kill me. Now I aim to offer him the satisfaction of doing just that if he's man enough to face me."

It became an intolerable situation for Reece McCandless as men shouted their approval. If a man was called out and refused to go, he was branded forevermore a coward. Those in the saloon began to bull-rag him, while Sheriff Duro tried in vain to stop it. Danielle stepped out on the boardwalk, looking over the saloon's batwing doors. McCandless was literally shoved toward the door and out onto the boardwalk.

Danielle waited on the other side of the street, then issued a challenge.

"When you're ready, McCandless, make your play."

"I'm no gunfighter," McCandless whined. "I won't do it."

"You cowardly, back-shootin' coyote," said Danielle, "the next time you come after me, you'd better make it good, or I'll kill you."

It was a calculated risk, and Danielle took it. For a split second, she turned her back on Reece McCandless, and then she did something none of the onlookers had ever witnessed before. She whirled, drawing her right-hand Colt as she did so, and dropped to one knee. Three times McCandless fired, the slugs zipping over Danielle's head. She fired once, and the force of it slammed McCandless back against a hitch rail. The rail broke, and McCandless fell to the boardwalk on his back.

"Damn you," Sheriff Duro shouted, "I ought to lock you up for forcing a gunfight."

"I don't think so, Sheriff," said Danielle. "Would you have jailed McCandless if I'd let him back-shoot me?"

It was a question Sheriff Sam Duro dared not answer. Red-faced, he started up the boardwalk toward his office. But as he rounded a corner and, out of sight of those who had witnessed the gunfight, he headed straight for the town's bank and the office of old Simon McCandless. Somebody had to tell McCandless that his cowardly son had been gunned down while trying to shoot another man in the back. Sheriff Duro sighed. Hell was about to break loose, with the lid off and all the fires lit, and there was nothing he could do.

Chapter 17

Nobody spoke to Danielle after Reece McCandless had tried to shoot her in the back and had been gunned down. It was an undeniable case of self-defense, for McCandless had fired three times before Danielle had gotten off a shot. Nobody followed Danielle, and she had no idea what to expect. She stopped across the street, watching the house where she hoped there were two outlaws who might lead her to Snakehead Kalpana.

Sheriff Duro had no stomach for what lay ahead, but he had little choice. Somebody had to tell Simon McCandless that his gutless son had been gunned down after he'd tried to shoot another man in the back. Duro knocked on the door.

"Who is it?" McCandless asked.

"Sheriff Duro."

"Come on in," said McCandless gruffly as Duro closed the door behind him. "Now whatever you have to say, speak up. Don't waste my time with trivial things you could have taken care of yourself."

"Some things I don't do," Sheriff Duro said, "and standin' between two *hombres* with guns is one of 'em. That loudmouth boy of yours just got himself shot dead after he tried to shoot another man in the back."

Simon McCandless's expression didn't change. He was overweight, with gray eyebrows, gray hair, and a ruddy complexion. Kicking back his chair, he got up and walked to the window. For a long moment he looked out, seething, and when he again turned to Sheriff Duro, his face was white with rage.

"Just where the hell were *you* when this was taking place?" he thundered.

"Watching Reece go up against the fastest gun I've ever seen," said Sheriff Duro. "He started it, and besides being a damned fool, he was a coward too."

"Nobody guns down my boy and lives to talk about it," McCandless shouted. "Nobody. Do you understand that?"

"I understand that it was a more than a fair fight," said Sheriff Duro. "Reece had a mad on because when he was stripping a girl in a saloon, this young gunfighter buffaloed him. It didn't do a hell of a lot for the McCandless image. Since then, the saloon girl has had her throat cut, and I think we have the brave Reece McCandless to thank for that."

"Are you done?" McCandless asked in a low, dangerous voice.

"For the time being," said Sheriff Duro. "I put up with a lot in this damn town, but I won't side with a yellow, back-shootin' coward, even if he is a McCandless."

"Then you just tell me who this young gun-thrower is," McCandless said, "and I'll see that he pays."

"His name is Daniel Strange," said Sheriff Duro. "He's after the outlaws who murdered his pa in Indian Territory. Snakehead Kalpana's one of them."

"Kalpana's the gun-happy bastard who shot a ranger in Laredo," McCandless said, "and you let him hang around here?"

"Hell, I didn't know about the ranger in Laredo," said Sheriff Duro. "You ain't in the habit of checking references on none of these owlhoots. Why should Kalpana be that much different from the others?"

"He shot a ranger, and the rest of them will trail Kalpana all the way to hell and then go in after him," McCandless said. "Where is he now?"

"Across the river," said Sheriff Duro. "Dirk and Malo, a couple of his *amigos,* have a room here in town. I reckon they'll know where he is."

"Then get them," McCandless said, "and see that they take a message to Kalpana. Tell him there's a gunfighter in town looking for him, and unless he gets rid of this troublesome kid, he'll get no protection from me."

"Suppose the kid, Daniel Strange, guns down Kalpana?"

"Then you can report to the rangers that Snakehead Kalpana's dead," McCandless said, "and that ought to keep the law off our backs."

"And if Kalpana guns down this Daniel Strange?"

"He will have paid for murdering my son," said McCandless, "and I'll see that Snakehead Kalpana is put where his reputation won't harm us."

"So either Snakehead Kalpana or Daniel Strange is to die in a gunfight," Sheriff Duro said, "and you aim to take care of the survivor."

"In my own way," said McCandless. "If this Daniel Strange survives a shoot-out with Snakehead Kalpana, he *still* must pay for killing my son. As long as Kalpana's alive, we're up against the possibility the rangers will come looking for him. I'm sure they'll be asking some embarrassing questions. It'll be better for us if Daniel Strange guns Kalpana down. It'll take ranger eyes off us, and I can still see that Daniel Strange pays. Now get out of here and find those men who have been riding with Kalpana."

All Danielle's suspicions of Sheriff Duro were confirmed when she saw the lawman mount the outside stairs of the boardinghouse she was watching. Sheriff

Duro knocked on the door, it opened, and he entered. Danielle would have given all her worth to hear what was being said. Sheriff Duro wasted no time.

"One or both of you have to ride across the river and find Snakehead Kalpana. You do know where he is, don't you?"

"Maybe," said Dirk cautiously.

"Damn it," Duro shouted, "you either know or you don't. Which is it?"

"All right," said Dirk, "we can find him, but he ain't the kind to spook easy. What do we tell him?"

"Tell him there's a young gunfighter in town, gunning for him," Sheriff Duro said. "If Kalpana don't shut this kid up, we'll have the rangers after us. McCandless said if Kalpana don't ride over here and cut the kid's string, that he can stay in Mexico until he croaks because he won't get protection from us. You knew Kalpana killed a ranger in Laredo."

"Well . . . uh . . . yes," said Malo, "but that's a long ways from here."

"Not when it concerns the death of a ranger," Sheriff Duro said. "Now get going. We want Kalpana on this side of the river when he faces Daniel Strange."

"That ain't hard to figure out," said Dirk. "You figure this young gunslinger can take Kalpana. Then you'll turn his carcass over to the rangers so's they don't show up here."

"Don't do too much thinking," Sheriff Duro said. "You ain't equipped for it. Just tell Kalpana this kid's got vengeance on his mind, and a draw as quick as a rattler. Kalpana's finished here unless he guns down this troublesome kid."

With that, Sheriff Duro stepped out the door, closing it behind him. He had no doubts that Dirk and Malo could find Kalpana, for they had ridden with him from Laredo after Kalpana had gunned down the ranger.

"What you reckon we ought to do?" Malo asked after Sheriff Duro had gone.

"We got to find Kalpana," said Dirk. "He's a marked man. If he can gun down this Daniel Strange, we can hide out here awhile longer."

Danielle watched Sheriff Duro descend the stairs, mount his horse, and ride away. Sundown was picketed nearby, and Danielle led the chestnut mare back to her vantage point, where she could see the outside stairs. Sheriff Duro had been gone only a few minutes when the two men she had been watching descended the stairs. Danielle watched them go to the nearest livery, which was two blocks away. When they rode out, she followed, keeping them in sight, but far enough behind that they wouldn't grow suspicious. The duo kept to side streets, and it soon became apparent they were headed for the river. Danielle followed them, convinced they were on their way to warn Snakehead Kalpana. Having the rangers after him, as well as a vindictive gunfighter, might convince him to remain in old Mexico, and Danielle couldn't abide that. She was breaking the law just crossing the border, and a gunfight with Kalpana could get her thrown into a Mexican prison. Still, she followed, not sure as to how she would get past the border sentries. But there were no sentries, and no evidence there ever had been. It seemed the border was open to Mexican and American outlaws, the alliance being sanctioned by corrupt officials on both sides of the border.

In less than an hour the two men Danielle was trailing reined up before a crude cabin. A tendril of smoke trailed from the mud-and-stick chimney. A single horse stood outside on a picket rope. One of the two men pounded on the door.

"Who is there?" demanded a voice from inside.

"Dirk and Malo," said one of the men, loud enough for Danielle to hear. "We got a message for you."

The door was opened, and Dirk and Malo entered. They wasted no time.

"There's a young gunfighter, Daniel Strange, looking for you," Dirk said. "Sheriff Duro brought the word from old man McCandless that if you don't silence this damn kid, you'll be stuck in Mexico for the rest of your life."

"Perhaps it is a trap to lure me into the hands of the rangers," Kalpana said. "Could this Daniel Strange be one of them?"

"No," said Dirk. "This kid ain't even old enough to shave. He told Sheriff Duro you're one of a bunch of outlaws that robbed and hanged his pa in Indian Territory."

Kalpana laughed. "And he seeks revenge. Well, my *amigos*, he will have his chance. Then you can bury him."

Dirk and Malo shuddered, for they had seen Snakehead Kalpana in action. He carried two thonged-down revolvers and could draw and shoot with either hand. He was as fast as the serpent whose name he had taken.

"Then saddle up and let's ride," said Dirk. "I always get the feeling these *Mejicanos* are watching us. It gives me the creeps."

Kalpana took his saddlebags, and the trio went out. Dirk and Malo waited until Kalpana had saddled his horse. Mounting, the three of them rode north. Following, Danielle sighed with relief. She had every reason to believe the third man was Snakehead Kalpana, and it appeared, for whatever reason, that he was riding back across the border into Texas. She would have gunned down Kalpana south of the border, had there been no other way, but the threat of Mexican prison was very real. Now Danielle concerned herself with where Kalpana would go once he reached Brownsville.

"What do you aim to do first?" Malo asked Kalpana.

"I aim to have me a talk with old man McCandless," said Kalpana. "I ain't takin' orders from that old buzzard."

"Then you ride on over to the bank and have it out with him," Dirk said. "We already locked horns with him once."

The three outlaws separated, Dirk and Malo riding back toward their rooming house. Virtually certain the third man was Kalpana, Danielle followed him. He reined up outside the bank, tied his horse to the hitch rail, and went inside. When he reached McCandless's office, he didn't bother knocking. Closing the door behind him, his cold, hard eyes met those of Simon McCandless.

"Don't you *ever* again walk into my office without knocking," McCandless hissed.

Kalpana laughed. "You scare the hell out of me, old man."

McCandless struggled to control himself. However arrogant and disagreeable Kalpana was, McCandless had need of him. He swallowed hard, managing to speak in a near-normal tone of voice.

"There's a loudmouth kid gunning for you. Not only does he have a damn good reason, but he's seen fit to tell others why he's after you. Now you got two choices. You can gun down this Daniel Strange, or you can ride out of Brownsville and keep going."

"You wasn't so high and mighty when Malo, Dirk, and me rode in," said Kalpana. "You was only too glad to take a cut from the horses we sold after running 'em across the river from Mexico."

"That was before I learned you had killed a ranger in Laredo," McCandless said. "That put a considerable price on your head, and one way or another, this Daniel Strange knows you're here. If he keeps shootin' off his mouth about you and what you done in Indian Territory, we'll have the rangers in here. I don't aim for that to happen. Now you can silence this Daniel Strange, or you can get the hell out of here. What's it gonna be?"

"I got a feeling Dirk and Malo didn't tell me everything," Kalpana said. "Why don't you tell me the *real* reason you want me to cut this gun-thrower's string?"

"Besides spreading the word about you—a ranger killer and first-class bastard—are in town, he shot and killed Reece, my only son."

Kalpana laughed. "Why? Was your kid playin' with his marbles, or did he stand up on his hind legs like the big boys do?"

Again McCandless struggled to control his temper. Lying would gain him nothing, for Kalpana would learn the truth. Finally, he spoke.

"Reece got into a quarrel with this Daniel Strange, and pulled a gun," McCandless said. "The kid carries two guns, and he's fast as greased lightning."

"There's a chance he might be faster than me, then," said Kalpana. "I don't aim to risk my neck just to avenge your idiot son, and I can't see it's to my advantage to silence this Daniel Strange. If the town ends up neck-deep in rangers, I can just ride on. It'll be you and your pet sheriff that gets kicked off your thrones."

Things weren't going right at all. Snakehead Kalpana had stayed alive by always being a cut above the average outlaw. McCandless sighed and spoke.

"All right, I'll admit my argument with Daniel Strange is twofold. I want him silenced permanently before he endangers my position here, and I want him to pay for killing my son. I'll pay you five hundred dollars."

"Double that," Kalpana said, "and we'll talk."

"Half now, and half when the job's done," said McCandless.

"Deal," Kalpana said. "Show me your money."

From a desk drawer McCandless took a small canvas sack and he counted out twenty-five gold double eagles. He shoved the money across the desk to Kalpana.

"Now," said McCandless, "when do you aim to take care of him?"

"Soon as I can find him and force him to pull iron," Kalpana said.

Kalpana then left the office, mounted his horse, and rode back to join his companions, Dirk and Malo. Danielle followed. Kalpana reached the boardinghouse, mounted the outside stairs, and knocked on the door. He was let in, and Danielle settled down to wait. Whatever the trio did, it seemed highly unlikely they would remain in their room very long.

"Well," said Dirk when Kalpana entered, "I see you met the old grizzly and come out with a whole hide."

"I done considerably better than that," Kalpana boasted. "McCandless wants this Daniel Strange to pay for killing that fool kid, Reece. He wants it bad enough to pay me for the job. That's a thousand in gold."

"That's somethin' to your credit," said Dirk, "provided this kid don't kill *you*. He's as fast as anybody I've ever seen, and he leads a charmed life."

"Yeah," Malo agreed, "and I reckon McCandless didn't tell you that his fool kid tried to shoot Strange in the back. McCandless wouldn't draw, and when Strange turned his back on McCandless, the yellow coyote went for his gun. But Strange was expecting that. He hit the dirt, and all three shots McCandless fired missed. Then the kid shot him dead."

"He won't have to worry about turning his back on

me," said Kalpana. "I'll face him in an even fight. Where do I find him?"

"Generally at the American Saloon," Dirk said. "He's as lucky at the faro table as he is behind a gun."

"The saloon don't open for another two hours," said Malo. "You might as well take a rest until then."

Danielle waited impatiently, realizing the trio probably wouldn't venture out until the saloons opened. In Brownsville there was absolutely nothing to do except frequent the saloons, drinking and gambling. It was a few minutes past noon when the trio left on foot. By the time they reached town, the saloons would be open. Reaching the American, they went inside. Danielle waited a few minutes before following. She went in through the batwing doors, stepping aside until her eyes grew accustomed to the dim interior. Besides the trio of outlaws who had just entered, there were four other men bellied up to the bar.

"That's Daniel Strange that just come in," Dirk said quietly. "He must have followed Malo and me across the border and then followed the three of us back to Brownsville. He must want you almighty bad."

"I'm still not convinced he ain't a ranger," said Kalpana, "but they can't string me up any higher for killing a second one. You, there by the door. I'm Kalpana, and I hear you have been looking for me. Is it asking too much for you to tell me why, *señor*?"

When Danielle spoke, her voice was low and deadly, and even in the gloom of the saloon, her eyes were like green fire.

"You and your bunch of yellow coyotes hanged my pa in Indian Territory last spring. I'm going to give you more of a chance than you gave him."

"No gunplay in here," the barkeep shouted, taking a sawed-off shotgun from beneath the bar. "I'll cut down the first one of you makin' a move. Take your fight outside."

None of the three outlaws moved. Quickly, Danielle stepped through the batwing doors to the boardwalk outside. Crossing to the other side of the dusty street, she leaned against a hitch rail, waiting. Snakehead Kalpana stepped out on the boardwalk, his two companions moving out of the line of fire. Something about an impending disaster drew men like flies to a honey jug, and observers were already everywhere, some of them looking out upstairs windows for a better view.

"When you're ready, Kalpana," said Danielle, still leaning against the hitch rail.

A chill crept up Kalpana's spine. The kid was just too confident. But Kalpana had taken money for the job, and he had placed himself in a position where he dared not back down.

"This will be a fair fight," Sheriff Duro shouted. "Any man pullin' a gun besides these two and I'll gun you down myself."

Most of the observers were aware that Kalpana was an undesirable who had killed a Texas Ranger, and they waited in anticipation. Eyes darted from Kalpana to Danielle, and back again. Danielle made no move, for Kalpana had issued the challenge. It would be up to him when he chose to draw. Finally, just when it appeared he might not draw, he did. He was fast. Incredibly fast. But Danielle Strange was faster. Without seeming to move, the butt-forward Colt from her left hip was in her hand, spouting flame. Her first slug ripped into Kalpana's chest as he pulled the trigger, and his shot went wild. Stumbling backward, he leaned against the saloon's front wall, raising his Colt. Danielle fired again, and Kalpana collapsed on the boardwalk. Her eyes on the bystanders, Danielle punched out the empty shell casings and reloaded her Colt, returning the weapon to its holster on her left hip.

There was murmuring among the crowd who had observed the fight, and Danielle chose to wait until it subsided before making a move. Sheriff Duro came to her aid.

"All of you break it up and get back to what you was doing," Duro shouted.

Dirk and Malo stared in disbelief at the body of Snakehead Kalpana.

"By God, I wouldn't have believed it if I hadn't seen it," Dirk said.

"Me neither," said Malo. "I've never seen a cross-hand draw as fast as that. I wouldn't go up against that little hellion with anything less than a Gatling gun."

Sheriff Duro had Kalpana's body taken to the carpenter shop, where a coffin would be built. He then returned to the bank building and knocked on the door to McCandless's office.

"Come in," McCandless said.

Sheriff Duro closed the door before he spoke.

"Kalpana's dead," said Sheriff Duro. "This Daniel Strange is the fastest gun I ever saw. He didn't get a scratch. What do we do now?"

"Kalpana had five hundred dollars of my money in gold," McCandless said. "I want it back."

"I took it off him," said Sheriff Duro, digging a handful of coins from his pocket.

The sheepish look on Duro's face told McCandless that the sheriff had intended to keep the money, but McCandless let it pass. Feeling the need to change the subject, it was the sheriff who spoke.

"Strange has done what he come here to do. He'll be leaving."

"He won't be goin' anywhere," McCandless said. "I want you to find me a dozen men, all good with guns. I'll pay fifty dollars a day and provide ammunition.

The man who guns down Daniel Strange gets a thousand-dollar bonus."

"Kalpana was no slouch with a Colt," said Sheriff Duro, "and him layin' dead may make it hard as hell finding gunmen to go after the kid."

"I'm leaving that up to you, and I want it done today," McCandless said. "We have to get the kid before he rides on."

"I'll do the best I can," said Sheriff Duro. "You want me to send these *hombres* to see you?"

"Hell no," McCandless growled. "The last thing I want is a bunch of killers coming to and from here." He handed Sheriff Duro a canvas sack. "There's six hundred and fifty dollars in here. That's enough for a first day's pay for a dozen men, and fifty dollars for you to buy the necessary ammunition."

It was clear enough, and Sheriff Duro had his hand on the doorknob when McCandless spoke again.

"One more thing. I want you to telegraph every Texas Ranger outpost. Tell them that Snakehead Kalpana, who killed the ranger in Laredo, is dead. That should keep them away from here."

"There's a price on his head," said Sheriff Duro. "Suppose they want proof?"

"Then they'll have to dig up his carcass and study it to their satisfaction," McCandless said. "If they got to know who killed him, all you know is that it was a gunslinger who was passing through and has since rode on."

"Yeah," said Sheriff Duro, "you're layin' it all on my back. The damn rangers are goin' to wonder how long Kalpana's been here, and why, when he got his, it was at the hand of another outlaw."

"Then damn it, tell the truth," McCandless snarled. "Tell 'em it was a revenge killing for Kalpana's part in a murder in Indian Territory. That won't reflect on us, and we'll see that they don't find Daniel Strange. Now get going."

Danielle returned to the Delaney house, let down and without any sense of triumph. It had been the anticipation of avenging her father's death that had led her on, but when a man, even the likes of Snakehead Kalpana, lay dead, she was strangely remorseful. To her mind came some Bible scripture she had learned long ago: *Vengeance is mine, saith the Lord.* She found Ephiram and Ethel Delaney on the front porch.

"We heard shootin'," Ephiram said. "We wondered if you was involved."

"I was," said Danielle. "Snakehead Kalpana heard I was looking for him and came after me. I reckon I'll be ridin' on tomorrow."

"We'll miss you," Ethel said. "I hate to rent to this dirty, unwashed bunch around here and from across the border. I'd swear some of 'em ain't had a bath since the flood."

"Wake me for supper," Danielle said. "I'm going upstairs to rest."

"I didn't want to say anything," said Ephiram when Danielle had gone, "but I simply can't believe old man McCandless won't try something to avenge his no-account son. This young man, Daniel Strange, ought to be riding out today, getting as far from here as he can."

"It's curious you should speak of that," Ethel said. "I'm wondering if somebody didn't *pay* Kalpana to kill Daniel Strange. Someone with a reason for wanting Daniel dead."

"We know who that someone is," said Ephiram, "and it's best we say no more about it. We got to live here."

Removing her boots, gun belts, and hat, Danielle

stretched out on the bed. Dead tired, she found herself
unable to sleep, for a sense of foreboding had her in
its clutches and wouldn't let go. After several hours
she got up. Donning her hat, tugging on her boots,
and buckling on her gun belts, she went downstairs.
There was no sign of Ephiram, but Ethel was in the
parlor.

"Do be careful," Ethel warned. "It may not be
over."

"That's what I aim to find out," said Danielle. "I'll
be back for supper."

The town seemed strangely silent. Danielle visited
some of the saloons, receiving only curious looks.
Meanwhile, Sheriff Duro had a dozen hard-eyed men
crammed into his small office. They leaned against the
walls, avoiding the windows. Every man packed at
least one revolver, while some had two.

"Fifty dollars a day, plus ammunition," Sheriff Duro
said, "and I got your first day's pay. All you got to
do is gun down this Daniel Strange. The *hombre* that
cuts his string gets a thousand-dollar bonus."

"I reckon we know who's bankrollin' this," said one
of the men. "I think the *hombre* we're bein' paid to
kill done the town a favor. I ain't never liked McCandless's big-mouthed kid."

"Me neither," another man said.

"This is business," said Sheriff Duro. "Money
business."

"Well, I ain't about to brace this Daniel Strange in
no standup, face-to-face fight," one of the men said.
"Kalpana was a fast gun, but he didn't have a prayer."

"Nobody said you got to face him," Sheriff Duro
said. "Hell, there ain't nothin' honorable about bushwhacking a man. Shoot him in the back."

"I've seen some dirty, stinking, low-down coyotes
in my day," said one of the men, "but this is the first

time I've seen a lawman pay to have a man dry-gulched."

"This is a wide-open town," Sheriff Duro said, "and things are done different here. If it wasn't for me and certain others, the whole damn lot of you would be rotting behind bars somewhere. If this Daniel Strange is allowed to ride out of here, he's likely to go to the nearest ranger outpost and tell them he gunned down Kalpana. Rangers have a way of figurin' things out. They're likely to wonder how long Kalpana was here, without the law layin' a hand on him, and how many more there may be just like him."

"I reckon that makes sense," said one of the gunmen. "We got to stop the varmint."

There was mostly agreement among the rest of the outlaws, except for Malo and Dirk.

"Duro," said Dirk, "you'd better be right. If I end up with my neck in a noose, I aim to see that you're hanging beside me from the same damn limb."

"Damn right," Malo said. "You ain't pullin' the trigger, but you're as much a killer as any one of us."

Sheriff Duro swallowed hard. If the worst happened, and Daniel Strange escaped, the town might be invaded by a company of Texas Rangers. Simon McCandless had wisely used Duro to arrange the killing of Daniel Strange, and would in no way be implicated, unless Sheriff Duro talked. He quickly reached the unhappy conclusion that even if he talked, he would still be neck-deep in trouble. There was no way he could accuse McCandless of anything without admitting that he, Duro, had arranged it.

Chapter 18

Brownsville, Texas. December 21, 1870.

Danielle lay down across the bed to rest, and the longer she lay there, the more she was sure that Kalpana had been brought back across the border to kill her. His having failed in no way lessened her danger, and she sat up, tugging on her boots. She would leave Brownsville tonight, taking word of the situation there to the Texas Rangers in San Antonio. But she had waited too long. There was a knock on her door, and answering it, she looked into the frightened face of Ethel Delaney.

"Daniel, there's a group of horsemen across the street, watching the house. Ephiram believes they've come after you."

"I reckon he's right," said Danielle."I should already have ridden out. Now I'll have to face up to them."

"But they're here to kill you," Ethel protested. "You can't go out there."

"I can, and I will,' said Danielle. "They haven't yet surrounded the house, but there may be men watching the back door. Is there a way out, without going through the front or back doors?"

"Through the cellar," Ethel said. "Come on. I'll show you."

Carrying a lighted coal oil lamp, Ethel Delaney led the way down the stairs from the kitchen to the cellar below. The door was barred from the inside, and Ethel lifted the bar.

"As soon as I'm out," said Danielle, "put that bar back in place."

"Go with God," Ethel said through her sobs.

Danielle stepped out into the night. There was no moon, and she could hear the mutter of voices across the street. Finally, there came a challenge.

"We want Daniel Strange," a voice shouted. "If we have to come in and get him, you Delaneys are gonna be sorry."

"He's been expecting you," Ephiram said, "and he ain't here."

"Duke," said the voice across the street, "look in the stable behind the house and see if his horse is gone."

Duke made his way around the house, his Colt drawn. Danielle stepped out of the darkness behind him, slamming the muzzle of her Colt against the back of his head. Without a sound, he collapsed. Taking his revolver, Danielle slipped it under her waistband, then waited. Her next move would depend on the men hunting her.

"Damn it, Duke," a voice shouted impatiently, "what's keepin' you?"

Only silence greeted him, and Danielle could hear angry voices. Obviously, the men were deciding what they should do next, and the gruff voice that had spoken before again threatened the Delaneys.

"You Delaneys, we're goin' to surround the house. You got ten minutes to get Daniel Strange out here. If you don't, we'll set the place afire and drive him out."

There was no reply from either of the Delaneys, and Danielle knew she couldn't allow them to suffer for her deeds. She moved away from the house into

the shadow of a huge oak tree. Finding a stone the
size of her fist, she waited until two of the men began
to make their way along her side of the house. Once
they were past her, she threw the stone against the
side of the house. The two men whirled, firing at the
sound. Danielle fired at their muzzle flashes, and they
fell, groaning.

"The bastard ain't in the house!" a voice shouted.
"He's shot Turk and Bender."

Danielle heard the sound of running feet and
stepped back into the shadow of the oak. Her trick
had worked once, but it would not a second time.
There would be too many of them, and before she
could cut them all down, some of them would be
shooting at *her* muzzle flashes. Six men crept through
the shadows alongside the house.

"Damn it," said one of them, "here's Duke, and
he's out colder than a bullfrog."

One of the pair Danielle had shot groaned, drawing
their attention.

"A couple of you help Turk and Bender back to
the horses," a voice commanded.

"Bender's dead, and Turk's hard hit," said another voice.

"Then take their carcasses away, and then get the
hell back over here."

Danielle waited until the two fallen men had been
removed. She then stood behind the huge trunk of the
oak and issued a challenge of her own.

"You're covered. Drop your guns."

The four drew and began firing. Lead slammed into
the oak. Danielle, leaning to one side, fired around
the trunk at the muzzle flashes. She then hit the
ground, rolling into a new position, belly-down.

"Oh, God," a voice moaned, "I'm gut-shot!"

Two of the men were down, and the other two stood
there, waiting. They well knew their muzzle flashes

could be their undoing. Slowly, they began to back away toward the front of the house, and Danielle let them go. When they reached the far side of the street, an argument ensued, and Danielle was sure she recognized the gruff voice of Sheriff Sam Duro.

"Sheriff," Danielle taunted, "you're done. The rest of you men, if you come after me, be prepared to die."

"Come on, damn it," Duro bawled to the rest of the men, "we're goin' after him."

But only two of the men followed. Dirk and Malo mounted their horses. They left town, riding north. Two other men watched them uncertainly. Then, mounting their horses, they followed Dirk and Malo. As Sheriff Duro and his two companions crept alongside the house, there was a shadow directly ahead of them. The unconscious Duke had staggered to his feet, only to have Sheriff Sam Duro cut him down at close range. It was all Danielle needed. She fired at the muzzle flash, and the force of the slug slammed Duro against the side of the house. He slumped to the ground, and the two men who had accompanied him ran back the way they had come. Seconds later, there was the thud of hooves as the survivors of the ill-fated ambush galloped away. Danielle walked around the house, mounted the porch, and knocked on the door. Ethel Delaney opened it.

"Is it over?" Ethel asked fearfully.

"Not quite," said Danielle. "I want to get my saddlebags, and then I want to talk to Ephiram."

When Danielle came back down the stairs, the Delaneys were waiting in the parlor.

"There are at least six men wounded or dead," Danielle said. "Sheriff Sam Duro is one of the dead, but he's not the head of this damn snake. Ephiram, who is the man who runs this town?"

"Simon McCandless," said Ephiram.

"That explains a lot of things," Danielle said. "He brought Kalpana in to gun me down and, failing in that, sent Duro after me with a bunch of killers. Where am I likely to find McCandless?"

"He's got an office at the rear of the bank," said Ephiram, "but he lives at a hotel. It's The Rio, I think."

"He'll be at the office, then, waiting to hear that I'm dead," Danielle said. "I'll be back for my horse." She stepped out the door, leaving the Delaneys speechless.

The bank building, having three floors, was the tallest building in Brownsville. There was a back door, and to one side of it a coal oil bracket lamp burned. Danielle turned the knob, and the door opened on silent hinges. At the end of a short hall was yet another door with lamplight bleeding out beneath it. Danielle made no noise, for the hall was carpeted. Standing to one side of the door, she turned the knob. When the latch let go, she kicked the door open, slamming it against the wall. Simon McCandless sat behind the big desk, staring at her unbelievingly.

"Your pet sheriff's dead, McCandless," said Danielle, "along with some of the other owlhoots you sent after me. The rest of them ran like the yellow coyotes they are. Since you want me dead, do your worst. It's just you and me, McCandless."

"You've got sand, kid," McCandless said, "and I wouldn't kill you if there was another way. But you gunned down my boy, and as soon you could get to a ranger outpost, I think you'd tell the rangers all about me. What do you aim to do with me?"

"I'm going to put you on a horse and take you to the rangers," said Danielle. "I want them to see the daddy skunk in the flesh, and then I want to hear your excuses as you try to save your miserable hide. Get up. We're riding out tonight."

"You won't deny me a last cigar, will you?" McCandless asked.

"Go ahead," said Danielle. "Just be damn careful what you do with your hands."

McCandless opened a desk drawer and took out a cigar box. Danielle was barely in time, dropping to one knee as McClandless raised a Colt from the box and fired twice. The lead went over Danielle's head, splintering the door behind her. Danielle drew and fired twice, and McCandless was driven back into his swivel chair. He lay there, blood pumping out on his white ruffled shirt. He was trying to speak, and Danielle leaned across the desk.

"We'd have . . . made . . . an unbeatable team, kid. Too bad . . . you was on . . . the other side . . ."

Those were his last words, and Danielle left him there. The town had some cleaning up to do before the rangers rode in.

The Delaneys were still in the parlor when Danielle got back to the house. They waited for her to speak.

"McCandless drew on me, and he's dead," said Danielle. "You decent folks in town had better get together and take control of things. I aim to report all this to the rangers just as soon as I reach San Antonio. There must be one honest man you can elect sheriff, and I hope your bank's got no more skunk-striped varmints like McCandless."

"McCandless has kept the town terrorized and under his thumb for years," Ephiram said. "Without him and his hired guns, we'll manage, I think. But tell the rangers we'll be welcoming them, just in case there are some undesirables who don't want to leave."

"I'll tell them," said Danielle. "I'm going to saddle my horse and be on my way."

"I hate to see you go, Daniel," Ethel said.

"In a way, I hate to go," said Danielle, "but I still have some man-hunting to do."

Danielle saddled Sundown and, mounting, rode north toward San Antonio. It was more than two hundred miles, and she took her time, for it was a two-day ride.

San Antonio, Texas. December 23, 1870.

Danielle rode in just before sundown on her second day out of Brownsville. She hoped to find Captain Jennings in his office, for it was important that the rangers reach Brownsville before the rustlers and killers had time to reorganize. Jennings was there and made no move to conceal his pleasure when Danielle entered the office.

"Captain," Danielle said, "we have to talk. There's been hell to pay in Brownsville, and the decent folks there are going to need some help."

"Then let's go eat," said Jennings. "Supper's on me."

They went to a small cafe where the ranger was known, and since it was early, there were few other patrons. While they waited for their food, sipping coffee, Danielle told her story.

"I thought there was something unusual about the telegram informing me that Kalpana had been gunned down," said Jennings. "It carefully avoided telling me who actually did the shooting, but I suspected it was you."

"I don't think I'd have had a chance at him," Danielle said, "if I hadn't been forced to shoot Reece McCandless. I think after Reece was shot, Simon McCandless hoped Kalpana could finish me. When he failed to, Sheriff Duro and maybe a dozen men came looking for me. In the dark, Duro shot one of his own men. I accounted for five others, including the sheriff himself."

"There's nothing worse than a lawman selling out," said Captain Jennings. "I'll need the names of some honest folks in Brownsville who will stand behind what you've told me. Not that I doubt you, but the rangers who'll be riding down there will find it helpful in getting at the truth of it."

"Ephiram and Ethel Delaney," said Danielle. "They stood by me through it all, even as Sheriff Duro threatened to burn their house to drive me out."

"We'll talk to them," Captain Jennings said. "I'll have two rangers on their way in the morning."

Their food was ready, and Danielle ate hungrily, for she had eaten little, the situation in Brownsville bearing on her mind. When they were down to final cups of coffee, Captain Jennings spoke.

"It's interesting, what you've told me about Simon McCandless. I've heard of him. He was one of the carpetbaggers who moved in after the war, and I suspect he may have been wanted by the law somewhere up north. I aim to find out. By the way, there's a three-thousand-dollar price on Kalpana's head, dead or alive. I aim to see that you get it."

"I don't really want it," Danielle said. "You know why I was after Kalpana. The reward had nothing to do with it."

"I know that," said Captain Jennings, "but I want you to have it. If you don't need it, send it to your ma and your brothers in Missouri. It's been hard times there, too."

"You're a thoughtful man, Captain," Danielle said. "That's exactly what I'll do."

"It'll take maybe a week to get the money," said

Captain Jennings. "Why don't you just rest here for a few days, until I make the arrangements?"

"I'm thinking of riding back to Waco," Danielle said.

"Rucker's still sheriff there," said Captain Jennings, "and it'll be the same old Mexican standoff, all over again. There's still too many folks around who haven't gotten over the war, and they resist all authority, even to hiding their outlaw kin."

"I know," Danielle said, "but when I return, I won't be the same *hombre* who rode in there before."

"Disguise?"

"Yes," said Danielle, thinking of the female clothing in her saddlebag.

"Since you'll be in town for a few days," Captain Jennings said, "how do you aim to spend Christmas Day? It's the day after tomorrow."

"Christmas," said Danielle with a long, painful sigh. "It'll be the first time I've ever been away from my family at Christmas. I don't know what I'll do. I feel like I'm so old, Captain. A thousand years old, in just the few months since leaving Missouri. I've ridden so long on the dark side, there's no light to guide me."

"All the more reason why you need a few days' rest," Captain Jennings said. "I have two friends in Austin—Rangers Elmore and Williams—and like me, they have no family. They generally ride down here on Christmas Eve, and just for a day or two, we become as close to being a family as any of us will ever get. This Christmas, I'd like for you to join us."

"I . . . I don't know, Captain," said Danielle, touched.

"My last Christmas at home, I was seven years old," Captain Jennings said. "A week later, the Comanches struck and burned our house. Ma and Pa died in the attack, and a kindly old aunt took me in."

While his eyes were on Danielle, he wasn't seeing her. His mind was far away, at a different time and place. Danielle spoke, breaking his reverie.

"I'll spend Christmas with you and your *amigos,* Captain. I think I'd like that."

"Bueno," said Jennings. "Find yourself a hotel and get some rest. Elmore and Williams will be here sometime tomorrow, and we can meet for supper."

Danielle left Sundown at a nearby stable and chose one of the better hotels in which there was a dining room. There was a chill wind from the west, bringing with it a hint of snow that might blow in from the high plains. Removing her hat, gun belts, and boots, Danielle stretched out on the bed and slept. Far into the night, she awakened to the howling wind outside. Thankful that she and Sundown had a roof over their heads, she undressed and went back to sleep.

San Antonio, Texas. December 24, 1870.

Danielle joined Captain Jennings for breakfast.

"Be here at the office at five o'clock tomorrow," said Captain Jennings. "Our ranger *amigos* will be here by then."

The threat of last night's storm had past, and it being Christmas Eve, the streets were alive with people. Danielle had started across the street to her hotel when a shot rang out. Suddenly there was a blinding pain in her head, and she felt herself blacking out. At first there was only merciful darkness, and then through slitted eyes she could see daylight. A man in town clothes was bending over her. Captain Jennings stood at the foot of the bed, watching with concern.

"You have a concussion," the doctor said. "For the

next few days don't do anything foolish that might jolt you around."

"No riding then," said Danielle.

"Especially no riding," the doctor said. "Spend as much time in bed as you can. I'll be back to look in on you the day after tomorrow. Where are you staying?"

"Come by my office, Doc, and I'll take you there," Captain Jennings said. "Is he in a good enough condition to make it back to the hotel?"

"It all depends on him," said the doctor. "Young man, can you stand?"

"I don't know," Danielle said. "I'll try."

Holding on to the bed's iron footboard, she got to her feet, only to be engulfed by a wave of dizziness. But it soon passed, and she spoke to the doctor.

"I can make it, Doc."

"I'll go with him," said Captain Jennings.

"Take this bottle of laudanum with you," the doctor said. "There may be more pain, and this will help you sleep."

Captain Jennings said nothing until they reached Danielle's room on the first floor of the Cattlemen's Hotel. Then Jennings had a question.

"Do you have any idea who might have fired that shot?"

"No," said Danielle. "It came from behind me. Some of those outlaws who rode out of Brownsville may be here."

The bushwhacker had been firing from cover, and when Danielle fell, he didn't fire again. Only when someone helped Danielle to her feet did Leroy Lomax curse. This damn little gunman had shamed him in Indian Territory, leading to a falling out with the four men Lomax had been riding with. Now he intended to get his revenge. The kid seemed to have just been creased. When he was again up and about,

Leroy would try again, and this time, he wouldn't miss.

Alone in her hotel room, Danielle removed her hat, gun belts, and boots. She stretched out on the bed and was soon asleep. She was awakened by knocking on the door.

"Who's there?" she asked.

"Captain Jennings. I stopped by to see how you're feeling."

Danielle got up, unlocked the door, and Jennings entered.

"There's no pain," said Danielle, "but the side of my head's sore."

"Elmore and Williams are in town," Captain Jennings said, "and they'd like to meet you. That invite to supper still stands if you feel up to it."

"I'm hungry," said Danielle, "and I feel steady enough. I'll try it."

"I thought you would," Jennings said, "so we're eating in the hotel dining room."

After meeting Jennings's friends, Elmore and Williams, Danielle was glad she had been asked to join them. While they were a little younger than Jennings, they showed no less enthusiasm for their work.

"Captain Jennings told us about you," said Elmore while they waited for their food, "but he's gettin' old. I got a feeling he left some of it out."

"Yeah," Williams said, "what you've done is worthy of a company of rangers. Tell us all of it."

Danielle told them, stressing the loyalty of Ephiram and Ethel Delaney. They listened in silence, and when Danielle had finished, there seemed little to be said. Captain Jennings spoke.

"Daniel, take off your hat."

Danielle did so, revealing the bandage around her head.

"That happened on the street yesterday, right here in San Antonio," said Jennings. "A bushwhacker, firing from cover."

"Then you have no idea who he is," Williams said.

"No," said Jennings. "It could easily be one of the outlaws from Brownsville. They had a death grip on the town until Daniel evened the odds."

"If he hated you enough to bushwhack you once, he'll try again," Elmore predicted. "I think we'll have Christmas dinner here at the hotel restaurant tomorrow, keeping you off the street for a while."

"Good idea," said Williams.

After supper, the three rangers saw Danielle to her room before departing.

"We'll see you at eleven o'clock tomorrow morning," Captain Jennings promised.

Again Danielle stretched out on the bed, restless. She was starting to regret having promised Captain Jennings she would remain a few days in San Antonio. The hotel had gone to great lengths to decorate the lobby and the restaurant for the holiday, but it did not cheer Danielle. She thought only of her family in far away Missouri, who had to spend this holiday not knowing if she was alive or dead. She drifted off into troubled sleep, only to be awakened by the distant clanging of a church bell. She sat up on the edge of the bed, listening. Finally, she pulled on her boots, buckled on her gun belts, and reached for her hat. When she reached the street, the sound of the bell was much closer. Following the sound, she came to a church just as the bell was silenced. From within the church came the glorious sound of several hundred voices singing the old hymns and Christmas carols. There was no music except in the melodious voices. Danielle stood there listening, and it was as though her feet had minds of their own.

When she entered the church, she slipped into a back pew. Some of the congregation, seeing the pair of tied-down Colts, looked at her curiously, but kept singing.

For at least an hour, Danielle lifted her voice in singing the old songs she had learned as a child. Long-forgotten memories came alive, and she closed her eyes, relishing the images. The words of the old songs, like long-forgotten friends, came rushing back to her. After the last song had been sung, Danielle slipped out the door during the closing prayer. She considered visiting the Alamo Saloon, but suddenly it seemed like a tawdry place, filled with boastful, cursing men. She returned to her hotel room and, with the joyful chorus still ringing in her head, was soon asleep.

San Antonio, Texas. December 25, 1870.

Many of the cafes were closed, so Danielle had breakfast in the hotel dining room. She wasn't surprised to find her three ranger friends already there. Danielle pulled out a chair and sat down.

"We forgot to mention breakfast this morning," said Captain Jennings, "and I thought you might want to sleep late."

"I can't hide out forever," Danielle said. "Sooner or later, the varmint that's out to get me will have to show himself. When he does, I'll be ready."

"If he doesn't shoot you from behind," said Williams. "That's one thing you can count on. A coward never changes."

After breakfast, lacking anything better to do, Danielle returned to her room, unaware that hostile eyes had been watching her. Leroy Lomax sat in the hotel lobby, an unfolded newspaper shielding his face. He watched to see how far down the hall Danielle was going, and then he went to the hotel desk.

"I want a room for the night," said Lomax. "Bottom floor."

Given a key, he was gratified to learn that his room was almost directly across the hall from that of the little gunman he hated. The kid had to eat, and Lomax would try again at dinner or supper. Lomax lay across the bed, waiting. The kid seemed to have a habit of eating with Texas Rangers, and Lomax didn't want to make his play as long as any of the famed lawmen were in the hotel. He would go after Daniel Strange after he had left the dining room and was on his way down the hall.

Danielle reached the dining room just a few minutes after eleven. Jennings, Elmore, and Williams were already there.

"Feeling better?" Jennings asked.

"Considerably," said Danielle. "I feel like I could eat a whole turkey, goose, or double portions of whatever's being served."

The meal was an occasion to remember. Prodded by Danielle, the three rangers spoke of trails they had ridden, outlaws they had captured, and violent brushes with death. Only then did Captain Jennings take from under his belt a Colt, laying it on the table before Danielle.

"It's a .31 caliber Colt pocket pistol, from the three of us to you," said Jennings. "It will fit neatly under your belt or under your coat. It's a short barrel, but no less a Colt. It'll stop a man dead in his tracks."

"I . . . I don't know what to say," Danielle said.

"There's nothing to say, except Merry Christmas," said Jennings.

"But I have nothing for any of you," Danielle protested.

"You gave us our Christmas early," said Williams, "when you salted down that ranger killer, Snakehead Kalpana."

"I'm obliged," Danielle said, slipping the short-barreled Colt beneath the waistband of her Levi's. When dinner was over, Danielle left her friends and started down the hall to her room. Softly, a door opened behind her, and a cold voice spoke.

"Unbuckle them belts and let 'em fall."

Danielle paused and felt the muzzle of a gun poking her in the back. Slowly she loosed her gun belts, allowing her Colts to slide to the floor.

"Now go on to your room, where you was headed," said the voice.

Danielle had her key in her left hand, and while fumbling for the key hole, she eased her right hand to the butt of the pocket pistol. Suddenly the door opened, and Danielle seemed to fall forward into the room. Rolling over on her side, she fired twice, slamming Lomax into a door on the other side of the hall. He fired twice, but his arm had begun to sag, and the lead plowed into the carpet at his feet. Men came running down the hall, three of them the rangers who had not yet left the building. Danielle's Colts lay on the floor in the hall, but in her hand she held the Colt pocket pistol.

"That's Leroy Lomax," Danielle said. "I had trouble with him in Indian Territory."

She stepped out in the hall, retrieved her gun belts, and buckled them on. She then slid the Colt pocket pistol under her waistband and, facing the three rangers, spoke.

"You gave me the best Christmas gift of all. My life."

"You still aim to stay a few days, don't you?" Captain Jennings asked.

"Yes," said Danielle, "but then I'll be riding on. There's six more killers I must find before my pa can rest easy. I want the varmints to know they're living under the shadow of a noose."

Rufe Gaddis
~~Bart Scovill~~
Julius Byler
Chancy Burke

~~Snakehead Kalpana~~

Newt Grago
Saul Delmano
Blade Hogue
~~Brice Levan~~
~~Levi Jasper~~

(Continue riding the vengeance trail with Danielle
in the forthcoming book, *The Shadow of a Noose*.)